ONE FOR SORROW

Sir John Lister-Kaye is a naturalist, writer and lecturer who has lived in the Highlands for twenty-five years. In 1970 he founded Britain's first private Field Studies Centre, now the internationally acclaimed Aigas Field Centre, near Beauly. He has lectured on wildlife and the environment on three continents and is a regular contributor to journals and periodicals in Britain and the USA. He served as Chairman of the RSPB's Scottish Advisory Committee for seven years, then the Nature Conservancy Council, and is currently the first North-West Regional Chairman of Scottish Natural Heritage. He lives at Aigas with his wife, four children and three step-children.

Other titles:
The White Island *(Longman, 1972; Penguin, 1976)*
The Seeing Eye *(Allen Lane, 1979; Aigas, 1994)*
Seal Cull *(Penguin 1979)*
Ill fares the Land *(Barail 1994, SNH 1994)*

ONE FOR SORROW

JOHN LISTER-KAYE

BALNAIN BOOKS

Published in 1994 by
Balnain Books
Druim House
Lochloy Road
Nairn IV12 5LF
Scotland

Printed and bound by The Cromwell Press, Melksham

Cataloguing in Publication Data:
A catalogue record for this book is available from the British Library

cover illustration and design by Simon Fraser

ISBN 1 872557 36 8

for
Robin and Anne Law
in gratitude

'If Laura had been Petrarch's wife
would he have written sonnets all his life?'

FOREWORD

On 8th December 1992, a small group of one hundred and ten crofters in the remote and rocky north-west corner of the Scottish Highlands heard that they had successfully purchased their own land on which they and their forbears had lived and worked for over a hundred and fifty years.

They are the men and women of the Assynt Crofters' Trust. No-one living in the Highlands in the 1990's can fail to have heard of this historic move—a group of locals buying out the foreign Property Development Company which, on speculation, obtained legal title to the Assynt Estate from a large absentee landowner.

The buying and selling of land on the open market is an established principle of our society. Yet in the Highlands that principle is sullied by the fact that in the 19th century many Highlanders were forcibly cleared from their land—the land upon which they had survived under the clan system for more than a thousand years.

The Assynt Crofters' inspirational bid becomes the more poignant when one realises that it is the poor, rocky, coastal land onto which their forbears were cleared, which they have now had to buy in order to gain control over their own destinies.

The Clearances came about because some landlords wished to profit from the fertility of the hills and glens by introducing large-scale sheep farming, and later by creating grand sporting estates for the pursuit of deer, grouse and salmon. Both land uses became cultures in themselves and are with us today, although the natural productivity of the uplands has plunged over the past century largely because of man's extractive use of the hills. In our time sheep farming remains viable only with the support of large sums of subsidy.

Since the Second World War hundreds of thousands of acres of impoverished upland have been planted with coniferous forestry, also heavily supported from the public purse. Forestry practices have often been environmentally damaging, further impoverishing the exhausted soils and cutting across the interests of hill farms and sporting estates. This has often resulted in the removal of yet more people from the land.

This Highland story is a blend of fact and fiction gleaned over twenty-five years of living in the heart of the Highlands and observing the ebb and flow of landownership and the sweeping systems which are applied to the land, so rarely to the benefit of the local people or the fragile rural economy.

Neither Glen Corran nor Ardvarnish Estate exist, although their position can readily be identified on the map. Nor, to my knowledge, has there ever been a blanket afforestation proposal in that place. Yet Glen Corran stands for many glens and Ardvarnish for many estates right across the Highlands.

After a quarter of a century of living among these ancient mountains with their sighing corries and wide, whispering moors, and knowing and working with farmers and crofters in the long, narrow glens, I am forced to conclude that the continuing saga of the extractive land-use imposed upon this land and its people, is indeed, one for sorrow.

John Lister-Kaye

Aigas, 1994

—PART ONE—

One for sorrow,
Two for joy,
Three for a girl,
Four for a boy,
Five for silver.....

"More tea?" she asked, the memorable hair falling around her face as she bent forward. I watched her closely, searching for a clue, any change in her eyes.

"Thank you. Please go on."

She sat down, folding her hands delicately and precisely in her lap. "There's not that much more to tell. Van Fensing sold up and went away. Seemingly it was all too much for him, he'd not had any interest in the people here nor yet in the land. The estate was on the market for that many months—nearly two years it was—before these new folk came in." She stopped. Her eyes, mackeral-blue now turning to rock grey, were looking beyond me as though she was resigned to her homeland being passed from stranger to stranger, as though that's what Highlanders expected. "They seem nice enough," she said, with a lifting of the voice and a softening of the eyes. "They're big wheat farmers from Norfolk and they want to do the right thing, there's no doubt about that. Mac's already got them signed up to new woodland schemes, and they're building a new house here. But the sheep are gone, of course."

"Why?" I asked. (Surely the struggle hadn't been entirely in vain.) "Is there really no room for them these days?"

"Oh, aye, there's room for them, right enough. It's just that the land is scarred now, it's the ploughing that did that, and that's something we just can't put back. There's no grants for undoing furrows like that and it's all Father's best sheep walks were ploughed the first. That was the good ground."

"So what's happened to him?"

"Huh!" There was a shake of the wild red hair. "Father's not a shepherd any more."

"So what does he do?"

"Ach, he get's by with a bit of this and a wee bit of that." Again, that same resigned smile, pale lips austere. "He carves walking sticks for the tourists, and he helps at the mart with the lamb sales, penning stock, pushing them through to the ring. In springtime he'll do relief lambing round and about, and Mac also keeps him busy with spraying the bracken and keeping the fences tight." She paused; sighed a little. "A job here and a job there."

"Oh I see," I felt her disappointment. "But he's still in the cottage at Dalbattigh, isn't he?" I remembered how much she had loved that place.

"Ach aye. Yes. They're still there right enough. Lord Denby bought the house back from van Fensing. They say it was because he felt guilty, but I'm not believing that. I think it was because of what happened." She paused. For a moment I thought she was going to say more. I watched her eyes staring at the tea-cup in her hand; but then she seemed to correct herself and she carried on as before. "He's been good to Mother and Father, whatever his reasons—I have to say that.... But drink your tea."

"Oh, yes," I laughed lamely. The tea was tepid. It didn't matter. I was entranced, under the spell.

"What made you come?"

"I don't really know," I said. "It's funny, Rob and I weren't really close friends, not in the way that would have made us want to keep in touch after school. But I always liked him, and we got on well enough. He was different though, from the rest of us. Quieter somehow, reserved; as though he knew something we didn't. He was busy with his own world, although none of us had a clue what that was; and later on, when we were in our teens he was still apart and preoccupied as if he knew where he was going. And then after school I had no idea whether he'd gone to university or anything. Certainly nothing of all this until it was in the papers. Then one day recently I bumped into his parents. They live in Tunbridge Wells—of course, you'll know that—and his father and mine belong to the same golf club, even play together from time to time. It seems a thousand miles away from here."

"It is that," she said, too quickly—and there was the clue. A misting of eyes, and the sudden glance away, down to the fireplace and the hearth rug, reaching forward for her tea. Perhaps I'd said too much? Come too close to the hidden pain. I changed the subject.

"I must go. I've taken up far too much of your time. You've been so kind."

"But you'll come down to the bridge with me?" she asked. "Robbie'll be back from the school in a minute. It'll be fine to have someone to walk down with. How are you at pushing a pram?"

I laughed. "Not much good,"

She stood up and began to gather the tea things. "I won't be a minute. We'll take the pup with us." She turned to the back door and lifted the latch, whistling through her teeth as only a shepherd's daughter can. A puppy romped in, all fluff and tail, jumping up at my trousers and barking. "Down, down! Trick! " said she bending to him, rubbing his neck and ears. "That's a good lad. Good pup. Quiet now, steady now," and the puppy responded straight away. As they say in these parts of someone who knows and understands working dogs, she had his eye and his ear.

As we stepped out into the midgey, humid air, I saw the little cottage with new eyes. When I had arrived that morning, directed by Jessie McChattin in the village store back at the crossroads in Corran Bridge, I had driven down the twisty single-track road totally in awe of this great landscape of mournful hills rising steeply above the wide moors and the rocky river snaking beside the road. I had thought it then a place of great majesty; a land of rock and the harsh raven's cry. But I had not thought of its people, of those who are born here and live out their days in the solitude of the long hard winter and the brief, apologetic summer; whose lives were still governed by the wind and the rain, the acid rocks and the peaty soils, despite the glossy life thrust at them by television, made tantalisingly real by the smart cars they all seemed to own. I was still in awe of the land; but now, having discovered what I came to find, I was in awe of its people too. I was finding that the two were inseparable, the Highlanders and their land. They were like the Scots pines around the Lodge at Ardvarnish, holding out against wind and storm, against greed and power far beyond the ability of the individual to influence. I had seen for the first time that the belonging is both spiritual and temporal—just as the pine belongs to its Highland ecosystem whether it stands or is felled, whether it survives in a remnant forest or as a single tree alone on a knoll on the vast empty moor. So it doesn't matter who owns the land, whose name is written on the deed filed away in the fusty safe of a lawyer's office. Andrew Duncan the shepherd, Mairi his wife, and this girl, their daughter Shiona, with the sad eyes and the savage red hair, and now her children—were of this land and of this place in a way I was only just beginning to understand.

We began to make our way gently down the stone track through the rhododendrons. Lord Denby had been kind, doing up the old estate kennels and creating a new home for them so that they could stand aside from the past and start again. Beside the burn I could see the old Keeper's Cottage part hidden by the hanging birch leaves. It stood empty now, awaiting conversion into a holiday cottage. I could see it only as Jimmy Forbes's cottage. I paused for a moment eyeing its lifeless windows and its locked door, remembering that he was down for life—for good. I was glad they were going to gut the cottage.

"It'll be nice to have it done up," I said as lightly as I could.

"Aye, it will that. Mac hates it as it is. I hope they paint the woodwork bright red or something cheerful.." We passed on.

"You still have not told me why you came," She said suddenly.

13

I didn't really know how to answer her. It wasn't simply curiosity; there was much more to it than that. "I think it was something his father said," I began, cautiously.

"I'd like to know," her voice slow, the clear eyes, not cold but demanding and authoritive, made me look down.

"He said this land had claimed Rob. I think those were his words. I didn't understand what he meant."

"And do you now?" Her voice matched her look.

"Yes. Yes, I think I do."

"I shall go to see them this winter." The baby murmured in her sleep and Shiona rocked the pram gently. "Mac likes us to get away from the glen for two or three weeks in the winter if we can and I always try to see Rob's folks."

Just then the bus came. It was new, a shiny red minibus. It swayed round the corners before stopping at the crossroads. "Aye aye, Hughie," she called, smiling at the old man at the wheel, his chubby arms protruding from a short-sleeved shirt. A slender boy jumped down trailing a p.v.c. shopping bag.

"Hiya, Mam!" He ran across the road to Shiona, his fine fair hair flying across his face. "Where's Janet?"

"Hush! Don't waken her, she's sleeping," said Shiona as the little boy tried to peep into the pram.

"Can I see?" he said, forgetting to whisper. Shiona smiled, with a glance at me.

"The novelty of the baby hasn't quite worn off yet." She picked up her son and held him close to the midge net for a moment or two.

"She's asleep," he announced.

"Away you go! Up to the house." Robbie dropped his bag in the dusty road and ran on up the track towards the rhododendrons. I picked it up.

"Well?" she asked, her eyes, appealing and vulnerable, searched for confirmation. I stared down at the smooth round stones protruding from the track, groping in my head for the right words. Words which would not wound her. "Yes," I said, at last. "I see him very clearly, when we first went to school together, only older than Robbie is now. That is what he looked like." We walked on in silence.

A vehicle rumbled through the tunnel of rhododendrons ahead. It was Mac. The Landrover stopped and the little boy climbed in to sit on his lap and hold the steering wheel as they came on down towards us. Mac's sculpted face, wind-tanned like an old oil painting, his beard greying at the temples, grinned at us. "Well then, you two!" The smile seemed to come from behind his eyes. "I was hoping that I'd catch you before you left, Peter. We've been counting hinds and calves up on Carn Mor and I came on down to say goodbye."

14

"You've both been so welcoming to me. Thank you." I shook his hand.

"I'm just going down to the sheds to see Jockie," Mac spoke to his wife. "I'll take Robbie with me. We'll be back for our tea in just a few minutes."

"Fine," she said. I watched the Landrover pull away, dust pluming from its wheels and the birch fronds fluttering above the track.

At the cottage I threw my jacket into the car and turned to this girl I had come to find and whose story I wanted to tell. "Goodbye," I said, "and thanks..." I couldn't think of anything else to say.

—2—

There is a special healing in the hill. Shiona did not go there often, but on this occasion it was no good fleeing to her bedroom, or running out to the dog shed. Her dog Trick was long dead and she had never found such a friend in the others since. No, it was out and away she wanted, urgently, quickly, to the mountain she had looked at all her life through the little skylight in her bedroom ceiling; out, to struggle above the hurt and the crampedness of her home, and away, because it was for that she yearned the most, and for the moment, only the mountain could provide it.

She was climbing more slowly now. The burning anger was leaving her, there was less need to hurry. At first she had run, her feet pounding the well-worn path past the rowan tree, the fank, and across the burn. As the ground steepened she had forced herself on, hands on knees to maintain the upward surge. She was aflame. Her anger burned, her chest burned, her leg muscles burned.

Twice only she had paused on the way up. Now the cottage was far below, although still clearly in view and she turned to eye it from above, reassuring herself that it was far enough away. She sat down beside a large grey rock. It was warm to her hand. Leaning back against it she closed her eyes, lifting her face to the sun. Even through closed lids it was more than she could bear. Her mind became a redness of blood and heat from within and without. She felt dizzy; the pain of injustice and outrage indistinguishable from her searing lungs and aching legs.

The first time she had stopped was to turn back; her face

drained white against the flame of her hair, anger raging; she wanted to go back to her father and tell him that she'd had enough. She was leaving for the south where she would succeed a great deal better than he had ever done, away up in this glen.

The speech was well rehearsed. Practiced many times in her bedroom with the ceiling steep-combed and the two-paned skylight through which, from her bed, she knew the morning sun setting fire to the peak of the mountain; or again, down by the burn, at the swinging bridge made of rusty steel cable and planks, when the burn was thundering in spate and the creamy brown water crashed among the boulders, flecks of white spume flying.

But it was a speech never delivered. The presence of her father had always been too powerful; his huge hands rough like alder bark to hold, his bronze forearms matted with sandy hair, and the muscle-thongs in his neck bulging when he was angry. But this time, she could not tolerate it any longer. Yet the futility of arguing with him turned her to the hill. Ignoring the pain in her calves, she went on up the steepening path.

She climbed on, steadily now. The healing was with her and the mountain sucked her ever upwards, higher and higher among its whispering scree until, alone with the sliding sun she threw herself down and turned to face the glen.

Old Trick had been dead these six years. He was buried under the rowan tree at the bottom of the lambing park on a day she remembered in minute detail—the pile of gravelly earth beside that dark hole; the silence of her father and not wanting to catch his eye; the spitting rain on her white school shirt so that it stuck to her; and her mother in the green-flowered apron looking on from the cottage door. She had loved her father that day for his gentleness with the old dog; the way he carried Trick in his arms, placed him in an old sack and down into the deep hole. And his words: "I'll not have another dog like Trick. You only get one like him," as his shovel bit the earth pile with more than usual power and the stony ground flew in on the sack until it was gone. When she glanced up she thought she saw a shine in his eye she had never seen before or again.

But that was then. As the years passed and she grew into her teens, so she had become ill at ease in her home. She seemed always to be in trouble, playing her music too loud, being out too late, or shortening her school skirt so that her father in outrage threw her make-up bag in the fire where it melted in sputtering green and blue flames. Even when she did well at school and passed her exams he had seemed to scorn her, saying her generation knew too much and no good would come of it if they didn't get down to doing a job of work. Now she was through with school and she had worked these past sixteen months, in the household of Lady Denby, up at Ardvarnish Lodge. Yet things were little better.

Certainly her father listened when she brought home tales of extravagance at the big house, of the guests coming and going, sometimes famous names and faces she had seen in magazines. He was pleased when she came in with half a salmon from the kitchens or a share of port left over when the Denbys all went south, but those were rare moments of approval.

And now this. Lord Denby had caught what he called his May fish—a modest twelve pound grilse—and the family had all gone back to Yorkshire. She was working only part-time at the Lodge for Bella Forbes, Jimmy the Stalker's wife, who was bossy. She called herself housekeeper when she was really no more than a domestic, giving herself airs behind Lady Denby's back, quick to steal the credit for everyone else's hard work when she had done little herself. So Shiona was at home more than usual until the Denbys returned for the grouse in August, and her father took it out on her , saying "You'll no' get paid for sitting about the house. If you were worth a crust you'd have a proper job like other folk." She knew she should not have answered back. "If I wasn't trapped in this glen because of you and the damned sheep I would have a proper job and live in a decent house with a car and friends and a life of my own, instead of living here and having to work like a slave for those people." "Get out of my house!" he had roared at her. "And out of my sight 'til y'can keep a civil tongue in your head! I'll not have a daughter of mine speaking like that!"

So she came to be here, high on the mountain, looking down on her whole existence spread out below her. Nearly twenty years old and she knew little beyond the life of Ardvarnish Estate and the five families it supported. She had made good friends at school, some of whom were married now with wee ones. The journey to school in Lairg every day, twenty three miles there and twenty seven back again to drop off the MacFee boys, was in a rattly old bus with sticky seats, driven by fat Hughie Macrae who cycled from his croft to the bus every morning because it couldn't get down the track, and who, leaving his cycle clips on all day, was universally known as Hughie Clips.

Most of her friends had said they were going south, and some had done so. Meggie McLardy had gone to a secretarial college in Aberdeen and then on to London. Her brother Iain said she was earning twenty thousand and working in an office made of green marble. Everyone knew Ellen McChattin from the shop was a model because they had seen her in a magazine and her mother had the photos pinned up beside the till. But most of her friends lived in Lairg or Rogart and could get away out to Dornoch or Tain or even to Inverness, whereas she had to get a lift down the glen. Eleven lurching miles beside the river and the loch, before she even reached the main road. And lifts were not that easy to come by. Her family only had the shepherd's van that went with her father's job and he was always off up the glen to the sheep and her mother didn't drive. Her brother Andy had the use of a pick-up belonging to Dunc the fencing contractor he was working with just now, but he was away by seven-thirty in the morning, and being two years older he was out till all hours of the night with whichever of his three current girls was available. It rankled with her that he could do as he pleased. The rules were very different for her.

Even when she could get away she felt inadequate. She had used up all her savings on driving lessons in Dornoch and had passed her test first time, but with no car available she had spent all her money to no gain. She had been to Glasgow, to a football match with Andy and some of his wild friends who had got drunk and then been sick on her dress in the car on the way back; and to Edinburgh, with her mother two years before; and even to Ibiza on a package tour with her family, where they shared a hotel with a rowdy bunch from Leeds who ragged them about being Jocks until her father lost his temper and called them, "—Ignorant English bastards!" and Andy joined in saying if it hadn't been for the Highlanders, Britain would never have won the war. After that things became strained and Jodi, the girl from Leeds with whom she had made friends, said her parents had forbidden her to go to the beach with her any more.

Nineteen she was, and still a virgin, although not for want of chance from Danny Stott's rough hands on her in the back of his car, an experiment she had found both exciting and tantalisingly distasteful. Perhaps Danny had been a bad start. She was glad she had pulled away, although later she had winced to hear that he put it about that she was a teaser. She was pleased to have escaped from Geordie Hoggett after the dance in Ardgay. There was no doubt he knew what he wanted, and how to go about getting it. But just the knowledge that he had been with most girls between sixteen and twenty from Golspie to Dornoch as well as a good few older married women who should have known better, was sufficient challenge to let him venture just far enough.

Sex presented her with no real concern. She was attractive, that she knew—more than that, she knew she was striking, even good-looking. She had always turned the boys' heads—and she had overheard Danny say she was 'a cracker'. Sex was there and it was exciting, but for now she was content to wait. There were other far more pressing problems to sort out. Tied to Ardvarnish, living in the tiny cottage under the feet of her parents had to be overcome first.

Love, on the other hand, she had spent many hours thinking about in her little bed, looking out at the mountain, or at the moon on frosty nights when it was too cold to turn over, pretending that she was destined for a passionate love match with Lord Denby's youngest son Nigel, who had kissed her once, in the stag larder, placing an arm round her waist and pulling her up into his face firmly and gently, whispering, "I say, you're a winner, Shiona," and at the last moment his lips brushing across hers to land delicately on her cheek. Then he let her go, and was gone. She was left standing slightly dazed on the scrubbed concrete floor with meat hooks and tackle hanging all round her. Nigel was only thanking her for removing the evidence of excess left in the billiard room after a late night party with his friends, before Lord Denby came down and threw what the family called 'a wobbly.' Nigel had called her into the stag larder saying, "Give me a hand with these buckets would you, Shiona?" It was innocent enough, and his gratitude was real. Shiona knew Nigel was afraid of his father's anger, just as she was of her but at the same time it was the most arousingly provocative thing he could have done.

Not that she was under any illusion about Nigel Tansley-Fairfax. He was well known for the procession of girls who were constantly chasing him. Shiona had often watched them enviously with their expensive jewellery and patterned headscarves, the designer dresses they wore to dinner which she had found in the mornings abandoned in a crushed jumble of silk and sequins when she was 'tidying out,' as Bella Forbes called it. She would pick them up and shake them gently just to hear the seductive rustle, as she placed them on hangers, briefly clutching them to herself at the mirror and wondering if she would ever own such lovely things, before hanging them with a dozen others in a bulging wardrobe.

Love was a mystery to her because it was everywhere and yet it was nowhere to be found. It was permanently on the radio and television, pop songs throbbed out its importance, and yet, in the whole of her almost twenty years she had never seen the slightest evidence of its real existence. There were times when she had wondered whether it wasn't just an excuse for gratifying sexual or sometimes financial needs—a kind of game adults played to make the whole reproduction business seem more respectable. Or then again, perhaps it was just something very rare which didn't happen much in the Highlands. If that was the case it was another very good reason for leaving before it was too late. If what her parents had was anything to go by, or

Jimmy and Bella Forbes, Shiona simply didn't want it. She had never witnessed the remotest demonstration of affection between any of them.

And what Andy did to his women behind the peat stack had nothing whatever to do with anything she had ever read in a poem. She had seen them often enough, in the back of his car in a passing place down the glen, scarcely even pulled off the road. As far as she could see, her brother had spent the past five years indulging in quantity without any thought for quality of emotional experience.

And then again, when Morag MacKillup had married Davy Phimister, the salmon fisherman from Lochinver, she had said she was in love and that it was all wonderful. They certainly looked fine enough at the wedding in Lairg. The photographs are a good record of how much it all must have cost poor old Sandy MacKillup, but if their smiles recorded their tenderness for each other it bore no relation at all to what she found when she went up to Lochinver six months later to see Morag in her new home. All she had seen of the wonderful husband was a man staggering in, too drunk to speak at midnight, and in the morning, roundly cursing Morag for wasting time 'blethering with women,' instead of getting his breakfast.

Her youth was burgeoning and she wanted to test it on the world—the real world, that she had known all her life, sensed in things she had read and seen in films and on television, but which was not here among these mountains, nor in Lochinver, nor Lairg, nor even in Inverness, but far away in what was universally known to Highlanders as 'the south', which could mean London or Edinburgh, Northumberland or Cornwall or beyond, anywhere, in fact, not hemmed in, as she was, by the mountains and the inward-looking traditions of her parents and the church and the past.

A raven croaked loudly and Shiona started. The raven called again, a throat-rattling curse which told of crags and high places. It swept off across the corrie with a wind-scythe of black pinions. Shiona knew ravens well. If you lived on Ardvarnish estate you couldn't help but know the raven—alive and dead. Her father cursed them for killing his weakling lambs and Jimmy Forbes poisoned and shot them out of the sky because whatever was black was vermin and must die, and if it wasn't vermin its survival depended entirely upon whether there were fish in the river or grouse on the hill for the Denbys and their guests to chase. If the sport was poor, whether they said it or not, he felt he was to blame and he had to take it out on something.

Many a time Shiona had climbed into the back of the Landrover to find herself face to face with a heap of dead hoodie crows or a buzzard, or even a golden eagle. Once she found herself sitting beside an otter. Its shining fur so warm to the touch that she withdrew her hand sharply thinking that it might not be quite dead, but a glance at its crushed head revealed that would never bite anything again. It had been caught in a gin trap set just below the water level where otters had always slipped in and out of the Falls Pool. Jimmy's steel-bound heel had stamped on its skull before removing it from the trap. "Why d'you kill otters?" she asked, and regretted it the moment she saw Jimmy's face. "They eat bloody fish, don't they? lassie," he snapped. "If they eat his lordship's fish they get the same treatment from me as the foxes get from your father for eating his lordship's lambs. And that's the way of it." "Oh." she had said lamely, as her courage failed her. She wanted to point out that surely there was a difference, wasn't there, between lambs on the hill, which were farm stock put there by men, and wild salmon in the river Corran?

But Andy had told her there was good money in otter skins and she knew that since Jimmy was at that moment travelling in the direction of Lairg, the dead otter was destined for Willie MacFee at Braeside. She had once got off the school bus with the MacFee boys and peeped into the old steading behind the house. Hanging from the beams, stretched out on boards and in festering heaps were the skins of every conceivable beast which crawled the hill, from Highland cattle and black lambs to deer, wild cats, otters, badgers, pine martens, foxes and blue hares. A gut-churning stench of death and interrupted decay made her retch and turn back to Hughie Clips's chuckling face. The thought of the otter going there had remained with her for days.

She shaded her eyes against the sun and looked round the great vista of peaks spreading away to the west. This was a wild and beautiful place, there was no doubt of that. Mrs Trenchard at school, who was an in-comer from Cardiff, told them that they were privileged to be able to live surrounded by such beauty and that millions of people had to live their lives without space or clean air or any scenery at all. Today, however, was the wrong day for that argument. She would have swapped Glen Corran for Cardiff in an instant and without a care. Something had snapped and at last she could go back down and face her little world again. Her mind was made up.

She noticed the sun glinting on a vehicle moving slowly down the glen road far below. She shaded her eyes to look more closely. It wasn't her father because the van was still beside the cottage. Jimmy was away into town, and the tourists rarely came this far up until much later in the year. The car edged slowly closer. It couldn't be Mr Holdingham the factor because he never came up the strath on a Thursday afternoon unless Lord Denby was at the Lodge.

She could see it now. It was a strange car, definitely not a local. It was one of those cars they called a beetle. She had never seen that one before. She watched it intently with the magnetic fascination born to the inhabitants of all remote communities, a fascination which often became a fixation and then an obsession. She mused to herself, carefully storing the information away. Then the car was gone, away down the glen, away from her, away from her angry father and Jimmy Forbes and Ardvarnish Estate and her own troubled orbit.

She began to pick her way down the mountain. She wouldn't go back to the cottage straight away, she would go up to the Lodge and see if she could help Bella in the laundry—something she would normally avoid, but anything was better than going back to face her father. If she waited she knew he would be off down the glen to the Glen Corran Hotel where he would stay in the bar until after nine.

The bright mountain had given her strength and her head. She could see herself clearly now. She was a Highlander born and reared in a wild and lonely glen. She belonged to its people with their soft, benignant voices and turbulent history, all as much a part of her as she of it, and she knew that was something very good.

She walked calmly and quietly past the cottage. Her step was purposeful and she never faltered. She turned into the dusty road and on up through the ocean of mauve and crimson rhododendrons to Ardvarnish Lodge. Whatever happened tonight, or tomorrow, or the next day, one thing she had decided. She was leaving, and it was now only a matter of time.

—3—

Gerald Edwin Stacey Tansley-Fairfax, fourth Baron Denby of Garth, had not slept. He stood in his bare feet and pyjamas hidden by a long burgundy silk robe. It was a spectacular robe. It had a broad green quilted collar and tied around his middle was a thick cord of woven burgundy, green and gold silk strands ending in fat thistle tassels. They reminded him of the purple-flowered spear thistles which lined the hill track at Ardvarnish.

He stood in the library window looking out over the terrace and the Long Lawn where rabbits bounced about in the steely grey light. "The little blighters know they're just out of range," he mused idly, although his concern was not for the rabbits or the damage they might be doing to the gardens at Denby Hall. Lord Denby was troubled by a much deeper malaise. It was a problem which had worried him for years, but which now, in his fifty-eighth year, and nearing the end of his useful working life (what he called 'the opportunity span' which all men pass through between the ages of thirty and sixty) he saw as an unstoppable force which would eventually change everything he had known.

He gazed out over the tailored lawns and the elegant parkland of beeches and oaks positioned like the chorus on a ballet set, each great tree with a skirt of long branches trailing to the grass—a signal that whoever owned the land was rich enough to be able to afford to keep grazing animals away from the trees for centuries. His distracted eye passed over the intricate lattice of paved limestone paths, cut stone walls and arches; terraced rose gardens with elegant statuary gesturing among the blousy, scented blooms, and, the feature for which Denby was most renowned, the remarkable domed orangery, an extravaganza of Victorian glass and wrought iron.

Denby was everything to him. He knew it in tiny detail from the dipper's nest under the iron trellis bridge over the Ladies' Walk Gorge, which had never failed to fledge young in the fifty years he could remember, to the name of the bell-founders, Thorpe & Jessop of Tadcaster, on the huge brass bell in the clock-tower. Even at Ardvarnish his mind drifted back to Denby as he lay in the heather while Jimmy Forbes was spying for a stag. With more than a hint of disapproval Jimmy had said to him one day "You're no' supposed to be writing on the hill, m'Lord," when he had turned from the telescope to find him scribbling in a little black book. "If I don't write things down when I think of them, Jimmy, I forget them, and the chestnuts badly need the surgeon before the winter gets to them." Jimmy had never been to Denby. That side of his employer's life was probably shrouded in the fantasy and myth of huge wealth and power. He thought very likely that his lordship might be speaking about horses, which he knew there were at Denby, so he declined to comment, escaping with, "Aye weel, that's the way of it, m'Lord. Ye canna deny that."

That was the way of it, and that was the way which worried Gerry the most. His home was under serious threat. It wasn't his fault and he didn't blame himself, but there was apparently nothing he could do to prevent the Denby empire ebbing inexorably away from his control.

It wasn't the social order changing which was the problem, in fact Gerry found it a relief. He could cope with that perfectly well. He was neither arrogant nor vain. He wasn't even stuffy, for all his formal grooming, and it didn't much bother him whether he was Lord Denby or Joe Soap, but, since he had been cast in his role by the accident of birth, he had lived with it and done his best to uphold the values of his class as he had inherited them, carrying them forward in as sensitive and honourable a way as he could. Dinah felt differently. But then, like her mother, she was a fool as well as a snob, and since she couldn't see beyond the end of her over-powdered nose she wasted her entire life fussing about not receiving the respect she thought she deserved from waitresses in hotel tea-rooms. Gerry knew that only he was to blame for that. Long before he married her he had known she was inherently bourgeois despite the vigorous shield of pretention her parents erected by double-barrelling their name and financially crippling themselves with too big a house and too many servants in a last-ditch bid to marry their daughters well. His fault, because he had seen through it too late. The allure of her body, which, he confessed, had been considerable and more or less permanently available, (egged on, he was sure, by her mother, whose own morals were opportunistic to say the least), had persuaded him to adopt a charitable view. Money was not in short supply at the time; its carefree application and the buoyancy of youth had fooled him to believe he could iron out any affectations he found disagreeable. How wrong he had been about that.

While Dinah was salt in the wound of his discontent, she was not the problem. He had learned to cope with her and had even developed a bogus temper which he could turn on at a moment's notice over any trivial annoyance to ensure that she backed off and left him in peace. At least she ran an efficient household and was good to their three boys. With skilful support from what he rudely called 'putty and paint' she could still look very good, even though her charms were not available these days. No, the problem was purely material.

For centuries the Tansley-Fairfaxes had managed their estates in a paternalistic and slightly pious feudal way, carefully sitting on political and religious fences until they could see which way to jump. The family upheld a respectable but uninspiring profile until the Industrial Revolution turned the West Riding of Yorkshire into a treadmill of exploitation for short-term gain. With seven thousand acres running from Wakefield to Barnsley with high quality coal underlying most of it, it was hardly surprising that Queen Victoria's government had deemed their contribution to the industrial core of the Empire to be worthy of the barony Gerry now proudly held.

His forbears had opened up little surface pits in the seventeenth century, deepened them throughout the eighteenth and expanded them into a labyrinthine maze in the nineteenth, through which it was possible to walk the eleven miles from Wakefield to Barnsley at an average depth of five hundred feet below ground.

The Fairfax family had succeeded, helped by a strategic marriage to a Tansley heiress, in increasing their wealth, their land and their influence for five consecutive centuries. In his lifetime all that had changed. While Britain was still reeling from the privations of the war effort, the socialists had nationalised the coal industry in 1948. In one vicious swipe the seven Denby coal mines and the capital heartland of their empire had been lopped off. They had received compensation for the loss of their assets, of course—and a heady sum it had seemed at the time—but overnight they had become preservers rather than creators of wealth. The introduction of capital taxes, like Death Duty, for which the Tansley-Fairfaxes were ripe picking, meant that the almost immediate death of his grandfather handed straight back to the exchequer nearly half the cash it had taken them five centuries to accrue. 'The redistribution of wealth' was the justification and the official euphemism. And so, with a great deal of bad grace and worse language, the process of selling off assets to pay the tax bill had begun.

Forty years later it was still happening. Gone were the racehorses and the fashionable town houses in Curzon Street and Newmarket, the Rolls-Royces and their liveried chauffeurs, his grandfather's yacht with its crew of sixteen, most of the Hall servants and the much loved Denby foxhounds. Gone was the Garthwaite limestone quarry, the light-engineering company they had developed to serve their own needs, and a good few hundred acres of development land on the outskirts of Huddersfield and Wakefield had vanished as well.

Gerry knew he was on a slippery slope and gathering speed. That was what kept him sleepless at night. He didn't know how to apply the brakes, let alone put it into reverse. His was the first generation in five centuries to preside over the break up of the dynasty which rows of his ancestors, all neatly lined up in their brass-bound and lead-lined oak coffins on stone shelves in the family vault below Denby church, had believed could never happen. "Some bloody privilege!" he barked out loud just as, unheard, Dinah entered the library door behind him.

"What are you grumbling about now, Gerry? Don't you know it's not yet six o'clock? I heard you come down at least an hour ago. I've asked you a hundred times to close your dressing room door behind you. If there's a window open on the gallery it always bangs and wakes the whole house."

"Damned rabbits are on the increase again." said Gerry quietly, not bothering to turn round. He knew perfectly well what time it was and seeing his gin-blotched wife at that hour of the morning was not going to help solve his problems and just might spoil his whole day. "Well then you must get Hardcliffe to do something about it," snapped Dinah, "Yes, I must," he said in resigned submission, adding "you can remind me again at breakfast and at luncheon and at dinner tonight, just in case I forget." It worked, and with a silken swish of whatever it was she was wearing, she was gone.

He spent the rest of the morning avoiding people. He made sure Dinah was not in the morning-room before going in to breakfast, and when Mrs Dudgeon came in to offer him bacon and eggs he said "Just coffee and toast this morning, thank you, Mrs D. If anybody wants me I shall be in the estate office later on, but for the next couple of hours I am not available."

Marjorie Dudgeon, having known him from the age of fifteen when she, not a lot older herself, entered service at Denby by marrying the under-gardener and moving in to the East Lodge, recognised the signals immediately, muttered, "Very good, m'Lord," and withdrew promptly. Half an hour later, hearing the coughing approach of Dinah and her scabby Yorkshire terrier which had chronic halitosis in total disproportion to its size, Gerry left by the French windows and slid out through the wisteria-scented orangery without being seen.

He walked the three quarters of a mile down the west drive between the long lines of majestically canopied limes and beeches. He walked in slow cogitative paces, savouring the place he loved and the kindness of the day. Young rooks racketed high above him as he crossed the pilastered stone bridge over Garth Beck he leaned over to see the wild flags in full bloom, their vivid yellow studding the tight packed fortress of green blades. A grey wagtail flashed past to land flickering on a stone.

Feeling much better and with an insouciant kick at a stone, he strode on down the avenue.

At the estate office he walked straight in to see Harry Poncenby, his agent, who ran the entire Denby empire—and looked it, in checked shirt and regimental tie, corduroys and heavy brogue shoes on what promised to be a hot day. He was as solid as a shire horse from Appleby Fair and as reliable as the Denby stables clock which just happened to be striking ten in high, churchy tones. "Morning, Harry. What's afoot today?" he asked chirpily, his mood transformed. He collapsed into an old leather armchair in the corner, leaning back and sticking his feet straight out. Harry stood up from behind his desk, pulled off his horn-rimmed glasses and smiled generously. "Good morning, Gerry. How are you?"

"Since you ask, I was bloody awful until the walk down here. I do love that avenue. Have you seen the flags in the Beck?

They're a delight just now. Dinah's been in one of her damned nagging moods for days, so I've escaped. What have you got brewing down here?"

"Oh dear." Harry sighed as sympathetically as he dared, looking down at his papers and wishing he hadn't asked. The very last thing he wanted was to be sucked into domestic strife. He knew perfectly well that if either of them ever got a sniff of him taking sides, his life would be intolerable. "There is one thing might interest you," he started, knowing that under normal circumstances he would not have brought it to Gerry's attention at all, but using it as a handy opportunity to change the subject. "I had a phone call yesterday from Derek Holdingham about the new fence at Ardvarnish running back into the hill to Carn Mor to see if we can't keep some of Duncan's sheep in place, and he mentioned that Forbes had intercepted some young fella camping in the old ruined croft at Dalbattigh."

"Good Lord!" exclaimed Gerry, "What a ruddy awful place to camp. It's full of sheep shit, isn't it?"

"Yes, I think it is. But some of these young chaps don't mind where they doss down. I should quite like to know just who he was and what he was doing there in the first place."

"I expect he was just one of these spring time hill-walkers, don't you think? Can't say I blame 'im, Ardvarnish is such a lovely place in June before the midge gets going. I'm surprised we don't get more of 'em."

"Could be it," said Harry, "but Forbes doesn't think so. He thought he was up to something. And you know what he's like, he has to know who everybody is and what their business is and if he doesn't like it they generally get sent packing in no uncertain way."

"Hmmph." grunted Gerry. "The trouble with Forbes is he does what he likes and there are those who don't always like what he does. Myself included. I hope to God he hasn't been loosing off at hooked beaks again. If he does that once more he can collect his cards. We can't afford to have the law down on us like poor old Iain Cumberland at Tordarroch." Gerry looked serious.

"No, you needn't worry about that. I've told Derek to make it absolutely clear to Jimmy Forbes that he's not to hit birds of prey. Anyway, I don't think that's what this is about at all. I expect it's some young chap interested in doing his own thing. The trouble is he's upset Forbes and if we're not careful we'll be in the local papers for throwing innocent walkers off the hill. If he's an archaeologist looking at some old Clearances ruins or something or other, I've no objection to him looking around. But he must do it through the factor, so I've told Derek to keep an eye out for 'im. Apparently he drives an orange beetle car so we should be able to spot 'im alright if he comes into the glen again. I don't think it's anything much to fuss about."

"Fine," said Gerry, getting bored.

"Now that I've got you, Gerry, I do need to talk to you about some of these industrial rents we don't seem to be able to collect these days..." Gerry Denby was not interested in industrial rents. He was already at Ardvarnish. He was walking on his own up to Loch Stac, trout rod in hand. "...I'm afraid it'll end in court, and that'll be the third time this year." Harry droned on.

"Serve the bastards right!" exclaimed Gerry jumping to his feet. "Fling a few writs about, Harry. They wouldn't waste any time doing it to us if we didn't pay our bills. I'll see you again later in the day." He was out of the door before Harry could reply.

He stood for a moment in the cobbled yard looking across the elegant parkland to the house barely visible in the distance. This place was where he belonged, a landscape lovingly passed father to son for more than eight hundred years. How could Harry understand that? Or anyone else for that matter. It was private, his belonging, a matter for him and his soul and no-one else.

Just then three magpies flew across from the stables, the first bird landing briefly on the coach house roof before pitching off again, chasing the other two. They laughed a loud, raucous cackle as they disappeared among the limes. Gerry threw his left hand in the air, holding three fingers aloft as he had been taught by his grandfather to make the superstition hold good.

"One for sorrow, two for joy," he said out loud, "three for a girl...well, well, a girl, eh?" He strode off up the avenue wondering who this girl could be and how she might affect him at this late stage in his life. Whoever she was, there was no sign of her here at Denby.

Then a sparkle came into his eye and a spring into his step. He had just decided to do something entirely different. He was the boy again, the taste of mischief sharp in his mouth, a little rush of pleasure across his shoulders and down his arms as he walked away from Harry and the rents and the leaden respectability of his existence. He was not going to tell a soul, least of all Dinah. In June, the month he loved most at Denby, he was skipping north. He would escape with his trout rod to Ardvarnish—without Dinah, without the boys, without any guests and without even telling the estate staff he was coming. He didn't care a damn about anybody else. He was going to have a few days on his own and leave the problems of old Denby to sort themselves out. And he was going now.

On the the overnight sleeper to Inverness he felt like a naughty schoolboy. In thirty years of marriage he had never gone off without telling Dinah to her face. He had left a note which was a blatant lie—that he had to go into York on business and that he might have to go on down to London for a couple of days.

His grandfather had bought Ardvarnish at the end of the last century from the estate of an estranged Duchess of Sutherland; forty-five thousand acres of mountain, heather moorland and wild, tumbling river. The second Lord Denby had dismantled the old Ardvarnish Lodge and built the present, not beautiful, but imposing white-harled building, which, if not in the full Balmorality style, had sufficient Gothic influence in its turrets and crow-stepped gables to give it a flourish of which the widowed and reclusive Queen Victoria might have approved. The house had two faces. One, looking down the river, garnering the morning light spilling in from the east along the Corran gorge, dancing silver-footed among the rocky pools; and the other facing west so that in long rose evenings the family could recline in the ample glass conservatory, safe from the rapacious Highland midge.

Three generations of Denbys had stalked the deer, shot the grouse on the purple moor, and flicked their romantically named and artistically manufactured flies over the peaty pools of the sparkling river. In common with many absentee owners of Highland sporting estates, for three generations they had scarcely ever been anywhere else. The penalty for owning your own mountains and rivers was that in order to justify the heavy costs of maintaining it all, you had to invite a regular succession of family, friends and guests to enjoy it for you.

Gerry had stalked and shot on a few other Highland moors and hills, and he'd fished a good many rivers in his time, but only for a day or two here and there so that he had seldom had an opportunity to spend any time anywhere else in the Highlands. As he lay in his bunk listening to names echoing around those tiny, drafty platforms where the train paused in the short June night, he found himself wondering who lived there and on what could they possibly survive.

———4———

If you were to choose a place for a young naturalist to kill time on a bright June morning, then the mouth of Loch Fleet where the tide jostles through the narrows at Littleferry would suit very well. Rob lobbed pebbles into the murmuring water twenty feet in front of him. He had no interest in where they landed. He was brooding. To look at him would tell the casual observer almost nothing. He might have been a tourist, or a birdwatcher, or a local unemployed youth sitting about on the shingle on a sunny morning. His saggy brown pullover and jeans, and a yellow and white spotted handkerchief knotted at his neck gave nothing away. He was unshaven but only by twenty-four hours, and wore round, thin, gold-rimmed spectacles which lent him a not-altogether-inaccurate, mildly studious image. His manner had a disconsolate air, like a lover who didn't know whether to go on or pull back, as if he looked without seeing behind the glasses slightly at odds with the clear morning and the shinkly blue sea. On the shingle beside him lay a pair of expensive-looking binoculars which, even in his present mood, seemed to be a part of him in a way which was the only real clue. They were essential to his trade and he never went anywhere without them.

Yet, despite the wide variety of seabirds and waders which rowed back and forwards across his view, he was not interested in examining them any more closely. That had been his priority when first he crawled out of his little tent pegged out on the rabbit-mown sward dotted with sea-pinks like confetti, a hundred yards up towards the dunes behind him. He had systematically surveyed the loch and its shoreline out of pure habit. It was as instinctive to him as cleaning his teeth and gulping the fresh sea tang.

Much of what he expected was there: eider duck cooing and bobbing in luminous rafts on the tide; the spiky wings of redshank and dunlin flicking across muddy runnels; cormorants and mergansers snatching fish in the ruffled water; rowdy oystercatchers in street gangs whose shrill insistence flailed the morning calm; a large flotilla of common gulls riding at anchor out on the loch, all pointing the same way as if controlled by some unseen conductor; the scratchy cries of common terns raking the air, alighting delicately and lifting off again in a tireless display of aerial grace; hoodie crows flotsam-picking on the tideline, ever capitalising on the misfortune of others.

Rob was a competent field naturalist. At the age of twenty-five he could identify at a glance, not only the twenty or so common bird species present on a north-east sea loch in summer, but most other British and European birds as well. He had spent thousands of hours examining them, prying into their private ways and their habitats, to achieve his high degree of competence. He was intellectually and philospohically wedded to the natural world in a way rarely understood by those who do not share the intimacy of knowledge such competence permits.

His knowledge had, with the experience of ground covered and time served, moved him into another ambit, away from being a bird-watcher or a hobby naturalist into someone who, at a thoughtful glance at the plants and animals present or absent on a piece of land, could expose its origins, its underlying rocks, its fertility, and its use or abuse at the hand of man.

He was not there to look at the birds. He had come out to the point overlooking Littleferry to get as far away from the mountains as he could. In a few minutes time, at nine o'clock, he planned to try to use his mobile phone to ring the office in Inverness. Mobiles were all very well in low country, but in the Highlands their use was limited. The crowding hills were as much a barrier to technology now as they had always been to man's pressing demands for communication. After discovering the only public phone box he had found had been vandalised, he decided to come right out to the coast.

Rob glanced at his watch. It was three minutes past nine. 'That should do it,' he thought as he pulled up the aerial and punched in the numbers. To his relief it rang first time.

"Rob!" exclaimed Mike Stone, pleased to hear from him. "I've been waiting for you to call. How d'you get on?"

"Bad, I'm afraid. We've got a trouble spot all right and I think I know who's responsible." "How bad?" Mike sounded anxious.

"Well, it's hard to say for sure, but there are no eagles at the Carn Mor eyrie and no peregrines in the Corran gorge. I've spent three days watching and there's been no movement at all."

"What about the Altborish peregrines?" asked Mike.

"Yeah. They're there okay. Three chicks and looking good."

"So it's just Glen Corran, is it? Is it that bugger Forbes at Ardvarnish?" Mike asked again.

"Looks that way. There's no-one else in the strath unless he's in cahoots with Andrew Duncan the shepherd up there. Hold a minute, will you? I just want to check something out."

Rob put the phone down on the shingle and snatched his binoculars to his eyes. He scanned the water out to sea. A speck rose and fell on the gentle swell and Rob studied it intently for several seconds. Picking up the phone again he continued, "Sorry about that, a diver just showed up."

"Where the hell are you?" demanded Mike indignantly.

"I'm at the mouth of Loch Fleet. It's the only place I can get this ruddy phone to work. It's a red-throat, probably from one of those lochans up behind Ben Bhraggie."

"You lucky sod! Why don't you come down here and do a desk job for a few months and see how you like it?"

Rob laughed. "Not me, thanks. I'll stick to the real work."

31

"You cheeky bugger! Now, listen. We need to be able to pin something on that man Forbes. Will you get back up there and have a good hunt round and see if you can pick anything up. Spend some time in the local bar and see what you can over-hear. But whatever you do don't raise a stink. If he is poisoning or trapping we want the evidence to nail 'im."

"Er Mike, I'm afraid I've screwed it up." said Rob. "Jimmy Forbes caught me camping in an old shepherd's bothy and threw me off the estate yesterday."

"Does he know who you are?"

"No, I don't think so. I managed to get my binos and maps inside my rucksack before he saw them and I said I was just hill-walking, but he was dead twitchy. I'm sure he's our man. He looked as guilty as hell." Rob lobbed another pebble into the sea and then went on, "I sounded indignant and insisted I was-n't doing any harm, but he wasn't having any of it. He made me leave straight away and I know he watched me drive right out of the glen. I stopped at the Glen Corran Hotel and put the car round the back and sure enough, minutes later Forbes came down behind me in a Landrover. He turned round at the cross-roads and went slowly back again, so I'm sure he was seeing me off his patch."

"Did you ask what the estate procedure was for hill-walkers?"

"Yeah, I did. He said Lord Denby didn't allow walkers on Ardvarnish without written permission from the factor. That's Derek Holdingham of Dank and Subtley's in Lairg."

"Oh, yeah. I know Derek, he's okay. You won't get much out of him but I think he's straight enough. I don't think he gives a damn about the wildlife, but he's not anti-people. You should get permission to hill-walk no bother. Go and see him today, and apologise for upsetting the stalker. Then at least you'll be able to go back without being molested. And you'd better climb a few peaks for good measure. You never know you might find a dotterel."

"Okay," he replied enthusiastically. He liked the idea of being paid to climb some of Sutherland's wildest and loneliest hills.

"And Rob, if you do find anything, follow the procedures by the book and phone in immediately. Leave it to us to bring in the police. It's all very well nailing Forbes, but if in fact it's the shepherd as well, and they're both acting under the direct instructions of Lord Denby, we want to know it all. This is the sixth year there have been no eagles breeding on Ardvarnish and the place is beginning to look like a black hole. This could be the big one we need to blow the whole thing wide open. Go at it gently."

"Will do." replied Rob. "I'll ring in again in a day or two."

Rob Pearce was a roving warden for the Scottish Society for Bird Conservation, working on the use of illegal poisoning and killing of protected species. It had taken him three consecutive summer contracts doing wildlife recording work to become trusted enough to carry out detection work in the field. Now he was on his own for the first time. He was enjoying it, although discovering the extent of the illegal destruction of wildlife angered and depressed him. He was well aware of the responsibility and the challenge. He turned his binoculars back to search for the red-throated diver. It was nowhere to be seen. Rob stood up and snapped the aerial back into the phone and headed back to his tent to break camp and return to Ardvarnish.

Jimmy Forbes knew he had over-reacted when he threw Rob off the estate. Just in case a complaint was lodged against him he had phoned the factor and reported the incident straightaway. He had painted a damning picture, making out that Rob had been behaving in a furtive manner and implying, if not actually suggesting, that he was a drop-out who, as like as not, would be light-fingered. Having him lurking around the estate when the Denbys were away could be a bad idea.

Derek Holdingham was not a fool. He knew Forbes of old and immediately sensed his guilt. It was also unlike Forbes to phone in on anything. It made him wonder just what he'd been up to lately and was anxious to hide. He had narrowly escaped a conviction for the illegal possession of strychnine a few years before and Derek Holdingham had heard from a colleague who factored a neighbouring estate that in the hotel bar, with a few drinks in him, Forbes had boasted to another keeper that Ardvarnish had less vermin than any other estate in the north. A conviction would reflect very badly on the estate and on the factor, and he was not at all happy about that.

The trouble was that Holdingham didn't like Jimmy Forbes. He was a stubborn and surly knave who did what he wanted when it suited him and yet when Lord Denby was around he was, "Aye aye, m'Lord" this and, "Aye aye, m'Lord" that, in a way which had long been an irritant. So he was not very surprised when his secretary came through to say that there was a young man in the front office asking permission to hill-walk at Ardvarnish.

Rob had shaved and washed in the burn and abandoned the saggy pullover and kerchief for a blue cotton shirt and tweedy tie. He had even produced a slightly crumpled sports jacket from the back seat of his car, thrown in for just such an emergency. He was polite and well-spoken. The interview went well and the factor gently uncovered that it was indeed this young man who had fallen foul of Jimmy Forbes. Holdingham even quite liked him and was keen to discover more, but without actually interrogating the fellow.

"...St. Andrew's? Really? How interesting, my niece is up there at the moment, reading history."

"I'm afraid I did Land Economy so any history I know has come out of books."

"Land Economy? Did you now?" smiled Holdingham, "They say that's a very good course. I had better watch out for my job, hadn't I!"

"Well, I am looking round..!" tried Rob, pushing his luck. Holdingham laughed and rose to his feet.

"You're welcome to climb some of those grand hills, June is an excellent month for it. Please try to keep to the paths on the low ground; keep well away from the buildings, and I'll tell the stalker. I'm sorry he was a bit abrupt. When you've lived up a glen for twenty years you get like that. Thank you for coming in."

Rob was excited. He knew he had done well. Now he was free. He had permission to go where he liked on Ardvarnish and instructions from his office to do a field investigation on his own. He sat drumming his fingers on the steering wheel. He was determined to do a good job, not just for himself or for the Society but because he really cared about the eagles and peregrines. He saw them as national assets, jewels in the crown of Britain's wild heritage, with as much right to be protected as a great cathedral or the trees of an ancient forest. Far from being a vigilante, Rob saw himself as an appointed instrument of the national conscience operating in an area in which the police were ill-equipped to enforce the law. If this man was destroying protected wildlife, it had to be stopped. There was nobody else likely to be able to do it.

Instead of driving straight to Glen Corran by the quickest route, Rob took the road back to Loch Fleet. He wanted to disappear. He knew that in a tiny community his old orange beetle would be spotted immediately. He plan was to take the coast road north through the neat 19th century townships of Golspie, Brora and Helmsdale, where the rows of cottages clung to the very edge of the land, crimped between the hills and the sea like barnacles. And then further north to turn inland to Kinbrace up the long and winding Strath of Kildonan. He would leave his car at the lonely railway halt at Kinbrace and walk the long track in, over shallow burns, past peaty dubh lochans where red-throated divers bred.

Rob planned to take to the hills and cross the high moors between Ben Armine and Meall an Chollie, dropping down into Ardvarnish to the north of Carn Mor. This would take him to the heart of the estate without once approaching a dwelling or a road. There he could find a discreet camping site from which to watch and explore. All he needed was a week's supply of food, his tent, bed roll and his maps. One stop in a village store allowed him to stock the car with tins and packets of dried food. He was victualled and equipped. More than that, his mind was narrowing into a channel of determination almost as though this challenge was somehow pre-destined—was what his life had been training for all this time.

Rob was the son of a civil servant. His father had served only one employer for the whole of his thirty-seven working years—the Ministry of Health. Released from the strict austerity observed by his self-employed green-grocer parents, he felt comfortable and secure and entered the buying department as a clerk. He married a nurse, and they bought their own semi in Theydon Bois. It was here that their son had been born and, on the edge of Epping Forest, first threw crumbs to the chaffinches and wood pigeons on afternoon walks with his mother.

When Rob was thirteen they had made the quantum leap from Theydon Bois to Tunbridge Wells. Ralph Pearce had been promoted to Deputy Chief Buyer. Their new house was an alto-gether smarter semi in a quiet and respectable cul-de-sac and with a quarter-acre garden backing onto the park. This was con-servative Kent in the turbulent seventies and the polarised polit-ical values of the parents revealed themselves in the classroom of Rob's secondary-modern. Rob disliked the go-getting set. Consequently he withdrew into himself and the private fantasy of being a backwoodsman in his late-lamented Epping Forest. He read widely, drawn to natural history and wildlife. He dis-covered Aldo Leopold, Rachel Carson and Konrad Lorenz. He joined the school bird club and, for his fifteenth birthday, his father bought him a pair of binoculars. The roots of green con-sciousness were spreading below the surface. Rob Pearce had no means of knowing it, but he was one of a new suburban genera-tion responding to their enforced separation from the soil.

He had chosen St. Andrews not so much for the course he was attracted to, but because it was in Scotland and away from the south in the now-booming eighties, and not in a city. He was active in the bird and botany groups and never missed a chance to get out to the coast with his telescope and binoculars. He began to witness the practical need for restraint in man's ever greater demands on the environment and his interest moved gradually to wider conservation issues.

At university he enjoyed a brief liaison with an earnest and bespectacled scientist called Tessa, a year older than himself, who was writing a thesis on 'The variable age of sexual maturity in gannets.' Together they travelled to Shetland where Rob stood on the wild cliffs at Noss and Hermaness open-mouthed at tens of thousands of those great white birds soaring and wheeling on the updraught, only inches from his face, and around him, stippled across the cliff like white stucco, a high-rise slum of wailing, haggling, bickering gannets, kittiwakes, guillemots and razorbills, all in an unforgettable stench of fish guano whitewash. He had never witnessed a spectacle like it and if he had had any doubts about his career direction before, he was certain now that a life conserving these magical creatures, so dependent upon the unreliable behaviour of mankind, was for him. Having clearly established the surprisingly bountiful sexual maturity of Tessa, they parted friends, replete in body and mind to pursue their divergent careers.

Rob drove north thoughtfully. He was in no hurry. He approached Golspie. Every student of land use in Scotland knew about the nineteenth century Clearances and in particular the enormity of Patrick Sellar, the ambitious and ruthless factor whose name is synonymous with injustice for his brutal eviction of the people of Strathnaver to make way for large scale sheep ranching a century and a half before.

Rob had read about it. Popular and emotive accounts of the Clearances had touched him. Since coming to work in the Highlands he had learned that the grievous cultural wounds inflicted by that whole episode of Highland history were thinly healed and often visible in the attitudes of the present day. In truth he did not know what to think.

In Helmsdale Rob crossed the old stone bridge over the river and turned inland along its northern bank, heading away out of the village, leaving the grey houses behind him with only the mountains and the wild river ahead. It was all new. He had never been given his head before. He drove slowly, savouring the rising and falling meanders in the single-track road. He knew that the hand of man had shaped this open landscape; that the trees themselves were but the remnants of woods long cleared, the moors a mosaic of heather and grassland dictated by the grazing regimes of centuries. But to Rob it was wildness. It was wilder than any of the countryside of his youth, of his bird club days visiting manicured nature reserves, duck-boarded and signposted to distance suburban man yet further from the land. It was wilder than the Brecon Beacons where he had camped with a school outing; wilder still than the Norfolk Broads where he had slipped away from his parents and nosed his canoe into the maze of reedy runnels.

After a few miles he stopped in a passing place and walked down to the river's edge. He sat hugging his knees on a large rock protruding into the stream and allowed the brandy-coloured water to mesmerise him, swirling and eddying in thin spirals of creamy foam. A dipper skimmed past and landed on a mid-stream boulder, immediately ducking under the water, air beads gleaming on its plumage as it rummaged across the pool bottom towards him. Rob was dizzy with the emancipation of his trapped spirit. The wild river was cogent and seductive. He felt as though he was coming home at last.

He was, for the first time, his own man. In a few short miles from Golspie to Kinbrace he had undergone his own personal catharsis. He was responding directly to the stimulus of the environment in which he found himself.

He parked at the deserted railway halt at Kinbrace, shouldered his laden rucksack and strode off down the dusty track.

—5—

Had Gerry Denby not had to wait an hour for his hire car to be delivered to the Station Hotel in Inverness, where he had had a substantial breakfast after leaving the night train, he might have arrived in Lairg in time to see Rob Pearce's orange beetle pass through the little town on its way east. The uncomfortable blue Ford had already given him backache so he was relieved to stop outside Dank and Subtley's offices and to climb out into the sunshine.

When he walked into the reception office Derek Holdingham just happened to be there with his back to the door, searching through a filing cabinet. "Morning, Derek. I'm glad to catch you in." Derek Holdingham jumped and was incapable of concealing his astonishment. "Good Lord!" he exclaimed. "Lord Denby. Er, how nice to see you,sir! To what do we owe this...er...unexpected pleasure?"

Managing only the remote Highland end of the Denby empire, Derek Holdingham had always stood slightly in awe of Lord Denby. He had only once been to Denby Hall when he was invited to the ball celebrating Gerry's fiftieth birthday and had been powerfully impressed. He knew virtually nothing of the machinations of the Yorkshire estates and felt very junior to Harry Poncenby whom he knew as the full-time managing director of several Denby companies. Derek worked for a firm of land agents and Ardvarnish was only one—although a very important one—of several estates he managed.

"Just passing through, Derek," said Gerry, mischievously, knowing perfectly well that he'd neither passed through in June before nor ever called in unexpectedly at this office in the whole of the eight years Derek Holdingham had been managing Ardvarnish. "I'm on my way up to the Lodge to do a spot of fishing for a few days and I thought I'd better let you know I'm there, and this blue Ford car I've hired—ruddy uncomfortable thing—will be parked outside the Lodge. If you get any more reports of strange vehicles in the glen I shall probably be one of them." he said pointedly, intending to let Holdingham know that he was up to date with the affairs of the estate.

"Oh, right, sir. Fine, I'll ring Forbes now and I'll tell him to ask his wife to open up the Lodge for you straight away. You'll probably be needing young Shiona Duncan as well, won't you?"

"Yes. If you say so," said Gerry indifferently. "As long as there's a bite to eat I don't mind who prepares it, what?"

"Will any guests be arriving, sir?" asked Derek cautiously.

"No, no. Not a soul. I'm on my own and that's the way I want it to be. I'm not here on business nor to play host to a lot of ungrateful youngsters," he added meaningfully, alluding to Nigel's incessant rotation of girlfriends. "I take it there's nothing pressing you need to tell me about?"

"No, I don't think so, sir." Derek was at last beginning to recover himself from the initial shock at seeing Lord Denby. "We've put out the contract for the new stock fence and I'm pleased to say it's gone to Duncan Macrail from Dornoch whom young Andy Duncan, the shepherd's boy, is working for, so at least some of the money will be coming back into the glen."

"Oh good. Did we get a grant for it, eh?"

"Yes indeed, sir, we got full grant on the fence, all right,"

"Good, good, glad to hear it. Anything else?"

"I can't think of anything else just now, sir," Derek Holdingham was anxious not to raise the doubts in his own mind about Jimmy Forbes but then, realising that he ought to mention something about Rob Pearce, he continued, "Oh yes, sir, there was a nice young chap in here this morning wanting permission to go hill-walking, so I've said he can go more or less anywhere he likes as long as he keeps away from the buildings. Of course, if I'd known you were coming I'd..."

"Fine," said Gerry briskly. "That's fine by me. I've no objection to one, it's a hundred I don't want. Right-oh, I'll get on then."

"Oh, there is one other thing while you're here, Lord Denby," said Holdingham, turning back to the cabinet behind him and rummaging amongst some papers. "I was just filing something on this a moment ago and I'll send copies down to Harry—we've recieved the final notification of your SSSI's."

"My what?" "You know, sir, your Sites of Special Scientific Interest that have been identified and now formally notified to us by the Nature Conservancy Council."

"Oh yes, of course," said Gerry, "I remember very well," slightly embarrassed that he hadn't known immediately. "All about the peat and the sphagnum mosses and things like that. Isn't that it? It's taken them a hell of a long time to get round to doing it, it's a year or more since we last spoke about all that."

"Yes," said Holdingham, "that's right, sir. The statutory period for consultation has just ended and we've received the formal notification papers. That's it finished,now, sir, we've got them whether we like 'em or not." He failed to conceal that he did not.

"...But we didn't object, did we?"

"Oh no, sir, no, not as such, although we did ask a few questions about the boundaries and things, and the size worried us a bit. They are very large. Between the two of them they cover about twenty thousand acres, sir, that's jolly nearly half the estate and...er..there are quite a lot of things we're not allowed to do now....."

"Yes, yes, I remember all that," Gerry interrupted, "we have to tell them when we're hill-burning for the grouse and we're not allowed to drain it or re-seed it and things like that, what? but as far as I can see there's nothing which interferes with anything we actually want to do. Isn't that right?"

"Yes, sir, that's...er...more or less it, sir, although it has considerably altered our ability to manage your property in the way you choose to." The note of reservation was clear in Derek Holdingham's voice and in the dour face he pulled.

"Well, we live in a changing world, Derek. One simply can't have it all one's own way any more. There are too many damned people on the planet. And besides, I thoroughly approve of keeping the hill as it is and looking after it a bit. We've had a whole lot of fun off it for a long time and I don't believe these Nature Conservancy boys really want to stop us doing anything in the sporting line. I think it's mostly forestry and farming spreading up into the hill they're concerned about, and quite right too. Ardvarnish is a sporting estate, and as far as I can see nothing they've proposed is going to do anything but good to our sporting interests. And that's the way it should be. I've often wondered whether all those damned sheep do any good on this place. We've spent a hell of a lot of money improving the ground for Duncan and the ruddy things are everywhere. They must be competeing with the deer for the better grazing," said Gerry forcefully.

"Yes, sir." Sounding slightly injured, Holdingham tried again: "I know your feelings on sheep, sir, but we do have wages to pay and agriculture is one of the ways we've managed to maintain employment on the estate. In this economic climate it is very hard to come up with anything else which attracts as much subsidy, and wipes its face."

"Yes, yes, I know all that," said Gerry impatiently. "So what do we have to do next with these SSSI's?" A hard line of sunlight cut across the green cord carpet at his feet making it look a different piece. Gerry tested it with his toe.

"Well, nothing, sir, really, that's it. We just have to keep their people constantly informed." "Don't they attract some cash?" "Er..not as such, sir, although there are probably a number of management agreements we can enter into with NCC to help manage the areas their way. I shall be investigating that with them and, of course, I'll keep you informed."

"Good. OK, that's fine. Anything else?" Gerry was impatient to get out into the sunshine. His span of attention for office work was rapidly drawing to a close.

Now that the cat was out of the bag, Gerry knew enough about bush telegraph to be sure that word that he was up in Scotland when he had said he was going to London would get back to Denby in only a few hours. "Ha!" said he to himself with a smirk, "Derek Holdingham has given me the perfect excuse."

A little less than an hour later he was standing in the study in Ardvarnish Lodge waiting for Dinah to answer the phone at Denby Hall. It rang and rang and rang.

"Damn her! Where the hell is she?" and then suddenly she was there. "Lady Denby speaking," she said slowly and with affected pomposity.

"Dinah, old thing, it's Gerry. I'm at Ardvarnish."

"What on earth are you doing up there?" she asked incredulously.

"I...er... had to come north to sort something out very quickly. These Nature Conservancy areas have finally been notified and I just have to tie up the details and sign the papers," he lied.

"I thought you were going to London," said Dinah petulantly. "I was," he lied again, "and then this came up and since it's much more important, here I am."

"Harry and I had no idea why you had to go to York or London," Dinah said crossly. "What on earth's going on, Gerry? You're behaving very mysteriously. Have you gone off with a local floosie and whisked her away to Scotland? You'll have to be careful up there, you know, there's nowhere worse for gossip than the Highlands," she chided.

"One of these days I jolly well will, and then you'll get the shock of your life and wish you hadn't joked about it for so many years. I'm particularly interested in what's going on up here just now. So I'll be here for a couple of days. I'll ring you again. Alright, old thing?—Oh, and Dinah, I'm not opening the Lodge up properly so don't let any of the boys come roaring up with their unruly friends, eh, what?"

"All right, Gerry," said Dinah long sufferingly. "I'll look after Denby for you and everything'll still be here when you come back. Have a good time."

A few minutes later there was a knock on the study door and Bella Forbes came in. "Guid morning, m'Lord. We weren't expecting ye here..."

"I know that, Mrs Forbes. I know that very well. I've come up at extremely short notice. I hope it isn't inconvenient for you to open up the Lodge for me?"

"Ach no, m'Lord, no' at all," she hurried to reassure him. "It's just that y'dinna generally come up in June and I hav'na got the hot water on or anything like that, and there's nae much t' eat aboot the kitchens."

"Don't you worry about that, Mrs Forbes. The water'll heat up soon enough, eh, and if you'd be kind enough to nip down to Corran Bridge and get in a few provisions, I shall only require very simple looking after. I won't be entertaining, and if you can give me coffee and toast at breakfast time, a piece to take on the hill with me during the day, and then one of your shepherd's pies at night I shall be more than satisfied."

"Will Lady Denby be arriving for dinner, m'Lord?"

"Oh, no. I'm here on my own, Mrs Forbes. There won't be anyone else."

"Very guid, m'Lord. Very guid," she replied, clearly puzzled, "And will you be wanting dinner at eight o'clock like when her ladyship is up?"

"Yes please, Mrs Forbes, that will do nicely," Gerry waited for her to take her leave.

"Will you be fishing the river, Lord Denby?" she asked, fishing herself.

"No, no, I won't, Mrs Forbes," said Gerry. But she wasn't satisfied with that and stood, hesitating, and then her courage seemed to return.

"We've no' seen you here in June for a gey long time, m'Lord," she said with as much of a question in her voice as she could reasonably manage without actually asking him what he was doing there. Gerry Denby knew perfectly well what she was up to and was determined not to give anything away.

"I've never had reason to before, Mrs Forbes," he said enigmatically, "but, there we are, what?" he added, rocking on his heels and toes as if to close the matter. "I shall be here for a few days."

Bella Forbes looked perplexed. What could he possibly mean? She realised she couldn't go on standing there and so she said: "Very guid, m'Lord. Thank you very much, and left the room. She walked slowly down the long pasage, past the gun room and the drying room, gathering pace as she pushed through the green baize swing door and into the servant's hall. She was almost running by the time she reached the broad Caithness flagged kitchen with its huge scrubbed pine table and high varnished cupboards round the walls, full of china and glass, every piece of which bore the elaborate Denby 'D' or the heraldic clenched fist, and its broad shelves of shining aluminium pots and pans, some of them big enough to sit in. She tore off her white apron which she had only put on seconds before going in to Lord Denby, hung it on the back of the scullery door and dashed out into the yard. She snatched her old bicycle with its front-mounted basket away from the corrugated iron back porch and pedalled down the track through the rhododendrons as fast as she could go.

Bella Forbes was sure that something was afoot. She was an obsessive gossip and she had already associated in her own mind what her husband had told her about that young man camping in the old ruined croft with Lord Denby's sudden and unexpected visit. When she reached the Keeper's Cottage she found him sitting in open shirt and braces at the tiny kitchen table, eating a cold pork pie with the boiled potatoes she had prepared for him earlier.

"Jimmy," she almost shouted at him, "somethin's gaeing on, that's for sure! His Lordship's up on his lone withoot saying for why and he's nae guests comin' neither." In her excitement her native Aberdonian brogue, never far below the surface even after twenty years living in Sutherland, blossomed again.

"Calm doon, woman. Calm doon for any's sake. You're no' helpin' matters by gettin' in a flap. Now, whit's it all aboot?" mumbled Jimmy through a mouthfull of pie, with his huge fists on the table and the knife and fork pointing skywards.

"Aah, Jimmy, ye shouldna have been so harsh wi' thon young man. I'm sure that's to dae with Lord Denby arrivin' here the day. I've never seen him here in June in twenty years and he wasna for tellin' me why he was up," said Bella, sitting down at the end of the table.

"I've no' done anything wrong, woman," said Jimmy indignantly, "I was just protectin' his lordship's interests as best I could. I didna like the look o' thon young man. He meant trouble and that was for sure. The best place for him was awa' oot the glen as fast as I could see to it." "Aye, Jimmy, but ye never ken who these folk are nowadays. It maybe he was a friend of young Mr Nigel's or...."

"Nae, nae, woman. You're just all wrong. Mr Nigel doesna mix wi' folk like thon. Thon young fella looked like a student or some such. I dinna ken what he was doin' into the bothy, but I'll tell ye this, he was up to nae guid. Nae guid at all," replied

Jimmy emphatically, popping a large boiled potato in his mouth.

Bella Forbes knew she was at the end of that conversation with her husband, but was by no means convinced the glen was not facing the most dire crisis since Sandy Bun, the mobile shop, (only ever referred to by his proper name, Sandy Peacock, on the kirk warden's rota), had run over one lamb of a pair of Andrew Duncan's best twins on the way up the glen, and the other on the way down.

Jimmy Forbes had never told his wife the full extent of his own misdemeanors. After the strychnine scare he had kept the details of his fell activities to himself, fearing that her peaceless tongue would be the downfall of them both. He had been a predator all his life. He was the son of the head keeper on a large Aberdeenshire estate and he had served under his father in the good old days of many keepers on the hill with clear instructions and complete freedom to preserve the game and destroy the vermin.

In those days vermin was everything except the prized grouse family: ptarmigan on the mountain tops, red grouse on the purple moors, black grouse in the birch woods and the forest edge, and the turkey-sized capercaillie, the largest grouse in the world, in those stands of ancient Caledonian pine which had survived the removal of the native forests for timber and sheep. There were also snipe in the marshes, golden plover and curlew on the open hill, woodcock in the winter birchwoods and whins, and several species of duck on rivers and lochs to add variety and interest to a day's bag. Deer on the hill were red deer; epitomised and romanticised by Landseer's Monarch of the Glen, a signed etching of which hung over the mantel in the dining rooms and drawing rooms of stalking lodges the length and breadth of the Highlands. The delicate roe deer, on their long, spindly legs hiding in the willow scrub or among the bracken, were vermin fit only for the crofter's larder or the keeper's own pot.

Everything else which ran or flew was condemned before it was born. There was an active trade in skins of all kinds. The polecat and the pine marten had both succumbed to the merciless toothed jaws of the gin trap; the polecat to extinction in Scotland and the pine marten driven to obscurity in a few remote peninsulas and glens. The most hated were the hooked beaks and talons of the white-tailed eagle and the golden eagle, both of which were reputed to rear their young exclusively on grouse and ptarmigan, red deer calves and lambs. The white-tailed eagle, or the erne, as it was locally known, also a salmon eater, had been systematically eradicated since the first world war. Next on the roll-call of the despised came the hen harrier and the peregrine falcon, which not only preyed upon the red grouse, but were also capable of ruining a whole day's shooting by just flying across the moor. Tacked on to the list for good measure were buzzards and kestrels, merlins, sparrow hawks and four species of owls. Greater black-backed gulls and all the crow family were charged with egg theft by the keepers, and the killing of weakling lambs by pecking out their eyes, by the shepherds.

Even after waging war on this impressive list of marauders, the keeper's day was not done until he had also accounted for the ubiquitous foxes and badgers, weasels, stoats, hedgehogs and rats which ranged over the whole estate and might steal an egg or gobble a chick or a hen grouse from her nest.

On the river, the otter, the heron, goosander, merganser, cormorant and the osprey were all condemned for eating fish. The osprey, being the easiest target because it chose to nest in prominent and exposed tree-top sites, was shot out with ease.

The tools of the trade were a shotgun carried night and day, snares, gin traps, box and pole traps, a cocktail cabinet of lethal poisons, and constant vigilance. The result often was that a conscientious keeper became an skilled natural historian, able to track and identify all kinds of wildlife at the slightest sign. He knew where vixens cubbed in the high, rocky cairns and the otter bitch reared her kits in the hollow roots of a twisted alder on the river bank. He became an excellent snap shot and could bring down the darting merlin which flew faster than any driven grouse, and he displayed his spoils on a gibbet at the roadside or on a shed door so that the laird could see and be impressed by his diligence—the putrid carcases of the merlin and the buzzard fluttering in the breeze alongside the lissome stoat and the naked, peltless otter.

Jimmy Forbes was fifty-six. He had only had four jobs in his working life. He served ten years under his father after leaving school at fifteen, first as a Keeper's boy and later as a full Underkeeper. He then went to Lord Marchmont in the Borders as Deputy Head Keeper with the prospect of taking over if he stayed the five years until the Head Keeper retired. He never completed the second year. He disliked the estate for the absence of grouse and red deer, and could not tolerate the fox-hunting fraternity who seemed to rule the countryside in a way which was quite alien to him. Their horses and hounds rollocked through the estate and scattered the pheasants to the winds at least once a month throughout the winter and he got roughed up in the pub by local boys for shooting and snaring foxes. He pulled out and returned to Aberdeenshire where he married Bella whose ample embrace he had been missing during his sojourn away.

He was a loner. He had always harboured a secret ambition to become a stalker, by far the more solitary of the two professions. Keepers were leaving the land in large numbers by then and he felt there was a much more secure future in working for a stalking estate which, as far as he could see, was always likely to be just that. He applied for a post as a ghillie on an estate in Wester Ross under a laconic and ill-tempered hard-drinker called Jock. Difficult though Jock was both to like and to work for, he was an excellent stalker. In the space of six weeks of the stag season Jimmy learned a very great deal. So promising was he that the estate owner, a whisky millionaire, asked him to stay on to help with the hind stalking through the winter. Bella came across from Aberdeenshire to join him in the blissful squalor of a corrugated iron bothy with an outside privvy. That winter Jimmy proved himself as a stalker. He was a crack shot with a rifle, and was intimately familiar with the habits of the deer from boyhood; he had no difficulty at all in emulating Jock's skills in field craft. By the following August Jock's preoccupation with whisky had put him paradoxically at odds with his employer and when he left in a huff, Jimmy was immediately offered his job and became Stalker for the next nine successful years. He had loved everything except the rainfall and he kept an eye open for an opportunity to return toward the east where the gound was drier and the grouse more plentiful. The Keeper was still in him and he hankered for the chance to practice the skills at running a driven grouse shoot he had learned as a youth. Ardvarnish was perfect. He heard of the position by chance and when Bella saw the substantial stone-built Keeper's Cottage with its own garden and outhouses, she gave him blunt instructions that he was to get the job or else. It was an else he never had to test.

Mairi Duncan was out. She and Andrew had gone to Lairg for their weekly shopping trip where Andrew would stroll on to the sheep sales to lean on the rails with a dozen other shepherds and crofters viewing the competition and passing derogatory comments on their neighbours' stock. When he was not selling lambs or cast ewes himself Andrew invariably repaired to the hotel bar where he remained until Mairi came looking for him in the afternoon. What might have been a short visit to Lairg to do an hour's shopping usually consumed the entire day.

So it was Shiona who answered the door to the breathless Bella Forbes. "Is there something wrong?" she saw Bella's fluster and pushing back her long red hair, held it behind her ear with one hand.

"I came down to see your Mam. Is she not in?"

"They're away to Lairg for the messages, you're awful breathless, Bella, come away in and sit down for a minute. There's nothing up with Jimmy, is there?"

"Ach, no, Shiona, not at all. It's just that Lord Denby's up and I was coming to tell your Mam I dinna ken what he's here for. I was wondering if ye'd heard anything yourself?"

Shiona could not imagine where she might have heard anything since all glen gossip emanated from Bella Forbes. She moved instinctively to the heavy kettle and slid it across onto the Rayburn. When she turned back Bella had evicted the cat from her mother's scruffy old chair in the corner of the kitchen and, firmly seated, continued: "I've no' seen the like in twenty years. He wouldna say what he was doing up and he's no luggage with him, so he must have come in a rush. Mr Holdingham said it was a surprise visit when he phoned and I dinna think he had any warnin' neither. What's he here for, that's what I want to know. I'm thinking he's heard something about the estate he doesna like, and he's here to see for himself."

Shiona knew very well that she was about to hear whatever was worrying Bella whether she wanted to or not, so she said, "Aye, well," and busied herself with making the tea.

"I think its to do with thon young man Jimmy found camping in the bothy. He was up to nae guid and Jimmy did right to see him off the estate and report it to Mr Holdingham."

Suddenly Shiona was interested. Jimmy would never have reported something like that unless he was covering his own tracks. "Here's a cup of tea for you, Bella. I didn't know Jimmy had reported it."

"Well he had to, ye see, Shiona, that man wasna nice at all. He was swearin' and cursin' at Jimmy, and Jimmy just asking him his business."

"Is that right, Bella?"

"Aye, Shiona, it is, and when Jimmy said to him he couldna stay in the bothy he was threatenin' and carryin' on like ye've never heard. I was sayin' to Jimmy he should've got the police."

Shiona smiled into her tea. She knew that was something Jimmy would never do, short of finding a corpse. Since they investigated him over the strychnine he detested the police. "I'm not seeing why Lord Denby would come all the way up from the south for that..."

"Well, maybe that young man didna like Jimmy and reported him to Mr Holdingham. There's nae tellin' what folk'll do these days."

"But what would he report Jimmy for?" Shiona asked with pretended innocence.

"I dinna ken, Shiona, but there's folk about dinna like keepers and stalkers and Jimmy's had a spot o' bother a few years

46

back. It could be thon man's made up stories about Jimmy."

"What kind of stories, Bella?" Bella looked embarrassed and her eyes cast about the floor, both hands cradling the mug of tea as if seeking comfort from it.

"Ach well, there's things keepers had to do when Jimmy was a lad ye're no allowed to do now—and my Jimmy's nae one for breakin' the law," she added as an afterthought.

"So you think this man's reported Jimmy for putting poison about the hill and Lord Denby's here because of it? Is it that, Bella? Is it that what's worrying you?" But she had said too much and she got up and returned to the teapot to offer more; but Bella was on her feet too, red-faced with indignance.

"I never said that, now, did I, Shiona! I never mentioned poison at a'. That's no' right! That's how rumours start and gossip like that could cost my man his job."

"Och, Bella, I'm that sorry. But if it wasn't poison ye were referring to, what was it?" Shiona asked, yet the chance to pursue it was past. Bella had grown wary and changed the subject.

"Ach, well, that's the way of it and we'll just have to wait and see what he's here for, won't we. I must get away down to Corran Bridge to get my own messages if I'm to have some tea for his lordship. Now you'll be up to the Lodge for six o'clock, Shiona, won't ye? And I'll need your help until he's away."

Shiona stood in the doorway watching Bella pedal away down the bumpy road and out of sight. Bella was right, she thought to herself, something was up and Jimmy was at the heart of it, she was sure of that. It was a lucky coincidence that Lord Denby should appear at just this moment in her life, now that her mind was made up. She had not expected to see him until August and all day she had been wondering from whom she might seek help. She closed the door resolved to use her new-found confidence to take the next step in her life.

Shiona dressed carefully when she was going up to work at the Lodge; in the first week of her employment Lady Denby had admonished her and sent her home to change into a longer skirt. She enjoyed working in the dining room because she could listen in to the chatter of the Tansley-Fairfaxes and their friends and could store away information about dresses she liked and many she didn't, or this type of pendant ear-ring or that type of necklace or choker. She watched the girls closely, especially their hair-styles, observing how very different they were to those available from *Vanessa's* in Lairg or *Get-a-Head* in Tain. She didn't know what she would be needed for tonight. She had a feeling that she was destined for the washing-up and pan-scrubbing. If that was to be the case she needed a ruse by which to speak to Lord Denby himself and on his own. She dressed extra carefully.

At five twenty-five she glanced anxiously at her watch. She was far less concerned about being late at the Lodge than she was about being seen by her father on their return from Lairg. She had blown her long paprika-red hair dry and then carefully pinned it in place with two velvet clips. She was pleased with the result. She wore a loose cotton frock in a blue floral pattern which, while being not the least daring, fitted her well, revealing the youthfulness of her figure.

There was a sniff of adventure in the air. Suddenly the oppression of her father and the restrictions of her home were pushed aside. She snatched up her bag, and, glancing anxiously down the track towards the glen road, she went out and away up the footpath through the crowding rhododendrons to the Lodge.

When she arrived in the kitchen there were eleven brown trout lying on the long wooden draining-board. Shiona dipped her hand under the cold tap and wet them one by one so that the golds and the browns came back, and the orange rings and scarlet spots gleamed again, and the streaks of yellow and silver beneath the belly fins shone. They were all of an excellent breakfast-size except one which looked as though it could be well over three pounds. It was a deep, heavy fish which Shiona guessed had consumed many of its sons and daughters in its time.

Bella Forbes came in, the swing door hissing shut behind her. "Ooh, there ye are, Shiona," she began, "Lord Denby's had a grand day on Loch Stac. He's wantin' two fish for his breakfast in the mornin' and all the rest can go in the freezer. He says not to gut the ones ye're freezin, just the two for the morning." Shiona reached for the apron and took a sharp knife from the drawer, and slid it into the belly of the first fish. "So it's just the fishing he was at today?" she asked casually.

"Aye, aye," said Bella stiffly, "so it seems." Shiona knew she was still bruised from the afternoon. "And when ye've done that, ye can go through and put a match to the study fire. Lord Denby isn't using the drawing room the night and it'll be cool later on."

Shiona did as she was bid, carefully wrapping the unwanted fish and laying them among the rigid salmon in the scullery freezer. Through in the study she laid sticks in the fire and arranged the peats around them before putting a match to the paper. The orange flame licked around the kindling which spat long, glowing sparks out onto the slate hearth. Shiona sat and caught them one by one, pushing them back into the grate until the first rush of the fire had died back and the peats began to smoke, wafting their dark sweetness into the room.

The door opened and Lord Denby came in. Shiona started

and began to get up. "Don't you move, young lady," said Gerry, "you just carry on. Take no notice of me. I'm just going to get myself a drink." He liberally splashed whisky from a heavy decanter into a tumbler. Shiona did as she was told and remained sitting on the hearth, and caught more sparks. She placed one or two more peats on the fire while she summoned her courage. She was not in the habit of instigating conversation with either Lady Denby nor her husband. But tonight she remembered the mountain and she was determined to try. "I've put your trout in the freezer, m'Lord. I see you've had a very good day on the hill," she began, "and I've kept back two very bonny-looking fish for your breakfast."

Gerry looked pleased. "Yes, indeed, I have had a good day. I don't remember such an enjoyable day at the trout for many years. I had no luck with the first two flies and then I seemed to get it just right. That big one's a beauty, eh, don't you think?"

"Ach, yes, sir, that's a grand fish. It's one of the best I've seen from Loch Stac..." and then she stopped herself suddenly, remembering that her brother Andy was not supposed to be fishing the lochs in the evenings. She cursed herself for the slip and hoped he hadn't noticed. "You'll be keeping them for when you've guests in the Lodge?"

"Yes, I will. They'll be very useful when the house is full, what?" Gerry moved over to the fire and took a long pull on his whisky. Shiona took her chance.

"Lord Denby, may I trouble you for a word of advice?" she asked tentatively, opening her eyes wide.

"Why, yes, of course, my dear, of course. What can I help you with, eh?"

"I've to help Mrs Forbes in the kitchen just now, but perhaps after dinner...?"

"Yes, of course, my dear," Gerry interrupted, "just as soon as you've finished through there you come back and I'll do my best to help you if I can."

"Thank you, m'Lord," she said and slipped away.

"Hmm. Wonder what she wants?" he mused. He was touched that she should want to come to him rather than to her father, or Forbes, or even Derek Holdingham. He turned his back to the fire and basked in its gentle warmth and in the success of the day, and of the freedom he had felt out in the boat munching his ham sandwich, watching the white-bibbed sandpipers flick and bob on the boulders along the shore. No doubt he would have been horrified had he known that he was being observed, scrutinised even, from far above on the shoulder of Carn Mor through Rob Pearce's telescope. But in ignorance he had had a magical June day which had restored his spirit and his faith in himself and his lot, and had made Dinah seem not so bad after all, and the whole world a perfectly reasonable place in which he was, at least for this evening, thoroughly content. And now there was a very pretty young girl asking to come and see him after dinner. A slow smile spread across his face and he chuckled. "That'd be a turn up for the books," he muttered, "and serve Dinah ruddy well right! And the papers would love it: 'Peer elopes with shepherd's teenage daughter.' It'd shake young Nigel rigid, too," he laughed out loud, and prodded the fire with his toe so that sparks flew and fresh flames engulfed the peats.

Shiona finished washing up without saying a word to Bella who was noisily eating her supper at the kitchen table. "That's it, Bella, all done."

"Grand, Shiona. That's just grand. Ye can go now. Ye'll be wanting to get away home."

"No, thank you, Bella," she said, nonchalantly hanging up the dish towels to avoid her eyes. "I've to go in and see Lord Denby. He's asked for me to see him," she said, unable to resist alarming Bella, turning to glance at her.

She was sitting with her mouth wide open in astonishment. "How d'ye mean?" she asked incredulously. "Lord Denby's asked to see ye?"

"Aye, he said to come through when I was finished."

"What for?"

"I've no idea," Shiona lied. "Perhaps he needs some information."

"Then I canna think why he would go to you," said Bella, unable to hide her rising indignation. Shiona was combing her hair in the scullery mirror. The red curls fell as she shook them free about her face. She heard the creak of Bella's chair as she leaned to get a better view through the doorway, and she applied just a touch of lipstick. "There," she said, coming back to the kitchen table. "I hope I look neat enough." Bella was speechless. "Don't wait, Bella, I don't know what his lordship wants, but it might take a little while," and she disappeared through the green baize door. "Y'wee hussy!" exclaimed Bella. She was most certainly not going home, she was going to wait up all night if necessary to find out exactly what it was Lord Denby wanted—which is precisely what Shiona knew she would do.

Shiona knocked and entered the study. Lord Denby was sitting in a huge tartan-covered winged armchair beside the fire. He stood up and held out a welcoming hand, beckoning her to the hearth. "Ah, Shiona, my dear, come along in. Come and sit down. Can I offer you a little drink?" he asked cautiously in his most paternal manner.

"That's very kind, m'Lord. Could I have a vodka and lemonade?" Jeannie Macronie had introduced her to vodka saying that was what all the girls were drinking in Lairg.

"Ah, well, now, I'm afraid I don't think you can," said Gerry apologetically, getting up and crossing to the drinks table in the window. "I'm afraid there's not much of a selection here just now. There's whisky or sherry or port."

"A wee sherry will do very well, m'Lord." She did not want to be difficult to please.

"Of course, my dear. Now, you come and sit down by the fire." Shiona had never sat in any of these chairs, although she had rearranged them often enough. It was deep,soft and relaxing in a way she was quite unprepared for. Gerry handed her a crystal glass in which there seemed to be more sherry than she'd seen in her entire life. She was determined not to show it. "Now, my dear, how can I help you, eh?" he asked, easing himself back into the tartan.

"M'Lord, I'm wanting some advice so that I don't make a fool of myself when I next see Lady Denby, in case what I want is impossible. You see, I like my job here fine, Lord Denby, but I am needing to get away. I'm twenty years old next month and I can't go on living my life in that wee cottage with my parents. It'd drive us all mad. So, I am wondering if Lady Denby would have a place for me at Denby Hall in the house there."

"Ha, ha! I see." Gerry laughed kindly, revealing a row of gold teeth. "So you've got parent problems have you? Yes, well I know all about those. They're just as bad in a big house as they are in a small one. And, of course, you're quite right. You have to live your own life sooner or later. When exactly were you thinking?"

Shiona felt as though a great load had been lifted from her shoulders. She'd had no idea that he was so human. It wasn't even like talking to the minister, she didn't feel she was being judged at all, and the doctor had always treated her like a fool. She had only asked Lord Denby one question and she had had a more sympathetic response than she could ever remember from her father. She sipped the sherry, holding the sweet liquid under her tongue and savouring the fullness of it and the huge chair together.

"I haven't really thought of a time, m'Lord. But I'm feeling that I can't go on here very much longer."

"Is it that bad?"

"Ach, yes, sir, at times it really is."

"Girls usually fall out with their mothers and boys with their fathers, or isn't it as simple as that?" he asked, genuinely interested.

"No, sir, it's my father. I just don't think he and I are in the same century."

51

"Humph," Gerry chuckled, "no youngster ever does."

"No, sir, that's maybe fine if you've lots of friends and can get away out from under your parents' feet, but I can't do that. Its very hard to get away from here if no-one happens to be going down the glen."

"I'm sure it is, my dear. I'm sure it is. You're quite right, what? Well, now. First of all, I think what you've suggested is a very good idea, but there is a problem. I don't think her lady-ship has a vacancy just now at Denby, and I can't just create a job for you because you're in a jam with your mother and father. I hope you understand that? But what I'll do, I'll have a word with my wife and we'll just see what can be done. It could be there's another Yorkshire house nearby could take you on."

"Oh, I do thank you, m'Lord. That's very kind of you." she said.

"Now, I'm afraid I shan't be speaking to Lady Denby during the couple of days that I'm still here and, er, as you know, we shan't be back up again until August. But don't you worry about that. You leave it to me and I'll see what I can do for you."

"So you'll not be here for long, m'Lord?"

"Oh no, I'm only here for a a breath of fresh air and to do a spot of fishing." ...He smiled, remembering the fight the big fish had given him, fully twenty minutes and half the length of the loch, before finally teasing it into the net.

"I'd better go now," said Shiona looking bleakly at her glass which was still three-quarters full. "Finish your drink, dear girl," said Gerry, who wasn't at all keen to lose his company so soon. Shiona leaned back again and sipped her sherry, eyeing his kind face over the rim of her glass. She liked him, he was gentle and friendly. He was so different from her father, and Danny Stott, and from Geordie Hoggett in Bonar. He was unlike any of the men she had ever known. She had been brought up to believe that he was a sort of god; that he owned whole towns and factories and thousands of acres of land and controlled hundreds of people's lives which he ruled with a rod of iron. He sat in Parliament and, Bella Forbes had told her, he knew the Queen and attended royal weddings and funerals wearing long scarlet robes edged with fur.

A little boldness had slipped into her with the sherry. "You have taken us all by surprise, Lord Denby. We've not seen you here in June before. Do you mind me asking what made you decide to come?"

"No, of course I don't mind," he replied amiably. "I quite simply wanted to get away for a few days. Nothing more sinister than that, dear girl. Everybody needs to break the mould every now and again. I wish I'd done it years ago. Ardvarnish is such a lovely place in June before the midge comes, eh?"

"Oh, I see...we thought maybe it was to do with the young man."

"Young man?" Gerry looked directly at her, "what young man?"

"Did you not know, sir, there was a young man found camping in the bothy up at Dalbattigh?"

"Oh, him. Yes, I knew about him. Why on earth should I come up for him?"

"Ach, I heard Jimmy Forbes had thrown him off the estate and I thought perhaps he had complained?"

"No, no! As a matter of fact I think he's back on the estate now. He went into the office this morning in Lairg and asked permission to go hill-walking,and Holdingham told me that I'd probably bump into him on the hill."

"I see," said Shiona.

"You look disappointed," Gerry asked her. "Were you expecting more?" This was the second time in one day that he'd been quizzed by a member of the estate staff. Clearly his presence had caused a stir and maybe there was more to this young man than had come out.

"Well, m'Lord, I think that everyone thought there must be some other reason for you coming here suddenly, with no warning and not opening up the Lodge and all."

"I see," said Gerry thoughtfully, "so I've thrown things off balance a bit, have I?"

"It's no' so much that, sir, it's just to have you here on your own is a bit strange. I don't think there's more to it than that, m'Lord." Gerry smiled.

Shiona finished her glass and stood up. "Would you like me to do the glasses before I go off, m'Lord?"

"Certainly not, young lady," said Gerry. "I have enjoyed your company and I wouldn't dream of letting you do anything of the sort. And as far as a job is concerned I'll do what I can for you, I promise you that." He liked the girl and he felt benevolent and congenial. The day of sun and birdsong on the hill loch, the fresh heather wind, the success with the rod, the whiskies and his dinner, had combined into a warm pervasion of well-being. "Thank you, m'Lord," said Shiona.

"Good night, my dear."

Shiona closed the study door behind her very quietly. She knew very well that Bella Forbes was still in the kitchen waiting for her and she had no intention of going in there. She turned right into the dining room with its long mahogany table and twenty-four matching chairs under its pale green dust sheet, past the huge oil paintings of stags strapped to the backs of ponies and slavering gun dogs, and tiptoed across to the French windows. She carefully eased the long brass bolts and stepped silently out onto the lawn. The cool azalea-scented darkness seemed to swallow her up as she leaned against the cold stone looking from left to right to make sure she hadn't been seen and to accustom her eyes to the gloaming before slipping across the lawn and into the rhododendrons.

—6—

The summer solstice presented itself to Rob by banishing the Ardvarnish night to a mere interlude; forty-five minutes of starless gloom after one of the most extravagant sunsets he had ever seen. Molten lava had slowly spilt from behind the jagged fringe of Coigach and Assynt, assaulting the hard land edge in both directions with deep glowing veins of crimson and gold. Rob had sat transfixed. It possessed him. It was an elemental pageant in which he was an involuntary participant, unconscious of time or being, as much a part of it as the mountain itself and the ocean of shadowy moorland below. Slowly the footlights dimmed to wine and then purple, deeper than the August heather, and the corrie beside him became huge and shapeless.

He could hear golden plover piping their thin, mournful call across the scree, and a little wind rattled the grass at his feet and whined among the rocks high above. He spread his bed roll and climbed into his sleeping bag with a shiver, not bothering with the tent under such clear skies. He lay watching the horizon in half expectation of an encore because the show had refused to go away. A steely glow remained in the north-west long after the first mercurial streaks of dawn stalked the northern rim and flooded across the moors. A vein of quartz shone back from the shoulder of the corrie and his last thought was that the sky above was but the softest grey-blue.

He awoke with a start. Was that a cough? He froze, his head an inch from the pillow of his rolled-up trousers. He must have been dreaming. The sunlight impaled his head and made him screw up his face. There it was again. A sharp, short cough like someone irritated or impatient. He rose onto one elbow and groped for his glasses. The sleep-muddled world came into focus around a pointed face staring straight at him. She was only a few yards away, her nostrils wide and her breath streaming from them in short misting plumes. Her angular muzzle was beaded with dew from the grass and her shining eye, as dark as a dubh lochan, spread wide with suspicion. She spoke again—a staccato cough edged with fear. A raised front foot stamped angrily and the hind threw an anxious glance backwards.

Rob knew immediately that she had a new-born calf very close behind her. He had seen red deer hinds below him the evening before. He had watched them and they had eyed him mistrustfully from a quarter of a mile away, but continued to graze undisturbed. He had decided to camp in the corrie, high up on its northern edge, drawn there by the sunset and the awesome view, hoping that he would be well above their calving grounds.

He sat up slowly. It was too much for her and she veered away downhill, running a few yards, stopping, looking back, stamping again and running on until she was gone. Rob rubbed his eyes and scratched his ruffled hair. He glanced at his watch. It was four-ten and the sun was already above the mountain and strong on his face. He pulled on his trousers and boots. Trailing long laces in the dew, he walked the twenty yards to where she had been standing. Casting about he walked on another fifteen and there, among the tussocks of coarse grass and straggly heather, lay a spotted calf. Its domed head and flattened ears rested between folded front legs and liquid eyes blinked at him from beneath long, curved eyelashes. He backed slowly away. It was only a day or two old and would remain where its mother left it, relying on the exquisite camouflage of its spotted coat and its complete scentlessness for the first ten days of life to protect it from the ever-present threat of foxes and eagles. He knew it would be fine until the hind returned to it; he removed his scant camp further up onto the summit ridge before brewing some tea in the brilliant morning sun.

Rob was clinical about his task. He went straight to the summit of Carn Mor and spread his map over the wind-smoothed rock beside the cairn, anchoring the corners with stones. He set his compass and rotated the map gently until he was satisfied it was correctly oriented. With his binoculars he then examined and identified on the map every feature of the great panorama spread around him. He searched out every burn and gully, every false summit and high lochan, every peat hag, each broad heather slope, where most of the grouse would be shot, and the wide green stripe of Andrew Duncan's re-seeded sheep walks. His eye moved on down to the Corran river. He took notes of the straggling birchwoods and swampy alders along the flood plain.

For his own peace of mind he felt that he had to know Ardvarnish estate. He had to assess its many varied habitats at every altitude. He needed to make up his own mind whether or not the land was likely to be able to support the wildlife he suspected should be there. He counted large numbers of red deer. On the south side of Carn Mor there were over six hundred hinds scattered across the steep shoulder of the mountain and out to the west. To the north he found the stag herd grazing their way back up the hill after foraging on the river flats during the night. They were in groups of a dozen here and twenty there, spread out over several miles of country. They were too scattered and too distant to count.

He needed to make an assessment of the land for his own purposes. He knew that the ultimate test of whether eagles, or merlins, or other forms of wildlife could survive, was the productivity of the land itself. His immediate task was to find out if the various birds it was his job to protect were present, and if not, whether they were absent because of the direct illegal actions of the people managing the land.

His initial survey done, he dropped down five hundred feet to a small corrie lochan and stripped to the waist. Kneeling on the spongy bank of sphagnum he eyed himself wistfully in the sky-reflecting pool before plunging his hands into the dark water and splashing it up into his face and over his head. He dried himself and felt good. He replaced his spectacles and drank in the strong sunshine bombarding his tingling face. As he did so, his eye caught a movement on the rough zig-zag track which led to Loch Stac, a thousand feet below him. He snatched up his binoculars. A man, apparently alone, was walking up the track. Rob ran to his telescope for a closer look. The day was still new and heat rising from the land had not yet started to vibrate the air; he could see the man crisply and clearly. He was holding a fishing rod and a net and walking purposefully to the loch.

Rob spied on Gerry Denby off and on throughout the entire day. He saw him push out into the loch in the little green rowing boat, watched him ship his oars and take up his rod. Twice he saw him change the fly on his cast, and take a nap in the boat; later in the day he witnessed the first catch, and his second, and his third. In the middle of the afternoon he saw him playing a fish up and down half the length of the loch, sometimes standing, sometimes sitting, now to the right, now to the left of the boat, letting it run and reeling in again until at last he landed it in the net at the boat's side. Even at that great range Rob could feel the thrill of the struggle and the excitement of securing the prize which captivated so many fishermen. Rob had no idea who the man was.

He spent the rest of the day working on his survey. He returned to the two eagle eyries he had checked out before, climbing down the steep rocky faces and examining the ledges closely for any sign of occupation. There was none. He began to realise that it could be an impossible task attempting to prove that there had been golden eagles on this estate in the recent past. He felt daunted by that, the reality of the task coming home as he sat munching oaty biscuits on a high knoll. He was certain it was going to be a long job.

Bella Forbes had waited in the kitchen for two hours. At one stage, burning with curiosity, she slipped out of the back door and tiptoed round through the rhododendrons until she was standing on the edge of the study lawn. But the ground sloped from the house down to where she stood and although the curtains were undrawn and the lights bright, she could see nothing. Later, she crept in to the green baize door and pressed her ear against it to see if she could catch their voices. She heard nothing. She eased the door ajar, but the spring creaked loudly and she let it close again, fearful that she might be discovered. She paced up and down the kitchen. She thought of going in and offering Lord Denby more coffee, but realised she had left it too late. She quivered with frustrated curiosity which increasingly turned to rage as the minutes dawdled by and there was no sign of Shiona.

Finally and reluctantly, as the clock approached midnight she left the Lodge, sullenly pushing her bicycle across the yard. As she turned the corner of the house she saw the blanket of electric light vanish from the study lawn. She stopped in her tracks. Abandoning the bicycle on the gravel, she rushed back to the kitchen, snapping on the light and sitting down hurriedly in the chair. She waited for Shiona to come in.

The house was silent. After a moment she called softly, "Shiona? Are you there, Shiona?" There was no reply. She went through to the baize door and pushed it away from her. The passage was in darkness. "Shiona?" she tried again. No reply. She went through to the servant's hall thinking Shiona might be sitting there in one of the worn Rexene armchairs, but the room was dark and empty. She returned to the kitchen and the scullery. "Shiona?" Nothing. Bella was mystified, and suspicious. She tiptoed down to the baize door again, slipping through into the darkness beyond. The house was silent. On she went to the study, pushing the door slowly open, half expecting to find Shiona there in the glow of the dying fire. She switched on the light and crossed to the fireplace. Three empty glasses stood on the mantelpiece. She picked them up and examined them closely; the one unmistakably whisky and of the others, one bearing the smear of Shiona's pale lipstick. "Yon wicked, wicked girl!" swore Bella in a curdling whisper.

She glanced round the room. Lord Denby's chair was

depressed and ruffled as usual. The other fireside chair was crumpled too, and there, tucked into the side was Shiona's little red bag. Bella gasped, her hand rising to her lips in disbelief at what she was seeing. "Oh, my Lord, she's still here!" She was out of the room and down the passage in a trice. She turned off the lights in the kitchen and hurried back out to her bicycle. On the back drive she stopped only to look up at the single light burning from Lord Denby's bedroom in the west wing.

Elated by her success with Lord Denby and the prospect of escape to Yorkshire—which had the same romantic ring as Paris or Monte Carlo—Shiona slept little. After leaving the Lodge she had walked in the cool of the night, up the dirt road past her home, towards the Dalbattigh bothy. She wanted to be alone again with the friendly looming hill and the night sounds she loved. She stopped beside Lady Margaret's Pool, where, as a little girl she had sat hugging her knees on the bank, watching the Denby's elegant tweed-clad guests enact the curious annual fly-fishing ballet. The long, whip-like rods, and the line curling back through the air like the looping ornamentation of an Elizabethan manuscript. Where she had watched Jimmy Forbes at his most obsequious: "Aye, aye, m'Lady, ye're into a big fish now. I told ye that was a skillful cast," and, "that's a beautifully placed fly, sir. That'll bring ye a fish as sure as I'm standing here." And the sadness she had felt as the great shiny fish was finally beached after a long, exhausting struggle, to be bashed on the head by a nasty little truncheon called 'a priest'— the incongruity of which had long puzzled her.

A flight of teal sprang out of a marshy bay as she passed, startling her; high above, somewhere unseen, up on the dark moorland she could hear the curlew's long slow whistle gradually building towards a bubbling crescendo. The darkness had no sooner settled around her, turning the river into a ribbon of silent blackness, than it was fading again. She stood and watched the dawn creep back across the mountain and listened to robins and blackbirds among the alders begin their tinkling song. By the time she had reached her home it was daylight and the sun was struggling to burst out from behind the mountain.

Making plans to move to Yorkshire had been a triumph; inadvertantly deluding Bella Forbes had been a retribution for the contempt Shiona held for her senseless babbling tongue and her self-importance about the Lodge. The greatest triumph of all, she thought, lying in her little bed staring up through the skylight at the blue sky and the mountain, was conquering her fear of the demi-god; meeting him face to face at his own fireside, where she had discovered that far from being a deity of any kind, he was, in fact, a perfectly normal human being who was really very nice. He had listened to her, which was something her father never did. And he had about him a gentleness which had impressed her more deeply than the bogus front of good manners so often practiced by his class or those who sought to emulate it. As she fell asleep she remembered her bag left, tucked into the armchair and made a mental note to retrieve it early, before Lord Denby was up.

When Bella arrived at the kitchen there was nothing for her to do. Shiona had been there an hour. There was jaunty music playing from the kitchen radio and the morning chores were done. She had cleared and re-laid the study fire, fluffed up the cushions and removed her bag and the dirty glasses. She had laid the breakfast table for Lord Denby in the dining room, and the two trout and a pan lay ready beside the Aga stove.

Bella came in without a word. Shiona knew the signals were bad. She stood in the kitchen doorway tying the strings of her white apron behind her back without looking or responding to Shiona's cheery "Morning!" She walked straight through the kitchen and into the body of the house pushing the green baize door aggressively so that it swung backwards and forwards several times before coming to rest. A moment later she was back again.

"I can see I'm not needed here this morning," she said, her little eyes flashing meanness and jealousy.

"I couldn't sleep," said Shiona, casually lifting the lid on the Aga hob.

"I'm no' surprised you couldna sleep, my girl," snapped Bella, shaking her head meaningfully, "I'm no' surprised at all."

"It is a beautiful morning, though," continued Shiona, ignoring Bella's aggression, pulling the heavy frying pan onto the heat. She dropped in a pebble of butter. "Oh, I have nae doubt it's a beautiful morning for you, my girl, I have nae doubt of that at all. But what have you got to say to me, and to your parents? That's what I want to know."

Shiona didn't understand what her parents had got to do with it, but ignored it, saying, "Ach, Bella, I'm hoping you didn't wait for me last night. It really was quite late." She stole a glance at Bella who was rearranging dish towels on the rack. She felt Bella's obvious discomfort with mischievous enjoyment.

"Och, no, of course I didna wait up. I've nae reason to wait about half the night. I have nae doubt at all if there was anything important for Lord Denby to say he would have said it to me himself." Her eyes darted about the room landing everywhere except on Shiona's face.

"You're quite right, Bella," she said, "Lord Denby had nothing of any importance to say at all."

Bella was outraged. She nearly cut herself slicing bread and rammed it into the toaster. "You can turn that off," she snapped, silencing the radio herself. "You know perfectly well Lady Denby doesna permit music in the kitchen."

"Lady Denby's not here," observed Shiona, with a broad smile as she placed the first trout into merrily sizzling butter.

"You're right, Shiona Duncan, Lady Denby's not here. No, indeed she's not," she said meaningfully, "and things just might be very different if she was."

The bell rang. Bella went through. "Good morning, Mrs Forbes," Gerry smiled amiably.

"Mornin', m'Lord." Bella said coldly, looking glassily past him with her jaw set in a defiant line. "I'm having my trout this morning and a bit of toast and some coffee. And I should like egg sandwiches for the hill today, please. I'm going to try Loch Meiklie."

"Very well, m'Lord. I'm doing your trout for you just now," said Bella, damned if she was going to let Shiona get any of the credit.

The swing door slapped angrily back and forth and Bella was in the kitchen again. "Give me those trout. Lord Denby's ready for them now," she barked at Shiona.

"They're just ready. I'll take them through, shall I?"

"Ye'll do nothin' of the kind. Give them to me, and you get on and do the job ye're paid to do, which is scrubbing out the pans. I can smell ye've burnt that butter and it'll need a right good scrub."

Jimmy Forbes had also had a peaceless night. Bella had come in late, fizzing with indignation about Shiona's shameless behaviour in the Lodge, which had been neither of interest nor consequence to him. What had worried him was that Bella had said that Lord Denby had been seeking information from young Shiona. What sort of information could he want from her? And why her? If it was information about the workings of the estate surely he would have come to himself or to Mr Holdingham or possibly to Andrew Duncan, but not to Shiona. What could she know about the grouse or the deer, or the fishings? Lurking in the back of his mind was the certain fact that through her childhood, Shiona, more than anyone else on the estate, knew about him and some of the things he had been up to. It gave him an uncomfortable feeling. So it had to be something which he couldn't ask the factor or the shepherd or the stalker about. Jimmy was very perplexed and the sunlight streaming in his bedroom window at half past four in the morning had driven him from his bed.

Something deeper was troubling him. He pulled on his boots and his old tweed jacket, through at the elbows and tattered at the cuffs; he snatched his stalker's bonnet off the antlers on the back of the door and his long crummack from inside the porch and stepped out of the cool cottage into the strong morning sun. A number of years before, Jimmy had shot two buzzards in the birchwoods beside the river, lying in wait for them until they were both at the nest together, and then blasting them out of the tree, and putting another two cartridges through the bottom of the nest for good measure. He had buried the birds in the peat along with two hoodie crows which had met a similar fate, well out of the way, some distance from the house. To his horror, passing by that place two months later, he had found that foxes had sniffed out the carrion through the peat and dug it up. The dismembered corpses were scattered around the entire area; straggly brown wings and chunks of tell-tale feathers, and a yellow leg with black talons clipped neatly off by sharp vulpine teeth.

When he first discovered Rob Pearce in the Dalbattigh bothy it had crossed his mind that the same thing could have happened again. He had meant to go and check his most recent grave then, but, having satisfied himself that Rob was just a hill-walking camper, and seen him off the place, he had not yet bothered to do so. But, with the new threat of Lord Denby interrogating Shiona Duncan—or whatever else it was they were up to, he never knew whether to take his wife at face value or not—he had become increasingly ill at ease. Now was his chance. It was not yet five o'clock, and anybody else being around was extremely unlikely.

The hill came easily to his powerful stride. He was hurrying and his long crummack swung out in front of him piercing the heather and pushing him firmly and surely up the steep slope. With these particular corpses he had decided to go well into the hill. He had taken the stalker's path from the swing bridge over the Corran up towards Carn Mor and then, leaving the path, headed north into the shadow of the mountain.

Rob was cleaning his teeth in the burn. He was up early on his second morning for the same reasons as Shiona and Jimmy. The streaming sunlight on his face had pierced his sleep and dragged him blinking and yawning into the day.

He had decided to use the time before the world awoke to check out some of the low ground much nearer to the Lodge and the heart of the estate. On his way down the mountain from his high camp he had crossed over to the burn to use its soft, tortoise-shell water for washing the sleep from his face. He stood up and stretched. A speck in the sky caught his attention and he instinctively reached for his binoculars to check it out. It was a hoodie crow heading across the moor below and in front of him. He watched its slow, leisurely flight and wondered where it was nesting. Quite suddenly it swerved to the left, doubled its wing beat and flew off across the glen in a completely new direction.

"Funny," said Rob to himself, "I wonder what caused that?" He climbed out of the burn and scoured the moor below him. A few seconds later he saw what had alarmed the hoodie. A man was walking briskly up the stalker's path parallel to the burn. He focused in. From the hat and the stick and the broad shoulders Rob knew immediately it was Jimmy Forbes. He did not want to be seen. He knew just how sharp-eyed Jimmy was, and it would destroy his plans completely to be discovered at this hour, very obviously up to something, and within a mile of the Keeper's Cottage.

Jimmy was still two hundred and fifty yards away but heading rapidly towards him. Rob backed quickly down into the burn and cast around for a hiding place. A little further upstream the burn flowed out of a gully with steep ferny walls of damp rock. A curtain of stunted birch trees on either side of the gully met above the burn creating a tunnel. Rob entered the tunnel and pulled himself into a cleft in the rocks and sat still.

His heart was thumping. Only a few minutes later he heard the swish of the heather and the dull thud of boots on the path as he strode up beside the burn. Rob could not see him. He lay very still. If Jimmy had a dog with him it could easily bark at the slightest movement. The footsteps passed him by and then faded. Rob came out slowly. He grabbed a birch branch and pulled himself carefully up to the lip of the gully. He could see Jimmy's broad back rising and falling as he swung away from him with the same steady pace. Rob breathed more easily. He levered himself out of the burn and watched Jimmy's bonneted hat disappearing above the heather.

Suddenly, Jimmy turned left, leaving the path and heading out into some dead ground. Rob had to climb higher up and settle himself into the heather to keep him in sight. Jimmy strode on out into the moor, his pace never quickening, never slowing. Only then did Rob begin to wonder what Jimmy Forbes was doing out of his bed and into the hill at five o'clock in the morning, so purposefully, out in the great expanse of heather beneath Carn Mor. "Perhaps he's just out on his rounds? Perhaps he does this regularly?" he thought. "What luck that I've spotted him before he spotted me!" He began to worry about extricating himself from the position he was in without being seen. He began to look around for an escape route which would take him back up the hill out of Jimmy's line of vision. Before setting off he raised his binoculars once again to check Jimmy's position. To his horror he saw that he was heading back towards him. "What the hell...?" Rob muttered. He crouched lower in the heather as the burly figure swung ever closer, the crummack prodding out in front with each stride. Rob was looking straight into his face; the eyes never looked up from the ground and his face glowered with a deep scowl. Rob crept backwards into the gully and down into his rocky hideaway. The heavy boots came pounding towards him, back onto the path, and on, past him, down the slope they way he had come.

He did not move for several minutes. When he did he peered up over the rim of the gully with extra caution. He was relieved to see the stalker now far below him, still striding back towards the river. Rob was now deeply suspicious. Satisfying himself that it was safe, he came out onto the path. He could see the imprints of Jimmy's heels clearly. He began to track him up the hill. Where had he been going? And at this hour? He had no difficulty in finding where he had left the path. The heavy boots had snapped the woody heather stems and Rob could follow his route with ease.

After about two hundred yards he came to where Jimmy had stopped and turned around. He could see the sharp round imprint of the crummack, where he had leant on it for a moment or two, looking about him. Rob could see no possible reason for walking to that place, nor for turning back just there. The whole thing was a mystery. He walked on a few yards, confused and puzzled. He walked slowly back to where Jimmy had stopped. He had not been carrying anything, no gun or traps or snares, and he hadn't collected anything. Perhaps he was checking out the deer calving in the corrie, but he wasn't even carrying a telescope and he had not climbed high enough to see anything with the naked eye, nor even to a vantage point. Perhaps he himself had been spotted by someone and reported to Jimmy? Could someone have seen the sun glinting on his own telescope the previous day? The fisherman perhaps? Rob scratched his head and idly chewed a heather twig as he looked around him.

A few yards up the slope was a peat hag where the deer had broken the surface of the peat and wallowed, creating a black scar in the moor. Rob wandered over to look at it out of curiosity. Instead of finding the footprints of a red deer stag in the fresh black peat, he saw the clear full form of large hobnail boots. They were not fresh; they were not Jimmy's that morning. In fact they were possibly weeks old, but there had been so little rain that spring that they had remained clearly stamped into the dry surface.

At one side of the crescent-shaped hag, close against its edge of overhanging heather, he noticed that the peat surface was freshly broken. He dropped down onto his knees and sunk his fingers into the cool, moist peat. It came away easily. He knew something was buried there. The ground had been turned to a considerable depth, not by the action of any animal, but by the sharp steel edge of a shovel.

Rob dug like a dog with his hands, spraying the peat out, first to the left and then to the right. After a few minutes work, now immersed in a hole to the elbows, his hands touched something different, something coarse and fibrous. He pulled away the remaining peat to reveal a potato sack bulging with the uneven shape of something inside. Rob's heart thumped almost audibly. The sack was bound with a short length of orange twine. Carefully he picked it up by the neck and eased it out of its grave. It was heavy. He shuddered at what he was about to find inside. Gingerly he lifted it up onto the dry peat and picked at the knot.

He couldn't guess how long it had lain there. The bag was moist but not wet; anyway, he knew it would take years for anything to decompose in the sterile peat. Excluded from oxygen and flies, decomposition of whatever was in the bag would be extremely slow. He loosened the neck carefully. Picking up its bottom corner, he allowed the heavy corpses to roll shapelessly out into a heap at his his feet where they lay in the pathos of their own destruction.

"You bastard! You miserable, criminal bastard!"

Rob was close to tears. He stood looking at the ragged corpses of two adult golden eagles and a raven. For all their tangled and crumpled appearance, they were untouched. Rob knew in his bowels that all three were the victims of a scurrilous poisoned bait. The carcase of a rabbit, or a hare, or perhaps a deer or sheep, which had been laced with a lethal dose of strychnine or alphachlorolose or possibly phosdrin.

The great soaring wings lay stiff and twisted and the long pinion quills bent and broken. The gripping scaly feet, as yellow as the gorse flowers beside the Corran, were drawn together, black talons curled in upon eachother in contortion. The soft feathers of the proud, golden mantle, the colour of a summer wheatfield, fluttered gently in the breeze above the hooded brow, the clouded, sunken eyes, and the mighty curving bill. A silent scream issued from the gape of the second bird, its spiky tongue protruding to one side. The glossy blue-black raven lay beside them with its wrinkled jet eyes staring lifelessly at the sky.

The events of the previous day gyrated inside Bella Forbes's head. When she had something to make known, it was as unstoppable as the Dalbattigh burn which thundered past the Keeper's Cottage in summer spate. It was something which just had to come out and away, regardless of consequence to herself or anyone else. With it came a manner of speaking, a quaver and a bother. To make matters worse that morning, she was denied an audience. When she returned to the cottage her husband had gone. The Landrover was bumping its way up the track to the estate workshops where Jimmy had his 'store'—a dark, locked room with a fertilizer bag nailed up over the only window to keep out prying eyes; the executioner's dim cell in which he honed the grim weapons of his trade.

Bella was undaunted. She cycled determinedly back to the Lodge and took the house car, an elderly estate kept for servicing the household, and set off down the eleven miles to Corran Bridge. "I canna say what's going on up at that Lodge," she said to Jessie MacChattin at the stores, doing just that. She leaned forward and lowered her voice as if, completely contradicting her intention, the information she was about to impart was private and ought not to be overheard. "I swear that young Shiona Duncan is turnin' into a right hussy. I'm very glad ye didna see her yesterday, Jessie me dear, the make-up was clarted on and her skirt hitched away up above her knees, and away in drinkin' wi' Lord Denby after dinner on their own. She was in there with him 'till—weel, I canna say what time o' night! I wasna waiting around to find oot what was going on. I just went awa' home to my bed."

Jessie's eyes were round and she listened with intense concentration and a fixed expression of disbelief. She was apparently oblivious of the fact that she stood there surrounded by photographs of her own twenty-year-old model daughter, Ellen, wearing a great deal less than a short skirt, employing all the art of a professional make-up team, and in a sequence of poses which were designed for blatant arousal rather than mild flirtation. " No! Is that right?" she said, clearly expecting more, "I was wondering myself what was going on."

Bella was still uncertain about what had happened. She couldn't understand why Shiona had been there for so long, why Lord Denby should have given her a drink, and just to where she had disappeared when the lights went out. She could not really bring herself to believe that either Lord Denby, in his late fifties, for whatever reason he had suddenly broken with habit and come to Ardvarnish on his own, or Shiona, still nine-teen, the daughter of her neighbours whom she had known since birth, and had always been such a nice quiet girl, had committed the original sin. Although, of course, she was well enough aware that there were regular 'goings on' up at the Lodge when there was a house party. For her it was one of the most attractive aspects of the job that there was a continuous patter of salacious gossip in the kitchens about who was tiptoe-ing along the corridor to whose bedroom, and who arrived with one partner and departed with another a week later. But she did not like what had happened and was determined that the world should know it. The Lodge was her responsibility, and, while she was working there, so was Shiona. She also knew that telling the world would help to absolve her in advance of any row or scandal which might emerge.

On her way back she called in to see Mairi Duncan. She was in the kitchen where she had spent most of her married life. Mairi looked fifteen years older than her forty-six, and her shapeless greying hair was scraped together in a knot at the back. "I wouldna have said anything, Mairi dearie, but you know I'm that fond of Shiona, and I am real worried about her. I thought you should know...."

As well as being downtrodden by her husband, Mairi had always been spineless. She had never been able to cope with any of the problems life had thrown at her and had learned over the years that breaking down and crying was an effective way of avoiding most responsibility. She withdrew a crumpled tissue from her apron pocket and pressed it to her nose, at the same time uttering an almost inaudible sob. "Ooh, now, I didna mean to upset ye," said Bella, "I'm sure nothing's happened, Mairi dearie, but I just thought ye should know."

The door thrust open and the tall, lean figure of Andrew Duncan filled the doorway.

"What's goin' on?" he demanded, seeing his wife weeping into a mug of tea.

"Och, Andy, it's yourself," said Bella trying to smile, "It's nothing to worry about, I was jest telling Mairi about Shiona up at the Lodge yesterday. I'm that worried about that young lass of yours. She's nae acting right just now and it's no credit to you folk at all. I felt it ma duty to come and say so."

"Shiona? What's the matter with Shiona? She's doing her job isn't she?"

"Och, aye, she's doing her job all right, it's what else she's doing that's the bother."

"And what's that?" demanded Andy, his brow puckering and fiercely darting his eyes from face to face.

"I was just saying to Mairi, Lord Denby's up on his own just now staying in that big house and it's no' right for a young lass like Shiona to be dressing herself up like—well—like she shouldna."

"What d'ye mean by that?"

"Weel, Andy, you ken how attached I am to young Shiona. I've known her all my life and I feel responsible for her in that household, and I've never had this trouble before."

"Speak your mind, woman!" "Well, her skirt's far too short for one thing, and she's making herself up like—well—like she's..."

"A hussy. Is that what ye want to say?"

"Aye, weel, I wouldna have chosen to use that word," said Bella piously, averting her eyes as though she was shocked, "but ye could put it like that, right enough."

Andrew Duncan took the mug of tea his wet-eyed wife held out to him and moved to the corner of the little kitchen. He eased his long, fit body into a high backed wooden armchair. "I've told her often enough no good'll come of her painting her face," he said sharply, "but what's this to do with his lordship?"

"Weel, ye see Andy, he's there on his own just now and Shiona was in with him last night for—well—I just dinna ken how long."

"What the hell d'ye mean, woman, 'in with him'?"

"Weel, y'see, that's what I don't understand, Andy. After dinner she did her self up in the mirror looking like—really, well, y'know—as though she was up for sale or something like that." Bella threw a glance at Mairi and back to Andy to see if she had gone too far and then hurried on: "She said to me that his lordship had asked to see her. He wanted some information of some kind, whatever that meant."

"And what happened then?"

"Well, ye see, that's what I canna work out. I waited up for a wee while, but Shiona never came back."

"Where'd she go then?" Andy demanded, looking confused.

"I don't know. Ye see, I canna say. When I came down all the lights were off except upstairs. And this morning when I went up I found two empty glasses in the study. One of them definitely had Shiona's lip-stick on it. It seems they'd been drinking together."

Andrew Duncan stared incredulously at Bella. His dark look betrayed anger and dislike of Bella and at the same time an uncertainty and an innocence about the world and his daughter which made him momentarily vulnerable. "Are you making this up, woman?"

"No, no, Andy, no, I wouldna do such a thing as that, no. I'm just concerned for Shiona."

Andy turned to his wife: "Did you hear her come in last

night?" Mairi looked bleakly at her husband, shaking her head. "No, Andy, I didn't," she answered lamely.

"I'll find out just what's going on when she comes in here." Andy glared at them both. "Get away upstairs and see if her bed was slept in last night," he barked at Mairi. She rose and scurried away.

"Oh, Andy, I'm sure she's not been up to anything," said Bella uncomfortably, fidgeting in her chair. She was concerned that things were getting out of control and she began to wish she could get up and go.

Andrew Duncan sat staring bleakly at the hearth, lost for words. Mairi returned. "Well?" he asked.

"Her bed's made, Andy, and I canna tell."

Her husband looked blank. "I'll find out soon enough,and if need be I'll go and ask Lord Denby to his face what's going on."

"Oh, I shouldna do that, Andy," said Bella quickly, sounding alarmed.

"And why not?" he barked.

"Weel, ye know, he is our boss and it might be unwise to cross him until we ken exactly what happened. D'ye not think so?" said Bella desperately looking to Mairi for support.

"Aye, that's as may be," said Andy unsure of himself. "I'll not have you breathe a word about this, Bella Forbes. This is between me and ma daughter and her mother, and we'll not have your prattling tongue causing trouble."

"Och, Andrew, you know me, I wouldna dream of doing anything of the sort," Bella said gathering up her bag and wishing she had never entered the Duncan household. She rose and turned to Mairi. "Mairi love, you come and see me one of these days when Lord Denby's away south and we'll have a nice cup o' tea together." Her hand grasped the door knob and as she made her escape she turned back to Andy, "I'm sure everything'll be perfectly all right."

"Old besom!" spat Andrew Duncan as soon as the door had closed behind Bella. "There'd better no' be a word of truth in this, or it'll be the back of my hand that young madam'll get. Just who does she think she is?"

The golden eagles were back in their sack now under a pile of stones high in the corrie on Carn Mor, their new, temporary grave marked by a prominent boulder. The raven, wrapped in a polythene bag was in Rob's rucksack as he hiked out of Ardvarnish the way he had entered two days before. He was on his way back to civilisation a week earlier than expected with the chilling results of his short but effective investigation of the estate.

His first, most important step was to get the raven analysed.

If it had been poisoned he could then mobilise a police investigation. If the same poison could be found about Jimmy's house or person, there was a fair chance the SSBC could make a prosecution stick. His own evidence of Jimmy visiting the site of the peaty grave was worthless. He had no witness to corroborate his story and Jimmy only had to produce an alibi to say that he was never there at all. The key to success, it seemed to Rob, pounding back along the moorland track to Kinbrace, was surprise.

He reached his car with a sigh of relief. He had met no-one and seen only one distant vehicle on the track into Loch Fitich. He had sat on a rock and watched it out of sight; a coil of yellow dust pluming out from its wheels, wafting slowly upwards on the warm air. As it dispersed the great open moorland drifted back to emptiness and silence broken only by the occasional trilling meadow pipit. He was glad of the rest. It had been a fierce trek of determined walking, not sparing himself, so anxious was he to get the news out and swing events into action.

The trout fishing success of the previous day was not to be repeated. Gerry Denby was a victim of his own surprise visit. When he arrived at Loch Meiklie he found the boat full of water. He cursed, at the same time acknowledging that Jimmy Forbes had acted correctly. If the old clinker-built dinghies were left high and dry in hot weather they contracted and leaked when next put in the water. Jimmy had intentionally sunk the boat in the shallows to prevent it drying out. Had he known Lord Denby was coming to fish he would have bailed it out and had it ready. Gerry was not inclined to spend his first hour in back-breaking manual labour.

Instead, he fished from the bank. All he caught in the first half hour was heather on the back stroke of the cast. He cursed again, and again. He found himself losing interest; he wandered round the loch, standing in the little sandy bays and walking out on the heathery promontaries to half-heartedly dip a fly here and there. He caught a small brownie and eased the hook from its mouth gently and carefully, kneeling on a boulder to release it back into the shimmering water. It lay in his hands momentarily before darting into the shadowy depths. It pleased him to see it go; he was enjoying himself, after all.

Gerry's mood was levitating. The desire to kill more fish had left him. The epic of yesterday's big fish had, for the moment at least, sated him. It had been a privilege to catch that fish. He had not known it existed. He had applied his skill with optimism in an intelligent presumption that such a quarry lurked there. He had enticed it and fooled it with his fly, played it patiently up and down the loch wherever it took him, his concentration as taut as his line, until he judged it tired enough to ease the net beneath and triumphantly take it. Now he was basking in that glory. A lesser fish was of no interest to him. He would not kill little brown trout today. Slowly and thoughtfully he dismantled his rod. He was at peace. The troubles of Denby Hall were of no consequence. The loneliness and the grandeur of the moors had plucked him away from the petty nuisance of self-made drudgery and he felt both humble and benevolent. He spied a little knoll about a mile off and decided to have his lunch there.

It was, he mused, a very beautiful place. He could not remember thinking about it in quite the same way before. "Perhaps one has to earn one's true appreciation of a place?" he thought. Perhaps he had got it wrong all these years? All those demanding guests showing off to each other; and the factor, pushing him into this scheme and that new plan, and trying to make everything pay all the time. Perhaps that had never allowed him to be a proper sportsman before? He sat down on the knoll and looked about him.

What was it, he wondered, that really made him love the place? It certainly wasn't owning it—that just meant work and worry. Nor was it the status being a large landowner brought, even to those to whom such things were important. Apart from the one or two old friends he had known all his life, he had a low opinion of all of them. In his eyes they were expensive hangers-on of questionable worth. "Damned parasites," he called some of Dinah's acolytic gin-drinking friends. No, it was nothing to do with any of that. It was something to do with the land itself.

A single file of red deer stags appeared on the shoulder of Carn Mor away to his left. Although they were a long way off Gerry could see each one in sharp silhouette against the sky. They were grazing their way up into the hill, walking a few paces, stopping to pluck at the moist grasses and the young green heather, jostling each other forward in constant competition for the best pasture and for position in the stag herd. Gerry watched them intently for a few moments; he smiled inwardly at the parallel between man and beast, of his own sons competing with each other for the attention of their women and simultaneously testing the authority of the old man. He knew these spring weeks were crucial to the success of the stags. Antlers were still forming beneath the hot velvet fur, dependent upon the quality of feeding for their eventual shape and size which would dictate the success of the stag amongst its rivals when the rut came in October.

He rummaged in his fishing bag for his elderly Zeiss binoculars. He could see far more deer now. There were dozens of them scattered over the moors in little groups. Some were lying

70

contentedly in the sun, and as he watched so he became more deeply interested. "I wonder how many stags we've got?" he muttered to himself. Forbes had told him that there were less than a thousand deer on Ardvarnish. He knew they stalked about forty stags each September and Forbes did a hind cull every winter accounting for another sixty hinds, but he had no idea how many there were.

He found a group of deer much closer to him, below and to the south of Loch Meiklie. They were twenty-two stags of what appeared to be a wide range of ages. He found himself fascinated. He moved from beast to beast assessing each one carefully, attempting to age them from their size and gait and working out which was the dominant animal in each group and which the underdog, ever challenged by the others, the bullied weakling never given a chance to graze for more than a few seconds unharrassed.

After eating he placed his fishing bag beneath his head and closed his eyes on the streaming sun. "I must do this more often," he said to himself, revelling in the peace and freedom from a nagging wife. Sun, fresh air, food and contentment, and then a strong pull at the brandy from his hip flask. He snored loudly.

He did not sleep long. He awoke with a frown and a sensation of guilt—a sort of growing unease. He sat up and looked around him to make sure he had not been observed. Some of the stags had grazed nearer to him and they saw him now, their heads up and half-grown antlers looking mildly ridiculous. He examined them again through binoculars before they panicked and ran, streaming away on powerful legs effortlessly up the slope and out of sight. The realisation that he had owned Ardvarnish for all these years and never spent an afternoon watching deer before embarrassed him. A thought struck him. He put down the binoculars and sat bolt upright, frowning crossly. He stared critically at the vast expanse of moorland in front of him, then down at his feet. He was sitting on heather. He parted the woody stems and looked closely at the ground. There was nothing else growing there. To his right there was a patch of thin moss with the heather straggling up through it, and below him he could see a stripe of damp ground where the heather gave way to a pale yellow-green grass and more sphagnum moss. He walked slowly towards it examining the ground.

Something entirely new had pierced through to his consciousness, which made him distinctly uncomfortable. What if the deer were slowly changing this place? He had heard much talk of overgrazing and never really bothered to try to understand what it was all about. He certainly never imagined it might apply to Ardvarnish. Most of the deer they shot each year, and Duncan's sheep were in good condition and so general accusations of overgrazing in the Highlands had fallen on deaf ears. Derek Holdingham had reassured him once by saying "As long as the bodyweights of your stags are as good as they are and Duncan continues to get top prices at Lairg, I don't think we've anything to worry about."

As he watched the more dominant stags bullying the others off any bit of grazing they seemed to be enjoying, Gerry suddenly imagined himself as a blade of succulent grass or the seedling of a young tree. His chances of survival were virtually non-existant. The deer were everywhere. They were criss-crossing this whole landscape night and day, back and forth, scouring the land for the plants they liked and wanted. And this was June, grasses and burgeoning young heather shoots were abundant; yet still the deer were competing with each other for the best grazing. How much more effective must that search be in winter when the heather was as brown as burnt cork and the grass scorched yellow and lifeless by the frosts. And then what about the added pressure of Andrew Duncan's sheep?

The revelation which had buzzed into his consciousness like an angry bee was that perhaps there were whole species of plants or possibly whole plant communities which should be present on these moors but which had been selectively removed by the deer over a hundred and fifty years of the sporting use of this land. What if what was there now was the lowest common denominator? What if at the end of this long period the land was reduced to its poorest state; that these plants, epitomised by the romantic purple heather, were the ones which had dominated the moor only because everything else had been removed by the deer and the sheep and by man? And what if, as a result of the underlying acidity of the peaty soils and the cold wet climate, the fertility of the land had gone down and down until it had reached an all time low?

These were uncomfortable questions which passed across him like heavy grey clouds pressing in from the west. What if the wild flowers he so loved were slowly disappearing? And what if there should be trees and shrubs on these hills, and that they had been steadily and systematically removed by the deer, each succulent young seedling being nipped off by the hungry animals until there was no seed source and so they never had a chance to return? He knew too well how very damaging to trees deer could be from some of the woods at Denby where they'd had young beech and oak saplings chewed out of existence by marauding fallow deer. What if the lack of vegetation and fertility in the land was responsible for the decline of the grouse, and the harvest of insects their chicks needed to survive? And what about the lapwings and curlews which used to be everywhere in the spring at Ardvarnish? They had almost all gone, and there were definitely fewer duck than when he was a boy. He was worried.

Perhaps these Nature Conservancy people were right to be concerned about the welfare of the hills. He recalled his conversation with Derek Holdingham. Maybe that's what the Sites of Special Scientific Interest were about and that there was more to it than just protecting the land in its present state. He felt exposed. He knew none of the answers. It was an uncomfortable feeling. Perhaps he should make it his business to find out more and to see that Holdingham co-operated with them fully, after all, weren't they the only organisation which had ever shown an interest in caring for the long term health of the land? He stood up and brushed the brown flecks of last year's heather flowers from his tweeds. Maybe they had been blind and they had got it wrong, but he was not going to be guilty of negligence from now on. He strode off down the hill with a new determination in his step.

"Yes, that's it," he thought, that was what he so loved about the place—it was the deep sense of responsibility it imposed upon him. He loved the feeling of mutuality; that he was dependent upon these great, moody hills for his recreation and his sport and his spiritual well being, and they were dependent upon him for their welfare. It was a custodianship he had always taken a pride in, like that of Denby. For decades it had been sufficient reward to rest his head at night secure in the knowledge that he was looking after the place as his father and grandfather had done before him. Now, in one brief trip to Ardvarnish in June, on a whim, unplanned and unpremeditated, a handful of idle hours alone on the hill had stripped that smugness away.

Shiona was late finishing her morning's work in the Lodge. Bella had taken revenge by giving her a long list of tedious chores, culminating in the polishing of the large, hexagonal brass door handle on the ecclesiastically-arched front door. Shiona had enjoyed it. There was a challenge in making it gleam and she was outside and the birds were singing and the air was fresh and clean. It had not occurred to her that life in Yorkshire might not be so clean, nor had it crossed her mind that the next job might not include the perks of food and accommodation and the security and shelter of a community such as she had known at Ardvarnish all her life. The determination to fight away from her home and her people was, for the present, blindingly powerful. She hung up her apron, closed the scullery door behind her and set off down the track mentally packing her belongings with every step.

She could see her father working his dogs, Jess and Bran, up

73

in the Brae Park. The lambing had gone well enough. The late spring had been kind when it came and the lambs grew strong and ran in unruly gangs of a dozen or more, exuberantly chasing each other.

Andrew Duncan's quick eye saw his daughter approaching the cottage. He stopped for a moment to lean on his crummack and watch her open the little garden gate and pass into the house. He looked up at his sheep and the keenly-panting dogs lying obediently where they had been whistled down.

He was out of his depth, he knew that. Shiona had first become difficult aged sixteen, three and a half years before, and he had felt himself losing his grip on his daughter, just as he had with his son two years before that. Young Andy had just walked away from his parents' authority when he left school and had never taken any notice of them since. He had gone where he wanted without reference to home or parents, abandoning the kirk and his family together almost as though they had never existed. Now, at nearly twenty-two, it was as though they had a lodger who only paid rent when it suited him and who came and went without a word or a wave. He could not remember the last time he had sat down at the family fireside with his son. If they met it was usually in the Glen Corran Hotel when they threw each other a glance and a nod and joined their respective drinking partners at opposite ends of the bar. It was no good approving or disapproving of what Andy did, or with whom.

But with Shiona it was different. A young girl couldn't just do what she liked, and he, as her father, was responsible. Besides, if she brought the family into disrepute it would damage them far more than if Andy did. Girls were expected to behave, especially when it came to men and morals. He had never been happy about young Danny Stott. Those Stotts were a bad lot and he had disliked Danny's father for many a long year for the rough way he handled his livestock. Many's the time he had seen him kicking them and throwing them about at the mart, and in the bar they said other things about Grigor Stott, about how he had fiddled his livestock returns and made a killing out of the drainage grants, half the tiles still stacked in a heap behind his barn. Andrew did not like the idea of Grigor's son messing with his daughter, but he had never been able to stop it. He had found himself expressing his anger to her in other ways and passing the problem to his wife. "Will you not stop Shiona seeing that Danny Stott? It's a mother's job and you're not doing anything about it, woman." Mairi had continued to do nothing.

But this time it was different. If what Bella Forbes had been saying was true, Shiona was putting the family's name at risk. Never mind the propriety of it, it was not her place to be drink-

74

ing at night with the laird and the gossip would rebound on them all; it could even be that she was threatening his job and their home. He didn't know what to make of it. He whistled in the dogs with two long shrill calls and strode away from his lambs with his eyebrows knit and his jaw locked.

"...eem...Shiona," her mother turned from the stove to face her as she came in. Her voice on edge and her face revealed the uncertainty and tension of the past few hours. Shiona looked startled. "What's amiss, Mother?" she asked, wide eyed.

"Oh, Shiona! What have you been at?" Mairi was close to tears; her lip trembled. "Your father's that sick with worry about you, Shiona."

"How's that?"

"Bella was in here this morning very worried herself about what's going on up at the Lodge, you drinking with Lord Denby till all hours, and it's not nice at all what she's saying."

"Oh, is that right?" said Shiona coldly.

"Aye, and we don't understand, Shiona, you've not told us anything."

Shiona felt a strange confidence arise within her. She remembered the sense of elation she had experienced after talking to Lord Denby and the wondering why she had ever been in awe. The little girl was gone; she would not now stand apologetic and submissive before her elders, nor become a wimpering drudge like her mother. That was not for her. There was too much of her father in her, and now, in an instant, in the kitchen of her home she came of age.

"No, Mother, I haven't told you anything at all, because there's nothing to tell. When will you stop listening to that wicked, blethering wifie? Have you no faith in me at all?" Now she understood Bella's reference to her parents. So she had hurt Bella by creeping out of the Lodge last night, and in revenge Bella had lost no time in concocting a malicious tale about her and Lord Denby and transmitting it around her family and her friends. She crossed to the Rayburn and stood with her back to her mother grasping the rail with both hands, her knuckles white and her wide blue eyes staring distantly.

It was more than Mairi could take. The tears flooded down her pale cheeks and she sobbed helplessly into her apron. She knew in her heart that they had not been close to each other for several years and she had failed to be able to help Shiona in the perpetual conflict with her father. Mairi was the double victim of two strong wills neither of whom she could deflect from their set courses. She sat miserably at the bottom of the family pile. Tears were a relief to her, an escape for her own frustrations and despair, as well as from having to face the world. Without turning round the icy calm of Shiona's voice broke into the sobbing. "I don't know what Bella Forbes has said to you, but I can guess fine, and it's about as much as I would expect from her, but if you and Father have listened to her, you're both as bad as she is. And if that's all you think of your own daughter there is nothing I can say."

The back door sprang open. The tall silhouette of her father loomed in from the doorway. The rich, familiar smell of sheep and sweat engulfed the room. Bran, the younger of the two collie bitches, slunk in around her master's legs, Jess obediently lying on the doorstep outside.

"Get by!" Andrew snapped at the dog. The collie whipped round and was out again in an instant. He closed the door. He stood looking from his daughter to his wife and back again. Shiona turned to face him, staring at him in a way he had not seen before.

"And what have you got to say to me, my girl....?" he demanded, but Shiona interrupted him sharply.

"No, no, Father, you've got it wrong," she exclaimed defiantly, her eyes the coldest blue and the angriest, "you've got it all wrong. It's you who've to do some explaining to me, the both of you," she threw a glance at her mother, "for listening to the rubbish that woman speaks. So, what will you be saying to me?"

Andrew Duncan was shaken. He was certainly not expecting this. He glanced from Shiona to his wife and back again. Mairi had stopped crying and stood with the hem of her apron clutched to her mouth and her wet eyes round with surprise.

"Don't you be giving me any cheek, young lassie. I'll not have you speak to your parents like that."

Shiona advanced across the room towards her father, hands on her hips, her red hair around her face drained white, and her eyes flashing. "Is it all right for you to listen to this bad talk from Bella Forbes, about your own daughter, can you tell me that?! Well, I'll ask you this, Father, and you, Mother, what word have you got for turning against your own daughter and listening to this lowest gossip?!" Flushed now; she stood in the middle of the room without a hint of submission to the years of authority her father has imposed upon her.

Andrew was off balance. This had never happened to him before, least of all from a woman in his own family. His mouth opened, closed again, soundless and wordless. Shiona saw his weakness and drove fearlessly forward, her voiced steeled with a cold authority, peaking with a steely cold assertion.

"And before you order me out of this house, Father, as you usually do, you should know that I'm going anyway. Lord and Lady Denby are offering me a job in Yorkshire and I'm taking it. I'll be away out of your house and from under your feet just as soon as I can make my arrangements. I had hoped I could leave this house with your blessing, but seemingly it's to be with the stain of Bella Forbes's gossip laid on me by my own parents. I'll thank you to stand aside Father, and let me out!"

"Oh, Shiona!" cried Mairi, streaming uncontrollable tears. Andew Duncan went to his wife's side, still without a word; Shiona stood in the doorway and faced them both. "I shall be back this evening to collect my things." And then she was gone.

Andrew Duncan put his arm around his wife's shoulder. She buried her face in her apron and wept. Words returned to him only slowly. He spoke softly. "Wheest, Mairi. Don't be crying now." He pulled her closer, staring glassily over her grey, wispy hair. They stood in the silence of their shock for several minutes. Then he spoke again. "She had to go, you could see that, but I'm proud of her, lass, I am that."

—8—

Gerry crossed the cattle grid on the back drive which, within its circular deer fence, enclosed the oasis of the Lodge and fifty acres of woods and rhododendron-dominated gardens from the open hill. He had not stopped looking and thinking all the way down from the loch. He stood at the edge of the grid and stared up each side of the fence leading away from him to the moor beyond. "Hmmph," he grunted. He laid down his rod and bag and picked his way slowly up inside the fence, closely examining the ground at his feet.

After a few yards he stopped again. His right hand reached out for the cold mesh of the fence. He stood resting and contemplating. His brow was creased. "I am a bloody fool," he muttered. At his feet the ground was dense with heather and grasses. The pale pink flowers of Lady's Smock struggled up through the forest of vegetation and the tufted heads of cotton grass dotted a wet patch to his left. There were young rowans with frondy leaves and slender, paper-barked birches springing thickly from among the heather, of every size and age from a few inches high to mature trees of forty feet, their fresh green leaves hanging like a pastel cloud against the sunlit hill and the sky. To his right, through the fence, there was an open ocean of heather, purple moor grass and sedges. He returned to the grid and crossed to the moorland again. This time he walked up the outside of the fence searching among the heather for any sign of a seedling tree. He found nothing. The ground was punctuated with little piles of fibrous khaki deer droppings. He looked out to the moor and shaded his eyes with his hand. The nearest tree was way out on the first burn which crossed the landscape in the middle distance. He knew instinctively that it sprang from the steep side of the burn, out of reach of the remorseless teeth of the deer and the sheep.

It wasn't that he hadn't noticed it before, of course he had. Every fool knew that if you wanted trees round your house in the Highlands you have to fence the animals out. It was just that he had never properly understood the full significance of that principle before. He had never really given any thought to the obvious fact that the great open moor could perfectly well grow wild trees if man gave it a chance to, and flowers, and lush grasses, and, now that he had seen it, and thought of the whole forty-five thousand acres all subjected to the same ravening persecution by teeth and jaw, he was troubled by it; troubled by the knowledge that he had encouraged it to be like that without planning it or thinking about it, or being aware of its other potential, just because that is what it had always been like and he had never seen anything wrong with that; and troubled by his ignorance. He just didn't know what to think. The revelation was forcing him to re-examine his very ownership of the land in a way which had never even crossed his mind before.

On the one hand he did not like to admit his stark lack of knowledge, and on the other he knew he could not go on owning this land without finding out whether what he suspected was true. And he wasn't at all sure how to go about that without making an even bigger fool of himself. He picked up his rod and bag and walked ponderously back down the track towards the jungle of rhododendrons which enshrouded the Lodge.

Up at Loch Meiklie a shaft of light had penetrated the long years of his experience at Ardvarnish. The decline of the grouse, which he had witnessed all his life, and which Forbes blamed on the wretched tick—which buried its evil little insect head into his shins and which would only let go if you singed its body with a cigarette, and even then left an itchy sore—was almost complete. In his boyhood they had shot a hundred brace in a day, any day they chose from August the twelfth until October. Those had been magnificent sporting days of many keepers in matching tweed suits and caps, and panting pointers, setters and retrievers straining at the end of leashes and chains; and of lunch brought onto the moor by the servants who set up chairs and a long trestle table with a white damask cloth, glass and silverware, for his parents to entertain their guests in full Edwardian splendour.

After the war the extravagance had seemed inappropriate.

The grouse had been good some years and bad others, but life went on much the same but with fewer keepers and servants, which everyone accepted because both world wars had sucked so much life-blood from the Highland glens. Capital taxation had snatched hungrily from landowners' pockets so that the economies imposed by fewer staff and guests had been welcome. All that had come and gone, year in and year out, the heather blooming bright over the moor and high into the hills to the delight of their friends who shot the grouse, flicked their elegant and colourful flies into the river Corran for a salmon, and slithered on their bellies through clouds of powdery heather pollen to stalk up to a stag under the imperious thralldom of the stalker, to take it or miss it according to the luck of the day or the will of the gods. All this and never a thought of any kind that all he had known and loved might not be able to go on forever, that something might be seriously amiss; something bigger than the welfare of the deer and the sheep, more important than man's sporting needs, and something altogether grander than Carn Mor and the great solemn peaks of Ben Armine and Ben Klibreck.

Gerry made up his mind to go home to Denby. As he approached the Lodge still deep in thought he saw the lone figure of Shiona walking slowly towards the back door. He stood and waited for her. "Why hullo there, young Shiona, I was hoping to bump into you or Mrs Forbes because I've decided to go home. I shall be leaving in about an hour, and you two can close the Lodge down again. We shan't be back until the second week of August."

Shiona smiled a wan, lifeless smile. "Very good, m'Lord," she said in an empty voice.

"Is there something wrong?" he asked, quietly. Shiona looked straight at him, seeming to study his kind face and the filigree veins which surfaced on his cheeks and told of too much good living, and the little grey moustache, his curling ginger eyebrows and those friendly grey-green eyes. She struggled to control her quivering lip, the colour flaring in her face as she fought back the overwhelming tide of tears, which shook through her whole body, rising from deep within her. "My dear girl!" said Gerry, instinctively placing a hand on her shoulder. Whatever barriers remained were instantly dispelled by the power of touch. Shiona let go. She cried from the very core of her being.

Perhaps it was a minute, perhaps longer before her will returned. Raising her head and opening her eyes, she accepted the silk handkerchief Gerry held out. "...Thank...you," she said, holding the crumpled silk to her eyes. "I'm so sorry, m'Lord, I'm so sorry..."

"Don't you worry about me, young lady. Whatever all that was about is a lot better out than in. I think we should go inside and then, if you would like to, you can tell me all about it." He turned and walked in through the back door.

Gerry instinctively sat at the end of the big kitchen table while she slid the heavy kettle onto the aga to boil and arranged fine china tea cups on a tray.

"Same old problem, what?" he said cautiously.

"Aye, m'Lord, it is that," Shiona replied, managing a little smile. "But I think it may be the end of the problem."

"Ah," said Gerry, "that sounds encouraging. Why all the tears then?"

"Because I've left home, Lord Denby, I cannot go back, not to live. I've told them that I'm leaving the glen. It's only just happened and I know I can't go back."

"I see. So the bubble has burst, has it? And have you any plans?"

"No, sir, I've none," she said, sitting down across the table from him staring blankly at the colourful wet silk in her hands. "I've made a mess of it, m'Lord, haven't I?" She looked up.

"Not for the first time nor the for the last, dear girl," said Gerry sagely. "Life often is blundering forward without really knowing what the consequences will be. Do you know where you're going—tonight, for instance?"

"No, m'Lord. I only know that I'm leaving this glen."

"Hmmm. I see. Well in that case you'd better come with me," he said decisively. "I'm driving down to Lairg and then on to Inverness to catch the night train. Have you friends you could go to, or a relation nearby?"

"Aye, m'Lord, ...I'd like to go to my friend Jeannie in Lairg. If I could use the telephone and then take a lift with you, I know I could stay with Jeannie for a day or two while I think what to do next."

"Yes, of course. That sounds an excellent plan. And you will tell your parents, won't you, eh?" Shiona was silent. She poured the steaming water into the pot and stirred it thoughtfully. "You know it will only cause them more pain and worry if you don't tell them where you are. Whatever you feel about them just now, you do owe it to them to spare them that. ...If you would like me to," he offered, "I will tell them for you."

Shiona looked up at him. "Oh, could you, m'Lord? Could you do that? I'm not wanting to be a nuisance. I've troubled you enough already."

"Nonsense, girl. I am your employer, and although it seems that you will be leaving your job here at the Lodge today, I am quite happy to assume that responsibility for you."

Shiona hesitated. "The trouble is, m'Lord, I told them I'm

going to Yorkshire. I told them I'm going to work for you."

"Oho, you have, have you? I see!" Gerry laughed. "You've really plunged in the deep end, haven't you, and dragged me with you? What? What?"

"Well, m'Lord. I had to say I was going somewhere. I couldn't just walk out of the door. But don't worry, I'll be alright. I'll get a job in Lairg, or Inverness or somewhere."

"Well, I think the best thing we can do is for me to tell them that you're going to stay with your friend in Lairg for a little while, and that we're trying to fix up something for you down at Denby Hall." Gerry could anticipate that Dinah was not going to be amused by this little episode, particularly if he tried to interfere with the staff arrangements at Denby. He knew he had to tread very carefully. "I will get Holdingham to pay your wages up until the end of this week in full, and that will give us a bit of breathing space to see if we can move forward sensibly. I don't know if or when we can offer you anything at Denby, but I promised you I would do my best, and I shall. You have some tea and I'll go and pack my bag and then we'll go down to your parents. You must have a bag or something to collect. You can't just walk out without any clothes, eh? and, if you can bring yourself to accept a little fatherly advice from me, it would be far better if you could say goodbye to your parents and leave with a smile on your face."

"Aye, m'Lord. I know you're right..." A warmer, brighter smile touched the edge of her mouth.

When the phone rang Rob had woken with a start. Mike was pleased, there was no doubt about that, but he was also coldly professional. "Have you told anyone?"

"No, not a soul. I haven't seen anyone to speak to."

"Good. Keep it that way. You'll screw the whole thing up if it leaks. Now, we need to act fast. I'll meet you at the Lairg Police Station in two hours time. I shall contact them now and have them ready for us."

"Right, I'll be there," said Rob.

"Make sure you bring the raven and I'll get the police to get it off to the lab pronto. We'll almost certainly have to wait for a result, so lying low and keeping silent will be bloody important. You know what Highland communities are like for gossip. Get going then! See you in a couple of hours."

"Yes, sir," said Rob emphatically as he snapped the aerial shut and started the car.

"Shiona has applied for a job in the household at Denby Hall, Mrs Duncan," said Gerry to a bewildered Mairi.

To the unspoken relief of both Shiona and Gerry, Andrew

Duncan was back on the hill. "I have agreed to give her a lift to Lairg where I understand she plans to stay a few days with her friends the Macronies." He could hear her rummaging upstairs in her little bedroom, throwing her few possessions into a suitcase. Mairi did not know whether to sit or stand. Lord Denby had never been into their little kitchen before and all she could manage to say was, "Aye, well, m'Lord, that'll be fine." until Shiona appeared in the doorway.

"I'll be in the car," said Gerry, tactfully taking his leave.

Mother and daughter stood looking at each other. "No tears this time, Mother. I've no doubt I'll be back soon enough. Tell Father that I'll be in touch before I go down to Yorkshire." She stepped forward and kissed her mother quickly on both cheeks, snatched up her suitcase and left. Mairi stood in the little porch and watched the car out of sight.

High on the hill above Andrew Duncan watched too. He thought of the little girl whose tiny, hot hand he had held in his for so many years, and the way she used to fling her arms around his neck and hug him, and the excitement of lambing together, and the surge of pride when she drew her first slimy lamb and they helped the exhausted ewe to her feet. He knew that his years of claiming were over.

"God go with you, Shiona, my bonny, bonny lassie," he said to the wind and to the dogs at his feet. And then he was back to sorting his lambs. "Hey on, Bran! On, Jess! Get up by!" The dogs sprang to his command and bolted forward unaware of the blur in his eye.

—9—

Rob met Mike at the police station on time. Sergeant Bane had done his job and procured a search warrant from the local JP. The raven had been officially handed over, sealed with a police tag in a polythene bag and posted off to the government laboratory for analysis. The police considered the evidence to be strong enough to proceed with a search without having to wait for the result. It was inconceivable that two eagles and a raven could have died simultaneously of natural causes, and the fact of burying them in a hiding place was sufficient incrimination of Jimmy Forbes to satisfy the rules. It was agreed that they would move into action at five o'clock the following morning.

They found rooms for the night in a bed and breakfast household just off the main street. It was a solid old stone villa and they were warmly welcomed by Mrs Macronie who showed them to twin attic bedrooms with dormer windows under a grey slate roof.

"We've had our tea," said Mrs Macronie, "but I can easily do you some bacon and eggs or some sandwiches if you lads are hungry." "Yes, please," Rob and Mike responded in unison "Come and meet the family."

They followed her into the front room where her husband was sprawled before the fire in a crushed armchair. He jumped up with surprising agility for his girth which was buckled inside a broad leather belt. He thrust his glasses back onto his nose and held out a big hand and a wide-toothed smile.

"This is Rob and Mike, and this is Jeannie, my daughter," said Betty Macronie. A shy, slender girl, made shyer by the scattered pimples of late teens on her nose, smiled at them. "You sit yourselves down and make yourselves confortable."

"Are you in Lairg for long?" beamed Sandy. "Probably only a couple of days," Rob answered, "we're keen hill walkers and we will be up and out very early in the morning." "Och aye, I see, very good," said Sandy enthusiastically, although he had never climbed a hill in his life and certainly never would now. "Are you..." but his question was broken by an angry door bell.

"That'll be your friend now, Jeannie," said Betty, and to Rob, "she has a friend coming to stay for a few days as well. We're a full house tonight."

Jeannie and her mother went out to the hall. Rob could hear someone being welcomed and helped with a suitcase. Their voices were excited and Betty Macronie was saying, "you're all right are you, pet?" And then Jeannie asked in a reverential tone, "Was that Lord Denby in the car?"

Rob began to listen intently. "Aye, that's him, right enough." said a new Highland voice, a girl—Rob guessed of similar age to Jeannie. "He's been so very good to me."

Mike had heard it too and a look flashed between them. The door opened and the two girls came in with Betty Macronie who said with obvious glee, "Now then, here's some nice company for you girls. This is Shiona Duncan. Shiona, these young gentlemen are staying with us the night; it's Rob and Mike." Both smiled and nodded. "Shiona's from Glen Corran and is an old school friend of Jeannie's."

"I'm very pleased to meet you," said Shiona politely, trying to conceal her dismay that she and Jeannie were not to be in the house alone.

"They've not seen each other for a wee while and I expect they'll blether away half the night if they get the chance," Betty

Macronie continued, and then to her daughter, "Jeannie, just you remember we've guests in the house, now."

"Ma-am!" complained Jeannie.

"Have you had your tea, Shiona?" asked Betty who was never content unless she had fed a full meal to everyone setting foot over her doormat.

"No, I'm afraid I have not, Mrs Macronie," said Shiona, "I only had an apple for my dinner, and that seems like days ago. I'm starving!"

Nothing could have pleased her more. She bustled out to the kitchen saying, "I'll no' be more than a few minutes."

The girls disappeared upstairs chattering. Rob was fascinated: this had to be Andrew Duncan the Ardvarnish shepherd's daughter and Lord Denby was up in the Highlands, too. He needed to talk to Mike urgently and in private. Betty Macronie came to his rescue. "Sandy," she yelled from the kitchen, "I'm wanting more eggs. Would you see if the hens have laid the day?"

Rob briefed Mike in whispers. "I don't know that much yet about the people on the estate, although it could well be that the shepherd is as hard on the eagles as the keeper. It would be very useful if we had some inside information. I should like to talk to this girl."

They were interrupted by Sandy carrying a tray with steaming tea dribbling from the spout of a large china pot, fat scones as yellow as the thick butter, homemade oatcakes and a pot of rasberry jam. He nearly tipped the whole lot on the floor as he struggled to clear the little table and Rob noticed that this delightful man's huge hands were scarred and leathery and puffy from half a lifetime of what he later discovered to be joinery. He was the Lairg self-employed joiner who, following his father before him, fashioned everything in wood the community needed, from roofs and rocking-chairs to coffins and cart-wheels, in a black corrugated-iron workshop at the end of the street. "You lads get started on that," he said, still grinning cheerily, "Betty's just cooking those eggs for you. You'll no' get them any fresher than that!"

When they came they were like twin orange suns on a white plate, two each, with a round slab of black pudding, broad rashers of crisp bacon and two large sausages accompanied by a thick cutting of fresh white bread. Shiona and Jeannie returned and conversation lapsed while they ate. There was no space for talk. The eating was earnest; the warmth of their welcome and the generosity of their plates encouraging all three to indulge themselves, happy that they were pleasing their hostess and her perpetually-smiling husband. The ample girth of Betty and Sandy bore witness to the priorities of the Macronie household.

While they ate he observed Shiona closely. She had the most strikingly red hair he had ever seen. At first he thought it must have come out of a bottle, but a second glance dispelled so irreverent a thought. She was a redhead in the way only a true redhead can be, with mackerel-blue eyes and skin as pale and refined as ermine. She was very close to being beautiful, but too youthful for that. And she looked tired and troubled. He burned to know why Lord Denby had brought her here. The chance meeting of someone so closely woven into the fabric of his own plot was an extraordinary twist of fate even in this little community. He was fascinated by her. She looked up twice and found him watching her so that she forced a weak smile. He knew he was going to achieve nothing in the cottage.

"I've been cramped up in a car all day, I should love to walk down the road to the Sutherland Arms and get a beer before bedtime. How about you, Mike?"

"Yeah. Great idea."

"Would you two girls like to join us? We'll only be an hour."

Shiona looked at Jeannie. This never happened at Ardvarnish. This was why she was leaving home—for some freedom, some opportunity to meet new people with new ideas and to make her own decisions. If she could enjoy a sherry with a peer then she could enjoy a beer with a hill-walker. She was not going to wait for Jeannie, whom she knew never to have taken a decision in her life, to ask her parents. "Thank you very much, that'd be fine. We'll come, won't we, Jeannie?"

The bar was almost empty. Three regulars leaning over drams and chasers clustered round the barman who left the conversation reluctantly to take Mike's order. Rob made for a corner table and sat down, ushering Shiona to the seat opposite him. He studied her again. She was—what was the word?—not beautiful, and certainly nothing lame like pretty or attractive, she was something in between, something much more powerful... he abandoned the search. Twenty, he guessed, or perhaps a little older. Her eyes were large and she wore almost no make-up. It certainly didn't matter. Her shoulders were neat and set well with an air of confidence as if she were in no doubt about herself. And she looked straight at him when she spoke in her soft Highland voice, which held for him a peculiar magnetism.

"So you live in Glen Corran?"

"Not any more, but that is my home. I'm staying with Jeannie's family for a while before going to take up a job in Yorkshire."

"Oh, I see. Have you just left home?"

She glanced at Jeannie and smiled, "I have—today."

"So this is you loose on the big wide world, is it?"

"Aye, well, I've been working on the estate for the last sixteen months and now I'm going south to work for them down there."

"Is that the Ardvarnish estate?"

"D'you know it then?"

"Er, no, not really, but I have climbed there in the past," Rob hurried on, "I've done all those big round hills, Ben Armine and Ben Klibreck as well as Carn Mor. I love them, they're so different from the jagged peaks of the west."

Shiona laughed, throwing back her hair from her shoulders in a way which seemed to amplify the smile and the flame of her blue eyes. "I've lived there for twenty years and I've never been up Ben Armine. If you live among them you've no need to rush about the hill like you folk from the south. Are there no hills where you come from?"

"No, which is why we're so keen on yours. I'm from Kent. It's all farmland. Do your folks work for the estate?"

"Father's the shepherd there."

"Up at Dalbattigh?"

"So you do know the glen?" Shiona half-questioned as a look of recognition spread through her eyes. Rob hoped he hadn't made her suspicious. "Is that your orange car parked outside the house?" "Yes, why?"

"I saw that car up the glen only a few days back. Was it you Jimmy Forbes found camping in the Dalbattigh bothy?"

"Er, yes. Yes, it was." Rob had not expected to be identified so readily. What they say about a stranger in a small community was evidently true. He shot a glance at Mike who eyed him warily across his beer. "I was hoping to climb Carn Mor, but the stalker made me go and get permission from the Factor first."

"Aye, well, that's Jimmy Forbes," Shiona laughed, flashing a smile at him. "He likes to be king of the hills, right enough. I hope he wasn't too rough on you?"

"He wasn't exactly polite, but I escaped with my scalp."

"Ach, he can be a bastard if he's in a bad mood."

Things were progressing well. Rob wanted her to open up about Forbes. He sensed that she didn't like him and she might well be teased into helping them. "I don't think I want to experience that, although I don't pretend to understand it. Why do these stalkers object so strongly to walkers and climbers in the hills? As long as we don't interfere with their shooting or their sheep or anything I can't see the reason."

"They're just not used to it. Folk like Jimmy have had it to themselves for most of their lives except for when the Denbys come up, which is only about ten weeks a year, and he thinks he owns it. They're all like that, and some of them's got a good deal to hide as well."

"What d'you mean?" enquired Rob as innocently as he could. Shiona looked down. She reached for her vodka and sipped it thoughtfully. Dislike Jimmy and Bella she might, but she was not a gossip and she was too close to home to be malicious about people she had known all her life. There was plenty she could say which would both shock the world outside and condemn Jimmy Forbes as well. Now was not the time for that. "Ach, stalkers and keepers are always taking a stag for the pot, or a salmon from the river when the laird's away. They were mostly poachers before they became keepers anyway and they don't want prying eyes on the hills..."

"Oh, I see what you mean." Rob did not want to sound disappointed, but he did.

"What did you expect me to say?" She gave him a hard, straight look. This girl was not to be trifled with. He tried to joke. "I thought you were going to say he had an illicit still up in a cave in the Dalbattigh burn!" Shiona and Jeannie laughed and the moment was past. "What will you be doing in Yorkshire?"

"I hope to be working in Lord Denby's house there. That's all I've done, work in the Lodge at Ardvarnish."

"Is he nice? I've heard he's a very large landowner."

"Aye, he is. He's been very good to me. I wouldn't be sitting here now if it wasn't for him. I had a row with my father and had to leave home before I went crazy. Lord Denby came to my rescue and brought me down to Lairg. He's a very considerate man, you know. Now he's away south to see if Lady Denby can employ me in the big house there."

"Is that what you want to do?" asked Rob, who could think of nothing worse.

"Ach, no. I just want to get out of the glen and away to other places before I decide what to do. It's a stepping stone, that's all."

She shook her hair back again. Rob was entranced. She was remarkably confident, this Highlander who had never been anywhere. Or was it naive? No, he thought, not that. Unspoiled, yes; inexperienced too, but there was something else there, a poise, a sort of knowing, almost an arrogance as if she'd got something no-one could take away. Maybe it was the flagrant red of her hair? Perhaps that's what rare quality does to a woman? But it was not that. He knew it was more than skin deep. It was within; a presence like the great hills around her home, an undeniable self-possession which remained constant, regardless of wind or storm, winter snows or the fiercest summer sun.

"We'd better head back if we're to be up early." said Mike. "We want to do some serious climbing tomorrow."

"Where are you planning?" asked Jeannie. Rob and Mike looked at each other for a second.

"We'll likely head up to Altnahara and climb Ben Klibreck if the weather holds," Rob replied, "Mike's never done it and it's a hell of a good hill for a view to the north and west."

The sun had gone from the street when they stepped outside, but the sky was still bright and they laughed and chatted their way past the little closed houses with their tidy front gardens and shiny paintwork. It was so different, Rob thought, so very different from Tunbridge Wells. Somehow this place was real. He knew that even if Shiona spent her entire life struggling through the human soup of some Yorkshire city, she would always be a Highlander within herself. No-one could ever deny her that. Bonny—that was it! That was the word he'd been searching for. Bonny, that's what she was; in their own unchallengable idiom, she was a very bonny lass.

—10—

Standing at his bedroom window in the bright morning looking distractedly out at his lambs and the familiar world he knew and understood, Andrew Duncan was surprised to see a police car and the orange car he had seen in the glen once before, cross the stone bridge over the Corran and sweep up the track towards the Keeper's Cottage.

"Mairi! Wake up, woman! What's Jimmy been up to now? There's a police car gone up the back road."

"What d'you mean?" Mairi sat up in bed and looked startled.

"Just what I say. There's two cars, the police and that orange car that was up at the Dalvourar bothy a few days back."

"What do you think they want?"

"How the hell do I know, woman? It wouldn't surprise me if that bloody bitch hasn't blethered once too often. I hope to God Shiona's no' in trouble."

Sergeant Bane thumped on the cottage door. Jimmy answered it in an open-necked shirt and old tweed trousers supported by frayed blue braces. His face was wet from washing but he was as yet unshaven. It was five-thirty. "James Forbes?" asked the sergeant.

"You know fine it's me, Archie Bane. What d'ye want at this hour o' the morning?" His voice betrayed nothing, but his eyes, flicking past the two policemen to Rob and Mike standing behind them, revealed instant recognition and the blood began to drain from his face. The sergeant ignored him and holding out a white printed document for him to see he continued.

"James Forbes, I have a warrant here to search your house and your out-buildings and any other place of work you may frequent...."

"What the hell for?" demanded Jimmy, but the sergeant carried on.

"...in your duties as keeper and stalker. Myself or the Constable will remain with you and Mrs Forbes in the cottage here throughout the search. We have reason to believe you are in possession of illegal poisons. I hope you will agree to cooperate.

"I will not! Ye've no evidence against me Archie Bane and until ye have to hell with your warrant! It's that bastard stirring up trouble," he growled, jabbing a caloused finger at Rob. "I knew ye were up to no bloody good!"

"These two men are licenced officers of the SSBC. At about this time yesterday morning you were observed to walk into the hill not a mile from here to a place where you buried the corpses of two golden eagles and a raven recovered and identified by Mr Pearce here. These birds are being analysed by the police to ascertain the cause of death which we believe to be poison. Have you anything to say?"

"Aye, I certainly have at that! Ye've nothing on me. This nosy bugger's jest making it up. I know nothing about any grave or any damned eagles. I went into the hill yesterday to check out my calving hinds, as I do every morning at this time o' year, and where I'd be now if ye'd jest bugger off and let me get about my work. Search where ye bloody like. Ye'll no find any poison here. I wouldna be surprised if this bugger killed the birds himself and planted them there just to cause trouble. Ye'll pin nothing on me. You do what y' like!" He turned back into the cottage.

Sergeant Bane followed him straight in, signalling to the constable and Mike to start the search in the corrugated-iron outhouses where terriers sprang snarling at the wire of the kennel run in a frenzy of bristling aggression. Rob was sent straight into the hill to collect the two eagles and bring them down while the search was going on.

From their window Andrew and Mairi Duncan watched him pass their cottage, Mairi in her nightdress, out of bed now and anxiously clutching her husband's arm. "Andy, there's something going on. I don't like it at all."

"Aye there is lass. We'll know soon enough."

In an hour and a half Rob was back down from the mountain. He met Mike and the Constable outside the cottage. They shook their heads. "We've done the cottage and the out-houses top to bottom and there's not even a gin trap," said Mike. D'you get the eagles?"

"Yep," nodded Rob, "they're in the car. Did you find rabbit snares and fox wires and all the other things keepers use?"

"No, not really, there's nothing here except a woodshed and a bit of a workshop with a bench and some tools, and, of course the dogs," said Mike, "and inside the cottage is as clean as a wood chip."

"You'd not expect it to be in the cottage," offered the constable, "these kind of folk are no daft."

"Then there has to be another shed or something. There must be a keeper's store of some kind. Where does he keep his winter feed for the deer? That must be a decent sized shed or barn somewhere?"

"Aye, aye. There is that," said the constable, "my brother-in-law used to ghillie for this estate a few years back and they had a room down at the sheds where the vehicles are kept and the stag larder is. Wait and I'll get the Sarge to ask for the keys."

Sergeant Bane did not ask Jimmy for the keys. He turned straight to Sally who, in uncommon silence, was sullenly sipping tea with her husband at the kitchen table. "I'll trouble you for the keys to the sheds Mrs Forbes," he said. Just as he hoped, Sally's eyes went straight to the dresser.

"There's nothing o' mine in that sheds," snapped Jimmy, but he was too late. The sergeant was lifting the keys from the hook before the words were out of his mouth. "You stay with Mr and Mrs Forbes, constable." Outside he joined Mike and Rob who were standing over the two eagles tipped out onto the ground. Hardened by twenty-two years in the force, Archie Bane was moved by the sight. "That's a bloody disgrace," he muttered. "Let's get down to these sheds."

The key turned arthritically in the lock. The door to Jimmy's private store creaked open, light spreading across the dusty boarded floor. Mike snapped on the single bulb which lit the dingy room. It was a small room with no furniture except a bench built under the only window sealed from the outside world by a hessian sack and a fertilizer bag which read Superphosphate upside down in grey letters. Around the walls there hung from rusty nails dozens of coiled snares with dangling pegs for rabbits and twisted heavy wire ends for foxes. An assortment of spring traps hung there too; some, old and rusted, were illegal gin traps from a previous era, apparently unused for a long time. On the floor under the bench lay a dead badger, a trickle of blood from its nostrils had left a dark patch on the floor, its mouth just open and its little piggy eye wrinkled and dry. It was a victim of the long light days, forced to roam in broad daylight and shot from the land rover window as it foraged for bluebell bulbs.

There were two shovels and a crow bar leant in a corner, and a bundle of sacks in another. A box of shotgun cartridges lay on the bench. There was a variety of lidless boxes and tins on the window sill, most of which contained nails and screws and spent brass shells from a high velocity rifle. There was an ancient green can of Rangoon gun oil and some cloths, and a ball of orange bailer twine.

The three men looked about them. It was orderly and yet random in a way which suggested its godless incumbent came and went answerable to no-one but himself. There was nothing there. Rob paced heavily round the room pressing down on floorboards looking for one which creaked or had been tampered with. There was nothing. He looked up into the rafters and the sarking boards above. Some bamboo canes had been stored there across the joists, and thick cobwebs straddled the timbers in undisturbed strands laden and sagging with dust. No-one had been into the roof for years.

They moved from shed to shed. There were stacked bags of deer feed cobs left over from the winter and empty pallets, and an all-terrain vehicle made from green plastic with six bulbous wheels on each side. They rummaged through the storage boxes in its cockpit and found nothing. There were rolls of fencing wire and deer netting and a stack of posts with long sharp points facing outwards from the pile like some mediaeval assault device. They searched through Jock the mechanic's workshops and the boat store, with coils of ropes and mooring blocks of concrete stained white-green with dried algae and brown from the peaty lochs. They found no hint of poison, nor anything one might not expect to find in such a place. Their mood slipped into despondency.

"Sod it!" cursed Mike.

"Aye, he's a cunning devil," Archie shook his head knowingly. "We never found anything the last time and two walker's dogs dead with strychnine from a rabbit carcase." They walked silently back to the keeper's cottage.

"Well then you smart-arse English buggers! What d'ye say now?" Jimmy taunted them. They said nothing. Sergeant Bane cautioned him and told him they would be back for a written statement about the eagles.

"I know nothing about yon bloody eagles," he cursed at them. "Ask those bastards for your statement! They planted them here."

"Let's go," said Mike. They climbed into the cars and slowly drove away.

A hundred and fifty yards round the corner Rob stopped abruptly. The police car pulled up behind him. They were out of sight of the cottage behind some alder trees. Rob leapt out and came to the patrol car window. "Let me and the Constable stop here for a few minutes? I'd just like to see if he comes out of the cottage and which direction he goes in first."

"Aye, right enough, if that's what you want."

"Mike, drive my car on would you?"

Rob and the policeman stood under the trees beside the river and watched the cottage. There was no movement for several minutes. Then Jimmy came out and looked up and down the road. He went back into the cottage asif to say something and appeared again seconds later. He climbed into the landrover and drove slowly up towards them. They crouched low behind the knarled trunks of the old river bank trees and watched him pass.

"I thought so," whispered Rob. "He's following the cars out of the glen to make sure we've gone. That's what he did with me the other day." They stood up as the land rover disappeared from sight.

"That's it then," the constable said dejectedly. "He's got away with it again." Rob looked at him in silence.

"The land rover!" He shouted, clutching the constable's arm. "We never checked the bloody land rover! Quick, radio through to Archie and get them to stop him and hold him in the vehicle. Let's go," shouted Rob already running up the road after him.

Over the rise and round the bend the three vehicles were stopped in a line. The police car had turned and was facing back, bonnet to bonnet with Jimmy Forbes's land rover where they had abruptly met. Mike had reversed the beetle back into a passing place. Sergeant Bane was standing at the Jimmy's window as Rob came panting up.

"I'd be obliged if ye'd come into the police car with me," said the sergeant.

"What the hell for now?"

"We intend to search your vehicle." Jimmy made no sign of moving from the driver's seat. Sergeant Bane opened the door and motioned to him to move. Jimmy folded his arms and sat still.

"This is bloody harassment, that's what this is! Ye've done your search, now why don't ye get down the road and let me get about ma work?"

"Into the patrol car, please sir," said the sergeant stiffly.

"Shits!" said Jimmy glaring angrily at Rob and Mike as he passed them. They started work on the vehicle.

The crude pockets along the front were stuffed with the flotsam of country living. There was an empty half-bottle of whisky, used rifle shells and cartridge cases, string, several screwdrivers, a can of crimson stockmarker, an old hammer with a broken claw, a roll of green insualtion tape, a plastic pen, crumpled cigarette packets and cellophane and a leaking tube of insect repellant. In the back were more old sacks, bloodstained from deer and other carcases thrown on top of them, a rifle and a shotgun with the scratched and dented look of hard use, hanging on a rack, a stick with a forked-antler top, a pair of black wellington boots and a roadman's black and yellow PVC jacket. Beneath the bench seats in the back were the usual assorment of rusting vehicle tools. There was no sign of poison. Rob lifted the bonnet and peered into the engine space. He slammed the lid down again with evident exasperation. The three of them looked at eachother in empty silence.

"Is there not a compartment under the driver's seat in this model?" asked the Constable. Rob looked.

"Yep, there is," he said, "And it's locked."

"Try the ignition keys," said Mike.

"No luck," said Rob tersely.

Sargeant Bane turned to Jimmy who sat clenching and unclenching his fists in the back of the police car.

"I require the key to the seat compartment, Mr Forbes."

"There is nae bloody key. I've not been in that box since years."

Archie Bane spoke quietly to his constable. "Smash the lock."

With two sharp blows from Jimmy's own hammer the padlock was sprung and clattered to the floor. The metal lid lifted. Inside was a small, old biscuit tin with a hinged lid. Rob eased it open.

"Got you!" he spat through his gritted teeth. He tilted the tin towards Mike and the two policemen.

The first little black ribbed bottle he lifted out had a label. He read it aloud, looking Mike hard in the eye as he did so. "Mevinphos." The second he held gingerly between his finger and thumb. A frisson of fear ran down his spine. It was a clear glass bottle of the size aspirins were once sold in. It contained a white powder, about half full. On the white screw lid, crudely scrawled in black ink, was a large 'S'.

—11—

In Corran Bridge Jessie McChattin was swabbing the shop doorstep in the morning sun. It was hardly necessary to do so every day. It was a routine far more to do with the opportunity it afforded to cast a predatory eye up and down the street, to record the early movements of the other villagers in the tiny cross-roads community, from which to add spicy morsels to the inexhaustible pudding of glen gossip upon which she thrived. This morning rivalled her happiest expectation.

It was still only seven-thirty when the police car came through. It stopped at the crossroads just long enough for her to see Jimmy Forbes glowering in the back seat. She stood, transfixed to her mop handle while the two cars disappeared from view. In an instant she was inside calling for her husband.

"Doolie! Doolie! You'll not believe what I've just seen!" she screamed up the narrow stairs. Doolie believed very little his wife told him, but he had long since learned to humour her permanent preoccupation with other people's lives.

"How's that now?" he called back from in front of the bathroom mirror where half his face was still white with shaving soap. But Jessie had not waited for a reply. She was dialling the Forbes number with the telephone already pressed impatiently to her ear.

Down the glen Mairi Duncan was also dialling a number. She knew that by seven-thirty Betty Macronie would be up and getting Sandy his breakfast. Her anxiety for Shiona's welfare was too urgent to wait any longer.

"Oh, Betty, I'm that sorry to ring you so early, but I'm just checking to see how our Shiona is. We had the police up here this morning at Jimmy Forbes's, and we are hoping everything is all right with Shiona."

"She's no' up yet, pet, no more's Jeannie. They went out to the Sutherland Arms last night with two lads we've staying here just now and they weren't in till late on," Betty exaggerated. "But she's fine. What's she to do with the police up at Jimmy's?"

"Oh, I cannae tell, but there's been so much going on lately, with Lord Denby up on his own and Bella herself upset and Shiona leaving so sudden—we were thinking that maybe there could be somethin' wrong?"

"Aye, aye. Well, I can assure the both of you Shiona's in her bed and just fine. But for what are the police up the glen?"

"We cannae tell! They came up at half-past five with another car, an orange one Andrew says he's seen in the glen a few days back. He thinks it belongs to a young man Jimmy found camping in the bothy and sent on his way. If this is him back again with the police something's up."

"Aye, right enough, it is." Betty replied, "I wonder what?" and then, "- what sort of a car's this orange one?"

"Andrew says it's a foreign one. Is it a beetle they're called?"

"Aye, that'll be it," said Betty knowingly, "and a young lad with fair hair called Rob Pearce owns it. He's a hill-walker by all accounts. And I'll tell you something else, Mairi, that young man and another one's staying in my house just now and they got up at the back of five o'clock this morning saying he and his friend were going hill-walkin'. Now there's a funny thing, if that's them up at Jimmy's house with the police. I'd like to know what's goin' on mysel'."

"Oh my!" said Mairi, her voice beginning to quail. "And Shiona was out with them last night, you say?"

"Aye, she was that, out till all hours. We were in our beds long before they came in. I think I'd better go and ask young Shiona what's goin' on." Betty said, sounding alarmed herself. "I'll ring you back in a wee whilie, Mairi, mi dear."

"Aye, if you would," said the faint voice behind the handkerchief, and the line went dead.

"Bella, aye, it's Jessie here. I'm awful sorry to be botherin' you first thing the morn, but I'm just after seein' Jimmy go up the road in Archie Bane's patrol car. I'm hopin' there's nowt wrong?" Nothing gave Jessie McChattin greater pleasure than to think there was a drama unfolding and that she had been the first to spot it.

"Oh, Jessie, I dinna ken what's goin' on, at all!" Bella answered in clear distress and lacking her usual glee at the prospect of gossip. "Archie Bane was here just now wi' two young men, one of them was the one Jimmy found up in the Dalbattigh bothy a whilie back. Jimmy thinks they've come back to make trouble because he saw them off the estate. He went away in the Landrover about a half hour ago and he hasna come back. He's in Archie's car now, ye say? Oh, I dinna ken what's going on at all, that I do not," she lied.

"Aye, he is that, right enough, I saw him myself just this few minutes past."

Jessie McChattin knew full well Jimmy had diced with the law for many a long year and that she would not get the full story from Bella. Confirmation that her eyes had not decieved her was sufficient. She offered a word of consolation and rang off as quickly as she could with the express intention of phoning a friend who lived next to the police station in Lairg, to warn them that the car would be along in a few minutes and to be sure to find out what was afoot and ring her back. It was not yet eight o'clock and the glen telegraph was fizzing wildly.

"I shouldn't wonder if Jimmy hasna gone too far this time," Jessie speculated to her now-shaven husband who appeared in the kitchen, more interested in his breakfast than in Jimmy Forbes. "I shouldn't wonder if its assault they've got him for. I heard he was too rough on that young man he found camping."

"Ach, well, that'll be it, then," agreed Doolie.

Shiona knew better. Over a mug of tea in the Macronie kitchen she was piecing the story together with Betty and Jeannie. "Oh! The rat!" she exclaimed bitterly. "Then that was a pack of lies he told us last night. I knew he was after something more about Ardvarnish than he let on. Wait till I see him. Early start to go hill-walking, my foot! They knew fine they were going up there with the police this morning."

She was not at all amused. She had quite liked him, had secretly hoped to see more of him. No longer. If that was the way lads from the south treated their friends, lying and cheating, even if they were only first-time acquaintances, she wanted nothing more to do with them—except to tell him just that.

By ten-thirty the story had broken. Mike's office in Inverness had put out a press statement that following an investigation by the SSBC and the discovery of two dead golden eagles and a raven, James William Forbes of Ardvarnish Estate, Glencorran, had been charged with the illegal possession of strychnine and phosdrin. The birds had been submitted for analysis by the Department of Agriculture. The Society would be bringing further charges under the 1981 Wildlife and Countryside Act if analysis proved that either of these illegal poisons was the cause of death. A police report was being submitted to the Procurator Fiscal.

Sergeant Bane had officially informed Derek Holdingham as soon as he arrived in his office in Lairg and Holdingham immediately telephoned Harry Poncenby in the estate office at Denby. Gerry at that moment was driving himself stiffly back to Denby from Wakefield station, having spent a uncomfortable night on the sleeper from Edinburgh. He was not looking forward to seeing his wife whom he knew would give him little peace about skipping off to Ardvarnish. His humour was worsened by the sight of Harry's car at the front door as he scrunched up the yellow gravel drive in his Range Rover.

"What the hell does he want at this hour?" he growled to himself. To make matters worse Dinah was standing on the marble doorstep , clutching the abominable terrier in her arms. He had phoned Mrs Dudgeon to say which train he would be on, but it was most unlike Dinah to turn out to greet him and the added presence of Harry warned him that something was wrong.

"Gerry, dear," said Dinah, kissing him perfunctorily on the cheek, "we've got such sickening news from Ardvarnish. It's rotten to greet you with it when you've only just come from there, but I think you'd better hear it straight from Harry."

It had not occurred to him that it might be about Ardvarnish. He was taken completely aback. Had he not just spent the whole night thinking about Ardvarnish, about how he was going to get to the bottom of the over-grazing conundrum; how he was going to jolt that complacent factor into setting up some research projects on the estate? The revelation on the hill had struck deep and he had been unable to shake it from his mind. Now, to arrive home and be told there was a serious problem which had mysteriously appeared while he had been on the train was bewildering.

"What? Ardvarnish? What d'you mean? Has someone died? Eh?" he spluttered.

"No, no. It's not as bad as that. Come along, dear, Harry's in the library." Gerry entered his home without relpying. He threw his tweed cap onto the hall table and crossed the black and white squared marble floor to the open library door. Harry was standing in the bay window with his back to him.

"What the hell's all this, Harry, old man?" Gerry demanded. Harry turned sharply to face him.

"Gerry, I'm so sorry to greet you with this."

"Never mind that," snapped Gerry, "What's it all about? That's what I want to know!"

Harry told him straight. He had not been idle since the phone call from Holdingham. He had spoken to Sergeant Bane in person, and to the SSBC headquarters in Edinburgh. He knew exactly what the full position was and left Gerry in no doubt as to the gravity of the situation.

"Oh, shit!" said Gerry quietly, collapsing into a buttoned leather chair, his eyes fixed on a distant point way out beyond the orangery lawn.

"We have three problems," continued Harry in his most business-like voice, pacing across the deep red carpet. "The first is what to do with Forbes, and I think we know the answer to that; the second is how to limit the damage this will do us all when it hits the papers tomorrow; and the third is how to replace Forbes in time for the grouse in August—that's only about six weeks off, and how to handle the stalking and the hind cull later on."

Gerry flicked his tired eyes across to Harry for a second. He spoke in a voice expressionless and muted. "This is my fault. I knew something like this was going on and I've been too damned smug to chase it up. I haven't seen an eagle on Ardvarnish for years." He stood up and crossed to the window. With his back to them both he continued. "That whole place is a disaster. We've been running it all wrong for decades. There's scarcely a tree growing on the whole forty-five thousand acres, there are no wild flowers worth mentioning and we've been ripping the natural wealth out of the place in venison and grouse and salmon and wool and lambs without ever putting a damned thing back. And now we've poisoned all the eagles, and just about everything else which crawls or flies I shouldn't wonder.

We're fools, Harry, you and I, bloody fools! and ignorant with it."

Harry blinked. This was not what he was expecting at all. A tirade, yes, and the blame dumped squarely onto him and Holdingham, but not this.

"Hold hard a minute, Gerry. Lets sort out one problem at a time. It's a bit tough to say everything we've been doing for decades is all wrong. If we've got it wrong then so have a hell of a lot of other people. Who have you been listening to anyway? I've never heard you talk like this before."

"As a matter of fact I haven't spoken to anyone, and I think it's very likely a great many people have been pretty blind, but that's no excuse. We've been cropping that estate of wild game for a very long time. You know as well as I do that the salmon are in trouble, the grouse have declined to almost nothing and the ruddy deer are everywhere. Added to that we've a thousand odd sheep as well, crawling like maggots all over the place. What have we put back during the last three generations? Answer me that! We don't even keep accurate records of the deer numbers. How do we know they aren't responsible for the decline in the grouse? And what about the sheep? Aren't they competing with the deer for the grazing? We've never given that a thought. We 've just let Duncan put on as many sheep as he can handle to pull in as much subsidy as we can get. We'd never get away with that sort of management on any of the farms here. I'm not happy about it, Harry. I've thought about it all night. We're ignorant, Harry, there's no other word for it, and it hurts." He spun round to face them. "Downright bloody ignorant about our own place!"

Harry opened his mouth to speak but Gerry cut him off, looking him straight in the face, his expression stern and determined. "In fact I'm glad this has happened. It's a damned shame about the eagles, and Forbes must go, today, but perhaps it will turn out to be a good thing. We needed something like this to jolt us into thinking a bit instead of taking it all for granted."

"So you agree that I should dismiss Forbes today?"

"Too damned right! I want that made public as soon as possible. At the very least we shall be seen to be reacting responsibly to what is a serious criminal offence. We should have done it four years ago when those dogs died of strychnine poisoning."

"Hmm," grunted Harry. "I just hope we can get away with it without a fuss. They've been there about twenty years if I remember rightly, and his wife works for you in the house. It may not be as simple as that. You can't just go throwing people out these days, and a tribunal is not likely to favour the likes of you and me. I shall have to look into it carefully before we serve notice on them to get out of the house."

"You can't sack her!"Dinah's voice was horrified, "I need Mrs Forbes for the Lodge in August." Gerry ignored her. She continued in resigned acceptance, "I suppose at least we've got young Shiona Duncan who knows some of the ropes."

"Ah, no, you haven't, she quit yesterday. She's already left the glen."

"What!?" Dinah was aghast. "What about my house party for August? We've got a dozen guests arriving!"

"To hell with the guests. I don't give a damn about them or the house party. No-one'll want to come anyway after this. You wait till you see the papers tomorrow. This'll be headline stuff in the Highlands and all the Yorkshire locals will carry it quick as a flash, and the nationals too, very likely, and you and me, dear Dinah, will be held responsible for Forbes's dirty deeds. It'll be a long time before the Denby family forget this bloody mess."

"I'm afraid Gerry's right, Dinah," said Harry tactfully, "no-one will believe we didn't instruct Forbes to kill the eagles and as like as not he'll say we did. It's the only defence he's got."

"Oh God! Why on earth didn't Holdingham know what Forbes was up to?"

"That's a very good question," added Harry pleased to redirect the finger of blame. "We pay his firm a hell of a lot to know what's going on. I do think he's let us down jolly badly."

"Yes, he has," Gerry agreed solemnly, "but that still doesn't get us off the hook. The buck stops right here with me, and I don't intend to duck it. There are going to be some very big changes at Ardvarnish."

It was midday before Rob and Mike had finished making statements at the police station and had concluded their business with the outside world by telephone. Jimmy Forbes had been charged and released. Derek Holdingham, red faced and flustered, had come round to the station and received the full facts from them both. He looked worried and upset, more, Rob thought, for his job than for the eagles. Finally they stepped out into the street. It was another hot day.

Rob felt drained. The early start and the excitement and the strain of such rapidly unfolding events had left him emotionally exhausted. They walked down to the Macronie's house in silence. Mike had to collect his things and get on back to Inverness, and Rob was to stay on for a day or two to monitor events on the ground. He was not prepared for what awaited them.

Jessie McChattin had not wasted time. The story was out. The whole community knew who they were and what they had done. Betty Macronie and the girls were still sitting in the kitchen where they had listened to a midday news bulletin on the local radio when the door bell rang. Jeannie rose to let them in.

Rob sensed instantly there was tension in the house. Jeannie was silent and unsmiling. Betty stood in the kitchen doorway. "You've come for your things, I expect. You'll be wanting to get away now you've done your business." Gone were the warm smile and the welcome they had received before. Rob knew that he was not invited to stay on. He had not expected this and he tripped over his words.

"Er, yes...well, erm... I think so..." Mike took over. "Thank you, Mrs Macronie, we'll just be a minute or two upstairs and then we'll be off." They bundled their things into their bags without a word. Rob lead the way down into the little hallway. Shiona was standing there watching him manoeuvre his bulky ruck-sack round the bend in the stairs. She was blocking his path. He saw it was intentional. Her blue eyes held the flame of anger, her face was palid and her lips drawn. "Excuse me," he said lamely.

"I'm asking you for an apology," her voice fierce with defiance.

"For what?" asked Rob innocently.

"You know fine well for what! For your lies, that's for what!"

Rob put his ruck-sack down with a sigh, leaning it against his legs. He looked blankly at her for a moment before he spoke. He had liked this girl, and he admired her now; she was right to be angry. He wished they did not have to part like this. Her red hair shone against the fine satin of her cheeks and he found himself wondering if it was the warring blood of Gaeldom or of the Vikings, or of a fearsome blend of both he was facing. His voice was gentle and calm and there was a look of sadness in his eye. "I am more than sorry we lied to you. Our work has to be very secretive and it was vital we remained anonymous. I could not have told you who we were."

"That's no kind of an excuse. You led me on a trail of deceit hoping to get more information out of me, did you not? Admit it! You thought I was just an ignorant gullible Highlander!"

"No, no, that's all wrong. I never thought anything like that, I promise." Rob pleaded. " I'm very sorry I misled you, but you must understand we had a job to do. That's all there is to it." But it was no use. Whatever blood it was, it was up and surging and roaring like the Corran Falls after a summer storm. There was no stopping her.

"Well, I'm glad I've learned what the English are like before ever I go down there to a job—at least I'll know not to trust any of you. Rob Pearce, a good riddance to you!"

—PART TWO—

....Six for gold,
Seven for a tale not to be told.
Eight for heaven,
Nine for hell,
Ten for the devil's ain sel'.

—12—

There is a special healing in the hill on a good day. It was October and the first frosts had touched the great grassy hills with ochre and the heather moors were the hue of burnt cork. A wind moaned in the high corries and from the summit of Carn Mor Rob could hear the primaeval roaring of stags echoing back and forth over the vast emptiness of the glen. He was seated on the thin alpine mat of lichen and moss beside the cairn on the roof of the world, his jacket buttoned to the chin and his hands clasped around a steaming mug of tea from his flask.

It was three years since he had climbed Carn Mor, a day and a chain of events which were branded upon his memory despite many incidents in the intervening years of his work up and down the Highlands. The Forbes case, as it had come to be known, had been the making of his career and he had been promoted quickly to Investigations Officer for the Highlands and Islands with his own office in Perth. He had travelled widely, constantly on the move, working with landowners, farmers, crofters and keepers in the ceaseless struggle to conserve the precious wildlife of the hills and glens from those who sought to destroy it.

He sat in contemplative mood. He had returned to Ardvarnish on impulse. He had three days leave to stretch his legs in the hills and escape from the pressure of work. The constant travelling and endless demands from head office to follow up this lead or that tip off, or to monitor the breeding success of ospreys before they all left on migration, or eagles whose nests he had been unable to check out before the young flew, had left him weary and distracted. Much of the glamour of working for a modern, high-powered conservation organisation had worn off and the hard work and fierce commitment of his colleagues had stretched him to the limits of his ability. He needed a break.

He returned to Helmsdale and sought out a friendly bed and breakfast house on a grey side street, from which he climbed Ben Armine and Ben Klibreck, feeling his spirit spiral skywards with each step, away from the acid reek of the sphagnum marsh, drawn upwards to the silent majesty of the domed peaks ahead. On the top of Ben Klibreck he faced the wind and the sky and watched in a trance as the huge banks of white and grey cloud tumbled past as inexorable as ocean rollers.

Mountain tops had always moved him. He loved the insignificance they imposed over him and his moment of time; he found the enforced humility both cathartic and cleansing. His senses became keen again. He stared into the wind until his eyes ran with tears and his cheeks shone with tingling chill. He felt real again. He felt good. There is a special healing in the hill.

Looking away inland he could see the dark bulk of Carn Mor towering over the broody moors of Ardvarnish, now purple-brown, now bright grey-green as the sun jabbed through the cloudbanks in shafts of brilliance, spotlighting a few acres of mountain grass here or there. He felt himself magnetically drawn by the need to see the golden eagles back in place on the north corrie, and to revisit the ground which had changed the course of his life. He swung his rucksack onto his back and purposefully set off down the ridge, taking the long, lonely, hike in, retracing his steps of three years before, over the high moors to Carn Mor itself.

Jimmy and Bella Forbes were long gone. Jimmy had been convicted on two charges and fined a record two thousand pounds. The sheriff had publicly damned the use of poison, calling it "an unconscionable public hazard" and "a no longer acceptable hang-over from the dark ages." He cautioned Jimmy that if he was convicted again he would be in for a custodial sentence. The SSBC were jubilant. It was the high profile case they had long awaited and it sent shock waves reverberating throughout the sporting world.

Jimmy had lost his job long before the case ever came to court. Harry Poncenby had acted swiftly and with surgical finality. On the same day that Jimmy was arrested Derek Holdingham served notice on him that if he was found guilty of either illegal possession of poison or of poisoning the eagles, or of both, he was dismissed.

The news roared through the glens like a heather fire on a windy April day. Bella was unable to tolerate being the subject of gossip herself. She delivered an ultimatum to her husband: either they got out together or she was leaving on her own. Three weeks later they had gone, still two months before the case came to court. They pled guilty with their shame—departing in the middle of the night, back to Aberdeenshire without so much as a goodbye wave to the community they had belonged to for so long.

Relieved to find that he did not have to evict them from the Keeper's Cottage, Derek Holdingham phoned Harry Poncenby to tell him the news.

"That's fine, thank you very much," said Harry coldly, "I'm not sorry to see the back of them, nor, I'm afraid, of you and your firm. Lord Denby is bitterly disappointed that you permitted this whole episode to happen and I have written to your head office terminating your contract with Denby Estates."

Derek Holdingham was numb. The business of factoring Highland sporting estates was precarious enough without losing major contracts such as Ardvarnish. The Forbes case was widely covered in all the Scottish newspapers with large pictures of the dead eagles, and found space in the nationals as well. The axe fell on the Lairg office shortly afterwards and Derek Holdingham was relegated to the property sales and surveying division in Inverness.

But now not only a new stalker, but one of a new breed had come to Ardvarnish. Mac MacDonald was in his mid-thirties and was as skilled with a camera as with a rifle. His hobby was wildlife photography and he knew and understood the hills and their ecology in a way which was unknown in Jimmy Forbes's day. Mac was married to a strikingly handsome girl named Janet and they had brought to the glen two fine children, a boy and a girl, both just old enough to swell the Corran Bridge primary school to fourteen and so, at the eleventh hour, a reprieve from closure for the little school and its one teacher was achieved. It was the best start they could have wished for and the glen community welcomed them with open arms despite the vacuum of embarrassment the Forbes's had left behind.

Janet also filled Bella's job at the Lodge, but, with a new style stalker came a new style housekeeper. Gone was the obsequious 'Yes, m'Lord. Very good, m'Lady,' of the past. Janet faced her employers with a sparkle in her eye and a firm handshake. She shocked Dinah on the very first day by saying, "I think you should replace the dining-room curtains, Lady Denby. They're badly faded and let the house down."

Dinah had never noticed how the sun had bleached the glazed cotton, nor the frayed footings, and found herself saying, "Yes, er well, we'd better look into it, then." She rushed through to the sun-room and woke Gerry from his afternoon nap. "Gerry! Gerry, this is really too much! That woman Janet has demanded new curtains for the dining-room. Who does she think she is? She won't last long if she thinks she can boss me around."

"Now look here, old girl," replied Gerry irritably, "Harry and I scoured the length and breadth of Scotland to find a stalker as good as Mac and his wife's a real bonus. You're damned lucky to have help in the house at all. Let her put up some new curtains, she'll prob'ly make a damned fine job of it, and by so doing you will have let her put her stamp on the place."

"It's not the new curtains I mind," Dinah retorted petulantly, "it's being told what to do in my own house!"

"Stop being so stuffy, for God's sake! The only reason you don't like her is because she doesn't kow-tow to you the way that Forbes woman did. Swallow your pride and let her get on with it." Dinah departed without a word and maintained a cold disdain for her husband for a full week, a situation Gerry found entirely satisfactory.

The estate had changed. Not only had the social order thawed its barricades of formality, but Gerry had bludgeoned Harry Poncenby into effecting real reforms. He had resisted at first, but on seeing how summarily Derek Holdingham had been dismissed he thought it prudent to humour his employer's new thirst for knowledge, confident that it would burn itself out in a few months. In that he was wrong; now, three years later, at private dinner parties away from the immediate vicinity of Denby, Harry was sagely claiming credit for environmental awareness and the new ideas of stewardship they had introduced.

From where Rob now paused high on a mountain there was no visible evidence of reform except that the ancient eyrie on Carn Mor had been used that summer and a strong eaglet reared. He had seen the great birds twice, once on the long walk in, the white wing patches of the juvenile plain to see as it soared triumphantly overhead, still accompanied by a parent, both birds spiralling slowly upwards until, as tiny black specks, they were lost in the wispy edge of the clouds; and again an hour later in the vicinity of the eyrie below the north corrie.

He had checked out the nest ledge just to satisfy himself that the report from his young contract warden was accurate. There was no doubt. A tangled mass of bleached pine twigs and heather stems were crudely stacked into a huge nest. Rob climbed gingerly down onto the precarious north-facing rock shelf to examine the detritus of five months occupation.

There was the inevitable evidence of grouse feet and feathers which had condemned the eagle to persecution for a hundred and fifty years. There were remnants of both rabbits and blue mountain hares, the white feathers of ptarmigan, the curving bill of a curlew, and a fragment of scaly adder skin. Deer hair was everywhere and many bones looked as though they had been torn from the carcases of deer of all ages, but there was also sheep's wool and the tiny black hooves of one or more lambs. Two of these Rob examined closely and put in his pocket. He knew that when a lamb is born its hooves are unworn with flaps of soft keratin curling in from the edge of the hoof like overgrown fingernails. Within a day or two of use these quickly wear away and the hoof becomes hard and compact. That he had pocketed the hooves of newborn lambs with their soles unused was useful counter evidence to the perennial charge by shepherds that the eagles took healthy lambs. No ewe would allow the eagle to swoop in and remove a newborn healthy lamb, but stillborn or very sickly lambs which died shortly after birth were soon abandoned by their mothers and became valuable prey for the eagles desperate to nourish their own growing chick.

As he climbed back to the mountain shoulder Rob disturbed the eaglet which had returned to a rocky perch only a few yards away. He heard its long wings grab air as it pitched out into the void below. After a few frantic flaps it spread its pinions and soared back overhead and away out of sight behind the mountain. A wave of fulfilment came over Rob. He walked slowly over the delicate tundra carpet of lichens and mosses, up to the stone strewn summit. What reward, he thought, what payment could provide satisfaction such as this?

A rifle shot blasted across the mountain, and then another, and a third, echoing back and forth from corrie to corrie. Rob jumped. He knew very well there was stalking in the hills and he had taken great care to spy his way forward, scouring the land ahead through his binoculars every half mile or so to ensure that he was not walking into either deer or a stalking party. Only here, high on Carn Mor had he been unable to check out the land adequately. He had not looked over the ridge to the south where the shots had come from.

Snatching up his binoculars he moved over the shoulder of the summit and approached the ridge with care. Creeping on down through a boulder-field of huge, grey metamorphic blocks, some as big as houses, jumbled on top of one another, Rob found a good position and sat down.

It only took a few minutes to find them. They were very close, perhaps a quarter of a mile away, below and to the south, at the bottom of the same boulder-field; two figures, themselves in amongst the rocks. Far below on the moor deer were streaming away into the wind, running wildly, uncertain of which direction to escape to, veering this way and that in confusion and panic, suddenly stopping and looking back, heads and ears swivelling to locate the invisible agressor, and then running on again, in the blind hope that distance would bring them safety.

A curl of smoke went up from a small heather fire lit by one of the figures. Rob could see him crouching low and blowing into the pile of woody stems and the yellow flame flickering upwards. After a few minutes the figure tore up some sphagnum moss and placed it carefully on the fire. White smoke billowed from the moss and, caught by the wind, sent a plume across the valley, a signal to the ponyman two miles away down on the Corran flats who, on hearing the shots would be searching for their position.

The second figure picked his way slowly and carefully down the slope. Rob watched intently. After two hundred yards the figure stopped and bent down to gently tap the eye of the dead stag, a check for reflex if the animal was not dead. Then he moved on and Rob could see him repeat his check on a second stag sixty yards further on. The firelighter came down the hill to join him. This second figure, evidently the stalker, drew a knife and began to gralloch the first stag.

Rob wondered what to do. He could slip away the way he had come and probably leave undetected, or he could go down and introduce himself. He had heard about the new stalker at Ardvarnish and was keen to meet him. If they were angry at his presence he could justifiably argue that he had not interfered with their stalk in any way. His three years of experience in dealing with tricky situations had taught him to be forthright and open.

The figures were too busy with the gralloch of the second stag to hear his approach. Its abdomen was slit neatly open and the white and bulging grass-filled paunch tipped out onto the heather along with the other intestines. It would be cut open and left to decompose and inadvertently provide for the ravens and foxes and hoodie crows. Rob coughed from twenty yards away to avoid making them jump. They looked up in surprise.

"Good afternoon," he began, "I've watched your stalk from the top of the hill and very successful it was too." The stalker stood over the stag, jacket off, sleeves rolled up, blood to the elbows and knife in hand. He was young and bearded and strongly built with a smile in his eye and an honest face. The other man was much older, dressed well in a tweed suit and cap, and with a red and green silk handkerchief tied round his neck. He stood holding the two back legs of the stag apart while the stalker worked. Rob continued before either of them spoke, "I thought I'd better come down and introduce myself in case there is somewhere you don't want me to go. My name is Rob Pearce and I'm a hill-walker." Rob held out his hand to the man in tweed. The man looked at him intently for a split second and then took Rob's hand.

107

"How do you do, Mr Pearce? Not just a hill-walker, if you're the Rob Pearce I think you are, what?" said the man eyeing him closely and still shaking his hand, "My name's Denby, and this is my new stalker, Mac MacDonald." There was more than a hint of emphasis on the word new and Rob knew instantly that this man was no fool.

'So this is Lord Denby,' he thought. Rob was suspicious of sporting landowners. Many he had met in the course of his work had been the source of the illegal action it was his job to investigate, and consequently he had learned to treat them with caution. He had never been certain in his own mind about Lord Denby's involvement in the Forbes case. Representation for the estate at the trial had been handled by Harry Poncenby. All the circumstantial evidence pointed to Lord Denby condoning Forbes's actions for many years before he was caught, although they had strenuously and publicly denied it. Rob had good reason to expect hostility.

"It's my pleasure to meet you, sir, and especially you, Mr MacDonald," Rob used politeness to keep his options open. "I can assure you both I am a hill-walker today." The stalker looked bewildered; he looked from one to the other for a clue to the riddle being enacted in front of him. Gerry Denby came to his rescue.

"Mac, this is the young man who brought your infamous predecessor to court. He works for the SSBC," and to Rob, "I take it that is still correct, Mr Pearce?" Rob nodded.

"Oh...I see," said the stalker, uncertain what to say next. Gerry turned back to look Rob straight in the eye.

"You may be surprised to learn that you are very welcome on this estate," said Gerry in a slow, measured voice, as if he were checking the construction of his sentences very carefully. "I had not expected to meet you quite like this, but since I have, I should like you to know that you did us a very good turn. We had been negligent for many years in not investigating Forbes ourselves, despite our suspicions, and I for one am delighted to see the golden eagles back on Ardvarnish. I have no doubt you are aware that they have reared a chick this year?"

"Yes, I have seen it this afternoon. I'm delighted too," said Rob carefully. He had not expected that speech.

"You're very kind to welcome me. I am aware that I should have checked with your stalker first, before climbing Carn Mor, but I assure you I've been very careful not to move deer."

"Yes, yes. Don't you worry about that. We've done well and got this old beast who's well past his prime and that little switch over there. You've done no harm and I'm grateful to you for coming and introducing yourself. I think we have a good deal to talk about. If you would care to give us a hand pulling these two down to the ponyman who is heading up this way, I should like you to come and have some tea with us so that we can have a chat. We have a great deal going on I think you will be interested in. How about it, eh?"

It was too good an opportunity to miss. "Thank you, Lord Denby, I shall be glad to."

"My name is Gerry. I have no desire to stand on formality. May I call you Rob?"

"Yes, yes of course, everyone does," Rob answered, feeling himself firmly led into a relationship he had neither sought nor expected to achieve. It was too late to back out now. He grabbed the rope held out to him by the stalker and they heaved and stumbled their way down to the ponyman three hundred feet below. Rigorous physical activity is a worthy mechanism for the destruction of barriers. Rob had noted with interest the particular method for tying the rope to the head and antlers, looping it round the animal's jaw so that the antlers did not snag on the rough ground. He was surprised to discover what very hard work it was, even pulling downhill, and what a gargantuan effort was required to drag it up out of a hollow. Then he stood in silence and watched the ritual of loading the stags onto the high bridge-like saddles strapped to the backs of two sturdy white garrons, blinkered against the blood and the lolling tongues, as the deer were secured for their final journey.

It took two and a half hours to walk back to the Lodge. Over that short span and across the six miles they covered Rob moved from deep suspicion to astonished admiration. He was quite unprepared for the depth of conviction and committment which Gerry Denby held—apparently at odds with traditional values. He was amazed to learn that Mac MacDonald's first task had been to complete a detailed count of all the red deer in the area and then to commence a reduction programme to maintain the herd at a hind to stag ratio of ten to one. He told Rob of his involvement with the Nature Conservancy Council and how they had commenced a series of research projects to find out whether the hills were overgrazed. They passed by a number of newly fenced exclosures on the edge of the Dalbattigh burn to keep the deer and the sheep out and to try to get the birches and rowans and alders to regenerate themselves.

"We haven't scratched the surface of this yet," said Gerry with intoxicating enthusiasm. "We've gone on and on for years doing the same old things without every really thinking what the long term effects might be. Your eagles were a much simpler problem to crack. That just boils down to whether you accept that eagles have a right to be here or not. I happen to think they do, but the actual use of the hills is altogether different." Rob did not know what to say. He remained silent.

"How do we know whether the soils are in good heart? How do we know whether the selective grazing by deer and sheep is doing harm to the vegetation, eh? How do we know whether everything else that lives on the hill, the lapwings, the curlews, the wildcats, the meadow pipits or your eagles or my grouse for that matter, are surviving alright? The truth is we haven't got a ruddy clue most of the time. We just press on regardless doing what it suits us to do in the hope that poor old nature will mend any damage —at least, that's what I've done all my life and most others I know as well, what?"

"Are you saying that the way you and others like you have used this land for sport for the past one hundred and fifty years was wrong?" Rob was fascinated by the sudden change of heart.

"Not wrong, but certainly blinkered. You see, I don't think there was ever any great motivation to examine one's actions and policies because they had been pursued for so long. I suppose Queen Victoria really started off the fashion for grouse shooting, deer stalking and salmon fishing, and that was in about 1840. Ever since then we have followed our noses, copying what our fathers and grandfathers did before us and perpetuating their mistakes as well. Where we are now is suddenly re-examining our own inherited interests and traditions in the new and often critical light of science and, of course, public opinion. That's where you come in."

"You mean I am an instrument of public opinion?" Rob asked.

"Yes, of course you are. Your whole Society with its thousands of members is an implement of democracy which can impose its views on parliament and on the individual like me. Your Society's concerns have found their way onto the statute book by the process of public awareness. Poisoning wildlife is now illegal, and quite right too. I hope we don't need many more Forbes cases to make it clear to those who wish to flaunt the law that the public in Britain won't put up with it any more."

"I am astonished to hear you talk like this," admitted Rob, stopping and looking at Gerry. "Forgive me if I appear naive, but you and all you stand for are supposed to be doggedly resistant to change and new thinking, and, without wishing to be rude, many of your land-owning class are seen by the likes of myself to be the cause of what we conservationists perceive to be badly wrong with the way our countryside is managed. And here you are lecturing me on why I'm doing my own job!" Rob hoped he hadn't gone too far.

Gerry laughed, "And you are right, old chap, or at least nearly so. The mistake you must be careful not to make is lumping everyone together under the heading of 'wicked landlord.' Landlords we are, and some are no doubt wicked, but many aren't. Many are good and have always tried to do their best for the land and the wildlife—"

"—And have often failed dismally," interrupted Rob.

"Yes, sometimes, I accept that. I'm now embarrassed at just how long we went on doing the same old things without ever questioning ourselves, and that's why I'm so determined to put it right now. Conservation must work with the people who own and work the land, what! otherwise it can't hope to have the influence it needs to correct some of the wrongs of the past. Come and look over here."

They crossed the heather to the last of the fenced exclosures which surrounded a high dry heathery mound of about six acres with two ancient birch trees and gnarled and twisted scots pines standing over a jumble of rocks at the highest point. The birches were trailing bright golden ringlets among the yellowing green of the autumn leaves and the old pine's jigsaw bark shone orange in the thin sunlight. Gerry unhitched the gate and they stepped inside.

"Just look at this," he said, pointing to the heather at his feet."This fence hasn't been up three years yet, and just look at the results, eh!" He bent down and parted the heather. There were young birch and pine seedlings springing up everywhere. "I say, old chap, look! And look here! And here. You see, everywhere there are young trees coming. In twenty years time we will have a six acre wood here, just from one old pine and two birches all within the last ten years of their lives.

"Are you telling me that it is also public opinion which has made you want to do this?" Rob asked.

"Yes, it is, although not in a direct way. When my own land was designated by the Nature Conservancy Council—and we have some very big peatland SSSI's on Ardvarnish covering thousands of acres—I was forced, by statutory instrument I admit, to look at the issues and listen to the scientists—whom I used to think a bunch of narrow-minded eccentrics—much more closely. But it wasn't really until I spent a day on the hill actually watching the deer grazing that the penny dropped. I suddenly realized that we weren't managing the land, the deer were, and we were failing to manage them."

"So are you completely convinced that traditional sporting estate owners have been getting it wrong for a long time?" Rob was still shell-shocked by the revelations of this enigmatic, tweedy peer. He had heard all the arguments before, but never from this quarter.

"Not all wrong, no. That's not fair. Some aspects of sport have been very beneficial to the land; for instance grouse shooting has protected the heather moors very well, but negligent, yes, and blind to the obvious common sense of ecological principles which are not all that new. But I don't have to tell you that there have been ecologists around for the whole of my lifetime.

"We just haven't seen the wood for the trees—if you'll excuse the bad joke. If we're getting it wrong, we are going to be the losers in the long run. I've watched the native trees more or less disappear from the river banks along the Corran in my life time. We haven't caught any decent brown trout in the river for years. I can't help wondering if there isn't a connection there.

"Look at the hill here." Gerry stopped and swung an arm out across the moor. "Just think what humans have done to this land over the past thousand years or so. We've cleared all the native pines for timber, the deciduous woods for firewood or agriculture and then we've hammered it with sheep and then deer and now grouse as well. We've taken the timber and put nothing back; we've taken an annual crop of wool, mutton, venison, or grouse off it for decades and put nothing back. I'm uneasy about that deep down. It keeps me awake at night. So I've asked the experts to come and find out for me. That's why we've got scientists buzzing about all over the place."

"You're beginning to sound like a conservationist," said Rob facetiously. "I'm impressed!"

"I don't want to be called an 'ist' of any sort," laughed Gerry, " but I do want to be sure that whatever I'm doing here is being done with the best advice available and with some common sense. Come and have some tea."

"Thank you, I will, but there is one small problem."

"Really? What's that?

"My car is at Kinbrace, about sixty miles away by road."

"Good God! What the hell's it doing there, old chap?"

"I walked in from there," said Rob ingenuously.

"Well you're not walking out again tonight, that's for certain. It's far too late. You must have a bed here and we'll see if we can get you back to civilisation in the morning."

"I'm going to Lairg first thing, Lord Denby," interjected Mac, who had been their silent companion listening intently to the discussion. He was interested in this unexpected intruder and wanted to know more of him. "I'll take Rob down if you like—in fact he's very welcome to a bed with us and that'll not disturb the Lodge early on."

"There you are," said Gerry aimiably, "all sorted out, what? No problem at all. I'll send him down a bit later when he's had a cup of tea. What time would suit Janet?"

It had been an extraordinary day. Ardvarnish was a strange and beautiful place. Like falling in love, it had sneaked a hold over him without warning and in a way he could not comprehend.

He had sensed something of it on that first visit. Now, standing on the lawn outside the Lodge, bewildered by the verbal embrace of this proselyte peer who had turned out to be the antithesis of everything he had expected of him, he felt strangely at home. That old sense of belonging came flooding back—a feeling he could not avoid and for which he could find no answer.

He pinched himself to make sure he was alive and well. He followed Gerry Denby into the big house, into a hall lined with the mounted, dated and named stag's heads of a hundred years, past a rack full of sticks with antler tops, tweed caps and coats and hanging dog chains, along a corridor lined with all the trappings of a Victorian lodge—the faded tartan carpet, the grand oil paintings of slavering dogs and lifeless game, the gargantuan stuffed pike, a snarling and spitting wildcat with arched back, its whiskers quivering from within its glass prison. As they entered the huge sunlit drawing room with its pale chintz armchairs and crackling birchwood fire, Rob realized that not once, in all that long walk and conversation, had he brought himself to call this man Gerry.

—13—

"I don't believe it! Jeannie Macronie is getting married to Geordie Hoggett from Brora!" Shiona sat down on the edge of the bed in the tiny flat she shared with Angela Rennies, a Lowland lass from Coatbridge. She re-read the letter. "Who would have thought it!" she said to herself out loud as if to endorse her surprise, her hands falling into her lap and addressing the room. Geordie had had no intention of getting tied down when she had known him, he was having far too much fun. Who would have guessed that wee plain Jeannie would catch Geordie? This was one wedding she was not going to miss.

Shiona had gone south to Yorkshire, but not to Denby Hall. Gerry had been good to his word, but he had completely failed to persuade Dinah to take her on, and things had taken an unpleasant turn.

"Why should I give a job to your young floozie? You only want her here so that you can pinch her bottom." Dinah had mocked when he protested that he was only trying to help the girl. "If she's so damn good why don't you keep her at Ardvarnish? You could always pop up there again when you felt desperate," she jibed.

"You can be a vicious bloody bitch when you have a mind to," said Gerry angrily, "just like your mother. No wonder your poor father died a drunken pauper."

Denby was spacious enough for them to avoid each other for days on end. Gerry stamped off to his study where he determinedly phoned all his friends to see if he could get Shiona a position. Finally he achieved it at Womersby Hall, the elegant Georgian home of Lord Horrick, a claret-drinking squire in his fifties who belonged more to the mid-eighteenth century than the present day. A week after the phone call Shiona was there.

Her short time at Womersby was bitter-sweet. She worked in a happy atmosphere in the kitchens and the household much as she had done at Ardvarnish. Lord Horrick spent his life either out fox-hunting, or rushing purposelessly around in riding breeches and black boots and loud-check hunting waistcoats, pretending he was. He addressed everyone as if it were a fox or a pack of hounds or a combination of both. He swore indelicately and identically at both his family and the staff and at the two black labradors which were in constant doting attention at his heels, as though he did not want any of them anywhere near him, and then the moment they moved out of his vision, he bellowed for them to return.

At Womersby she met Sam, a twenty-six year old groom who fed and mucked out the horses. He cut a gallant dash when he galloped them hot and steaming across the park in the early mornings, walking them back into the yard, riding one, leading another, his hips sinuously moving to the pace of the powerful horse beneath him. He also rode a snarling and gleaming motor-bike. In her time off Shiona walked down to the stables and stood at a discreet distance watching him at work. "Get over, Dancer!" he would growl at a restless grey gelding which towered over him when he was picking out its feet, and "Hey-back there, Soldier!" at another which surged repeatedly forward as he manoeuvred around its cobble-clattering hooves. And then one day, "Hey Shiona! Hold this one for me will yer?" He handed her a slender lead-rope at the end of which was a prancing bay mare. Shiona did as she was bid and instantly regretted it. The mare flared her nostrils and snorted plumes of hot breath, tossing her head so that Shiona's arm was jerked savagely and she cried out.

"Steady there, yer silly bitch!" cursed Sam. Shiona wondered which bitch he was addressing. He took the rope from her saying sharply, "Never wind the rope round yer 'and. What would 'appen if she buggered off to Doncaster?" He waved graphically. " Now, try again, I shall only be a minute wi' this stable." He stood holding the horse's head while Shiona took the rope again. "Easy, Damsel, that's my gel, easy now." The mare stood quietly for him, her black eyes blinking calmly as he soothed her. Shiona felt herself and the mare being hypnotised by his quiet authority and fearlessness, his shoulder muscles flexing beneath the sweaty tee-shirt. She and the horse stood transfixed while he tossed straw about the stable, and then called, "Lead 'er in now, nice and gentle." The mare followed her meekly into the box and the ordeal was over. "There! That weren't so bad, were it?" he said as they closed the stable door. Sam strolled to his shiny red and silver bike and kicked it into a throaty roar. "Coming to the pub?"

Excursions to Pontefract and Doncaster, roaring through country lanes at dare-devil speed to the throb and throng of the night-spot of the moment where they danced out sensual jerking rituals under the flashing lights and throbbing rythmics of the disco. For a few short weeks it was everything she had dreamed it might be. After one such evening Sam throbbed and jerked his way past her underclothes and Shiona bade farewell to her maidenhood.

The relationship and the job at Womersby were short-lived. Satisfied with the conquest only for a few brief weeks, Sam ended the affair with characteristic Yorkshire bluntness. "Yer've bin great, lass, but yer not it," he announced early one morning as she made his toast in the stable flat.

"What d'you mean?" she asked, thinking he was referring to the toast.

"I mean it's over gel. You and me—that's it. No hard feelin's, eh doll?" He kissed her on the cheek and departed, leaving her to collect up her things and return to her lonely servant's bedroom in the big house. She thought she had been on the brink of falling in love and fate had handled her roughly. She was bruised and unhappy. She handed in her notice and left Womersby a week later.

She had nowhere to go. As she dejectedly packed her few possessions into a hold-all, fat Gladys the cook, bespectacled, plain and kind, and who had seen it all happen before, appeared in her bedroom doorway and offered to drive her to York station where she could get a train back to the Highlands and home.

"I'll not do that," Shiona replied resolutely shaking her head and remembering her painful departure from Ardvarnish. "I'll not run home the first time I'm out of a job." Inside she felt panicky and forlorn. She had no idea where to go.

"What'll you do then, dearie?" asked Gladys. "Where are you gonna live? I could ask my auntie to put you up for a couple of days in York if that'd help," offered Gladys. "Just while you have a look round for something."

It took Shiona just two days to find a job as a waitress in a one-star tourist hotel opposite the Micklegate Bar. She was allocated an attic bedroom of Dickensian austerity and paid a pittance with a cruel chunk lopped off for board and lodging. A new experience entered her life—one for which she was entirely unprepared. Nothing in her Highland upbringing nor her work for the Lords Denby and Horrick had even approached the continuous salacious vulgarity she was subjected to by the coarse and surly proprietor whose obscenely distended beer gut had so obviously precluded any normal sexual activity for so long that he had resorted to habitual verbal molestation of any girl over whom he had power. She was as much offended as shell-shocked. On top of her sense of inadequacy left by Sam, it came as a vicious initiation to the reality of womanhood in the wide world and she endured it only long enough to find a better position in a better hotel. As the months slipped by she moved again, swallowing insult and indignity with silent and growing self-possession, always slightly improving her lot.

Only now could she begin to see the innocence of her own sheltered upbringing. She had witnessed brutality and crime among some of the aquaintances she had adopted in blind faith. She had struggled with disillusionment and loneliness when forced to abandon those she thought she knew and trusted and she had also met face to face, and coped with, extremes of prejudice and bigotry which had made her father seem generous and charitable by comparison. And she had discovered and worked with cringing poverty and towering wealth.

And now she was going home, back to the glen for the first time for more than three years. A tremor of excitement whispered through her. She knew she was returning a different person, world-wiser than many of her friends. She was proud of her three years of life-training.

Now that she had found herself a secure position as deputy-senior receptionist in the Viking Hotel, looking out on the tranquil dignity of York Minster, where the American tourists loved her soft Highland accent and the paprika mass of her hair, and the management had come to trust and value her for her honesty and old-fashioned manners, she was earning a good wage. She had even managed to save a little money. On reflection Shiona felt that, all in all, thus far at least, life had dealt her fair.

Whether consciously for effect or not, she elected not to go home before the wedding. She was determined to arrive independently at the church in Lairg, rather than with her family, all of whom she knew would be there. She wanted to greet them looking her very best, and on her own terms. Only afterwards would she return to Ardvarnish for a few days.

What she wore would have to be good. A day's shopping in York delivered nothing. October weddings were a gamble, especially in the Highlands. It could be bright with warm sunshine, or frosty with icing-sugar snow on the hills, or diabolically wet and windy. "What am I going to wear?" she cried to Angela.

Angela was a slouch in her spare time, never wearing anything but jeans and baggy sweaters, but she worked for a national travel agency wearing every day a dapper uniform which, just in from work, she wore at that moment.

"I don't know, hen," Angie replied, kicking off her own shoes, "but you're welcome to anything of mine, you know that."

"Thanks, Ange," said Shiona forlornly, eyes tight shut and her hands clasped behind her head. 'I'd look a right drop-out in one of your sloppy sweaters' she thought, but decided not to say it. Angela brought her a mug of tea and set it down on the table. "Do you mean that?" Shiona asked suddenly.

"Aye, of course." said Angela, sounding surprised. Shiona looked her up and down. "What're you thinking, hen? This?"

Angela's uniform was modelled on that of an air hostess. The association was intended. It was a cunning ploy to make the unwary customer think they were already booking flights to their holiday destination when they walked into the travel agent's shop. It consisted of a tartan waistcoat and a pleated navy blue skirt with a panel of matching tartan down either side. It was worn with a fetching navy and tartan pill box hat.

"Aye, that! Angie, you're a genius! Will you let me wear it?"

"Aye. Aye, I will, I've got two. You'll look great and no-one'll ever know up there. Here, try it on."

The train dawdled the last few miles into Lairg station. Shiona's pale skin had a flush of excitement as she looked out over bracken slopes the colour of deep-fried batter and the snow-dusted tops of the distant hills pink in the sun. As she passed lonely houses and huddles of cattle and sheep dotted along the loch-side and moorland fields, childhood memories sprang vividly to her.

Sandy Macronie stood beaming on the platform. On this special day his ever-smiling face smiled wider than ever before and Shiona had to look twice to recognise his burly frame buckled tightly into kilt and black doublet.

"Och, now,!" he said, holding wide his huge hands. "What's this? This is surely not the wee lass I used to collect from school?" Arrival at the Macronie house and the sight of Jeannie in white with her mother and aunt trying to fix blue and white flowers in her hair was too much for both of them and for five minutes they laughed and cried out the shared friendship of twenty years. "Now look at the both of you!" said Betty, not far from tears herself. "I'll have to start all over again."

At the church Shiona was composed. She sighted her parents among the throng from way off and quickly looked away. She wanted them to see her first. She busied herself in conversation with an old friend, casting a furtive glance toward her mother from time to time.

Young Andy her brother had no hesitation. "Hey, little sister," he yelled, striding across to greet her, "look at you!" Shiona turned to see her brother dressed in a hired kilt and jacket.

"Hi, Andy," she said softly, tiptoeing to peck him on the cheek.

"Great to see you, lass," he whispered. "You look fantastic. Are you rich?"

"Not quite yet," she smiled, fighting an uninvited surge of affection for this brother she had not spoken to for years.

"You've not forgotten you're a Highlander, then?" he nodded at the waistcoat.

"Away with you! You just watch what you're saying." The laughter flashed in her eyes; and then suddenly her parents were at her side. They had not changed much. Her father was a little greyer perhaps, but as lean and upright as ever in his old blue suit, and her mother a little more lined about the eyes and in the same green coat she had worn on Sundays for as many years as Shiona could recall.

"Hello, Mother, Father," she whispered, stepping foward to kiss them both, embarrassed by their open-mouthed disbelief at the appearance of their daughter, her mother with customary handkerchief out for the inevitable tears. This was not the child who had lambed with her father behind the fank; nor the feisty teenager with whom they had struggled for so long. Nor was it even the girl who found her courage on the mountain and walked out on them three years before. This was a different person, a full-grown woman, made up and dressed in a way they only knew from television and magazines and guests up at Ardvarnish Lodge—strange to them and apart in a way they could not at once absorb.

Her father's hand stayed on her shoulder so that she could not step back. They looked directly at each other for a moment and she fell to him, hugging him, the strength of him passing to her. When they parted she saw his shining eye and she knew that words were not needed. She had none. They stood for a second only, and then he spoke. "You're looking grand, lassie."

"We still can't believe our luck," said Mac, sitting on the Caithness flagged hearth staring into a fat tumbler of whisky. "We wanted to be in this part of the Highlands but we never thought we'd find an estate as big and as wild as this and we never dreamed that we'd find an employer who was prepared to put up with me being a photographer and one who really believed in looking after the wildlife and the land."

Rob liked this man. He had about him a natural freshness — a smooth clean-ness like a pebble from the shingle banks in the Corran. There was kindness in his face, and understanding, not about money or politics or anything material, but about the everyday needs of people and the land and life as he and his wife and two children met it head on; it was the face of a man you could trust, a man who worked with the world, not against it. And there was patience in his eye and his voice. You couldn't be a wildlife photographer unless you had the patience of a stone. Rob was drawn to the paradox of the stalker-photographer. It demonstrated an openness of mind which he had learned not to expect from some other keepers and stalkers he had worked with and a lack of defensiveness which stimulated rather than cramped debate. He couldn't help wondering what Jimmy Forbes would have thought of him occupying his house and his job, the gin trap, the poison bottle and the snare replaced in the back of the Landrover by a bag full of expensive cameras—zoom lenses, filters, meters and tripods—and the long summer daylight at both ends of the day spent silently by the falls pool, not to bring home the silken otter pelt for the miserable fifteen pounds Willie MacFee would pay, but to capture the light shining on its spiky wetness and the pearls on its quivering whiskers, to share that split second of life, his and the otter's, through a photograph.

"It looks as though you came along just at the right moment," said Rob. "He seems to have gone through an amazing metamorphosis and he admits it."

"Oh, yes. He's proud of it. He boasts about it now, like he was to you today. Forbes had the place to himself and no-one ever dared challenge his actions because he'd run the show for so long and his wife had such a grip on the Lodge. He was never managed in any real sense. It's not surprising he did what he liked."

"Do you think he was killing everything?" Rob enquired, intrigued to be sitting in Jimmy Forbes's parlour, beside his fire and hearing this direct from the mouth of his successor.

"Oh yes. The place was a black hole for twenty years. Now we know the facts it's clear he was doing it both because he genuinely thought that is the way a sporting estate should be run, and to supplement his own income. He only buried your eagles because he knew he couldn't get away with selling them. Everything else went away to taxidermists and skin dealers on the black market. I've recently met up with one rogue near by who obviously took a great deal from Forbes over the years— although he now claims that he turned down everything illegal."

"Who's that?"

"It's an old scoundrel called Willie MacFee at Braeside."

"Oh yes, I've heard of him," Rob nodded, remembering another investigation which led there some months before. "Go on."

"It seems Forbes did a regular trade with MacFee in otter, wildcat and pine marten skins—they mostly get mounted for display or used for making sporrans—and also in birds for taxidermy.

Janet came in. "That's the bairns abed, Mac. Go and settle them down and don't be winding them up!"

Rob caught himself eyeing her analytically. She was confidently handsome; strong and fit and firm about the eye, and mouth which made him think she probably stood no nonsense from the kids. She flopped down in an armchair and relaxation spread a wide smile across her face. An exaggerated sigh released happy emotion and tiredness in measure. "The days get shorter and the work takes longer to do," she protested good-naturedly. Before he had time to comment she was sitting up, eyes flashing enthusiasm for the next task. "Did Mac tell you we've some friends coming in for a drink after supper? It's something we try to do to keep in touch with the other families in the glen.

"No—that's great!" Rob replied. "Who've you got coming?"

"Jockie Jack and Cathy, his wife. He's the estate mechanic and they live in the cottage just up beside the Corran falls. Jock plays the fiddle and we've had some grand ceilidhs with him; and old Lachie Gunn, he's one of the Corran Bridge crofters, and he'll come with his neighbours, Donald and Effie Swanson, they have a croft too, although they really belong to Caithness, and then two young NCC scientists who are living at the back of the Lodge, Lesley Scott and Tom Clifford—they're doing a research project on pine and birch regeneration in the strath— they're really good fun; and Andrew and Mairi Duncan, he's the shepherd who has the Dalbattigh sheep stock, although that's been run down lately. Andrew doesn't say very much," she made a long face and mimicked a dour voice. " Especially just now, I think he's that worried all the changes 'll put him out of work.

To be honest they're both a bit heavy going, but they've been here since years, born and bred I think—they really belong to the place, so Mac tries to involve them as much as possible."

"Yes, I've heard of the Duncans." Rob nodded, although it was only of Shiona that he was thinking at that moment. He had never forgotten how very plainly she had spoken to him. The memory was vivid and and he blushed to think about it again, sad that at their parting she had held him in such low esteem. "At one time we thought perhaps he was in cahoots with Forbes over the eagles. Shepherds are not well known for liking eagles."

Mac came back into the room and advanced with the whisky bottle in one hand. "Och, there's no fear of that. I don't think Andrew likes eagles much, but he's too clean-living to break the law. They're a family of high moral principles and regular church people. I'm certain sure they weren't involved with Forbes. As a matter of fact I don't think any of the folk here really liked Jimmy and Bella at all. No-one seems to have been sorry to see them go. Have another dram?"

Laughter rang out from the little cottage and the log and peat fire spluttered and the bright images of wildlife shone from Mac's dramatic colour photographs, mounted and framed with the eye of an artist and hung in profusion round the walls. A little while later Mac went out to feed his dogs and Janet to the kitchen. Rob stretched his legs before the fire and gazed into its beckoning flames. This Mac MacDonald, this new breed of stalker-manager, with his passion for wildlife and his profound understanding of the land was an enigma. His replacement of Forbes contained a culture shock Rob was still wrestling with, not because it seemed to have lurched from the ridiculous to the sublime, but because of the whole scene-change at Ardvarnish itself, of which Mac was only a symptom.

The Duncans were the last to arrive. The party was under way. With a knowing wink to Mac as he came in, Jockie Jack had slid his black fiddle case quietly behind a chair in the corner. The little room was humming with voices and the chink of glasses. Janet and Mac passed round drinks and sandwiches and crisps and threw in a joke here and a jibe there, laughter and well-being spreading across weather-reddened faces. Rob glanced up from a deep discussion about pine trees with Lesley Scott. He saw the tall lean-ness of Andrew Duncan fill the doorway, with the same high cheek bones and wide eyes, that strong jaw and the look of the Gael in his own land—a look which sees and garners and stores away and yet reveals nothing—that he shared with his daughter. He knew this was a man of firm opinions and quick anger, but a man of work whose supple body and broad forearms had given him an independence which lurked in the back of his eye; and there was his wife, a woman in his shadow, with a hesitant and apologetic face almost as though she ought not to be there, as if, married to Andrew there was only room in the house for one set of opinions and hers had been banished many years before. Then he saw there was someone else in the doorway.

"Oh hello, it's grand you could come," he heard Janet say, "we've heard so much about you." Shiona's eyes went quickly around the room, passing across Rob and back to Mac who was shaking her hand. He knew it was her, although it was not the girl he had met three years before. The unmistakable red hair cascaded to the collar of a simple slip dress of blues and greens gathered at her slender waist by a tied belt. On a ribbon choker she wore a round silver brooch of finely interwoven Celtic knotwork.

Rob was transfixed. He felt his chest tighten and a tremor came over him as though he was back in the little hallway in the Macronie's house and she was blocking his way out, lips whitely austere. Her words rushed at him again, "For your lies, that's what!" she had cried bitterly. He drew the whisky into his mouth and swallowed. 'This is crazy,' he thought, 'she probably doesn't even remember me.'

Suddenly he was aware of Lesley Scott's face staring at him at his side. "Are you alright?" she asked.

"Yes, yes, I'm fine. I'm sorry, someone I used to know has just arrived." Rob was still looking past her. She turned to see.

"Who is that?" she asked flatly.

"It's Shiona, Andrew Duncan the shepherd's daughter," Rob was still staring across the room. "I didn't know she was coming."

She was nodding and smiling at Cathy Jack, and Jockie, beaming across the width of his creased face, placed his hands on her shoulders and leaned to kiss her on the cheek with all the stored affection of someone who had known her for her whole life. Rob heard the word wedding and laughter and saw them nodding benevolently at her, the old mechanic still holding her, and looking her up and down. Finally Mac took her elbow and led her forward again.

"You won't have met Tom Clifford," he said. "Tom, this is Shiona. And Lesley Scott— Shiona Duncan, Andrew and Mairi's daughter who is up from the south just now." And to Shiona, "Tom and Lesley are working with us on a research project in the glen..." she smiled politely and her eyes passed to Rob. "...and you don't know Rob Pearce who is our guest for the night."

"Yes, I do," said Shiona quietly. The flare in her blue eyes impaling Rob with instant recognition which were neither warm nor cool. "We have met, haven't we, Rob?"

"Er...yes, that's right. We have, more than three years ago. You look well, Shiona." The smile had left Rob now and he was nervous, unable to free himself from her gaze. "Good to see you again."

"Have some more wine," Mac proffered to Lesley and they both turned away.

"Well, now." said Shiona. "I didn't expect to meet you again in this house!"

"Yes, I know, it's ironical isn't it? But I like the MacDonalds very much. Do you know them?"

"No. I've only just met them this moment. I'm completely out of touch. This is the first time I've been back to the glen since— well, since we last saw each other."

"Me too...and I'm only here by accident now—but that's too long a story." A little nervous laugh came to him. An impulse was rising within, he felt it coming on like a snowsquall on the mountain, dark and unavoidable. He cleared his throat and dragged his eyes down to his glass in his hand. "Er...Shiona, I think we have quite a lot of catching up to do...." his eyes came back to hers. He gripped his voice with all his strength. "...but first there's something I have to say to you. I have thought about it many, many times."

Shiona saw his hand was trembling and the colour rising in his cheeks. She wondered what might be coming. "What's that?" her voice was quiet.

"I never meant to trick you or decieve you that night. I was so wrapped up in the Forbes affair that..." But Shiona put out her hand to steady his glass, and her blue eyes looked straight at him. A warmth spread into them and a little smile flickered in her cheeks.

"It doesn't matter. It's years ago; we were both wrong. I should not have shouted at you like that; I've grown up since then. Please don't mention it again," her smile spread, "I've regretted it too. Often. Now, let's sit by the fire and you tell me what you've been up to all these years."

They talked all evening, stopping only when, to much rowdy begging from the whole company, Jockie Jack reached behind the chair for his fiddle and the room fell quiet. His nimble fingers and split, ragged fingernails, creased and lined with decades of black engine oil, danced across the strings with the speed and certainty of raindrops in a summer storm. With his eyes closed tight and his lips pursed he teased from that unpolished old fiddle the melancholy hopes and passions of a dozen

Gaelic airs. The room was still but for the lifting of a glass here and there as eyes stared at the fire or the carpet, thoughts private and emotions tingling to the old sadness of this land. Later, downing a heavy slug of whisky, he jerked and sawed it into hand-clapping, foot stamping jigs and reels which had old Lachie Gunn hopping around the floor like a red indian and Andrew Duncan slapping his thighs and shrieking with Lesley and Mac at the full pitch of their lungs. Without a signal Donald Swanson pulled a tin whistle from his kilt stocking and suddenly the room was alive with shrill piping, a firework display of exploding music, a bubbling jumble of thin notes rising and falling above the racketing throng.

At half-past midnight Janet yawned. "I am going to have to go to bed," she said, stretching. Only Rob and Shiona, and she and Mac remained, half-circling a wig-wam of birch-log embers slowly falling apart, sections of charcoal tumbling onto the flag-stone hearth where the glow left them, black and tinkling as they cooled.

"Me too," said Mac, standing up and collecting glasses from the mantle. "Do you two mind if we toddle off?"

"I must away, too," Shiona rose. "I've not seen Mother and Father for years, it's a bit much to drop them on the second night home." Rob felt a pang of disappointment.

"Can I walk you down the hill?"

There was that same bewitching smile. "That would be very kind."

Outside the sky was possessed by a crescent moon hanging hard and clear above the Lodge pines. Rob stared up at the plough and the bear and the pole star, like the eye of the night, glaring down at him as though he was being watched. He shivered. They set off down the track through the rhododendrons.

"So what do you make of all these changes, the MacDonalds and all Lord Denby's new ideas for the estate? Does it feel different after three years away?" Rob began.

"Aye, it does a bit. Mac and Janet seem like a grand couple and the glen needs the two bairns badly. It's great to have some younger folk in the community. Mother says it's brought the place alive. But I don't really understand all that's going on. What d'you think yourself? Has Lord Denby gone a bit potty in his old age, or what?"

"No, I don't think so. It makes very good sense to me, although I can't really believe it's all happening. Mac and Janet are tremendous. Lord Denby's really struck gold there. Did you see those photographs? Mac fair knows what he's doing with a camera."

"Aye, I did. They're fantastic. Jimmy Forbes'd have a fit if he could see them. The only good otter to him was a dead one."

"Did he kill everything?

"Aye, he did, I think, especially if he could get a pound or two for it. Over the years I've seen most creatures in the back of his Landrover on their way down the glen. But I'm not really understanding what all these scientists are doing. Is it some kind of experiment? Can you explain what's going on?"

Rob was pleased to have the chance to explain. As they walked quietly through the scented darkness he began to recount the saga of his day.

"Hmph! You know what's so funny about all this is that although I didn't know it was him at the time, when all this started buzzing in Lord Denby's head, I was watching him catch a trout on Loch Stac through my telescope."

"Where were you!?" asked Shiona incredulously.

"I was camping in the north corrie on Carn Mor."

"And you watched him fishing on Loch Stac in June that year?"

"Yes, he played a fish for half and hour or more."

"Well, I'll tell you something else—I gutted that trout and cooked it for his breakfast the following morning." Rob laughed with her.

"I don't believe it!" he said.

"Aye, that's when he was staying at the Lodge on his own and I went in to talk to him about moving to Yorkshire. That must have been only a day or two before we met, 'cause it was he who took me to the Macronies. But what's that to do with it?"

"Well, it seems that he got bored and spent half a day watching the deer. And for instance he wondered how many there were. He admits that the one thing he had noticed over his own fifty years of knowing the estate was that the few clumps of birches and rowans there were on the hill had almost all gone during his time. And then, he told me, he stopped to look at the fence round the Lodge woods and inside he found lots of young trees coming up, and outside not a single one. That apparently did it. It's what he calls his Conversion on the Damascus road. He became determined to get some boffins in to confirm his suspicions."

"What does it matter if there are no trees on the hill? I think the heather's very bonny."

"So do I, but perhaps even the heather is at risk. If you look at the slopes of Carn Mor you'll find more purple moor grass than heather, and the area of that poor quality grassland increases every year. Anyway, even if you took all the sheep and deer away, the heather wouldn't disappear, it would just become broken up into a patchwork of woods and moors. If people are to earn their living off the land, like your father does, they have to do it in a way which allows nature to restore the natural fertility of the soils and maintain the most productive vegetation, otherwise the place just becomes a desert. That's what's happened to most of Africa."

"But you're not suggesting Ardvarnish could become a desert, are you?"

"Not a sand desert, no, because we have high rainfall, but a wet desert, yes. It has already been called that by international ecologists. It is perfectly possible that the fertility of the soils here is at an all time low because of man's activities over hundreds of years, and the acid soils and high rainfall and cold climate don't allow the land to recover in the way it does further south on better soils."

They stopped at the old stone bridge over the dark, whispering waters of the Corran below. The moon and the silvery clouds were reflected dimly in its shiny black surface. An owl screeched shrilly from an alder on the bank. Shona jumped. "Its only a tawny owl," Rob reassured her.

"I know," she said, staring into the darkness. "It's a sound I know well enough; I used to lie awake and listen to them at the croft, but I must admit I just might not have been able to say which owl it was. You do know your subject, don't you."

"I should ...I've been studying birds for years."

"What happened next?"

"No sooner had Denby had his revelation than I came along with the Forbes affair, which rubbed salt into the wound of his ignorance about the estate."

"How ever did you catch him? He was a fly old devil."

"No, you're dead right. The very day after I had seen Lord Denby catch his fish I was up at dawn on the Dalbattigh burn, when I saw Jimmy coming up the stalker's path. I followed his tracks. A sixth sense told me there was something very fishy going on; and ten minutes later I had found the eagles." They stood in silence for a few moments before Rob continued. "I still don't know why he went up there that morning."

"I think I do," said Shiona slowly. "Wasn't it an old orange beetle car you had?"

"Yes. Well-remembered!"

"Well, it's funny you seeing Lord Denby catch that fish through your telescope, because I was watching you a few days before."

"When?" Rob demanded indignantly.

"I had stormed out of the house after a row with my father and gone away up the hill. I was sitting up there that I saw this car driving down the glen. Well, it was then that Lord Denby arrived at Ardvarnish without any warning at all. He just never did that. We were all taken by surprise and Bella was distinctly worried about someone having reported Jimmy for assaulting you and I think she warned Jimmy that the laird was up north to check up on him. She knew fine he was up to every trick with poisons and traps and all sorts and I think she told him to just make sure there was nothing about."

"I see." Rob added.

"Aye, that's it. And he may have been suspicious of you anyway. What did you tell him you were up to when he caught you in the bothy?"

"Just hill-walking."

"So you lied to him too."

"Ouch! That was below the belt, Shiona Duncan." Rob sounded hurt.

"I'm sorry, Robbie, I shouldn't have said that, I take it back," She placed her hand on his on the stone parapet; he knew she meant it.

"That's okay. You're right, of course. But what's this 'Robbie'? I've never been called that before."

"Ach well, if ye will mix wi' Highlanders ye must expect to be treated like een o' us," she teased him in an accentuated brogue, relieved that she had recovered herself from the unfortunate barb. Rob began to stroll on. The owl emitted a long two-noted, quavering hoot and then pitched into the blackness. They watched the silent silhouette waft past them and on down the river.

"Anyway, I was the last straw for Lord Denby, and at the same time he called in the NCC to mount research projects to find out exactly what state the land was in. And that's where we are today. He's reduced the deer by half and taken some sheep off too—I heard your Dad talking to Mac about that tonight—I gather he's not too pleased."

"Aye, that's putting it mildly. Dad's no conservationist; he's a shepherd and that's all he knows. He's scared stiff all this talk of trees and wildlife is going to do him out of a job. Do you think that'll happen?"

Rob was silent for a moment. "If agriculture in the hills and glens was in better shape just now I would say definitely not, but I'm worried that economic factors being what they are, if the subsidy on sheep goes so will the sheep. Do you know if the Ardvarnish sheep stock makes a good profit?"

"It certainly used to, but I'm not so sure now, and he's been forced to take two hundred ewes off, so that'll not be helping the profits."

Rob could see the lights of the cottage now. They walked in silence to the little gate. Up behind the house sheep were bleating in the darkness. "This is it, Robbie Pearce," she whispered,

"It's a lot I've learned tonight. Thank you very much."

The little gate creaked and was shut. "And Robbie, it was fine of you to say what you did when we met again this evening. I don't know many would have done that. Thanks." Then she was gone.

—15—

It was afternoon before Rob arrived back in the glen. The sun, a blood red orb, was slung low over Carn Mor as he drove due west. Mac had driven him to Kinbrace to collect his car and he was on his way back to take up their invitation to stay for another day at the Keeper's Cottage. The flat light of an early October afternoon, with the brightness in the sky held high above the glen by the darkening hills, made the Corran river look grey and forbidding. The boulders which studded its course were black and the current whispered past in silvery ribbons. He saw the bowed shape of a heron glide in and land in the shallows ahead of him and he stopped the car to watch it stalk noiselessly to the edge of a pool.

The rushing sounds of wind and river invaded the car as he wound down the window. He raised his binoculars to watch the bird, poised and statuesque above the pool. A stag, unseen and preoccupied with its own business, roared hoarsely from the shadowy alders only a short distance upstream. The urgency of the sound and then an answering guttural challenge from somewhere across the river sent a shiver down his spine. He scoured the trees for the second, closer stag. Suddenly it was there, not fifty yards from him, aggressively thrashing the bushes at the water's edge with its antlers.

The stag came on, wading through the shallows with its branched head high and alert. Well out into the stream it threw its muzzle forward and, antlers tipped right back on either side of its shaggy shoulders, hurled a breath-clouding roar out into the glen. It was quickly answered, closer now. A movement stirred to the right and he panned the binoculars across to see the other stag loping towards the car and the river, stopping in full view to roar again, angrily now, tailing off into a succession of indignant throaty grunts. He could smell them now. The air was rank with strong, sweet musk. The stag in the river surged forward into the pool, the silver water curling white from its powerful chest as it struck out to swim the few yards of deep water. It found its feet and rose up, dripping and steaming from the current to plunge forward up the bank between trembling alders to face its opponent.

They were now only a few yards from him. They stood off for seconds only with a short expanse of rushy green between them. To the right, the larger of the two, and, he thought, the one in possession of a harem of hinds and a rutting stand, powered forward with head high, showing no sign of checking. On came the challenger, out from among the dark trees in matching stance and pace. At the last moment, only two lengths apart, their heads flung down and antlers crashed together with a force which spun them sideways and made Rob wince. They parted and backed off, mouths open, breath coming sharply, eyeing each other. They came on again, the clashing rattle of hard bone echoing back from the alders as they locked and heaved in a vicious embrace. They spun, first to the left and then to the right, their hoof cleaves spread wide and churning mud beneath them. Tongues lolled, flanks heaved and steam rose in a cloud from their black, shaggy manes; they paused, apparently deadlocked, eyes staring wildly, waiting for the slightest hint of weakness, then surged again, shoulders arched, flaring nostrils almost forced to the ground as they inched back and then forward again, neither gaining nor losing in their desperate struggle.

Suddenly it was over. The splayed back legs of the challenger crumpled and he lurched sideways, antlers breaking free to recover his stance. But it was too late. The heavier stag pressed home, savagely lunging at his exposed neck and shoulders so that he staggered again, too late to do anything but run for his life. In seconds they were back in the river, splashing downstream at full tilt, as they chased away and out of sight.

Rob sat in silence for several minutes. It was a sight he had witnessed before, but never with such drama, so close and vital. No wonder Mac had wanted to come here. This place was a wildlife photographer's paradise and the privilege of working among such powerful natural images was rare and chilling. Content though he was with his own job he identified strongly with Mac and the whole Ardvarnish challenge. He wanted to see more of it. The knowledge that his actions had already helped spark off the whole metamorphosis now taking place on the estate had already awakened in him a sense of belonging. Since he had some leave time left he wanted to spend it here. He drove slowly on down the glen. At the Keeper's Cottage Janet gave him tea and girdle scones hot from the heavy iron on the Rayburn, and running in butter and honey. Then she left to collect her children from the school bus. He had arranged to meet Shiona at five-thirty. He left the cotttage and sauntered beneath a burning sky down the track. He paused at the bridge and looked to find the dead alder branch where the tawny owl had perched.

It was unavoidable that he should want to see Shiona again. He had never known a redhead before, least of all one so radiant, so flagrantly flaming —a redness which demanded more than casual attention; and then there was something about Shiona which un-nerved him, in a way which eroded his confidence and made him feel awkward and unsure. The tremble which had come over him at the ceilidh he had found alarming—almost a panic. He sat on the stone parapet and flicked a twig down into the dark water. Turning his palm upward and stretching the fingers wide, he held his hand as still as he could. The subtle tremble was still there, unmistakably, and he cursed softly to himself, "Damn it!" One thing was certain, if he was to continue a close involvement with the MacDonalds and the estate it was no use trying to avoid Shiona. Of course he would go on, but he would make damned sure he was late.

Two black and white collies ran panting to him and sniffed searchingly at his legs; the younger bitch rolled belly-up as he fondled her silken ears. A shrill whistle pierced the river murmur and the dogs sprang away from him and raced off down the track. Andrew Duncan's wiry frame paced towards him, crummack swinging out and his boots crunching hard into the dirt road, Jess and Bran now weaving at his heels.

"Hello, Mr Duncan." Rob was unsure of Shiona's father and politeness and formality was customary in the glens.

"Aye, aye." Andrew paused and eyed him, folding his arms and leaning on his long stick.

"That was a great ceilidh last night," Rob began, "Jockie can certainly make that fiddle work."

"Ach, aye, he can, right enough." Andrew nodded without smiling.

"I'm on my way down to see Shiona. She said she'd take me up to Dalbattigh to see that end of the glen."

"Aye, well, she's down at the cottage just now."

"Oh, don't let me keep you. Nice to see you again." Rob said lamely.

"Very good," came the terse reply and he strode away, the dogs chasing on ahead.

Shiona smiled. "It's late you are, Robbie Pearce. D'you keep all your women waiting? There's only an hour or two of daylight left in it. "

"Only those I'm testing to see how patient they are," Rob grinned back as he held the little gate open for her. She laughed and pushed the bracken-red of her hair from her eyes.

She was wearing jeans and her boots looked too big for her; the thick knit sweater was not hers either and she had rolled it back at the cuffs to make it obvious. She saw his glance.

"I didn't bring clothes for the hill, this is my brother's." Rob thought he saw a flicker of nervousness.

"You look great," he said, and meant it.

"I thought we could wander up to Dalbattigh to see the old settlement there. That's where it all started for you, isn't it?"

"Yes," muttered Rob quietly. "Yes, it is."

They walked up the river in silence. He was rummaging in his head for something to say. Nothing came. He felt the same panic he had felt at the party—chest tightening, pulse rising. 'Damn this' he thought, 'this is absurd.' Every time he formed words on his tongue they seemed ambiguous and awkward. He was afraid she might misunderstand him. The silence grew towards an embarrassment and he seemed incapable of stemming it.

"How long are you staying for?" She asked. Wasn't that the very question he had been wanting to ask her?

"I've only got another day, then I've got to get back to Perth. How about you?"

"And me, too, I'm due back in York on Saturday. Ach, I couldn't stay long, that house is still too small even after three years away. If I'm not careful Mother and Father will be back treating me like a sixteen year old. You'll not know what a time I had in my teens—I nearly went mad. D'you get on with yours?"

"No problem now," said Rob with a shrug, "they're a million miles away and very wrapped up in their own lives, and anyway I only see them for a day or two a year. They don't understand my love for wildlife and the hills. They'd probably have been much happier if I'd been an office worker in a city. They've accepted it now, but ever since I went to university we haven't had much in common."

Ahead lay the little stone bothy where Rob had camped that June. It was unchanged. The stinging nettles were frost-sick and the bracken burnt cinnamon in the fronds but still green in the long ribbed stems. Rabbits scuttled for cover among the tall, seedless heads of rose bay willow herb which grew thickly out of the ruined buildings around the bothy. Rusted corrugated iron lay about. "Come up here," Shiona called, running up a short heathery knoll.

They stood breathless on the top and looked down on the little bothy. Shiona asked, "What d'you see here?"

"I see a ruined croft slowly being reclaimed by nature."

"What else do you see?"

"A mess of rubbish, just like thousands of others I've seen all

131

over the Highlands. I've never understood folk leaving old cars about."

"Aye, you're right Robbie Pearce, just like thousands of others." There was something odd about her voice. Rob felt unsure again. She continued, " I know you'll not understand. None of the incomers ever do." Rob winced. He did not like the word incomer. He had never heard it used in anything but a derogatory sense.

"What d'you mean?"

She stared past him and out at the stone bothy and beyond. She took a deep breath, and turned to him and her eyes were dark and sad. "You're looking at a village, Robbie, a place where folk have lived and toiled for thousands of years. D'you not see them now, thirteen houses, not yet empty a hundred and fifty years? There, look there," she pointed, her finger jabbing at the air, "and there, and over by, and there, right down to the river. Every mound and pile of stones out there was a black house where babes were born and children ran barefoot to the burn."

Rob said nothing. He could see them now, easily enough. He felt a fool for not seeing them before. "The Clearances?" He asked quietly.

"Aye. They were cleared in 1839. Moved out in two days, so they say, and the houses burned behind them. They were made to leave the glen altogether to give up the land to the big sheep flocks and the laird. There were over forty families living on Ardvarnish. As you said, like thousands of others all over the Highlands—although that's not what you meant. ....There are only five families today."

"Where did they go?"

"Some went to new houses built by the laird in Corran Bridge, others to Lairg and further. Many emigrated to America. There's one or two folk round about who claim to be decended from families living in the glen, but not many. The Clearances are so bitterly resented, they shattered communities which had survived for centuries and once broken they quickly dispersed. The bothy here was never a black house. It's been built later from the stones of some of the other houses for one of the new shepherds needed to look after the huge sheep flocks. There was an old fellow living here when Mother and Father came to Ardvarnish twenty five years ago. He's long dead and Lord Denby has allowed the house to fall down. There are fewer folk employed on the estate now than ever before and Father's dead worried that he'll be the next to go." Shiona sat down on the heather and pulled her knees up under her chin; Rob scoured the moor facing them with his binoculars.

"I can see it all now," he said still looking. "That's a field system opposite us, isn't it? You can see the remains of old stone dykes running up the slope, and that huge expanse of bracken means the ground there has been heavily grazed by livestock for decades, if not centuries."

"Aye, it must have been their in-bye grazings."

"It must have been intensively cultivated," Rob sat down beside her. "If you think about it, Shiona, this settlement was very remote, and there was likely no road in, so almost everything they lived on had to be produced here or carried in on the back of a man or a pony. That means there had to be a huge area of fields and lazy beds. How many houses did you say there were, thirteen?"

"Thirteen that you can still count."

"Well, even thirteen probably meant a community of fifty people, maybe many more. To feed that lot there had to be well organised supplies of grain and potatoes and other vegetables. There had to be oats grown here, and bere, and hay for winter feed, as well as grazings for milk cows and sheep and goats. This place must have been buzzing with activity all the year round. It had to be for them to have survived, even if there were some barrels of salt-herring coming in from the coast to supplement their protein."

Shiona was impressed that Rob seemed to understand how they had lived. She fell quiet as she tried to imagine all those people bustling about in and out of the houses, up and down the hill. Rob went on. "And the fuel," he said, "think of that! There must be enormous peat banks up the hill there which have had thousands of tons of peats cut and carried from them over the centuries. A community like this would burn tens of tons a year, and sticks and firewood must have been collected from miles around. You wouldn't collect much now would you?"

"How d'you mean?"

"There aren't any woods, are there? They've all been grazed out by deer and sheep. It can't have been like that before because the timber was too valuable a commodity to these folk. They must have had a system for looking after their woods, coppicing them for firewood and sticks for making hurdles, beams for roofs, tool handles and every other need. Perhaps it was a crime to destroy a community wood? They needed them for survival, and for shelter for their beasts in winter. Where could you winter cattle here nowadays? There isn't a stick of shelter for miles around. The first big snowfall would wipe them out. There must have been huge areas of birchwood and pines too."

"I never thought of all that," Shiona admitted quietly. "I suppose you're right. It's all very fine to think of them on a grand day like this, but the winter's another matter." She looked at Rob, their eyes meeting. She smiled. "It's a fantastic thought. I can almost smell the peat smoke, can't you?"

"Yes," Rob nodded, staring out across the barren expanse of heather and bracken, "I can. And I can hear the children laughing and shouting, and dogs barking. And I can see women folk carrying baskets of dung and compost from the midden up the hill on their backs to where there are more men and women turning the ground with foot-ploughs and working it into the soil. I can see chickens scratching round the houses and far out into the fields and being chased off the oats by barefoot boys and girls -"

Shiona's voice was excited, "—There are banks of drying peats all along the ridge there, and more men and women carrying them down to the village to stack them against the gable of each house. And, look! Here come some teenage boys with a deer. They must have poached it from the hill. They're dragging it down to the byre. Look at all the interest, folk running to see from all directions."

"Poached it? Who from?"

"From the laird, of course. All the deer belong to the laird."

"They do now, I know that, but which century are you in? If as you say this community has been here for centuries there might well have been a time when the game belonged to the people, whoever their chief was, and was an important part of their diet. Brown trout from the burn, salmon from the river and the loch, gulls and plover's eggs, rabbits and hares, roe deer from the woods, and the odd grouse or capercaillie and blackcock on special occasions—sounds pretty good to me, eh? And what about some plump blaeberries and mushrooms in season, and a great variety of flowers and herbs for medicinal purposes? There was more to this life than toil, you know, but only if the people had the right to harvest the fruits of the land."

"You're right, Robbie Pearce, d'you know that? I do believe you're right. I never thought of all that. And I was thinking you're an ignorant incomer."

"—and you're right too, I am, but that doesn't stop me trying to understand this land and its people. That's a mistake you Highlanders make too often." His voice grew serious and Shiona knew she had touched a nerve. "I may not belong here, but I can love it too, you know, and feel for it, and want to see it restored, not ravaged like it is. That's why I like Mac so much, because that's what he wants. That's what he's here for, and it's a mighty task."

They fell silent for a moment, as though they had to let the emotion dissipate into the cooling autumn air. Rob stood up. "I'll tell you something else you might not have thought of which gives added poignance to your Clearances."

"What's that?" Shiona looked up at him, her blue eyes wide.

"Do you know why it made sense to move the people off and bring in the big sheep flocks to take over this place?" Rob didn't wait for an answer. "It's because this place was productive. These hills and glens had the fertility in the soils carried there on the backs of its people, and worked into the ground with the sweat of their brows and hands, century upon century, and it grew good grass, and the cattle grew fat in high summer. That's why there was profit in the land for the flockmasters and the lairds. They wouldn't have wanted it otherwise." He paused. "And look at it now." He paused again, staring out over the bleak moor. Shiona said nothing. "No people, no fertility, no fat cattle or sheep, and no profit." He began to walk away, down the heather slope, back towards the river. He had surprised himself. He cared much more than he knew and he felt anger rising within him. His throat tightened and his eyes stung in the cool wind. To himself he muttered, barely audibly, "and no woods,or blackcock or capercaillie, no lapwings, no curlews and bloody nearly no eagles."

Andrew Duncan leaned his crummack against the back porch of the Lodge and called in the two dogs. "Down Jess! Down Bran! Down and stay!" The collies obeyed instantly and lay at the back door to await their master's return.

Gerry and Harry Poncenby sat in the study in scruffy tweeds and stockinged feet sipping Lapsang Souchong from Dresden cups beside a bright fire of hissing birch logs. Dinah and the other guests were playing pontoon in the dining room, their laughter and ribald banter audible through the open door. A teenage girl in a pale-blue house coat knocked at the study door and entered. "Mr Duncan's here m'Lord. Will I show him in?"

Gerry looked at Harry, "Remember, old man, we do not want to lose him."

Andrew Duncan's heavy footfall announced his arrival. "Come in, come in," said Gerry. "Come and have a seat by the fire." Andrew came forward slowly, ill at ease.

"Good day, Mr Poncenby. Thank you, m'Lord." He placed himself stiffly in a leather armchair.

"Now what's all this about, Duncan? I understand from Mr Poncenby that you have asked to see me about the sheep, what?"

"Aye, m'Lord. That's it. I'll come straight to the point if you don't mind."

"Of course, of course, please do," said Gerry waving his hand generously.

"I put six hundred and seventy good lambs to the Lairg sales Wednesday past and we got top prices for half o' them, and the other half were not far behind. Now Mr Poncenby tells me I'm to put off two hundred and fifty ewes as well. That only leaves a ewe flock of eleven hundred. I can't see the sense of it, m'Lord, if you'll pardon me for saying so. If you take my breeding stock away how can I make a profit? That's what I'd like to know."

Gerry looked at him blankly for a second before he spoke. This was a part of being a landowner he loathed, but it was no good delegating it this time, it had to be faced. "Yes, well, I understand your concern, Duncan, and I'm grateful to you for coming and expressing it. We have difficult new policies here now, as you'll know very well, and Mr Poncenby and Mac MacDonald are working together to implement them. You might say we are feeling our way forward. I think it's better if I let Mr Poncenby explain."

Harry got to his feet and stood with his back to the fire. "As you know, we've pulled all the sheep back off Carn Mor and the south side. Mac is now reducing the deer there so that we can get some trees growing again, to improve the ground and provide shelter in the future. The north side of the glen gets much more sun and has always been much better grazing. That's where we want to concentrate the sheep stock from now on and we have to cut numbers back to match the grazing available. You can continue to have the whole of Dalbattigh and the hill behind your house, as well as the north river grazings, at least for the time being."

"Aye, sir, that's just it, for the time being. I hear tell that you're planning to let the river parks go back to alder woods, so I'll not have them for long. That's where I winter my ewe hoggs. Will I be told to put them off, too?" The colour was rising in his cheeks and his huge hands fidgeted nervously on the leather. Gerry and Harry looked at each other. Gerry put the tips of his fingers together thoughtfully and looked Andrew straight in the eye. He spoke slowly and carefully. "Are you afraid it's you we'll be putting off next?"

"Aye, m'Lord. That's about the length of it. I can see that day coming, right enough."

"Hmm. I understand why you're worried," said Gerry. "So you're asking me to predict the future?"

"Aye, well, a man has to know if he has a future. I've been here twenty-five years and I've seen the shepherds go from five to just myself. It's not very comforting to see the stock being put off and to be losing grazings at the same time. The sheep's my life, m'Lord, and I can't understand what you want with all these trees. There's no living in trees."

Gerry Denby rubbed his eyes and pursed his lips. "Right, old chap," he said decisively, "I'll tell you what I'll do. I shall arrange for you to spend a whole day with Mac MacDonald and

Mr Poncenby on the hill to go through the whole new policy. I will guarantee you a service contract for five years from today regardless of profit from the sheep, and I promise you that if I can possibly keep you and a viable sheep stock on Ardvarnish for the long term future, I shall do so. In return I want your help and cooperation with the new policy to see if we damned well can't make it work for you and for the sheep and for everyone else. How's that, what?"

Andrew Duncan gave nothing away. "Very good, m'Lord," he said getting straight to his feet. "Thank you very much. Good day to ye," He strode to the door. Harry followed him.

"Thank you for coming up," said Harry, but Andrew was already halfway down the corridor and did not turn back.

"Oh dear!" Gerry stretched his legs out in front of him and replaced the tips of his fingers carefully onto each other one by one. Harry returned to the fireplace. "You'll have to find out from Mac whether he is still upset."

"He's still upset alright, I'm jolly sure of that. The question is whether he will start to look round for another job," said Harry staring into the fire. "He is a damned good shepherd, that's the pity of it."

"I know that Harry, for God's sake! And he's given us twenty-five years of his life, but the fact of the matter is that sheep are not the be-all and end-all of this estate any more. We've got to break away from all that. Hill livestock has been in decline for years, you know that as well as I do. If it weren't for the subsidies and the availability of concentrate feeds the sheep would have been off these hills decades ago. The land is knackered and no amount of pouring cash into drains and re-seeds is going to put that right. You can't go on taking for ever. We have to start putting something back. We've to get the stock off it and let mother nature restore herself in her own time and way. I am completely convinced of that, and what's more we've made a damned good start. If we can do it as well as keep Duncan, then fine, that's what we must work for, but if we can't, then so be it."

Shiona ran after Rob. Catching him up she slid her arm through his . "That was one of the best half hours I've spent in years." He stopped and faced her. He wanted to hold her face in his hands and kiss her there and then. She was so close and her face so lovely, looking up into his. He felt his chest tighten and the same tremble came over him again, like chill destiny stalking his shadows. A long thin whistle sliced into their silence. Shiona instinctively let go his arm and they both looked to the river. A quarter of a mile away on the Dalbattigh flats they could see the lonely figure of Andrew Duncan working his dogs.

The Perth streets were dreich. November had spread a dripping blanket of chill over the entire Highlands. Traffic hissed past in a mist of grimy spray, and people, bent and huddled against the spitting wind, scurried about their business beneath buffeted umbrellas, their downcast faces cowering within upturned collars. Rob stared at the swollen river barely discernable through the rain stippled glass. There were times when he was grateful for the office. Writing reports was not exciting, but it gave him an excuse not to be out on a day like today and he was content enough with that. Opposite his desk the sharp brightness of a heron poised against the spume-flecked Corran river looked down on him. It was a moment of coiled expectation impaled by Mac MacDonald's predatory lens and trapped forever. The photograph was Rob's daily link with Glen Corran and it enabled him to relive the wild beauty of the glen he had come to love. It was a gift which had bonded their friendship and guaranteed his return.

The phone rang.

"Good lord! I was just thinking about you, Mac! I'm looking at the heron. I've had it framed and it's on my wall. It's got pride of place and keeps me sane on ghastly days like this. What can I do for you?"

"There's a problem brewing here I'm a bit worried about. It's Andrew Duncan. He's turned against us badly and is attracting quite a bit of support in the glen."

"Oh hell, no! What's it about? His job?"

"Aye, it is. He's convinced we want all the sheep off the place and has spread alarm among all the crofters up at Corran Bridge, and now the church. I had the minister here last night telling me everything I already knew about the importance of the community. Now I hear there's to be a public meeting in the hall on Thursday night to discuss the estate's policy. I think it'll draw quite a crowd."

"Oh my God! That sounds heavy. Are you going?"

"Aye, aye, I must, of course. The worst thing I could do would be to duck it, but I must admit I'm not that keen to go by myself. Some of those crofters have teeth."

"Yeah, so I've heard," Rob laughed grimly. "What about Harry Poncenby? I suppose he's away south is he?"

"Aye, and Lord Denby too and anyway their presence wouldn't be helpful. I need to handle this without the landlord and the factor."

"I can see that," agreed Rob. "What about those nice NCC folk? Are they still about?"

"Nope, they're away too. You know what it's like at this time of the year, there's nobody here at all and there's almost nothing going on. There's just myself at the hinds and Dunc MacRail the fencer is working at the new enclosures with Andy, Shiona's brother, but we've lost him, too. He's gone sullen and won't talk to me any more."

"Oh hell!"

"He said to me the other day, 'I suppose these enclosures are fencing out my own family.' I tried to talk it through with him but he wasn't hearing me. He's on the point of throwing in his job rather than work for what he sees as his father's downfall."

"What's the meeting really about? Do you know?"

"Not really, except that there's one or two local councillors coming and folk will be generally expressing their fears about jobs and the land. You know what it'll be like, it'll be the second clearances all over again. It'll only need one to get onto his feet and accuse conservation of working with the landlords against the people and we'll be damned for ever." Mac paused while they both pondered the prospect dejectedly, "It'll make my job impossible."

"I see that," Rob agreed. He knew he had to go. Mac and Janet were his friends. They were important to him; he couldn't desert them. More than that, he knew full well that the conservation reforms he had welcomed so wholeheartedly at Ardvarnish were on the line. "What do you think I can do?" he asked tentatively.

"Would you be prepared to come up to that meeting and put an outsider's point of view? You could do it much more objectively than I can. My problem is that I'm the manager here. I'm seen to be the laird's man and the one who has to implement the policy, so I am never going to be given a fair hearing."

"Yes, Mac, I'll come. Of course I will. If you think it'll help, I'll do what I can." Mac was seriously worried by this turn of events and much of the old sparkle had gone. Rob sat deep in thought. His fingers drummed urgently on the desk as he stared at the heron and the sky-filled pools of the Corran river which seemed alive and beckoning behind the frozen statue of the bird. What was it about that beautiful place which had haunted him all these years and would not leave him alone? His thoughts triggered an impulse and his hand shot out to snatch up the phone.

Rob had not contacted her since leaving Ardvarnish a month before and wasn't sure how welcome his solicitations might be. They had parted in subdued mood, both uncertain of the way ahead. Shiona's father had presented a daunting outlook they had neither forseen nor knew how to deal with.

They had walked down to see him that evening and had stood at the roadside watching him work Jess and Bran, back and forth, up and down the river park, teasing sheep out from among the rushy hollows and alder clumps, gathering them up into a bunch, bleating and jostling back down the glen away from the river which Andrew knew was likely to flood if there was another night of rain.

They had followed him along the road, a few yards behind, with him but apart, showing a genuine interest in him and his flock but rendered superfluous by the absence of any acknowledgement or recognition from him. They reached the hill gate and as he was busy untying the tangled wire, a few of the sheep broke back down the track with a scuddle of black hooves rattling on the stone. Rob had sprinted to hold them only to be scorned for his effort by Andrew's gruff command, "Stand away there, gi' the dogs their space!."

Back at the cottage her father's brooding presence had prevented any chance of relaxation. Then he went straight out again without a word. His disapproval was clear. Shiona was convinced it was her and this was a repetition of the bad old days. Rob felt heavy with doubt. He hoped it was only the problems with the estate. When he had gone Rob looked to Mairi for some sort of explanation but none came; she merely looked embarrassed and talked about folk of whom he had never heard. Shiona looked uncomfortable and said nothing more than yes and no to her mother. The bell was cracked and the resonance dulled. The vitality they had shared on the hill had evaporated as if it had never existed. The unpredictability of fate had barged into whatever private aspirations they each possessed, leaving them truncated and untried. They had parted at the gate with no more than a sad eye and a quiet word.

Somehow a month had passed. Rob had intended to ring or write but the rush of work had sent him scurrying over to the west coast on a poisoning case, and a court hearing in Nairnshire had locked up his best intentions in a flurry of briefing sessions and written reports which often sent him to his bed emotionally and physically exhausted.

"Viking Hotel, can I help you?"
He knew immediately it was her, for her soft Highland voice was unmistakable. "Shiona," he said, uncertain of the response, "it's Robbie."

There was an almost imperceptible pause. "Robbie Burns, I take it?" The release of tension was tangible.

"Och aye, who else?"

"I was beginning to think I had offended you. It's been a long month...."

Ten minutes later the rain outside was of no consequence. Hot-headed impulse had overtaken him. His papers bundled together, he left the office, jumping puddles in the cracked pavement and head down against the rain as he ran to his car. He was in Edinburgh within the hour and on the express train to York, and by six o'clock he was there. He found himself among a throng of commuters emerging from the station onto equally wet, darkening York streets. He knew Shiona's shift ended at half past and he demanded the way to the Minster from a startled traffic warden.

The Viking Hotel was bigger and grander than he had expected. He was impresssed. Its elegantly-lit facade and huge gilt lettering announced its importance to the whole square. He smoothed down his ruffled hair with his fingers and pushed through the etched glass doors into a miasma of light and heat and emollient music. Two smartly uniformed receptionists stood at the long desk, neither of whom was Shiona. Dismay struck him full in the face.

"I'm looking for Shiona Duncan," The closest navy blue and white clad girl calmly replied, "You've just missed her, I'm afraid. She left two minutes ago."

"Where'd she go?" Seeing the girl look him up and down he quickly added, "it's okay, I'm an old friend."

"She crosses the square to the bus stop on Fulford Road where she catches a number sixteen to Micklegate Bar. You'll catch her at the bus stop if you're quick."

Rob was out of the door and racing across the square before she had finished speaking. The Minster stood high and proud in its amber floodlights, its great tracery windows aglow with colour and history from within. He flashed past the Fulford Road sign running down past the great church toward a huddle of weary citizens standing dimly beneath a steel and glass shelter. He slowed to a walk, trying to control his heaving and pounding chest. His eyes flicked across face after face with no care or concern for their owners. He felt panic rising. No Shiona. There was a girl in a belted raincoat with her back to him at the end of the line.

"Shiona?" he said, trying to disguise the anxiety in his voice. The girl turned to look blankly at him. Suddenly he felt cold. "Sorry," he said, "I thought you were someone else." He cast wildly around. No Shiona. No sign of her.

"Does number sixteen stop here?" he asked of a stooped old lady with a black plastic shopping bag and a polythene bonnet tied under her wrinkled chin.

"It does that, dearie. There'll be one in just a minute."

"Thanks....has one just gone?"

"No. They run every ten minutes. There's one due just now."

A number twenty-three drew up and several of the queue climbed on board. Rob walked away dejectedly , back towards the square and the hotel.

"Oh, damn!" He cursed to himself. He felt more than a little foolish. He hadn't even got her home address. He hoped he could persuade the hotel to give it to him. He wished he had told her he was coming . What if she had gone off early? What if she had a date? He knew nothing of this girl. Certainly nothing of this end of her life. The realisation that she had lived here for all her adulthood—that this was her real life, not Ardvarnish which was her past and one which she had chosen to desert— even fought away from in desperation—slowly dawned on him. She had never even spoken of her life here. What if she'd been hiding something? He knew she had a flat, but he had no idea where. What if she was living with a boyfriend? It suddenly seemed to have turned from being an exuberant romantic impulse into a highly risky expedition courting humiliation.

Outside the great carved west doors of the Minster he stood for a moment in distracted thought, drying the drizzle from his glasses on his handkerchief. A Salvation Army band was assembling on the far side of the square and he could see the huge silver tubas and a euphonium emerging like gleaming moths from their black pupal cases. He watched in detatched fascination as the merry-go-round of this ancient city spiralled around him— of no consequence whatsoever.

The lone figure of a woman in a beret was walking towards him across the paved square from the direction of the hotel, her hands thrust into the pockets of her raincoat and a shoulder bag at her side. His hesitation was not of recognition but of control. "Shiona!"

As they met, the band struck up and the diffused strains of 'God Rest Ye Merry Gentlemen' engulfed the damp night in forced jollity. For several minutes they were lost, faces buried in hair, necks, rain-wet collars, lips burning and searching across cold, moist skin as the volcano rumbled ominously within them both. "Robbie, my Robbie," she whispered. "You came to find me." He held her face in his hands kissing her eyes and her mouth with trembling tenderness. "Of course I came. I had to. I'm a fool for not coming before. Where can we go? I need a drink."

"I don't want to go into the hotel, let's go to the wine bar just over there."

They sat opposite each other, staring at one another. Rob held her hands to his lips and kissed her knuckles. "Sorry," he said, "I'll recover in a minute. You've never been out of my thoughts since that night at the MacDonald's party. I'm a victim of chemistry. It'll wear off in a minute."

"It'd better not! And you'll not be thinking you're the only one who knows about chemistry..."

"This is crazy," said Rob, shaking his head, removing his glasses and wiping them again.. "This isn't supposed to happen to real people. We've only spent a few hours in each other's compnay and yet I feel I've known you all my life. What are these chemicals? Have I been drugged?"

"Aye, Robbie Pearce, if you're feeling like me then you have."

"When are you going to stop calling me Robbie Pearce?"

"Probably never." She looked at him with shining eyes, they were the living blue of the loch and the high Ardvarnish sky on a June day, and the paler, mystical blue of the distant hills, a blue that was neither land nor sky nor water but which came from the depths of her turbulent Gaelic ancestry, like her incandescent red hair which tumbled onto her shoulders in a riot of colour and femininity. "Probably never, Robbie Pearce," she leant forward running gentle fingers past his ear. She drew his face to hers over the middle of the table. Their mouths met in trembling softness which denied passion but cried of it with brain-swirling clarity.

"I didn't know this was going to happen," said Rob. He took a long draught of warm Theakston's ale, "and it's not what I came for."

"What d'you mean?" Her vulnerability was in her look.

"I mean I came about something else. I can barely remember this morning, it seems years away. I wouldn't change this for the world, but the truth is I came to see you to ask a favour."

There was the slightest hint of hurt on her voice. "I'm guaranteeing nothing." A smile hovered at the edge of her mouth.

"Have you been in touch with your folks lately?"

"No, why? —Has something happened?"

"No, no, it's just that your Dad is still convinced he is about to lose his job and has spread alarm up and down the glen. Now there's a public meeting about it on Thursday night in the hall. Councillors and the press are going to be there."

"Oh no!" Shiona stared wistfully at Rob. "Did Mac tell you all this?"

"Yeah. He's dead worried. It could make his job impossible."

"I can see that, right enough. Oh, poor Mac. If he gets the Corran Bridge crofters against him he'll get no peace. They can be a difficult bunch."

"He knows that, which is why he has asked for my help."

"What can you do?"

"I can go to the meeting as an objective outsider and support him. I have to. I believe in what he's trying to do and he is my friend." Shiona's look was suspiciously.

"Where do I come in?"

143

Rob looked down at the marble table top for a few seconds. He pulled her hand to his lips again and kissed her fingers. His eyes remained on hers. "When I phoned you this morning I didn't know I was. ..." he looked away.

"What did you not know, Robbie?" she whispered.

"I didn't know this was going to happen and now I feel a rat asking you this."

"You want me to come with you? Is that it?" Her voice sounded strained, "you want me to come and support you and Mac against my own father and my home glen? Is that what you're trying to ask?"

"Not against, Shiona, I wouldn't ask or expect that. But to come with me to show that at least someone from the glen is prepared to listen to what's being proposed and to see if we can't head off the clearances claims before they get running in the press. Mac doesn't stand a chance if that happens, and Lord Denby's very worthwhile and brave baby will be thrown out with the bath water."

"You really believe in what he's trying to do, don't you?"

"Yes, I do, because it is constructive and is genuinely trying to put something back." Exasperation crept into his voice and he looked flushed. "You know what the position is out there. We've been through all that. There's no future for anyone if we don't start to do something. Don't see it as just your father who is losing out, he is only the last in a long sucession of people from when Dalbattigh was a healthy settlement right down the centuries to today. Now there's no future for anyone at all except property speculators and commercial foresters, and that's yet another extractive system which will do still more damage to land and people alike." He stopped to drain his glass.

"So my Father is to lose his job, after all?"

"No, no, I didn't mean to imply that. I don't know what will happen, nor does Mac, but I am sure he will fight to keep a smaller sheep stock in place if he possibly can. Mac and Lord Denby both believe in the community and need the land to pay its way, but there are simply too many sheep and deer on it at the moment. They have to give it some breathing space to recover. Listen," he gazed intently into her eyes, "I will do everything I can to help your Father save his job, but I can do it better with your help."

Shiona gripped his hand. "Aye, I'll come with ye, Robbie. But I'm coming because I believe in you, not the cause. I just don't know enough about it to be sure of that yet. I've not had your training and I don't understand about fertility and the land like you do. I have to have faith in you not to trick me and my people with science. That's why I'll come, but I'll tell you something that I do know."

"What's that?"

"If I don't come it will be the end of you and me." Her eyes flashed with laughter. "You would never forgive me and I'd never forgive myself."

"Bless you, Shiona—and thank you. I need you, you know that, but I need you much more now than I did this morning."

"Aye, and I'm glad of it. I need you too, and I'm not giving you up without a struggle." She squeezed his hand once more. They laughed together but they wanted neither the wine bar nor the patter of small talk. They dined on tagliatelli in a bistro smelling of garlic and candle wax. They laughed and teased each other through two courses and abandoned a third unseen. Outside in the shiny street they walked hand in hand back towards the Minster and the square. The traffic slid past unseen. Waiting to cross the road Rob kissed her earnestly, surprising himself at the forces gathering within, greater than he had known before, and slightly frightening, as the tightness of chest and throat and the trembling fingers returned. The band was packing up its instruments to go home. They looked wet and miserable. Thin drizzle drifted like smoke through the floodlights as they approached the hotel doors.

"There's the Minster, in all its glory." Shiona said as she stood with her back to him staring up at the great building shining majestically through the night, and at its ancient city wall. Rob stood behind her sliding his arms around her waist, his face resting on her hair.

"It is very beautiful isn't it," he whispered, breathing in the fragrance of her hair and her silken skin. "And so are you."

Shiona turned in his arms and faced him, kissing his neck and pressing her forehead to his quivering lips. "You're trembling again, Robbie Pearce."

—17—

At Denby Hall, late November had been memorable only for the demise of what Gerry called 'The Halitosis Hound'—the scrawny, yappy and badly house-trained Yorkshire terrier which had been Dinah's preferred companion for eleven years. In a moment of provoked but inspired malice Gerry had once observed, 'Between the two of you you've tried and tested every vice and bad habit known to man.' From what it died, was a mystery. It had failed to eat its food in the middle of the day, despite the dangling of slivers of fillet steak in front of its dry nose, took to its chintz covered bed and died in the night, all within the space of twelve hours. The maid who brought her ladyship tea at eight o'clock in the morning found it stretched out on the pink and blue silk Aubusson carpet on Dinah's bedroom floor.

From the wailing distress this discovery evinced, Gerry, enjoying a solitary breakfast in the morning-room at the time, assumed that at the very least one of his wild sons had been killed in a car crash. In a rare display of concern he ran upstairs with a mouthful of toast and Dundee marmalade. He met Dinah shuffling along the gallery in her nightdress and satin robe clutching the rigid pet to her visible and ageing bosom, crying loudly. Since he cared very little for her and nothing at all for the dead dog he found it hard to be sympathetic in anything like the appropriate proportion. "Oh dear," he said lamely, stopping well short of dog and wife in case he should be expected to take it from her. "How sad. I'll tell Hardcliffe to dig a grave." He turned about and headed off towards the stairs again.

"G-G-Gerry," sobbed Dinah. "I think he's been poi-poi-poisoned." Gerry stopped and waited for the new crescendo of sobbing to ebb.

"Dinah, my dear," he began in a coldly matter-of-fact tone, "just because we once had two eagles and a raven poisoned at Ardvarnish there is not the slightest reason to imagine that, out of spite, Forbes has travelled to Yorkshire to poison your dog," and then as an after-thought he added, "and since the dog never managed to make it to any of the six doors out of this house, it is exceedingly unlikely that it picked up something outside. I think its much more probable it died of being over-cossetted." He headed for the stairs again to the accompaniment of more unrestrained grief. Then he softened and came back. "Look, old thing, I'm very sorry your little dog has died without giving you any warning, but it doesn't appear to have suffered and anyway, I must say I hope I can go the same way." Then he thought to himself 'and I bet you wouldn't make half this fuss if I did,' but he refrained from saying it. His conscience absolved he made as rapid an escape as seemed dignified.

It was to be an inauspicious day. At ten o'clock Mrs Dudgeon brought the mail to the library and laid it neatly in two spearate piles on the desk blotter in the wide bay window. Gerry was reading *The Daily Telegraph* in an armchair beside the fire liberally heaped with glowing coal, free from Denby pit, one of the few perks the family had retained after nationalisation.

"Thank you Mrs D." He said without looking up. A few minutes later Dinah came in and went straight to the desk. She peered nosily at his letters and, removing her own, she departed without a word. Gerry folded his paper and tossed it onto the long embroidered stool in front of the marble fireplace. He rose slowly and crossed to the desk. There were eight items. Four he knew immediately were estate office business and he pushed them aside unopened. A large brown envelope from the House of Lords he knew contained the Motion Papers for the forthcoming debate on National Parks, which interested him, but which could be read later; a sixth envelope he tore open to reveal an engraved invitation to the marriage of the very unexciting daughter of one of Dinah's more sycophantic friends. He had absolutely no intention of attending. Resisting the temptation to toss it into the bin, he placed it on Dinah's side of the blotter. The last two letters were both from Lloyd's. He recognised the insignia on the back of the crisp white envelope immediately. He wondered why he qualified for two letters in one day.

On the point of opening the first of these, Dinah returned brandishing a letter herself. "Gerry, will you read this?" She thrust the paper at him. "It is too much to bear on top of losing poor Trinket all in one day." Muted sobbing began behind a lace-edged handkerchief. Gerry took the letter and read without a word.

After a glance he put it down and hurredly opened the two of his own. They were all from Lloyd's. As he suspected, both he and Dinah had received the same letter from their Member's Agent. It contained a sickening warning about the performance of two particular syndicates of which he and Dinah were prominent underwriters. They had clearly been intended to arrive in advance of the really bad news itself. The second letter addressed to Gerry announced the results of one of the troubled syndicates—one about which Gerry had been secretly worried for some months because it underwrote hurricane damage claims in the Gulf of Mexico. News of widespread devastation had been widely broadcast when two major hurricanes within one year hit Florida and Texas.

He skimmed over the letter and the accompanying figures. It was serious, he knew that. How serious was not yet clear.

"You needn't think this is going to interfere with my spending February in Capetown with Elsie Mountgarron. If there are going to be more losses to pay this year you'll just have to stump up again." She cried plaintively as she walked away, adding fatuously, "I never liked the sound of that syndicate anyway. Why the hell should I pay for someone's damn roof if they're stupid enough to build their house in the path of a hurricane. You put me into it—now you can get me out of it. I don't want to hear another thing about it," with which she stalked out.

When things went seriously wrong Gerry never lost his temper. His was not a real temper anyway, more an evolved escape mechanism from his aggravating wife, his unruly sons and his lot which, it had always seemed to him, looked so cosy from the outside and yet which, from within, for all its material consolations, had never made him happy or contented or fulfilled. As a mechanism it worked well; a short savage explosion sent the irritants scuttling for cover and then he was left well alone for several days. But when something dire happened, he forgot the tirade and went silent, withdrawing into himself to consider his options alone. On such occasions he leant heavily on the stoical Harry Poncenby. He snatched up the letters and stalked out through the hall.

In the estate office he threw the letters onto Harry's desk and picked up the phone. "I don't like the look of this, Harry, not one bit." Harry, startled, began to read.

The number rang out and Gerry stared anxiously at Harry across the desk. He pulled a large red and green silk handkerchief from the breast pocket of his tatty tweed jacket and blew his nose noisily. "Dennis Ransom, please." He blew again and stuffed the silk back into its pocket so that it spilled out untidily. "That you, Dennis, old boy? It's Gerry Denby here, I've got your letters. Are we in a hole or what?"

It was several minutes before Gerry came off the phone. He sat down slowly and wearily in the leather armchair in the corner of Harry's office. "Bugger!" He said quietly, nibbling at his bottom lip.

"Do you know how much?" asked Harry cautiously, still fingering the letters.

"Not exactly—prob'ly won't for another year, but it can only be a disaster. This is the big one we've all been afraid of."

"A major disaster or a nuisance disaster?"

"It depends what you call major, my old friend. Is a million and a half major in your book? That's what it could be between me and Dinah."

"Dear God!! You can't mean it." Harry stood up, jerking his horn-rimmed glasses from his face.

"Oh yes I can! And that's not the full story. Dennis also warns that an asbestosis award in a Chicago court last month has set every sort of alarm bell ringing in the Carlsson syndicate, and I'm in that up to here." He whisked a finger across his throat. His hand flopped despairingly back onto the arm of the chair. "It's major all right."

"Can any of these losses be carried forward or offset in any way? You aren't going to have to find that much are you? Not all at once, surely?

"No, we can duck and weave a bit, I'm sure. There are delaying tactics, of course, but even if I only have to find five hundred thousand this year, can you come up with that for me, Harry? How's the petty cash these days? Eh?" He laughed feebly. "And then if I get a year or two's grace before having to find the next half million, which of our companies can pay that out? What have you got up your sleeve, Harry? I don't remember seeing much to spare from Denby and Garth Farms last year, do I?"

"Hmph! The estate overdraft is close to half a million as it is, without this. The bank are not going to like it one little bit." Harry came round to the front of the desk and perched on it, spinning his glasses in agitated circles in his right hand.

"No, Harry, it's no good pretending we might be able to scrape it together, however long we're given, and it's senseless to borrow any more. I shall have to sell, there's nothing else for it."

For a few seconds the chill fingers of self-interest gripped Harry by the throat and he saw his job in danger. He looked alarmed. 'Surely to God he doesn't mean Denby?' he thought to himself. And then the wave of panic passed and he got things back into proportion. He knew Gerry would sell Denby Hall and the Yorkshire estates last of all. They were, after all, the tribal heartland and what would Lord Denby be without his stately pile? Anyway, they'd been through all this before, every time they had a bad harvest and the farms made a loss. When it came to it he always fought like hell to keep it all together around his beloved ancestral patch. He swallowed noisily. "What are you thinking of, Gerry?"

"None of the industrial sites in Wakefield would fetch anything like enough, and farmland is pretty worthless just now." Gerry was looking at the ceiling as though there was something fascinating up there. "I could sell those two Stubbs in the dining-room, or the Gainsborough of Lord Fairfax on the gallery stairs, but if we ever had to open the house to the public they would be an essential attraction. Besides, I like them too much and they would leave a hell of a hole. I don't want to do that."

Harry Poncenby was a factor. He was also a friend and he enjoyed his relationship with Gerry and the family very much, but first and foremost he was interested in himself. Many years before he had made the telling observation to his wife, "Since I haven't a hope in hell of ever owning my own farm, far less an estate, I may as well get my kicks out of running someone else's." The job had nurtured him well. He had a fine Victorian house on the edge of the Park and he enjoyed real authority and control as manging director of Denby Holdings Limited and as managing trustee of several family trusts. He was well paid by land agency standards and he had long since taken for granted the expensive perks of having a four-wheel drive estate car, a full gun in the Denby shoot, a week's salmon fishing on the Corran each summer, a go at the grouse over dogs, as well as a few days deer stalking in October. Denby was one of those rare estates with a wide spread of assets which were constantly challenging to manage, so he was equally well fulfilled in his professional capactiy. As the years ticked by he looked toward his retirement and a welcome wind down of responsibility with considerable pleasure.

The complication in his life these past three years had been Scotland—a generic term by which he actually meant Ardvarnish estate. Not only was he uncomfortable about what was going on there, but he also considered it a bloody nuisance. He hated the journey up and down and could never sleep properly on the train. Now that Holdingham had been sacked and he had had to manage it himself, the wearisome trail back and forth once a month disrupted his home life and made him irritable, although he was careful never to reveal a hint of that to Gerry. "What about Scotland?" he tried cautiously.

"Ardvarnish!? After all we've been through? You must be joking!" Gerry dismissed it, but Harry had surprised himself with so brilliantly convenient a solution which was just beginning to consolidate itself in his mind's eye.

"You wouldn't have to sell the Lodge, or Carn Mor." he mused. "And you could keep the Corran salmon fishings."

"What d'you mean? Are you suggesting I break the place up?"

"Yes," Harry sounded enthusiastic now, "Dalbattigh and the north side must be worth well over a million on its own, and you'd be able to sell the sheep unit with it, and leave Duncan in place as its manager. It'd solve that problem too." His scheme was gathering pace and he could see that Gerry was listening to him. "What's more, if you banged up a lodge at Dalbattigh, on the site of that old bothy—you know, a kit house of some kind we could put up in a couple of months, some of them look bloody good these days, costing, say, a hundred thousand all in—it would push the value of the south side up to about one and a half. There's about fifteen thousand acres there, good loch fishing and ten or a dozen stags and a few grouse on the high ground. I believe it'd look damned smart in a glossy brochure."

Gerry looked at him hard. He could feel his heart beating inside his chest. He felt light-headed, a touch dizzy and unreal. Surely this wasn't happening to him? He would wake up in a minute and it would just be another bad dream like the hundreds he had had all his adult life as asset after asset had been scrutinised, valued, dismissed as too precious, argued over and finally wheeled out to the auctioneers to be haggled over by the world's vultures, fingered, gossiped about in the local papers— 'Lord Denby sells racehorse string'; 'Peer sells off town house to pay debts'; 'Baron gives up quarry after two hundred years'— and finally, ignominiously relinquished to the hand-rubbing lawyers to wield the legal scalpel and sever yet another extremity from the mutilated corpse. He rounded on Harry sharply. "That may make commercial sense to you, Harry, but I care deeply about that place and I'm damned if I'm going to be bullied into hacking it to bits to suit bloody Lloyds."

"All right, Gerry, I hear what you say, but if your sums are right we don't have many options. I think you should give it some very careful thought." Harry had his glasses back on his nose and he knew he had scored a hit. He walked thoughtfully back to his chair and sat down again. He was back in the driving seat. As Gerry got up to go he was flicking through his phone book to find the name of Dank and Subtley's senior partner in the north. He would need a very quick valuation.

—18—

"It's really decent of you to come," said Mac with a grim smile as he kissed Shiona on the cheek. An icy rain spat upon Glen Corran. The Glen Corran Hotel lounge was deserted. They could hear the hubbub from the public bar and knew it was full. There was a nervousness about them all. Mac looked strained. The laughter was missing from his brown eyes.

"Where's Janet?" asked Rob. "Is she not coming?"

"Aye, she'll be here in a minute. She's on her way back from Inverness. She's been down to the Inverness hospital for a check up."

"Nothing wrong, is there?" Shiona looked anxious.

"No, no." Mac assured her. "It's a routine woman's thing." He smiled, shaking his head, "Have you told your folks you're moving up to Perth? "

"I've not had time, we've driven straight here from Perth just now, and I've never been able to talk to them properly on the phone." She paused, acknowledging her problem. "Father'll not like me even knowing a conservationist, let alone living with one. I'm sure of that, but there's nothing I can do about it." Shiona looked at Rob with resignation and they smiled.

The door swung open and Janet came in, breathless and shaking the rain from her hair. "Ooh, what a night! Sorry I'm late." Mac kissed her lovingly, his hands on her shoulders. "Okay?"

"Just fine," she answered dismissively and turned to Rob and Shiona. "Well, you two, how grand to see you here. How kind of you to come. It means so much." She looked lovely, Rob thought, with her cheeks apple pink from the stinging rain and her chrysanthemum radiance. She was everything to Mac and his work in this tiny community. He imagined himself in Mac's position, with Shiona as his wife, working busily in a place where she was active in her own sphere, widely known, admired, loved; respected by those folk who brought their troubles to her privately, confiding in her because she never indulged in gossip like the rest. What was he doing to Shiona, bringing her here? He hoped it wasn't a mistake. "Are you sure you wouldn't prefer to go in on your own, ahead of us?" he asked her. She looked from Rob to Mac to Janet and back again.

"No, Robbie, I'm here because you asked me to come with you. I'm not going to desert you now. I've my own life to lead and I've to make my own decisions. That's the way of it and we may as well get on with it."

"It might not be as bad in there as we think," said Janet hopefully. Shiona laughed dryly.

"I know my father. However the meeting goes he'll brand me a traitor and he'll storm out without speaking to me. I'll put good money on that."

"It doesn't look very good." Mac sat down heavily in an armchair. "The whole glen's convinced Lord Denby's trying to get the people off the land, starting with your father."

"Are we sure there's no truth in that, or is there a chance we're being used?" Rob looked anxiously from Mac to Janet.

"I'm as sure as I can be. I've asked him direct, and Harry Poncenby, and they both assure me that's rubbish. They have offered Andrew a five year contract regardless of profit from the sheep, at the end of which he'll be re-trained and offered a new position if, after all, the estate decides to get out of sheep altogether. The estate lawyers are drawing up an agreement now."

"It isn't the five years he'll be worrying about," Shiona said quietly, perching on the arm of Rob's chair, " it's having to give up the sheep after that; for he knows nothing else and he'll be dead against re-training. I'm not thinking that Lord Denby understands, he doesn't want to be anything else. He's a shepherd. That's his life. If you take that away from him he's nothing left."

"I understand that, but it's still a very defeatist attitude, and no employer can be expected to have business policy dictated by the limitations of one employee," said Rob.

"Aye, that's maybe so, but, I know my father, he's too proud to even think about re-training. He'd rather leave and be a shepherd somewhere else, and he'll be saying that now."

"Aye, that's it," Janet added, nodding, "the re-training'll not be seen as a real offer, it'll just be thought to be a trick to get rid of both him and the sheep."

"And why should all this bother anyone else? Why do we have to have a public meeting about it?" Rob asked naively, already knowing the answer. Mac spoke in a slow, matter of fact tone.

"Oh, because of the threat to sheep farming in the hills. It's been the principle source of employment throughout the Highlands and Islands for generations. The Lairg sheep sales are famous all over Britain. There's folk come up from Dorest and Devon and all over to buy at Lairg. If an estate like this is seen to be going out of sheep it will be assumed that others will follow. It's the trend they'll be afraid of, with nothing coming along to replace the role sheep played in the local economy. And then there's about fifteen crofts on the Corran Bridge common grazings which are all part of Ardvarnish estate. Lord Denby has no power to interfere with their policies for sheep or anything else. They could keep elephants if they wanted to, but many of them rent extra grazings from the estate which could be taken away from them, and, of course they all subscribe to the sheep culture of the area like everyone else. It's their way of life, just like it is Andrew's, and they look to him as one of the best. He takes top prices at the sales every year and if the Dalbattigh stock are not worth keeping, where does it leave them? They'll be an unhappy bunch, there's no doubt about that."

"Aye, and I understand exactly how they feel," added Shiona flatly. Rob reached out for her hand.

They had been through all this in the car on the way up. Rob had tried to dispel her fears before they arrived. He knew he had failed. She was torn. She was right to point out that their position was flawed. They were offering no real alternative. It was all very well to say the land was exhausted, but the subsidies and the government grants available for reseeding and draining from time to time had kept the sheep economy afloat for years. Why not allow that to continue? What was the use of trying to restore the natural productivity of the land if at the end of it there were no people left? Shiona was trapped between loyalty to her own origins and a long and troubled past of being sold out by landlords and policies from far away, and her trust in Rob, which, he well knew was based on an emotional irrationality only a few days old. Her position was made the more difficult by her lack of understanding of the environmental issues at stake. On several occasions she had freely admitted that until she met him she had never given the condition of the land a moment's thought, nor the wildlife, except for feeling uncomfortable about the death and destruction which had surrounded Jimmy Forbes. It had never crossed her mind that her own father's activities, at the very core of her upbringing, might be damaging to the long term health of the land. It was too new a concept, too devastating for her to simply abandon everything she had known and loved about her people and her home for an untried philosophy she didn't properly understand. He also remembered, grimacing inwardly as he did so, that their own friendship had started three and a half years before with his blatantly deceiving her for his own ends.

"How's the time?"

"Three minutes to six. We'd better go across," said Mac.

They pulled long faces at the rain and scuttled across the puddle-strewn road to the little corrugated iron hall, built, Rob noticed from the plaque on the wall, by the second Baron Denby of Garth for the benefit of the people of Corran Bridge and Ardvarnish Estate, April 1927. Old Lachie Gunn stood at the porch door grinning toothlessly and leaning on his crooked stick. "Aye, aye, Mac. I was thinking you were not coming," he observed wistfully. "Oh, now! there's young Shiona!"

"Hullo, Lachie, how are you?" Shiona said, blushing.

"That'll please your father, right enough. Have you come up from down south? I heard you've got a good job down there?" Shiona did not want this. It had been hard enough to come to terms with the knowledge that she was already a subject of gossip in the glen because she hadn't been back for three years. She had despised Bella Forbes for gossiping. She was reacting to a childhood asphyxiated by the clinging smoke of bush-fire gossip. She wondered if Rob really understood how much she dreaded this second return, not only in the heat of controversy involving her whole family, but with the opposition. "Aye, aye, Lachie. I'll see you again," she smiled weakly. She pressed on into the hall and slid into a chair next to Rob at the back.

The hall was packed. A dull murmur filled the long room. Rob whispered to Shiona, "There must be sixty or seventy people here. I had no idea."

"Aye, it's all the Corran Bridge crowd and a good few from Lairg and round about. There'll be plenty here hoping for a good row. I can see quite a few who couldn't care less about the land or a sheep and have never been up a hill in their lives." The room fell quiet. They had been spotted and word passed through the seated rows like a bad smell, faces turning blankly to stare and then back to whisper their surprise or nod knowingly or to shake their heads. Slowly the level of chatter rose again.

At the front, beneath a bare bulb hanging from the roof on a long flex, at a wooden table too small for the purpose, sat Andrew Duncan and two other men. On the wall above and behind them hung a faded and water-stained photograph of the young Queen Elizabeth in 1953. The roof had leaked a little in this distant corner of the realm, but little else had changed in nearly forty years.

Andrew looked stony faced and pale, straight off the hill in baggy trousers and a thick-knit sweater beneath a tweed jacket. One of the other men leant across and spoke intimately to him. He stared coldly towards the back of the hall.

"Your father's seen us," whispered Rob. " Who're the other two?"

"The one next to Father is our Regional Councillor, Willie Ritchie, Drumruin, he's very good. And next to him is the District Councillor Bob MacHurdle—he's a nasty piece of work who's into everything. He gets in unopposed—that's the trouble when you've no choice of candidates."

"Why's he up there?"

"He's one of the crofting tenants Mac was referring to from just outside the village. He rents hill ground from the estate. He's not from these parts—Cumbernauld I think, or thereabouts— and he's only been here about ten years, but he got the croft at Balinreach from his great aunt. Now he's the spokesman for the rest of them and just says what he likes."

Shiona had scarcely finished speaking when Willie Ritchie, looking official in a white collar and tie and a tweed sports jacet, banged the table loudly with his clenched fist. The hall fell quiet. He got to his feet, the chair scraping loudly on the bare boards.

"Quiet now, please, everybody!" He called firmly in not quite a shout, taking his glasses off and putting them back on again as if to make it clear he was seeing everyone properly. He pulled impatiently at his little grey moustache while he waited for a late-comer to tiptoe in to a seat at the back.

"Thank you very much. It's very good to see so many folk turned out on a wet night to discuss some very important—shall we say 'developments'- in Glen Corran which are of interest to us all." He spoke slowly and solemnly with the air of one who addressed formal meetings regularly, but seldom had anything significant to say. "I have been asked to chair this meeting by Bob here, who is a District Councillor and Chairman of the Community Council and a crofter in the Strath as well. And by Andrew Duncan, who you all know for his excellent lambs at the sales." There was a buzz of general nodded approval from the whole assembly. "And I'm very pleased to see Mr Mac MacDonald and his wife at the back there—thank you both for coming along—Mac's the estate manager at Ardvarnish these past two years and very active they are in the community...." He broke off and bent down to refer privately to Andrew and Bob MacHurdle. They nodded to each other. Willie continued "...perhaps you would care to come up and take a seat at the front here, Mr MacDonald, since I'm thinking you're the best person to throw some light on the subject of this meeting?"

Mac rose and went forward without a word. Bob MacHurdle scraped a spare chair noisily to the table and Mac sat down next to him. Willie went on. "Now, I think first of all I shall call upon Mr Bob MacHurdle to explain what the meeting's all about." He sat down. Bob stood up. Formality was not for him. He wore an old grey anorak torn on the sleeve and a sweater which sagged at the neck. A thin hand-rolled cigarette smouldering in the ash tray in front of him sent a curl of smoke up in front of his face. He began to speak in a thin edgy voice which failed to conceal the hostility within it.

"Thank you, Mr Chairman." He cleared his throat. "Well, ladies and gentlemen, I'm here to speak for the community of Corran Bridge and Gen Corran and to voice concerns which have been raised at the Community Council by Andrew Duncan here, about a new policy on Ardvarnish Estate to put off the sheep from the whole of the south side of the glen and to reduce the stock to an uneconomic level at Dalbattigh on the north of the river. Now we all know what a good shepherd Andrew is, and how successful he's been at the sales for many years. The Dalbattigh sheep unit is one of the best hill farms in the north and the loss of the stock will be felt by the whole agri-cultural community.

"I don't think there's many of us here tonight can see any sense in this decision especially when the estate agree that the policy is likely to be uneconomic since it's for conservation pur-poses—whatever that means. Andrew's afraid it'll lead to the complete removal of sheep from the glen and his job with it. We can't afford to lose the sheep nor jobs and it's up to us to make that clear to the estate now, and that he has the full support of the community, before it's too late." The pitch of his voice and the tempo were rising. There was general approval again from the floor, with much nodding and ayeing and a shuffle of feet.

"Thank you, Mr Chairman, that's all I have to say just now,

perhaps you'd care to call on Andrew himself to put to the meeting the exact situation he's facing."

Willie Ritchie nodded authoritatively and looked over his glasses at Andrew. He rose slowly to his feet. Shiona's hand moved instinctively to Rob and he took it in his, feeling the tension in her. Her father looked uneasy. Shiona guessed he had been pressured into calling the meeting by Bob MacHurdle. She could not imagine him ever wanting to speak to any kind of meeting, least of all one about his own job.

"Thank you, Bob, Chairman." He looked up at the crowd and down at the floor. He spoke loudly and in rapid bursts, punching out each sentence as it came to him, as if they were unconnected and being fed to him one by one.

"It's not my job I'm here to talk about...... .It's more the life of the glen and the hill sheep we all depend on.....It makes no sense to me to put the sheep off, no sense at all....It's only the sheep that make any money on the estate now that the price of venison's dropped so low.... the economy of the glen's too fragile to play about with....If there's no sheep where's the living to come from?....No-one has given me an answer to that....What use is wild trees? It's only firewood they're good for and where's the jobs in that?....Conservation doesn't create jobs, it keeps folk off the land....It's no use talking about re-training folk if there's nothing to re-train for....There used to be five shepherds on Ardvarnish and I'm the last....If my stock goes it'll be the end of hill-farming in the glen....Perhaps Mr MacDonald can provide some answers..." Then he sat down. He folded his arms across his broad chest and stared severely down the hall.

There was a stir in the audience. Everyone began talking at once and one man called out from under the window, "We're with you Andrew!" Others shouted "Aye" and "He's right enough!"

Willie Ritchie rose to his feet again, banging on the table. "Quiet please, settle down now!" He waited for silence. "Thank you Andrew. Now, ladies and gentlemen, before I ask Mr MacDonald if he would be kind enough to speak to the meeting I'd like to ask if there's any questions from the floor." There was an uneasy calm for a few seconds before Jockie Jack rose to his feet.

"I'd like to say that I'm here tonight to support Andrew in his concerns. I've worked alongside him since many years and I can testify as to what a good shepherd he is. There's not many hill flocks as well cared for as Dalbattigh and none of us who work for the estate can understand what's behind putting them off. Why can you no have conservation and the sheep? That's what I'd like to know?" He sat down and there was another round of nodded agreement. Silence slowly fell over the hall. Suddenly young Andy Duncan was on his feet. Shiona had not seen him in the far corner at the back surrounded by a group of his drinking friends. He spoke in a nervous shout and everyone turned to see who it was.

"I don't think it's any good asking for more questions until we've heard what Mac has to say. I'm working wi' Dunc just now fencing the hill for trees. Land my father has grazed all my life. That land'll be out of grazing now for fifty years. I'll not live to see sheep on it again that's for sure. Is that what's going to happen to Dalbattigh as well? If that's it then it's my own family I'm fencing out! I'm not happy wi' that, no' happy at all. Mac MacDonald's not come up with any answers for me. I want to hear what he's got to say to the whole community tonight!"

Mac did not wait for any more questions. He stood up and looked about him. There were more shouts of "Aye!" and "Good on yer, Andy!" The hall fell quiet again.

"Mr MacDonald," announced Willie Ritchie, not wanting events to usurp his authority. Mac placed his knuckles on the table in front of him and leant on them, staring earnestly forward at the audience.

"I'm very pleased to have this opportunity to speak to so many members of the community Janet and I live and work in here, and a good few others besides. Let me say straightaway that it is always wise to discuss and debate matters of importance to the local economy and I shall do my best to provide some answers, although I am the first to admit I am not a prophet and I can see the future no clearer than many of you. I'm no Mr Fixit either and I certainly can't provide the instant solutions Andy Duncan is looking for." He drew breath and stood fully upright as though he was getting to grips with his task.

"I'm an employee of the estate just the same as Andrew here. I am just as dependent upon the landlord and the economy of the whole glen as he is. Anyone who works for a Highland estate knows they are in the hands of outside forces we have little, if any, hope of influencing. Both Andrew and I should never lose sight of the fact that if Lord Denby went under a bus—God forbid!—and the estate had to be sold, the next owner might well decide to farm ostriches here, or mine peat, or plant the place rigid with forestry. That is the lot of an estate employee and no amount of shouting is likely to change that, whatever our feelings are.

"So I don't want to talk about my job or Andrew's. The current position is that he has security for his job and his home for several years yet—more, in fact than Janet and myself. What I do want to talk about is the land itself. Everyone here knows about the Dalbattigh settlement which, like so many others, was cleared of its people to make way for sheep in the last century.

Before that happened there were hundreds of folk living in these glens and on these hills. Here we all are, a hundred and fifty years later and there's just a handful of us left, clinging on, dependent on the goodwill and the wealth of an absentee landlord. That situation's the same all over the Highlands. At Ardvarnish we consider we're very lucky, compared to many other estates. Lord Denby's family have owned the estate for three generations and have put a great deal into it—millions of pounds at today's values—and have always been very responsible landowners. Yet, despite all that, the productivity of the land has gone down and down, and the employment with it. We have to ask ourselves why that has happened." He paused again for his words to sink in. The hall was as still as a tomb.

"It is because all the systems of land management this past century and a half have been extractive. They have all taken and taken from the land without putting anything back." Andrew Duncan shuffled his feet restlessly and Mac was onto it like a shot. " I know you have done re-seeds and spread lime on some of your best ground, Andrew, that's why your lambs are so good, but the crop you take in lambs and wool is drawn from over the whole forty-five thousand acres, so that what you've done is like a drop in the ocean. That's our problem, and it's one somebody has to face up to before there are no jobs for anyone and the place is a desert. The reason I've been employed and the reason for the new policies is that Lord Denby has had the courage to face up to the needs of the future and to begin to put something back....."

"This is good," whispered Rob. "This is vintage Mac. He's getting really fired up now." Mac pressed on. He made the analogy with the fishing industry "....we all like eating fish, we all go on expecting them to be there in the supermarket or in the chip shop week after week, and yet we all know very well we are over-fishing our waters . One day we'll run out of fish and the fishermen's jobs will go and there'll be nothing for anyone. That's not wise policy. It's just grabbing profits for short-term gain and to hell with the future! Someone has to be brave enough to say stop! And mean it! It's the same with the land...."

He explained the nutrient cycle and how the trees restored fertility to the soils; how a good growth of vegetation slowed the rainfall down and improved the rivers and burns, preventing flash floods; how the wildlife was a thermometer of environmental health and how it was now at an all time low; he spoke of the lost sporting potential because the land was so poor and that the over concentration of deer and sheep were likely to be damaging to the grouse and other game.

"....and you're asking me to predict what will happen to the people living here *now* while the land is slowly restoring itself?

That's the hardest part of the equation and I don't pretend to have answers, but I do believe the right way forward is for us all to join together and support this initiative and put pressure on government, local and central, to come to the aid of folk who are brave enough to address the future for their grandchildren. If we do it together we have some chance of getting somewhere. If all we do is fight amongst ourselves we are likely to do no more than damage ourselves in the process." Then he sat down. For a moment Rob thought he'd won support. There was a pregnant pause but it was cut short.

Bob MacHurdle was on his feet in a flash. "Mr Chairman," he began in an exasperated tone, "all I've heard so far is a lot of waffle about restoring the land. To me it stinks! I think Mr MacDonald here is being used by Lord Denby. I don't believe in this great new policy for a minute. If there wasn't a profit in it somewhere you can't tell me he'd be doing it, and he doesn't give a damn for the likes of Andrew here or the tenants! I'm no fooled by this conservation lark for a minute. All they're inter-ested in is the capital value of the estate so that they can sell it on for millions. If the sheep are off it, they're keeping their options open. If the Dalbattigh stock goes I think it'll only be a few weeks before there's our grazings being withdrawn. We can't survive that! If Mac MacDonald believes in what he's been say-ing then he's a bigger fool than I thought he was! He's been duped by the laird and the factor, either that or he's been put in there to do their dirty work and is being well paid for it! We've seen all that before and I'm not fooled, not for a bloody minute!"

Rob withdrew his hand from Shiona, and stood up. "Chairman," he called out, "may I speak please?"

"The gentleman at the back," said Willie, pointing to Rob. Faces turned to see who it was.

"My name's Rob Pearce and I am an outsider and I work for the SSBC. The only connection I have with this glen is that three years ago I led an investigation into the stalker here who was prosecuted for poisoning eagles. That episode is long over and I congratulate the estate for replacing Mr Forbes with someone as knowledgeable and committed as Mac MacDonald. Everything Mac has said here tonight is true, and what Mr MacHurdle is saying is entirely wrong and blatantly alarmist. But there is another angle to this I think you should be aware of. Jimmy Forbes was prosecuted because a few years ago the public concern about the abuse of poisons pressured parliament into making it illegal. There are millions of people out there who contribute taxes to the subsidies which support every aspect of the Highland economy, none more so than agriculture, as you all very well know. I believe there will soon come a time when public pressure will once again, if it isn't happening already, impose its views on your lifestyles by demanding that the land is cared for better than it is now. We have already seen the NCC designate large areas of SSSI's, which is nothing more than part of that process. The next step is for government to take control of subsidies and make it illegal to overgraze or to operate extractive and damaging land policies. The Highland population is minute. It must be better to be seen to be trying to do something positive and constructive about the problems of the land, rather than sit back and wait for regulations you don't like to be imposed over your heads.

"I care very much about these glens and hills, and I want to see people living in them again, but that has to be done through systems which are sustainable, which they certainly aren't at the moment. We have to give it a try and, as Mac says, it's better to do that together."

Bob MacHurdle was up again. "I want a straight answer to a straight question. Is Ardvarnish estate going to withdraw my grazings at Balinreach?"

"Mr MacDonald, can you answer that?" asked Willie Ritchie, trying to keep control.

"As far as I'm aware there is no suggestion of a policy to withdraw grazings from the Corran Bridge end of the glen, nor do I think the estate will come out of sheep altogether. I don't want that, but I do want the hill to be farmed in a sustainable way, which it isn't at the moment. It may be that the stock will have to come off for a while to give the ground a rest." said Mac cautiously.

Bob shouted back without bothering to get up. "Bah! 'As far as I'm aware'," he mimicked. "What kind of answer is that? As far as I'm aware it's not going to rain tomorrow! But you'll not be worrying yourself if the grazings are withdrawn, will you, Mac MacDonald? Stock might have to come off! What's that mean? For ten years or fifty, like Andy Duncan says? And where does that leave the rest of us, eh? Answer me that?" Mac did not answer. Another man was on his feet in the middle of the hall. It was a new face, someone he had never seen before.

"Who's that?" whispered Rob.

"Well, well!" Shiona said softly, "that's Willie MacFee's eldest boy Alec. I've not seen him since school in Lairg. They say he works for Bog Forestation. That family were very thick with Jimmy Forbes."

"Mr Chairman, I have reason to believe someone here tonight's not telling the truth!" The hall fell silent again.

"If you've something to say you'd better say it, but let's have your name first," insisted Willie Ritchie.

"Alec MacFee, I drive a plough for Bog Forestation and I didn't like Mr MacDonald's remarks about forestry. There's nothing wrong with growing timber and to my mind it's a sight better than sport for the rich and wilderness for the conservationists. But that's no' what I wanted to say...."

"Just a minute, just a minute, Mr Chairman," complained Mac, getting to his feet again. "I never said a word against forestry. For the record I believe commercial timber is very important in its place, but I also believe it should be grown on land which will produce good timber for the nation, not on deep peatland like the flows. Is Mr MacFee saying the Dalbattigh ground should be forestry? Because if so, that will remove Andrew and his sheep quicker than anything else!"

"What is it you wanted to say, Mr MacFee?" asked Willie, struggling to keep up.

"My girl works in an estate agent's office in Inverness and two days ago she heard Ardvarnish estate was coming up for sale. We've heard nothing about that from Mr MacDonald. I was expecting an announcement here tonight." There was a gasp from the audience and everyone started talking at once. Willie rapped sharply on the table.

"Order! Order, please! Continue Mr MacFee."

"If that's true then it's in Lord Denby's interest to get the sheep off quick so that the ground can be sold for forestry. It's the second Clearances, that's what it is!" There was hubbub again. Willie banged loudly on the table again and again. Slowly the racket subsided.

"Quiet! Quiet please, ladies and gentlemen. I think we should ask Mr MacDonald to respond to this information."

Mac stood up and glared at Alec MacFee. He spoke slowly and deliberately. "I can categorically state that I know nothing of this except that I believe it to be rubbish and blatant rumour-mongering to cause trouble in this community!"

At that Alec MacFee leapt up and shouted, "Are you calling me a liar?"

"I'm saying you came to this meeting tonight to cause trouble!" Mac shouted back, angry and red in the face.

Andy was up and shouting from the back, "If what Alec says is right we've to make it damned clear to the next owner that we're not to be pushed off the land by some bloody incomer!" Then another man was up, "If the estate's to be sold we're all wasting our bloody time here." There was widespread commotion in the hall now. Everyone was talking and shouting to each other across the rows and taking no notice of Willie Ritchie's calls for order. Rob was up again and it was some time before Willie could subdue the assembly sufficiently for him to speak.

"Ladies and gentlemen, there's a lot of jumping to conclusions going on which is not helpful to finding a sensible way forward. All I can say to you is that I am absolutely certain that the suggestion that the estate is to be sold is a dangerous rumour. I have spoken to Lord Denby recently, and seen all the work he is having done—Andy Duncan can testify to that," he threw an appealing look across to Andy, "I just don't believe he would be spending all that money if he was planning to sell the estate. And I am absolutely sure Mac is speaking the truth to you here tonight. I have come all the way from Perth to be here to support him because I really believe in what he is trying to do. I think we should dismiss the suggestion that the estate is to be sold and concentrate on finding a way forward."

"So you're calling me a liar too, are you? Ye're just like all the other incomers, you always think you know bloody best! Well this time you're wrong!" shouted Alec MacFee, and as he did so he barged past the others seated in his row and stormed out. At the door he paused to shout, "We'll see who's telling the truth. We'll bloody see soon enough!"

Andy Duncan went next. He pushed past Shiona and Rob stopping long enough to stab a question at her, jerking his head at Rob, "What the hell are you doing with him?" He didn't wait for an answer and the door slammed behind him.

"Ladies and gentlemen, please! Please will everyone sit down!" Willie Ritchie tried to regain order, but it was too late. People were up and leaving in a surge with chairs falling over in the rush. Rob sat uncomfortably between Shiona and Janet as they pushed past. Three minutes later the hall was empty but for the three of them at the back and the four at the front table. Willie Ritchie began to speak. "Well, I'm very sorry..." but Andrew was not waiting either.

"Goodnight," he said sourly as he snatched up his cap from the floor. He strode loudly across the hall and out of the door without even a glance as he passed three feet from his daughter.

"I knew it! I knew it!" said Shiona with her teeth gritted.

"It seems there's more to this business than meets the eye," commented Willie, trying not to look embarrassed.

"Aye, it does that!" spat Bob MacHurdle angrily, glowering at Mac. "That's the least of it. There's treachery afoot and that's for sure! Alec MacFee's right, it's the Clearances all over again."

"Come on, you guys," said Mac staring down the hall and ignoring Bob MacHurdle, "There's nothing more we can do here. Goodnight, Willie, thank you for doing your best." He was simmering with rage and frustration.

"Oh God!" muttered Rob, rolling his eyes to Shiona and shaking his head.

They followed Mac outside. He turned to them, a dejected huddle standing in the rain. "What a bloody disaster! God, I could ring that bugger MacFee's neck! They've been wanting to get their own back on this estate ever since Jimmy went because they don't get otter skins any more."

"So you don't think there could be any truth in the sale story?" Janet sounded confused.

"Bloody hell, no!" said Mac. "It's a lot of malicious rubbish! Come on, let's away home and drown our sorrows. No wonder alcoholism is rife in the Highlands!"

—19—

Roddie the Post thrust the little bundle of mail at Janet through the window of the red van with his usual badly-shaven grin and said, "It'll be a grand day later on if the rain keeps off," which was the most appropriate of three or four similarly anodyne predictions for such a damp, grey November morning. She stood for a moment flicking through the letters and listening to the roar of the Corran as it crashed into the Falls Pool. There must have been more rain in the night, she thought. Highland burns can break into angry spate in only a few hours after heavy rain in the hills. The roar was much louder than the previous evening and the birches dripped menacingly in the cloying grey mist. The children were away to school an hour before and, for a moment, the house was tranquil—insulated from the world beneath a shroud of mist.

She carried the letters through to the others who were lingering over coffee at the kitchen table. The mood was like the day outside, downcast and chill. It had been a breakfast at which they had churned over the unhappy events of the previous evening.

Mac saw the Wakenfield post-mark and knew straightaway it was from the estate office. There was nothing unusual about that. Letters from Yorkshire were regular and frequent, although usually in brown manila. This was the firm white vellum reserved for Lord Denby's personal use. It was in just such an envelope that he and Janet had received the triumphant news of their appointment to Ardvarnish and the one he now held possessed the same slightly ominous aura of portent. The rest looked like bills. Mac slid a knife under the flap and cut it cleanly open along the top.

The previous evening they had reconciled themselves to the disastrous meeting in an over-indulgence of whisky and self-pity at the fire-side. Shiona was once again at total odds with her father, and now, for the first time, with her brother as well; Rob was branded an interfering outsider; and Mac had failed to win the support of even one member of the community. They were isolated and injured. Wound-licking had persisted into the early hours and breakfast was correspondingly late. They were all feeling fragile. The only element about which they felt secure was that history would reveal Alec MacFee's Machiavellian ploy to discredit them, and their bona fides would ultimately emerge the stronger for having survived such a scurrilous smear.

"Oh! my God!" Mac threw the open letter into the middle of the table and got up all in one movement. He walked through into the living-room and hurled himself into an armchair. Rob picked up the letter and scanned it in silence. He looked up at the two girls who waited wide-eyed and alarmed. Then he read it in a slow, flat voice.

> *Denby Estate Office,*
> *Denby Hall,*
> *WAKEFIELD,*
> *Yorkshire*
> *November 16th 1988*

My dear Mac,

I am writing to you personally because I know how disappointed you will be to learn of the very sad decision I have been forced to make today.

Denby Estates have suffered serious losses in a number of sectors in recent years and we have been forced into a level of corporate borrowing which is unsustainable at current high interest rates. Heavy personal commitments have recently compounded this situation so that I feel it is necessary to raise a substantial capital sum with which to secure the economic future of the estate.

I have decided to do this by dividing Ardvarnish and selling Dalbattigh as a separate sporting estate and hill-sheep unit of fifteen thousand acres. Dank and Subtley's have been instructed to prepare a brochure for immediate sale. It is my sincere hope that Andrew Duncan will be taken on by the new owners. We shall therefore not insist on the reduction of the ewe flock this winter.

It is of paramount importance to me that this decision does not interfere with your work, nor with the reforms we are undertaking on the remaining thirty thousand acres of Ardvarnish. This action will, in fact, make the estate more manageable and will enable us to concentrate on the task in hand. I have asked Harry Poncenby to write to all the Ardvarnish employees today advising them of this decision.

Yours very sincerely,
Denby

> *P.S. I hope Janet and the children are well.*

The kettle rattled metallically on the Rayburn. Rob put the letter down carefully. He looked first at Janet and then at Shiona. Their faces were blank with disbelief. Janet slowly got up and went to her husband, closing the door behind her.

"We must leave," said Rob soberly. "This is such a severe blow for them we must leave them to themselves. There's no role for us here now."

"Aye," murmured Shiona wondering what this would do to their own relationship.

"Do you want to go down to your parents before we leave the glen?" Shiona shook her head. Her eyes had a distant look; and Rob knew she was thinking about her family. When she spoke her voice was resigned.

"I've no desire to go there again for a long while. I've not done anything nor said anytthing to harm them, it's Father and Andy who have taken against me and if that's what they want there's not very much I can do about it." She paused and then added, "and I can get on fine without them."

"You don't mean that."

"I do." A look of steel was in her eye. "I lived without them for three years before this. I can do it again. There's no place for me in this glen just now, nor in my family either. That's the way of it and I shall just have to get on with my own life."

"Not on your own," said Rob softly. He pulled her to him and kissed her knuckles delicately. "I shouldn't have asked you to come, I've made things much worse for you with your folks...Perhaps I shouldn't have come myself."

The door opened and Mac came back to the table, Janet behind him red-eyed from crying and blowing her nose. "Well, that's it then," he said baldly, "It's all over. We are the laughing stock of this whole glen and we may as well pull out."

"No, Mac, no! You can't do that!" Rob rose to his feet. "You've still got thirty-thousand acres and a job to do. It's a cock-up, of course it is, a bloody awful one, but nothing you can't overcome. Don't throw in the towel, please don't do that!"

"Oh Rob, come on! I canna do the bloody job without any credibility at all. It'll just be an uphill struggle all the way. They'll never believe I went to that meeting in innocence. I'm a liar and the laird's lackey in their eyes, and that's that. I don't want Janet and the children to have to live with that."

"No, Mac, you're wrong. I'm sure you are. Look, no-one else will have got their letters until today. It's perfectly feasible that you didn't know. Jockie and Cathy Jack will believe that, so will Old Lachie Gunn and plenty of others who know you well. And you can always get Denby and Harry Poncenby to confirm that, and what the hell if Bob MacHurdle does think you're a shit?

You think the same of him, so it's quits. I bet if you had another ceilidh in three weeks time they'd be back in here dancing to Jock's fiddle better than before."

"Not the Duncans," interrupted Shiona who had been quietly thinking about her family and their own letter and how they would take the news. "You don't know my father. He may want to blame Mac and the new policies for the estate being broken up. He bears grudges and he'll not speak to Mac for months if he can avoid it. Andy's the same."

"And what about you, Shiona?" Mac asked.

"Don't be so daft, Mac! Take a hold of yourself!" The anger flashed in her eyes only for a moment. She spoke again softly, "I'd stay here like a shot, so would Robbie. It's not deserting you we are, although I think we should go just now." She looked at Rob.

"Yes, she's right. We'll come any time you ask us, but we should get going anyway. We have some thinking to do and some plans to make and you two need a little peace and quiet to gather your wits."

"Thanks..." said Janet. "I'm sure you're right, it's all come as such a shock. I'd never have guessed it. Even when we heard it last night it never entered my head it might be true."

"It's a cock-up, not a conspiracy, of that I'm sure. It was just bloody bad luck and bad timing. Don't forget Denby and Poncenby didn't know about the meeting, and it was your decision not to tell them because you were afraid they'd come up. If they had known I'm sure they'd have told you they were planning to sell. In fact there wouldn't have been any need for a meeting. A chunk of land's coming on the market with a sitting sheep stock and shepherd. There's nothing unusual about that. It happens all the time. Denby is right in the letter," he snatched it up to read it again, "it will make your job easier because you won't have to worry about Andrew and the sheep. It's not all bad, Mac. Promise us you won't make any rash decisions. Please?"

"He's right, Mac," added Shiona, "don't you be making any rash decisions." She turned to Janet. "Folk may not speak to you for a while, but most of them'll not blame you for what's happened for long. Everyone in the Highlands knows that estates change hands every now and again. That's part of life here and it happens all the time. They'll get over it, you'll see. Believe me, I know my own people."

They sat in silence as the car wound slowly through the rhododendrons, down the track from the Keeper's Cottage and over the stone bridge to the road. They were both lost to their own thoughts. Rob was entirely preoccupied by an overpowering sense of disappointment that his new friends, with whom he had identified so strongly, had run up against such daunting problems so early in their task. His lips were tense and he gripped the steering wheel tightly, white knuckled as if he were struggling with it. Shiona stared out of the window.

She was leaving the glen again, as she had done in Lord Denby's car three years before. Then she was burning to leave, desperate to distance herself from the hurt and frustration of her father and her home, excited by the prospect of the adventure ahead. She remembered it in precise detail, although at the time she had never looked back—the dark-leaved alders along the meandering river then expendable from her consciousness like the wallpaper on a long corridor in which one is only interested in the room which lies at the far end. But centuries of belonging to these mournful hills could not be so lightly dismissed. Now it was different. As the trees flicked by they seemed to be old friends whose own future was in doubt, and a sense of sad farewell came over her.

As they turned right at the fork she looked up to Dalbattigh, towards her home just out of sight round the bend in the river. She could see the rowan at the fank, and the sheep studding the yellow winter grass. She knew her mother would be in the kitchen there, wearing her floral apron peeling potatoes or neeps for her father's lunch. Perhaps Andy was home with them now, after the meeting, drawn back into the family by the threat she herself felt so deeply? Perhaps he was leaning against the Rayburn rail rolling himself a cigarette with one hand in the way he had, her father pacing the floor, and her mother in tears as they discussed the contents of the letter open on the table? Maybe she should go to them now, walk through the door and say to them, "Look, I'm with you, so is Rob. Don't read us wrong now, when you need all the help you can get. We're as devastated by this as you are," And Robbie, her Robbie, holding out his hand to them, saying, "We'll do everything we can to support you, Mr Duncan."

She glanced at Rob but his eyes were staring ahead, far beyond the road, and she knew the moment must pass. It wouldn't work. It was too soon; and anyway her father and Andy were too proud. She knew it would take them weeks to come round to recognising that they had been hot-headed, or mistaken, or just plain wrong about anything. Even then there would be no chance of an apology, just an unspoken shift of emphasis to signal that life could go on again. Saying sorry was not part of her heritage; clan feuds had perpetuated for centuries because of the stubborn reluctance to stretch out a hand and settle differences with a smile and a dram. No, the moment must pass.

At the Corran Bridge junction old Lachie Gunn and Doolie

McChattin stood jawing outside the hotel bar. Shiona smiled for the first time since leaving the Keeper's Cottage eleven miles before. As they passed their faces turned to follow the unfamiliar car with concentrated curiosity. "They'll be waiting for the bar to open," she said, "if they've recognised us they'll be at least two hours speculating whether or not there's been a family row. Once Doolie tells Jessie we've been seen leaving the glen together there'll be a dozen wild rumours buzzing up and down in no time."

"Poor old Mac really is up against it, isn't he?" said Rob darkly.

"Aye, he is that," was all that she could reply.

The car left the village and climbed the brae towards Lairg. Suddenly she said, "Stop, Robbie, stop—pull in over there," pointing to a peaty lay-by on the edge of the moor. "I want to get out and look back from here. When we came home from school the bus always stopped here to let Rory MacFail Balmonie off and I used to look down the glen from here. You can see right back to Carn Mor."

Rob pulled over and they both got out. It was cold. A bitter wind scurried round them, tugging at their clothes from several directions at once. Shiona pulled up her collar as she pointed into the grey distance. "There," she said, "Carn Mor's in cloud, but you can see the moor sloping down to the glen. We walked it once, straight home over the hills because the bus broke down. It's eight miles in a straight line and it took me and Andy four hours. We got lost several times and didn't get home until dark."

"How old were you?" asked Rob putting an arm round her and pulling her to him.

"Nine, I think. It was the longest walk I've ever done." Her voice became as distant as the grey clouds and the dark shapes of the hills to the west. "It was so different then. I knew nowhere else, this place was my whole life. Lord Denby was a God we spoke about with hushed reverence, it was inconceivable that he might ever think of selling up, such thoughts never entered our heads as children. Nor that there mightn't be sheep one day." Rob hugged her tightly to him. "You know," she said, "I have a stronger sense of leaving now than I ever had before."

Shiona returned to York but only to work out her week's notice at the hotel, pack up her flat and partake of a farewell to Angela Rennie.

It was an inevitable decision. It was as spontaneous as the eruption of their passion and as irresistible. They both knew that there was a rare fatality about their relationship. To deny it was to destroy it; denial was out of the question. They had sat at breakfast that first morning in the Longship dining-room eyeing each other over their coffee. Rob munched croissants and marmalade and Shiona studiously ignored the waitresses who tittered behind the serving screen. Rob wiped the pastry flakes from his lips and said with forced nonchalance, "I want you to come and live in my house in Perth, it's too big for one."

"Is it now, Robbie Pearce?" she had tried not to show her nervousness. She knew she was in love. She could not identify a moment in which it had happened. Had it been the unexpected apology for deceiving her three years before? Was it on the hill at Dalbattigh when he had surprised her with his knowledge and understanding of the Clearances? Perhaps it was afterwards, when they had parted uncomfortably, leaving a nagging void which had kept her awake at night. Or was it just the swamping sense of relief when he phoned a month later?

It was slightly frightening. She had never dreamed it would be like this. It had crept up on her and engulfed her in a helplessness for which she had no defence. She smiled mischievously at him.

"Are you saying you wouldn't move to York for me?" She feigned injury.

"No, I'm not, but my employer wouldn't like it and I'm not abandoning my career." He took another bite of croissant, looking at her over the top of his glasses. He was strangely confident. He was nervous, certainly—but that was because he knew his life was careering off on a new course, unplanned and into uncharted territory. Not being in control was unnerving to him too, but not because there was any doubt in his mind that he and Shiona were in love and would be living together almost immediately. Nor was there arrogance in that confidence; he had known it on the train to York, on walking into the Viking Hotel for the first time, seeing her crossing the square. Their meeting there had been but confirmation of an inevitability—as it were, the signature on the deed. He gazed at her thoughtfully. She was dangerously attractive. He had often wondered what a *femme fatale* was. Perhaps that was it?—an irresistibly fascinating woman, whose irresistibility pierced all armour. He continued talking as calmly as he could—in a matter-of-fact sort of way.

"I know you could get a pretty similar job in Perth, there must be five big hotels all crying out for really good receptionists. Besides, I need a housekeeper."

"Robbie Pearce! You have the cheek of a hoodie crow! You'll go too far in a minute."

"Then you'll come. Good! That's settled."

There really was no option, nor any opposition. Shiona knew she was going. She had vaguely planned to move back to Scotland. After all, her Highland-ness was important to her and something deep down had always told her that's where she should be. To return to Perth, to the gateway to the Highlands, was better still—and the fact that Rob had a rented house to himself, in the middle of a genteel terrace overlooking the Tay, made it immediately possible.

By the first sharp December frost she was there. Like trying to visualise the bitterness of winter on a warm spring day of daffodils and soft sunshine, after a week together in the house they could neither of them have recalled what it was like to be alone; neither of them tried. Their former lives had disappeared beneath a blanket of contentment, out of sight and mind like the heather beneath a heavy fall of snow.

On the Tuesday morning Shiona had set herself the task of finding a new job, they awoke to just such a world —a silent, traffic-less world of white. The central Highlands had experienced its heaviest snowfall for decades. It had come on a wild wet wind from the west which had collided with an icy Siberian airstream over the Grampians. Power lines and pylons tumbled under the weight of wet snow and all roads and railways to the north and east were amputated within the space of a few hours. The telephones were dead too. He walked to work and was home again within an hour. Only one other employee had appeared and since they had no phones nor any heating, and the computers were down, he had closed the office by pinning a note to the door saying 'Try again tomorrow.'

They had a gas fire and some candles. In fur boots Shiona padded the two hundred yards to friendly Mr Patel who ran the licenced grocery on the corner and returned with enough food to see them through a week's siege. They were as sufficient as hibernating dormice, as happy as Christmas children and just as excited. It was as though God had said, "What this couple would really like is to be locked up together for a week." For three more days Rob kept the office shut. Although power and telephones recovered falteringly they were inadequately co-ordinated to be able to function reliably. A semblance of normality returned for the week-end with traffic creeping about in slush and trepidation, but Rob and Shiona had no interest in mobility. The candlelight added to the inherent romance of their insulation from the outside world; in its flickering flame Shiona's hair shone and burned as if it, too, was on fire. They lost track of the time and the date, eating little and sleeping only locked in each other's arms.

A fierce frost fell upon Scotland from a bright moon-filled night. In the morning the sun shone triumphantly from a lapis lazuli sky. In their brief sallies out into the keen air they walked through the park and along the frozen river bank, mingling their crunchy footprints in the pristine drifts of snow, running and laughing, hurling snowballs at each other. They were as oblivious of the fastidious step-sweeping and pavement-shovelling citizens of Perth as of their Calvinistically-disapproving faces whenever they stopped to snatch a kiss in the sparkling sunshine.

"Where do you want to go for Christmas?" Rob asked suddenly, as they lay awake in the darkness.

"Ach...wherever you go..." came the sleepy answer, and then she sat up, "Why? Have you made a plan with your family or anything? What d' you normally do?"

"Yes, I s'pose I do usually go home, just for a day or two, but I don't have to. It's no great ritual or anything like that. How about you?"

"Nothing...anyway Christmas never used to be celebrated in the Highlands—it's only since television came that it's caught on. My folks disapprove of it because of all the materialism and they never knew it when they were children. I've no plans." She settled down beside him again and yawned.

"That's settled then," said Rob enigmatically.

"What's settled?" She sat up again.

"We'll be having Christmas here, on our own!"

"Oh good! I'm not thinking anything could be nicer. What are you going to give me for Christmas?"

"Never you mind! God! You're as bad as a ten year old. I wouldn't tell you even if I knew, which I don't." But that was not the truth.

At Ardvarnish there had been a flurry of activity before the snow came. As soon as they heard about the disastrous meeting and the unfortunate timing of their decision to sell, Gerry and Harry Poncenby flew up to placate Mac and Janet. Mac was offered a service contract and a rise which, without actually saying so, begged him not to leave. He was given the task of drawing up, with the NCC, a long-term management plan for the remaining thirty thousand acres, and he was removed from direct responsibility for Andrew Duncan and the Dalbattigh sheep unit until it sold, which with bad grace Harry agreed to manage himself from Yorkshire.

The incident of the public meeting had taken them by surprise. Gerry was astonished to hear there was so much local feeling about the sheep and that the memories of the evictions from Dalbattigh a century and a half before were still capable of surfacing so quickly. Now that the decision to sell had been made and announced he was curiously unmoved by it. The sense of dread and erosion which had depressed him so badly to begin with had evaporated as the idea began to take shape. He was still sad to see the property broken up, but it did sweep away a nasty little pile of problems with one stroke. Initial valuations had been very promising. Sporting estate values were riding high and properties selling well. Several, he learned, had been snapped up even before they were advertised. Because it had never crossed his mind to sell anything in Scotland before, he had taken no notice of market trends beyond raising his eyebrows when he read that such and such an estate had sold for six million or another, the river of which he had once fished, had changed hands for an eye-watering fifteen million. He was surprised to discover that the few paltry grouse they managed to shoot could be capitalized at £2,000 a brace; the stags they shot at £30,000 each; and that the sheep unit he had always looked down his nose at was worth over £120,000. The fact that the new estate he was creating drew on the long established reputation of Ardvarnish as a first class sporting estate enabled the game to be valued at a premium. Dank and Subtley's put a value on every last snipe and duck which could possibly be shot on the property. Even the corrugated iron barns and sheds where Andrew kept his winter feed were popped in at an astonishing £28,000. It all came to a glossy total of one million, six hundred and fifty thousand pounds. That, he thought to himself, was a useful way to dispose of a problem.

There would be a certain amount of capital gains tax to pay, but Harry had convinced him he could roll that over into the expenditure he was embarking upon on the rest of Ardvarnish. There was therefore a considerably greater sum to invest in the conservation reforms than he had previously been able to consider. Mac had been encouraged by that. It beefed up the management plan and made it all the more challenging for Mac. There was, however, one other consideration he wanted to attend to.

The community row had left Mac and Janet very exposed. They were on their own. Not only were they new incomers, but the incident had shown that in the whole glen, they alone believed in the reforms and properly understood them. The

NCC staff involved were very useful, but they didn't have to live up in that lonely strath and rub shoulders with the locals every day. What Mac needed was an assistant. He discussed it with Harry.

"It's a hell of an expense, Gerry, just to keep 'im happy!" was the response.

"Couldn't we share the cost with the NCC or some other body who might want to do research or something? You hear of that sort of thing happening from time to time." Gerry persevered.

"What, you mean a joint-funded contract post for a few years?" Harry asked.

"Yep. That's the sort of thing, old man."

"I'll try," said Harry looking sceptical, "there's no harm in asking."

To avoid stirring up further local resentment it was agreed that a lodge would not be built at the ruined croft at Dalbattigh, but that it would be sold with planning permission for one and the site cleared and services put in place. Andrew was permitted to winter his full complement of ewes and the tups went in as usual. It was hoped that an April lambing would occupy him so fully that he would have no time to fuss about the sale of the estate. Gerry and Harry were quietly confident that he would be taken on by the new owner and they promised Andrew that they would actively support him alongside the community if there was any suggestion to the contrary. They returned south pleased with the way things had gone and satisfied that, for the present at least, the crisis was over. They escaped the great snow blockade by only a matter of hours.

For five days no vehicle was able to get down the glen. The blizzard piled in from the mountains all night and on into the next day. The wind swept down the deep glacial trough in muffled splendour bowing over the broom bushes and birch branches into unrecognisable cushions of shining white. The road disappeared, leaving only the triangular passing-place signs protruding where it used to be. The vast heather moors became a gently undulating counterpane of brilliance and subtle silver shadow on which groups of deer stood about strangely obvious and static as if they had nowhere to go. Even the boulders in the river were white capped like iced buns studding the jostling stream.

Mac turned out each day to help Andrew find and feed his sheep which they brought down to the riverside for safety. After a day of exhausting leg and dog-work, Jess and Bran bounding through the powdery drifts, the air rent with whistles and shouts, as the flock was jostled and herded urgently downward, only seven out of thirteen hundred and fifty were unaccounted for. Andrew spent two whole days searching for them on foot, prodding deep into drifts with his crummack, walking every hour of daylight the brief days allowed and covering tens of miles at a time before he abandoned them. He knew they would not survive. They were buried deep, wherever they were, in some gorge or ravine of the burn, now filled in with snow, or in a peat hag which had filled over in the night to a depth which rendered the contours of the land impossible to tell exactly where he was. When the freeze came, sealing the snowfields with a hard crystalline crust, their fate was certain. Mac had dared to venture that Andrew should be careful himself and that he would turn out to look for him if he wasn't back by dark. For his trouble he received a baleful stare in condemnatory silence.

For all his inability to express it, Andrew was grateful for Mac's concern for the welfare of his sheep and the willing practical help he gave. Carrying bales of hay on their backs through the deep snow was testing work; over fifty a day had to be carried from as far as the tractor and trailer could get, for the remaining thirty yards to where they had erected emergency feeding racks out of wire netting and fence posts. Mac knew he was slowly regaining credibility and was pleased to do it. Once the hay was out he pitched straight into filling the feeders with ewe nuts from bags.

For Christmas lunch Shiona cooked one of a brace of pheasants given to Rob by a friendly landowner.

Afterwards, sitting cross-legged on the hearth rug Rob produced a little gift wrapped in red and green holly paper. Shiona took it carefully in her hands and fingered it suspiciously. She rattled it to her ear, shook it and sniffed at it. Then she began to pick the wrapping delicately undone. She knew it was special. Her pulse thumped excitedly inside her head, and a tremble in her hand.

"Oh Robbie..." was all she could manage in a small voice as she uncovered the little black velvet box. She stared at the closed lid for a few moments, almost afraid to open it. Rob looked away and reached for the bottle to pour himself another glass of wine. She sat motionless, and then she eased open the domed lid. A small square-cut emerald flashed its verdant brilliance from its setting on a thin gold band. A tiny label hung on a thread from the delicate ring. *'Second from the left, left hand, from Robbie Pearce.'* She lifted it from its box and held it out to him. She looked at him with candle-lit tears running down her face. "Put it on for me, Robbie."

The day in January when the Dalbattigh Estate sale brochure came through the post took Rob by surprise. Ardvarnish had temporarily passed out of his vision. Weeks had flicked by without noticing. They had phoned Mac and Janet at Hogmanay to wish them a happier new year and, with Shiona vigorously shaking her head in the background, he had admitted that their relationship was serious. "No firm plans," he said as Shiona looked aghast.

"If it gets to Mother and Father before I've told them..."

"They won't say anything," Rob tried to reassure her, "they're too tactful for that."

"Robbie. The glens are the worst places in the whole world for gossip, there's six other people will have heard it already."

"How could they?"

"Ach, you've no idea what goes on. Jessie MacChattin at the shop never passes the phone without picking it up in the hope there's a crossed line. If she gets one—and it happens all the time up there—she'll be listening to every syllable until the conversation is over and if there's the slightest hint of a story she'll be on the phone again in seconds to her circle of friends, making up what she hasn't heard. And she's not alone. There's dozens like her all over the Highlands. There's only one thing to do,"

"What's that?"

"I'll write to Mother myself tonight and tell her. Then it's done."

The brochure brought the whole drama of Ardvarnish sharply back into focus. Rob sat at his desk flicking through the glossy photographs and reading the glowing prose about its 'magnificent mountain vistas' and 'centuries of rich natural productivity' which made him laugh out loud. Then, on the next page was the agricultural analysis. There was a lovely summer picture of Dalbattigh, the little cottage and the rowan tree heavy in red fruit, and the fank full of ewes and lambs and the tall figure of Shiona's father leaning on his crummack. The sky was blue with cotton wool clouds and the rowan and the grass were strident green symbols of burgeoning fertility.

Suddenly he realised he was looking at his future father-in-law and his fiancée's home. This was her heritage, and it would, one day, not so far away, be part of his family. Then he saw the price. He could barely believe his eyes. He got up and left the office.

Shiona worked at the reception desk in the Station Hotel and it took him seven minutes running across the town to get there. It was bitterly cold despite the run, and the tropical heating of the hotel hit him in the face with a welcome blast.

"Got a couple of million to spare?" he asked.

"Och, away, not just now!—why?"

"I know a nice little place we could buy," he said passing the brochure to her. It fell open at the photograph of her home. Rob was not ready for the response. Shiona sat in a glaze of silence turning the pages and scanning the unrecognisable text. A large tear rolled down her cheek and landed audibly on the shiny page. "Shiona, my Shiona!" Rob sounded concerned. "I didn't think it would upset you. I'm so sorry."

"No, I have to see it and come to terms with it," she said solemnly. "It's just that it's not some piece of estate agent's property, not any old hill. It's not just any lonely rowan beside a fank. It's my home." Her voice wavered bravely before she gave in to the tears and sobbed quietly. When she recovered she looked back to the picture. "That's my father, that man there," and her voice had that same strange edge to her voice he had heard when they were looking down on the cleared village at Dalbattigh, as if she thought Rob didn't know or that he was a stranger who wouldn't understand. "And that's the fank where I learned to lamb and felt the heat inside a ewe and cried when the lamb lifted its little wobbly head and gave its first shaky bleat. And that's the tree old Trick is buried under, just there," she pointed to the page, "and those are the same as the berries I picked and laid on his grave. And d'you see that little sky-light in the roof? That's my bedroom where I slept for the first nineteen years of my life, and looked out at the stars, and the mountain and wondered who was out there for me, where I would go, who I would love and when?" She put her arm round Rob. She looked up into his eyes and kissed him, her cheek wet against his. "You will have to let me weep about my home, Robbie—it's happening, whether I like it or no'. With you to help me it'll no' bother me long, whoever buys the place. But if you're planning to marry a Highlander, you're marrying the glen in her heart too. That's the way it's always been wi' my people and that's the way of it. There's no changing it."

"So it's love me—love my glen, is it?" he smiled. "Then it's a good job I do, isn't it?"

Rob was distracted for the rest of the day. He was astonished at the price they were asking and couldn't get it out of his mind. Shiona had unsettled him in a way he couldn't quite fathom. He, too, felt a sort of grief, a longing which wouldn't shake off, to go back and take a long last look at the place which meant so much to the girl he loved, before some stranger came and put his mark on it and changed it forever. The phone startled him.

It was Mike Stone in Edinburgh. It was good to hear from him again. Mike was now assistant director and they seldom had a chance to see each other as in the old days.

"I'll tell you what it is, Rob, I thought of you immediately. You remember the Forbes case at Ardvarnish? Well we've had Lord Denby's agent on asking if we would be interested in joint-funding a post up there with the NCC. I've spoken to their people and they're very keen on the plan. Apparently Denby is a changed man and is spending serious money on a management plan to restore some of the woods. D'you know anything about it?"

"Er..yes, as a matter of fact I do, a bit," said Rob cautiously wondering what on earth was coming next.

"Well, you prob'ly know then, they've put in a new man called MacDonald who is running the place and he wants an assistant for three years. That's what this contract is about. What d'you say? Eh?"

"What do you mean, what do I say? What do I say to what?" Rob asked indignantly, knowing perfectly well what. He wanted time, air, space....Why did this place keep coming at him like this?

"Well? Will you consider it? We could second you from your job for three years. You'd live up there and work for them and NCC and for us. Our part would be to do a complete bird. survey of the whole area. You always said that's what you wanted to do: well, now's your chance."

There was silence. "Rob? You still there?"

"Yeah, Mike. I'm still here, I'm just taken aback and astounded, that's all. I need some time......"

Rob walked slowly home along the river path. It was dark and the Tay was black and shiny as it murmured past, swollen with melted snow from the hills. He took the long route through the park, delaying himself on purpose, sticking to the tarmac paths instead of cutting across the grass as he usually did. He was unable to think clearly. He knew he was going, that wasn't the problem. How could he not? The place had never allowed him any freedom of will ever since he first set foot upon it, so why should it now that he was engaged to a daughter of its hills? It seemed to him to be the more unavoidable for that—just another of those barbs of fate which had snagged him when he landed in the same guest house in Lairg that Shiona had run to that night; and when he was cleaning his teeth in the Dalbattigh burn and saw Jimmy Forbes striding up the path that morning. Who had ordained that? Who had led him to find the eagles which by rights should never have been found? And what trick had made him arrive there three years later at just the moment Gerry Denby was getting wound up about his reforms and the very same weekend—the only one in the whole three years—

that Shiona had chosen to go home? And now he was engaged to the girl....

He walked past the house and glanced up to see if the lights were on and if Shiona was at home. They were. He kept going. He would go and buy a bottle of wine from Mr Patel on the corner.

....And then getting sucked into the community row about the sheep when it was really nothing to do with him, and now, just when he thought they were about to part with Dalbattigh as they had known it, forever, the very same day as the brochure comes through the post, here he is accepting a job to go back there to work side by side with Mac and Denby and Shiona's father for three years. He was going all right, there was no doubt about that. But he didn't know how to tell Shiona. He had a feeling he was going to need that bottle.

"What's this?" asked Shiona, puzzled, as he held the Beaujolais out to her. "You're not thinking I'm cross with you?"

"No, no." Rob's smile was wry. He kissed her on each cheek and on the end of her nose. Her eyes, pale bluebell, looked up at him and he kissed her again, softly but meaningfully on the lips. "God, I love you!" he whispered.

"Robbie! I'm suspicious! A bottle of wine and a kiss like that before you've even got your coat off? What *have* you been doing?"

He threw his coat over the back of the sofa and flopped down into an armchair. "Nothing that I'm ashamed of," he said mysteriously.

"Ach, then you have been up to something."

"Yes, I have." He sounded sombre. Too sombre. Shiona, her look worried, came to him and sat on the hearth rug at his knees, clasping his hands in hers.

"Let's open the wine."

"Not until you've told me what it is."

How could he say it? Why was he afraid of her reaction? What was he expecting? She should be pleased. It was her home after all and she had told him how deep it ran just a few hours before. But something held him back, just a feeling, like that feeling he got sometimes leaving the office—that he had left something undone, but couldn't think what it was. An uncertainty because perhaps it was a step too far too fast. He sighed and looked at her closely before speaking.

"What is it, my Robbie?" she asked softly out of an open face.

"Where would you live if you could choose anywhere in the UK?"

"Here, with you," she said simply, "where else?"

"—and if you couldn't live here?" Her expression changed,

179

her face clouding momentarily as if she feared something dark and threatening from the labyrinths of her Highland past.

"Are we being turned out?"

"No! No, nothing like that," he said shaking his head and a hand. "Nothing to worry you like that. Let's be hypothetical, go on, just choose the first place which comes into your head."

"Mmm...mm..Corran Bridge!" she said abruptly.

"Good Lord! Why Corran Bridge?! That's a funny choice, isn't it?"

"No," she looked hurt, "you said it didn't matter. It was simply the first place I thought of."

"Was it? Really? Hand on heart?" he asked.

"Well, no....but it was the second."

"Aha! There you are, you cheated. What was the first place? Come on, own up."

Shiona looked into the sputtering gas fire. "The first place was my home. But I was not wanting to say that, because I wasn't fair on you this morning. I should never have cried like that, it was silly. It was just seeing it up for sale that upset me. It's sorry I am, Robbie."

He ran his fingers through the flame of her hair and over her forehead, drawing a gentle line down the length of her nose and across her lips with his forefinger. "Don't be so sorry. If you want to live at Ardvarnish, we could, you know."

"How do you mean?"

Rob took a deep breath. "This afternoon I had a phone call from Mike Stone at HQ.....if we wanted to we could be living there by March." They sat in silence. He'd said it all.... out of the blue...bizarre coincidence coming the same day as the sale brochure...the extraordinary way the place pulled at them both...had got them together...now was summoning them back. She had sat motionless looking from him to the flickering blue and orange flames of the fire and back again as he spoke. Her expression was of bewilderment and innocence. She got up without a word and began to open the bottle.

Coming back to him she held out a glass of red wine, and settled down beside him; when she spoke her voice was again resigned, far awa.

"D'you know your Bible, Robbie? D'you know that bit from Ruth? *'Intreat me not to leave thee, or to return from following after thee; for whither thou goest, I will go; and where thou lodgest I will lodge.'*"

"Yes, I know it," he replied, gazing past her at the fire, "But you haven't finished it: *'Thy people shall be my people, and thy God my God; where thou diest will I die, and there will I be buried; the Lord do so to me and more also if ought but death part thee and me.'*"

"I'm impressed, Robbie. You always impress me with your

knowledge. It's wondering I am sometimes how you get it all into that head of yours. But I wish it was as simple for us as it was for Ruth."

"Would going back there to live be a big problem for you?" he asked, knowing that despite the loyalty for which he loved her, her generous heart quailed at the thought.

"Not so much for me, Robbie, but for Mother and Father. He's a Kirk Elder and it'd be a disgrace for him to have his daughter living in sin in the glen, and with an incomer at that. He thinks I've deserted him as it is, going off with a conservationist and one who he thinks is against the sheep. If I came back and lived there, rubbing his nose in it I'd be. I'm thinking that he'd never speak to us again."

"Would it be okay if we were married?"

"Ach, aye, it would that, but I'm not agreeing to a rushed wedding before March just to please Father and the minister. It's our lives, not theirs and that's our decision and it's private. I want to marry you, Robbie, you know that I do, but on our terms and in our time, not to suit a God you don't believe in and a set of rules that I'm not respecting."

"That's my lassie!" He patted her her hand and squeezed it. "Would living outside the glen make a difference?"

She thought for a moment and looked at him, still thinking. "Aye. I think it would. Not Corran bridge, that's too near and part of the community, but Lairg or Rogart or somewhere thereabouts might make a big difference. Father never liked Andy bringing his women into the glen, but he could do what he liked anywhere else—and he did." She laughed. "Huh! Andy the Bull, he was called. D'you know, I didn't understand what it meant for years."

—21—

Ko van Fensing bought the Dalbattigh Estate 'sight-unseen'—as the estate agents describe such plutocratic high-handedness— from his office in Amsterdam. He was a successful self-made man who controlled his own chain of colour printing businesses spread across Holland. He was, like all successful businessmen, 'widening the base of his portfolio.' Property in the UK had proved to be lucrative in both of the London houses he had bought for renovation, and the Hampshire farm he had acquired twelve months before—an intensive calf-rearing operation—was coming along very nicely. Something in Scotland semed like a good idea. There were not many places in Europe, he had been told, where one could buy huge chunks of wild mountain land. The market was buoyant and there were an number of commercial options to pursue. The allure of capital growth and a development opportunity, at the same time as a chance to try his hand at famous English aristocratic sports was too great to resist. Dalbattigh was a big area for not all that much money and there was the added cachet of being a landowner of mountains and moorland which were famous all over the western world. Nor had it slipped his attention that he was buying from an English lord, a distinction which in itself added to the flavour of the investment for a man of his own undistinguished origins.

He was not a sportsman beyond enjoying the occasional day's shooting at a pheasant or a hare on a friend's farm. He had never been deer-stalking, although he was keen enough to try. He had learned long ago that in smart circles of wealth and influence it was more impressive to be able to say that you had done a thing rather than to claim to be good at it. But his true motives were purely financial—in the loose way that wealthy men can justify their whims and fancies under that heading—as long as there was a fair enough chance of getting his capital out again without suffering a large loss. He was a practiced buyer and seller of real estate on the international market and the reputation of sporting estates in Scotland was such that he didn't give it a second thought. Furthermore he was determined to get Dalbattigh. It was third time lucky and this time he was taking no chances.

"Listen," he snapped in impeccable English at his cautious London solicitors, "you have missed the last two estates I wanted by wasting time, buy this one today and if I don't like it when I see it I shall sell it again. OK? Do you understand? Good!" He slammed the phone down. "Why are these English lawyers so superior?" he growled at his secretary in Dutch, not wanting an answer.

Four days later he was thudding across the mountains at four thousand feet in a chartered helicopter. Once he knew he had clinched the deal he wanted to know what the options were. From signing the contract in London he went straight to Dank and Subtley's Piccadilly offices to talk to their Highland sporting estate specialist, a Mr Patrick Purdie-Steele. He had found the man pompous and affected. There was a self-important, silk-tie smoothness about him which barely concealed a contempt—even a sneer. He declined the expensive invitation to be escorted to Scotland to view the estate. Only two things stuck in his mind as he left their bogus-antiqued offices an hour later. One was a determination to challenge their fees, and the other was the suggestion, popped into the conversation as an alternative. 'If, after all, grouse shooting and deer-stalking didn't prove to be quite his cup of tea'—said in a way which even Ko could not mistake to mean that such pursuits weren't really the preserve of people like himself—commercial forestry, for which the British taxpayer would largely pay, was an excellent investment for anyone with interests in the paper and printing trade. Mr Purdie-Steele generously suggested that he knew one or two chaps in the far north who could advise him. Ko was no longer interested in their advice, he was going to see for himself.

It was a clear February day. A high pressure zone had sat motionless over the Highlands for a week. The anticyclone had sucked what little heat remained in the land up and away to the starry sky for six nights of savage frost. Mac had recorded minus six on the Farenheit scale on his porch thermometer, thirty-eight degrees of frost. It was the coldest he had ever experienced. He phoned the Met Office to see if it was a record. It wasn't, but it remained a startlingly new experience in his thirty-fourth year. The sun shone brilliantly but it made no difference. Its feeble heat was reflected back from the snowfields and the shiny ice casing which glazed the filigree birch twigs so that they tinkled in the scurrying wind. The cold was inescapable. The Corran Falls had stopped as if the grand conductor had stemmed the concerto in full forte, cancelling its power and passion in one flourish of the baton. It hung there with huge bulbous icicles overhanging each other from the towering walls of an ice-cavern, like a scene from an extravagant fairy tale where the white witch might appear at any moment. The burn, too, was silent, smothered by undulating waves of yellow, waxen ice.

Mac saw the helicopter go over and wondered, as did Jessie MacChattin in Corran Bridge, if it was a potential purchaser. He did not know the deal was done. Jessie didn't need to. She was on the phone in a flash to Mairi Duncan. "That'll be the new owner now, coming over in his helicopter. I heard he had one, right enough," she lied. "He'll land by you, I shouldn't wonder, and want a cup o' tea," she said spitefully, knowing it would panic her. Mairi looked out of the kitchen window and simultaneously heard the drumming rotors over the house.

"Oh my! Jessie, that's it, I can see it, I must go and get the kettle on."

On the frozen river flats Andrew watched it, stony faced and leaning on his stick as he surveyed his massed flock huddled together for warmth, their fleeces hung with dirty icicles so that they rattled eerily. Mac saw it, too, from the Landrover cab, up at the workshops where Jockie Jack was topping up the anti-freeze in the engine for the third time and putting paraffin in the diesel to stop it thickening to a glutinous gel.

It circled round in a broad sweep, up to the snow-filled corrie on Carn Mor and back down the river, now much lower. It passed over the Lodge pines and away to the east, only to reappear again seconds later skimming the birches and alders on its way upstream to Dalbattigh where a large digger had recently cleared and levelled the old bothy ready for a new building. The aircraft circled tightly once more, hovered for a few seconds before alighting delicately on the freshly cleared site. Mac saw that it had landed out of his vision and set off up the road in the Landrover to investigate.

Ko was big and solid. You could not call him fat, but it was immediately clear he enjoyed good living. He wore tight breeks and stockings, a thick loden jacket with the collar turned up and a sheepskin hat with ear flaps hanging down over his ears as he dismounted from the helicopter. The Landrover bumped up the track and stopped twenty yards away. Mac got out and strode across to the figure standing on the frozen mud. The rotors were still winding down, cutting through the air with a whining swish and a judder as the pilot applied the hand brake.

"Hello," said Ko, extending a hand to Mac and smiling broadly through a cloud of breath, "How do you do?" Mac knew straightaway from his correct English politeness and his tight vowels that he was Dutch.

"I'm Mac MacDonald. I am manager of Ardvarnish estate. Are you a prospective purchaser?"

"No, not any more. I'm Ko van Fensing," he was still grinning. He shook Mac's hand vigorously. "I'm the new owner. I signed the contract in London this morning. It's very nice to meet you."

"Oh. I see!" said Mac, taken aback. "Word hasn't reached us yet. How d'you do? Very good to meet you. Have you seen the estate, or may I show you around?"

"I should love to see around, but I cannot stop or the helicopter will ice up. Why don't you join us on board and you can tell me about the estate as we fly round."

"Great!" said Mac. "I've always wanted to have a good look at it from the air. It'd be a pleasure."

"Come on! Jump in," he opened the door for Mac to climb into a rear seat. "This is Roland, my pilot." The starter whined angrily to a crescendo and the jet engine exploded into life again. Ko plugged Mac's headphones into the intercom and helped him strap up. The rotors hammered and the ground seemed to quiver below them and then tumble away as they rose in a vertical column.

The helicopter hovered at three hundred feet while they chatted about the estate: where the new boundary ran; the extent of the old Ardvarnish holding; about the Duncans and the sheep stock; about Lord Denby; about the grouse and the deer. They swung away to the west to begin a systematic examination of the ground. As they did so Mac found himself looking down on the old settlement. He could see the string of ruins beneath their snow blanket. They were starkly obvious under snow, more so than without it because the rank heather confused the contours. Now each oblong hump was side-lit by the low sun and made clearer by the long blue shadows. He could see the field systems too; ancient dykes running up the hill in straight lines, partitioning the enclosed land from the moor beyond. And there were peat banks, row upon row of them in random terraces he had never noticed from the ground. Before his attention whisked back to the task in hand a powerful image passed through his mind. For a fleeting second he saw people there, dozens of them, busy about their work, scattered across the hillside in little groups, men, women and children, and their livestock, engaged in pastoral exchange of labour for life, a cyclical photosynthesis under the scudding clouds. It was an image which moved him in a way which unnerved him. It was like a catchy tune which imposed itself on the subconscious so that it kept returning in a mildly irritating way. 'People,' he thought, 'perhaps that's what's really missing from this land...'

Ko was speaking. Mac apologised. "What did you say? Sorry, I didn't catch that."

"I said, can you grow trees in the mountains here?" Ko bellowed at him through the headphones. Mac's mind sped straight to the wild birches, rowans and pines he was encouraging all over the south side below Carn Mor.

"Yes, no bother! Come back in the spring and I'll show you the fantastic growth we've got going in just three years." Ko nodded at him enthusiastically.

"Good! Good, that's what I wanted to hear."

The glen hummed with speculation. Before Mac had had a chance to check out van Fensing's ownership, wild and imaginative rumours were rife. He was an Arab, a Dane, a Belgian Count, as well as a Dutchman. He was an industrialist, a big-game hunter, and a property speculator. Even when the truth was available the Dutchman was still the subject of contortion and an inventiveness which would have done credit to a thriller writer. Fuelled by a bewildereing spectrum of possibilities from his wife, Doolie MacChattin assured old Lachie Gunn in the Glen Corran bar that night that van Fensing was really Denby's man. That was why he'd never bothered to survey the place properly before buying. After all, wasn't it true that Mr Nigel'd had a Dutch girlfriend not so long past? It was a cunning scheme by which Denby could appear to sell it and yet pass it to the next generation tax free.

Not an hour later Lachie, well lubricated by the excuse of an unusually eventful February day, passed this devious interpretation on to Bob MacHurdle who happened to look in to the bar with a couple of friends.

"So Denby's not sold it at all, right?" Bob asked to make sure he had heard it right.

"So they say." answered Lachie shaking his head sagely.

"Then the sheep'll still go off in that case. That bastard MacDonald'll still be in charge. Someone'd better tell Andrew Duncan about this. That's why he'll be using a Dutchman, it's to put off the sheep and get Andrew and Mairi out of Dalbattigh and not take the blame himself. That'll be it right enough! Someone should tell this to the papers."

"Aye, that'll be it," agreed Jimmy with a toothless grin, not caring what it was.

Back at the Keeper's Cottage Mac and Janet discussed the day's news more soberly. It was getting dark outside and the horizon glowed with a luminescent electric effect from the sunken sun and the omnipresent whiteness of the land. "Andrew'll be in now and I'd better go and tell him what's going on before he thinks we're conspiring against him again," said Mac.

"Aye, you're right," agreed Janet. "Don't phone. It'd be better to take a run down and see him."

When he arrived Mairi let him in with a worried smile. In the hallway Andrew stood leaning against the stairs with the phone pressed to his stern face. Mairi ushered him anxiously through to the kitchen. "Was that the new landlord in the helicopter?" she askedly as her hand strayed to the kettle. "Andrew'll be with you just now. You'll take a cup of tea?" Mac heard the phone ring off.

"Aye, it was that. I thought I'd better come and tell you both about him."

"Not before time," said Andrew curtly from the doorway. Mac thought that was a reference back to the information about the estate coming up for sale in the first place, and better to ignore it.

"I've only just had confirmation myself. I knew nothing about this man coming until I saw the helicopter like you."

There was something uncomfortable about Andrew's look. He didn't sit down. He had his arms folded in a defiant way as though he did not want to hear nor accept any news.

"I saw you were up in it quick enough." There was an accusation in his voice. Mac let it pass.

"It's a fantastic way to see the hill. It was a good chance to show him round. I saw things I've never seen from the ground, despite the snow. He wanted to see where the marches were and to know the extent of the sheep walks."

"Did he now?" Still the cold voice. Mac was losing patience.

"What's bugging you Andrew? I thought you would want to know who your new employer was. I came down here to give you the information I got from him and his Lordship first hand. You're the first to know. The man only signed the contract this morning. D'you not want to know? If I'm wasting my time, I'll go!" He could feel the blood burning in his cheeks. "Thank you," he said to Mairi in a calmer voice as he took the steaming tea from her.

"I'll only know who to believe when it happens," said Andrew cryptically.

"What the hell's that supposed to mean, man? When what happens?" Mac wished he hadn't bothered to come.

"I've just received information myself. The sheep'll be put off altogether and we'll be out of here in a matter of weeks. I'm told Lord Denby's done a deal with this Dutchman to get us out so that the blame doesn't fall on him. They say it's not a proper sale at all and that the estate'll pass to Mr Nigel once the Dutchman's got us out of the way. We'll not be able to fight him if he's a foreigner. You'll be in here yet Mac MacDonald, with your damn' birch trees and fences. The house'll be useful to you, I shouldn't wonder. You'll have some student from England to put in."

"Bullshit!" exploded Mac angrily, spilling his tea. He stood up and put the cup down. "You are your own worst enemy, Andrew Duncan, listening to all this bloody rubbish! When are you going to learn? All that'll come out of this nonsense is that you'll anger this new owner and he will put you out. And I'll not blame him!" He looked to Mairi for a flicker of support. She was on the brink of tears with her apron clutched to her mouth. "I've never heard such bloody rot! Who's told you all this?"

"That's my business," retorted Andrew beligerently.

"Then you must live with it! I'll not waste any more time with you." He took a deep breath. "I came here to tell you both that the estate's been bought by a Mr van Fensing from Holland who seems nice enough and is very interested in you and the sheep. He asked a lot of questions which I did my best to answer, but I said he should come back when the frost's off and spend some time with you himself, although I don't know why I bloody bothered!" He swallowed hard and began again in a more controlled tone. "I spoke to Lord Denby this afternoon to get confirmation that the sale had gone through and he asked me to send you

187

both his very best wishes for your future." He paused and looked from one to the other. They were silent. "Well, I've done my duty."

He made towards the door and Andrew crossed to the Rayburn and stood with his back to him. With his hand on the door knob Mac turned back. His voice was softer now, and open, containing no anger nor side. "It's done, Andrew. The estate's sold and you've a real chance now to get things right again for you and your family. Don't screw it up by listening to rumours from the likes of Bob MacHurdle. They're only interested in using you for their own gain. Give this man a fair chance and I'm sure he'll give you one in return. Good night to you."

There was no reply as he left. He closed the door firmly and stepped out into the cutting cold. "People! Give me strength!" he swore to himself, "who the hell wants anything to do with bloody people?"

—22—

Why was life so complicated, Shiona wondered? She was in love and the three months she had lived with Rob in Perth had been the happiest of her life. Now she was returning to the northern Highlands, to the hills of her childhood, to that bit of the earth which meant more to her than anywhere else. Rob was going there to do what he had always wanted: to live and work in one place long enough to get to know it properly—'to climb into bed with it and tease out its deepest secrets,' he had said one evening by the fire—and that in the company of Mac MacDonald whom he liked more than anyone else he had ever worked with. Yet the move was fraught with uncertainty and tension. She had written to her parents weeks before and told them they were unofficially engaged and that, sooner or later, they would be coming up to Glen Corran together to see them. She had received a post-card back from her mother which she noticed was posted in Lairg. It said little more than that it was nice to hear from her—no congratulations, no good wishes, no mention of Rob. She knew very well that her father had refused to discuss it, slamming the lid on the subject and pocketing the key, saying, "They'll not be welcome in this house!" and that was that. Her mother would have had to post the card secretly when they were next in Lairg.

She had not had the courage to tell them that they were moving to Rogart. She knew she had to. It would be worse for them to find out by hearsay, which they would any day now, even though she had only told one other person. She scrumpled up another sheet of paper and threw it at the waste-paper basket. It missed.

Rob came up behind her chair and put his arms around her neck, resting his chin on her head. "What's the problem? Just tell them straight. That's all you can do."

"I've tried, three times now, but it sounds so—I don't know—well, dead, really."

"Let me see." He picked up a ball of paper and opened it. He laughed loudly. "I see what you mean! Dead is right! Why don't I do it? Anyway, the whole point is to keep them informed so that when everything settles down at least we will have kept the communication channels open. Our conscience will be clear. It doesn't matter a damn which of us actually does it. Here, give me a pen."

By the second week of March they had moved to a lonely cottage near Rogart. It was equi-distant to Golspie and Dornoch, the two townships in which Shiona was most likely to find work, and well under an hour's drive to Ardvarnish. It was just about far enough away from Lairg and Corran Bridge for them to be able to live their own lives.

The cottage was a dream and a nightmare. Where the corrugated iron roof had rusted through it had been daubed up with black bitumen so that in warm, dry weather when the corrugated iron expanded in the sun it sealed well, and when it was cold and wet and the metal contracted, it leaked badly. There were two main rooms: a kitchen-living room to the left of the front door and a bedroom to the right. A crude lean-to bathroom had been tacked onto the gable end off the kitchen. It leaked too, but conveniently only over the bath.

A corrugated iron porch propped up by stout and knobbly birch trunks, sheltered from the east wind by an ancient rowan tree, covered the front door. A path which might once have been gravel, leading through the small, sometime-wire-netting-fenced garden to a one-hinged gate, and a doorless hen-house which lurched drunkenly away from the wind and which, while it might never house a chicken again, was well used by blackbirds and thrushes.

They bumped up the lonely track with long yellow grass brushing the underside of the car on a deceptively mild late-February afternoon. The cottage smiled benevolently at them with a look of contented abandonment, as though it had done its job well and was happy to slip back to nature, earth to earth, dust to dust.

A pair of jackdaws clattered from the chimney pot cawing in alarm as they got out of the car. From the blue above the hill a buzzard mewed its piercing cry and soared lazily on eagle wings. Rabbits bounced unhurriedly away into the rank grass and broom bushes, and a wren tripped along the fence, in and out of the undergrowth, chattering in shrill protest. Rob was ecstatic. "It's fantastic!" he said, struggling to untie the bailer twine at the gate. Shiona was quiet. "What d'you think?" He asked so enthusiastically that she had not the heart to be honest.

"It's not quite my idea of a modern married home, but we'll survive,"

He stood upright and turned to look at her. "You don't really like it, do you. It's too ramshackle."

"It's not that, Robbie, it's just, well..." she took his arm in hers as they walked through the straggling broom bushes towards the front door, "it's what we Highlanders want to escape from. It's derelict, it belongs to a time when the Highlands were the poor-house of Britain and no-one could afford anything new or smart. But it will do. I know you love it and I know why, so I'm not caring. Remember Ruth?"

She was smiling up at him, the red hair spilling over her old navy pullover and a bright blue scarf wound haphazardly round the soft paleness of her skin. "If you'll give it a go for the summer, I promise if we don't adore it by October we'll move out and into something of your choosing for the winter. How's that?"

"Whither thou goest..." she laughed, shaking her head.

She knew well why he loved it. It was wild. There was no other house for miles. It backed onto a hillside with a birchwood of delicate purple-stemmed tracery against the sky, one of the few old birchwoods remaining in the area after a century and a half of intensive sheep farming had claimed the woodland soils for pasture. She had seen the gleam in his eyes when they rounded the corner and it came into view. "Now that is what I call a birchwood! That is what we want to achieve at Ardvarnish," he had said admiringly. And the cottage faced across the valley, south-west into the sun and the wind, which contained nothing but mournful, undulating hills and moors for as far as the eye could see. To a young man from Tunbridge Wells it was as different from his parent's semi as a mud-hut on the Masai Mara. And it was free. They had been offered it by Jeannie Hoggett, the only person in whom Shiona had confided about the move and their engagement.

This cottage—a but and ben—had belonged to Jimmie Ban,

an old batchelor uncle of Geordie's who had been a much sought after ghillie on the river. He and his collie had survived together into their respective nineties in splendid and stubborn independence until, as if by mutual pact, they departed this life within a few days of each other. The cottage had stood empty for seven years. Geordie hoped to do it up one day and let it for self-catering holidays. It was unlettable so they were pleased to have it lived in rent free in return for Rob doing his best to stem the leaks and emulsion the water-stained ceilings.

First they had to undertake some ruthless evictions. The house had permanent residents who would depart neither willingly nor quietly. Not only did the jackdaws have designs on the chimney pot, but several generations of them had diligently filled the chimney with twigs, dead grass and leaves. It all had to be laboriously pulled out, both up and down, with an impromptu grappling iron of twisted fencing wire, Rob perched on the undulating ridge like a weather-vane and Shiona, red hair bundled up in a knotted tea-towel, collecting a fall-out of fine debris in a bucket below. Once clear and the fire lit, the cackling and cawing jackdaws circled rowdily. Then, at dawn, when the fire had died down, they maliciously tipped in new twiggery so thick and fast that by morning the rayburn could only billow smoke into the kitchen.

The fireplace in the bedroom had been boarded off and a lead hat crimped onto the chimney-pot. It was one of the first things Rob wanted to reinstate. All his life he had nurtured the image of a back-woodsman going to sleep in his lonely cabin to the flicker of the fire-light across the ceiling. It was a fantasy of wildness and adventure, a romance of the traveller and the explorer, the hunter and the frontiersman. It lurked, along with the fabulous white stag of Epping Forest, in the recesses of his inner consciousness, as irresistible now as when he was a boy. Shiona knew better than to counter his most ebullient enthusiasms. In no time at all he had lifted the lead hat and prized off the boards. To his delight the fireplace was complete and intact. He lit a newspaper and let it roar up the empty chimney. It worked. Moments later he returned with kindling and some bits of timber from the hen-house. As he layed the sticks in the old iron grate something stirred. He removed them again and peered into the dark corner of the hearth. At the back, sitting half buried in ancient red ash was an enormous toad. It stared wartily at him out of glassy eyes, motionless but for its occasionally pulsating gullet. He lifted it carefully in both hands and took it through to the kitchen. Shiona backed away.

"Isn't it magnificent?" he cried.

"No!" said Shiona meaningfully. "Where did you find it?"

"In our bedroom," he replied gleefully.

But the fire was a success. That night they climbed into the old mahogany bed, blew out the oil-lamp and lay in each other's arms watching the yellow fingers dance across the ceiling and the pine panelled walls, listening to the snap and crackle of the birch logs and the hiss of the peat.

There were also pipistrelle bats in the roof which made their way in and out beneath the corrugations of the iron sheets. To Shiona's alarm they flickered and swooped their way round the bedroom at night. A net curtain was the cure. The bats continued to hawk for moths outside the open window, but seldom attempted to enter.

High in the Glen Corran hills the golden eagles were paired and back at the eyrie on the north escarpment of Meallan Liath Mor. Mac had been watching them from the Landrover throughout February, noting their movements as he chanced to spot them while driving up and down the glen. When he had records of twenty or so sightings he spread the O.S. map on the cottage floor and plotted each one with pins and threads, from where he had first seen the speck against the winter sky to where it had wheeled or slid effortlessly out of sight behind the ridge. Several he had seen carrying sticks, and these were crucial clues. On one or two occasions he had witnessed both birds in courtship display, soaring together and tumbling, an apparently unco-ordinated jumble of talons and wings, falling together from a great height, to break and spiral upwards again on broad, finger-spread wings, or, once only, he had witnessed them tumble to the heather and mate there in the winter sunshine. Equally tell-tale were the times he had seen one of the birds crossing between the mountains in a series of huge undulations, wings half closed like a falcon on the plummeting stoop, to swerve gracefully upwards again in a wide arc, almost stalling, hanging on half-open wings before diving earthwards and into the next climb.

The simple exercise of plotting the sightings told him which of the several eyrie sites was the chosen one for this year. When Rob arrived to join him in March he knew the hen eagle would be laying eggs and together they decided to check her out. It seemed an appropriate start to his survey.

Meall an Liath Mor was no longer on Ardvarnish ground. With Dalbattigh it had passed into the undeclared management of Ko van Fensing. "Where do we stand with him at the moment," asked Rob as they trudged through the brittle heather.

"Access is no problem. He was very interested in what we were up to when I spoke to him last, but he hasn't given me a sniff of what his plans are for the estate."

"P'raps he hasn't got any."

"I think that's very probable, which is why we must get in there and convince him he should try to get some native woods coming back."

Rob was silent for a few paces and then asked "Do you think we can get Andrew to agree to a few small exclosures on poor ground the sheep don't use?" Mac shook his head and looked grim.

"He's still not speaking to me. I just don't know what's going on in his head. If we're to do it at all it has to be through van Fensing."

"There's plenty of room, for God's sake!" said Rob. "What about all the steep ground? And up the burns, and where the bracken is—that's removed from the sheep anyway it's so damned thick? Growing a few trees there would do the ground a power of good and shade some of the bracken out. If we can persuade van Fensing to start like that it shouldn't be a threat to Andrew or the sheep."

"Aye, you're right," Mac agreed. "What about Shiona? Are they talking to her again?"

"No, not a word. They've not even replied to our letter saying we were moving up. I'm afraid we've been excommunicated for the time being."

"Damned shame!"

"Aye, it is."

"Did I hear you say 'aye'?"

"Aye," said Rob with a smile.

"Well, well! So our English incomer is adopting the Highland way, is he?" Mac laughed.

"He has to!" Rob grinned . "I may not be married to her yet, but living with a Highlander is very infectious and if I'm to survive I have to adopt the mother tongue. Hey! What's that?" Rob whipped his binoculars to his eyes and scanned the moor. "Ho, ho! Mr van Fensing has a hen harrier!"

"So he has! And she's a female." Mac picked the bird up in his own glasses and they watched it waft gull-like across the heather ahead of them, twisting this way and that, never very high, swooping low and rising again, as it quartered the ground for prey. Suddenly it spun sideways and pitched into the heather and out of sight.

"Do they breed here?" Rob asked as they moved forward again.

"Not over this side. We usually have a pair out behind Carn Mor, but I've never found a nest on the sheep ground. I think it's too disturbed." As they spoke a white helicopter buzzed into view round the hump of Meallan Liath Mor. "What's this?" asked Mac. Their binoculars went up together. "It's not the charter firm van Fensing uses, but I've seen that one before. I wonder what he's up to." They watched it cross the ground like the harrier, coming well below the ridge and passing across the broad south-facing sheep walks where Andrew Duncan's ewes were hefted. It vanished round a bend in the valley and then appeared again, heading back and passing below them along the valley floor. Rob stared intently through his glasses, following it past as though it was a bird. "BF-26," he announced, reading the registration from its fuselage. "Bog Forestation."

"Bloody Hell! They've lost no time!"

"You don't think van Fensing's on board do you?" Rob asked, looking shaken. The helicopter was almost out of sight. They stared at each other for a few seconds.

"Why else would they be flying this ground?" Mac said slowly, his cheeks as pale as the pockets of old snow high on the hill above. "They came here for that very purpose, in from the east and out east again, back down the coast to Inverness. They've done nothing else but look at the Dalbattigh ground. That was no joy ride, they're up to something alright." He paused thoughtfully for a moment. "They're not interested in a shelter block here and there, they're looking for the big fish, the investor who will tie up a few thousand acres at one bite. A big scheme. That's what brings in the heavy grant money from the government. A scheme with a big management factor written into it—the sort of thing no resident landlord would go for, but which a foreigner, with no allegiance to the land or the people on it, just might."

—23—

"I never did like Dutchmen," said Dinah sourly, pulling on a Balkan cigarette in a long black holder.

"You really mean you didn't like Nigel's Dutch girl," corrected Gerry from behind the *Financial Times* as they sat on either side of the black Italian marble fireplace in the drawing room. "I don't think you know any other Dutch, do you? Unless you have a Continental lover as well as a Taffy." He couldn't resist jibing at her about an old boyfriend in the Welsh Guards with whom he had vied before they were married and who, upon the collapse of his career and his own marriage some fifteen years

later, had turned up in search of sympathy, a lonely and dejected Lieutenant Colonel with a face like a bloodhound, rejected
by wife and regiment. At what level he had received it Gerry was
unsure, but for a year or two the lugubrious Colonel had been
the cause of regular sniping between him and Dinah.

She exhaled, sending a plume of aromatic smoke high into
the room in a gesture of disdain. "She had heavy flat features,
and no manners. She was quite unsuitable." she said dismissively. "I knew it wouldn't last, Nigel has more sense and taste. This
man obviously has no manners either. Where on earth is he?"
She glanced up at the Chelsea porcelain mantle clock, "he's half
an hour late already! I don't know why I have to be here.
Couldn't Harry have handled him?"

"Certainly not! Pull yourself together for God's sake, Dinah!"
Gerry retorted crossly, crunching the newspaper into his lap
and eyeing her over the top of his spectacles with his headmas-
ter's face on. "The man has just paid us over one and a half million quid for a few thousand acres of sour old bog and bailed us
out of a very nasty spot! The very least we can do is to meet him
and answer a few questions about the place. He is going to be
our neighbour up there, we must at least try to get off on the
right foot with 'im, whatever nationality he is."

"It's still no excuse for being late," Dinah insisted as though
she had some pressing engagement she would now have to cancel. Gerry sighed in exasperation and folded up his paper,
throwing it onto the floor beside his chair. He stood up with his
back to the fireplace and his hands behind his back, rising and
falling on his toes and staring at the chandelier as if something
was wrong with it.

"He is coming from Amsterdam," Gerry laboured his words
as though talking to a difficult child, "perhaps his plane or his
train was delayed, what? It has been known to happen, you
know."

Just then the front door bell echoed through the marble hallway. Mrs Dudgeon knocked once on the drawing room door
and entered.

"Mr van Fensing to see you m'Lord."

"Please show him in, Mrs D." Gerry walked forward to greet
him. Ko appeared in the doorway looking a little unnerved at
the grandeur and formality of Denby Hall and the huge drawing room with its set of five full length portraits of Tansley-
Fairfax daughters and a 19th century Lady Denby in extravagant crinolined gowns, the lofty ribbed and medallioned plas-
terwork ceiling from which hung two enormous crystal chande-
liers, and the matching Louis Seize gilt chaise-longues and
chairs in pink and cream silk brocade.

"I'm Gerry Denby. How very nice to meet you." Gerry smiled

benevolently, shaking Ko's large hand. "And this is my wife Dinah."

"You are so gracious," Ko said, holding Dinah's ring-studded hand in both of his and bowing with a little nod and stoop of the shoulders. "You are so very kind to receive me, Lady Denby." Dinah smiled. She was almost embarrassed at this address. She couldn't remember being called gracious before. Perhaps, after all, the fellow did have some manners.

"Would you care for some tea? You've come such a long way, you must be rather hungry." She asked, reaching for the bell-pull beside the fireplace.

Mrs Dudgeon entered and spread a tablecloth over an occasional table. A girl dressed in a black tunic uniform with white apron carried in a tray. Silver teapot, silver kettle and stand, silver platters of neat cucumber and cress sandwiches, buttered scones and shortbread were laid out, and pink and blue floral cups and saucers of fine Coalport china. Mrs Dudgeon left and the girl remained to administer the English ritual.

"So what was your main interest in Dalbattigh?" Gerry asked after a few mouthfulls of sandwiches. "Are you a keen deer stalker?"

"No, I have never had that experience, but I am most keen to try. I should like to talk to your nice Mr MacDonald some more about that. If you wouldn't mind?" Ko added quickly.

"Of course not. You won't get better advice on deer than Mac'll give you. And what about the sheep? Do you have any plans for them?"

"It's too soon to say, Lord Denby, but, er, yes, I think I shall keep them going, so long as they don't lose money. I don't expect them to make much. I have a farm in Hampshire and my agricultural advisors will be looking at the sheep farm at Dalbattigh. Did you find the sheep very profitable?"

"No, no, they're certainly not that, but they do help pay the wages of someone to live there and you'll find Duncan an excellent shepherd. He's been there just about all his working life, y'know. He doesn't say much, but he's a damned fine stockman. I do hope you'll keep him and his wife on there."

"I certainly hope so too. It's good to have someone on the place who knows it so well. I have yet to meet him, the weather has been so bad, but I hear he is a very good man."

"Did Mac tell you about our plans for Ardvarnish?" Gerry asked keen to get off the subject of the Duncans.

"Yes, he did tell me something about it. I understand you are reducing the numbers of deer and growing some trees. It's very interesting. I want to know much more and would like to spend a day out with Mr MacDonald in the spring."

"Good, good! That's excellent."

"Trees interest me very much. How long do you have to wait before you can take a crop?"

"Eh what? of birch and pine, d'you mean?" Gerry sounded confused. "Won't be in our life time, that's for certain, and I hope not in my grandson's either! Although I s'pose we can cut a bit of firewood at some stage." Ko looked puzzled.

"Not in your grandson's life?" he frowned.

"Good Lord, no! A decent Caley pine's good for three hundred years. There'll be some thinnings, of course, after a hundred years or so, and we'll thin out the birches a lot sooner than that, but hopefully most of the areas we're enclosing will be permanent woods from now on."

"Oh, so you're not growing them for harvesting, for timber or for pulp or anything like that?" Ko asked, also sounding confused.

"Hell, no! We don't want any commercial forestry on Ardvarnish, it'd wreck the place. We're interested in restoring the soils and getting some of the game back, like black grouse and capercaillie."

"Oho," said Ko, a smile breaking across his round face, "I see, it's not commercial what you're doing."

"No, 'fraid not. Ardvarnish is a sporting estate and we're shoring up its future as just that. It's got very run down over the years and we're putting something back, a bit of giving rather than just taking. You must talk to Mac about it. No profit in it, I'm afraid!" Gerry said with a laugh, as if he'd given up all hope of ever making a profit on anything again.

Dinah replaced her cup on its saucer noisily and yawned a little too obviously. She stood up, rattling her bracelets. "Well, Mr van Fensing, it's been so very pleasant meeting you." She held out her hand. "I shall hope to see something of you in Scotland in the summer. I expect we'll coincide, don't you?" She didn't wait for an answer. "If you'll excuse me I must take my dog for his afternoon walk. Goodbye." Ko stood up and bowed again, shaking her hand delicately. Gerry resisted the temptation to ask whether the dog had returned from the grave.

Ko stood looking at Gerry as Dinah departed. He sat down again slowly. He didn't know what to make of this English lord. He didn't really understand what he was talking about. Not least because he had only just bought the place. He had done all the giving he planned to do for a long time. What concerned him most of all was that it shouldn't cost him anything to run and that he would be able to get his money back again, with interest, when he had finished with the place. The conversation had not gone the way he had expected. He was a little bewildered. He had imagined that anyone living as the Denbys obviously did would be arrogant—yes, aristocratic—of course, eccentric—very likely, but through it all he had been confident that he would have uncovered a common unity of hard-nosed purpose; that the bottom line would be money. Wealth. That was what the world was about, that and power.

These people could not have got to where they were without both. It was not possible that they were short of money. Not now that he had seen Denby Hall, and driven down the long avenue of beautifully maintained Spanish chestnuts, through the broad parkland with its great oaks and beeches, to discover this vast mansion at the end of the drive, a show-piece of stately opulence, adorned by its topiary yews and statues, and the forest of corbelled chimneys. The staff to greet him at the door, the chequered black and white marbled hallway and the sweeping staircase all spoke of huge wealth accumulated and enjoyed over centuries. And then the grand drawing room, and the magnificent paintings. He had expected, after the niceties of English society were over, to be able to cut through to the reality and talk straight. Perhaps now was his chance, perhaps it was not done to discuss money matters in front of one's wife?

"Lord Denby, I hope you don't mind me asking why you decided to sell Dalbattigh estate?"

Gerry was not ready for that question. Now he wished he had prepared an answer. He looked straight at Ko. Nothing showed on his face. "That's very simple," he started, "I have to put a great deal of money into the remaining thirty thousand acres at Ardvarnish to achieve what I want there, over a long time." He surprised himself how easily the answer came. "It made good sense to sell it off and re-invest the value in getting what we really want out of the ground where we have the fun."

An inner smile settled over Ko. So he was right. Money was the bottom line. This lord had his own funny ideas about restoring the land on his sporting estate and he was not prepared to dip into his liquid cash pocket to achieve them. He himself had done exactly the same in Hampshire. When he bought the farm there he had felled and sold an old oak wood in order to invest in the calf-rearing unit to bring the place into profit. Now he felt much better. It was all clear. He was not interested in the restoration programme, that was of no concern to him. Denby was obviously a much wealthier man who could afford to wait a generation or two to see the profit, or just take it in sport and enjoyment for himself and his family. He wouldn't need to operate like that—he was not in a position to. He was pleased. At least he had sorted that out.

Gerry was pleased too. The Lloyd's debacle was a humiliation. Besides, if it got out it could have serious repercussions locally. It was bad enough having to live with the slow break up of the Denby empire without admitting to having stepped into quicksand up to his neck. The answer he'd given sounded very plausible. He'd handled that well. He helped himself to another cucumber sandwich.

"Do you think the sheep farm can be brought into profit?" Ko asked, following on from his thoughts about the Hampshire farm. Gerry wasn't ready for this either.

"What? Sheep?" He spluttered with his mouth full. "Well, yes, I suppose so, if you watch the costs very carefully. The market isn't very good just now," Gerry suddenly thought better of that tack. He mustn't put the man off. "But Duncan the shepherd always gets the top prices for his lambs. You can't do better than that y'know," he nodded reassuringly. "And there's the subsidies and quotas and things like that. There's good money in those. You'll have to talk to Duncan about all that business."

"Aha, yes, of course, but you're not staying in sheep yourself?"

"Well, no, we're not." Gerry sensed a trap. What was this man trying to make him say? He trod warily, searching for a way out. "And you've got all the good sheep land now, our side of the glen doesn't get as much sun as yours—not much use for sheep," he added with a benevolent grin. He was even more pleased with that.

'This man is not a fool,' thought Ko. He was now deeply suspicious that the sheep were unprofitable and in decline and there was more to Denby shedding the sheep land than he was admitting. He had already made up his own mind that there were probably better options to pursue. The nice company with the helicopter had impressed him. They had good ideas, and the management skills to run the place without bothering him. He wondered whether to ask Denby about them. It was on the tip of his tongue.

"Andrew Duncan's a good man," Gerry continued, "he's one of the best and he's very much part of the community there—keen member of the church—all that sort of thing. He'll be a big help to you. He knows everybody for miles around."

Ko nodded. That wasn't what Bog Forestation had said. They'd said he was a difficult man, and surly with it, and that he would do well to close the sheep unit down before it lost any more money. Maybe Denby was just as keen to get shot of the man as the sheep? Perhaps the whole sale was because this man and his sheep were proving to be a headache? There was more to this, he was sure of that. No, he wouldn't ask Denby about Bog Forestation. That might not be such a smart idea.

"Lord Denby, you have been very helpful indeed. I am sorry to have taken up so much of your valuable time." Ko rose to his feet. Gerry reached out to press the bell. Mrs Dudgeon appeared instantly.

"Please show Mr van Fensing to his car," said Gerry, and to Ko, "it has been a pleasure to meet you. I look forward to seeing you again in Scotland. Don't hesitate to get in touch if there's anything more you need to know, my dear fellow." He held out his hand.

When the taxi was out of sight Dinah returned to the drawing room. Gerry was leaning against the mantle staring pensively into the fire.

"I suppose he could have been a lot worse. Where did he get his money from, did you find that out?"

"No, I didn't as a matter of fact..." Gerry shook his head despairingly without looking up. 'Just like her mother,' he thought, and then continued, "...and I'm sorry you couldn't spare more than ten minutes of your precious time with him. I trust the reincarnated hound is feeling better for his walkies?"

"I gave him tea, didn't I? What more did you want?"

Gerry didn't bother to answer. Something was troubling him. What did he mean 'You're not staying in sheep yourself?' Surely to God van Fensing hadn't already made up his mind to get out of sheep? Something was afoot. He had a queasy feeling that he had just been checked out and that he had himself fallen into a trap.

Rob and Mac had maps spread all over the floor in the Keeper's Cottage. They were dividing the estate into sectors for survey, to perform a systematic examination of the ground from the river to the high tops, collating data on vegetation and wildlife, which would be the primary task for Rob to undertake that spring and summer.

Mac went through to the kitchen to answer the phone. Rob drew heavy red lines across the map, naming and numbering each sector after a prominent feature or an event in each one. 'Eagle Carn 1&2' he wrote for the north corries on Carn Mor, and 'Alder Challenge' for the river flats where he had witnessed the two stags locked in combat. 'Forbes's Ruin' he named the open moor where he had found the poisoned eagles. Mac came in again.

"Oh...what next!" he said, flopping down in a chair. "That was his Lordship. He's just had van Fensing to see him in Yorkshire and he thinks he's up to no good."

"What d'you mean?"

"He doesn't really know, more a feeling than anything. Their meeting went well enough, but the boss says he's left with a nagging worry that van Fensing was checking him out before doing something—perhaps something which could rebound on us."

"Like what?"

"Like turfing out the Duncans and selling the sheep!"

Rob gasped. "Oh God, no! Why would he do that?"

"To plant it rigid with sitka spruce and lodgepole pine—the worst possible option for us." Rob was silent for a minute.

"Did you tell Denby about the helicopter?" he asked.

"Aye, I did. He was horrified. He said it confirmed his worst suspicions. We've got to stop van Fensing, somehow. I don't know, Rob. I just don't know how to tackle this." Mac gazed distractedly across the room. The words 'Forbes's Ruin' caught his eye. "Hmph!" he shrugged, "not just Forbes, the way things are going!"

Rob was on his knees folding up the maps, shuffling them together as quickly as he could. He knew he had to do something. The top map was Dalbattigh. It glared up at him, daring him to take up its cause, to fight for it alongside Shiona whom he loved and for their shared love of the place. There on the map was the little Duncan cottage, the fank and the burn. There was the old settlement where he had wanted to kiss her for the first time, with the word 'ruins', a cryptic admission of the past in this harsh and beautiful place. A deep sadness came over him. What had changed? A few less people, but still the same struggle for possession, still the same tangle of motives and opportunities, the rich and powerful manipulating the fortunes of the poor and powerless, the pawns in an endless game of landed chess.

Shiona was one of those. She had broken free, it was true, stepped outside and met the world head on, but she was still Andrew and Mairi Duncan's daughter, born of these hills with their mysterious Gaelic names. He was caught up in its magic and its drama, in Shiona with her wild red hair and snowy skin, her gentle femininity and her hot Gaelic passion. And in the place, the whispering alders at the river bank, the contorted old pines with their jig-saw bark and twisting orange limbs up inside the dark needly crowns, the last of the trees of old Caledonia which had watched the clans come and go, and felt the chill wind of the defeat of Gaeldom blow through the land after Culloden. The same trees had seen the Dalbattigh evictions and the broken people trailing past, watched the English landlords arrive with their loud voices and stove-pipe hats, horses, carriages, and carts, with teams of masons and joiners to build the Lodge in the height of her Imperial Majesty's baronial fashion.

He was enraptured, too, by the wildlife. The sharp-billed heron poised at the edge of the Falls Pool, and the shy otter bitch, returning to her three kits in the holt under the water worn roots of a knotty alder, and the golden eagles back on Meallan Liath Mor, building their huge nest of heathery twigs as if they had never been persecuted at all. And the red deer, favoured quarry of the powerful until Gerry Denby saw the lack of the wood for the trees and began his own brand of evictions. And the land itself; the high, wind-moaning corries and moors, places of solitude and majesty. He could not stand passively by in wooden indifference to Shiona, nor to her people, nor could he ignore his conscience which tugged peacelessly at him.

"What are you doing?" asked Mac, sensing a new mood.

"I'm going home to collect Shiona. I'm taking her down to see her father and we are going to tell him together that if he doesn't do something quickly to endear himself to this bloody man van Fensing, he will be be out."

"But what can he do?" Mac threw up his arms in a gesture of hopelessness.

Rob stood up and pulled on his old khaki coat. "I don't know, Mac. But I do know this. If we don't do something we are going to be too late. If those forestry people have got their hooks into van Fensing it will be for the biggest scheme they can possibly sign him up to. Most of that ground is plantable—ripe for it!" He swept a wave at the Dalbattigh map. "And look what they've done to a dozen other glens up and down the Highlands. You can't tell me there'll be any room left for an economically viable sheep unit. Of course there bloody won't! Shiona's folks will either be sent packing now, or squeezed out more slowly and painfully as the scheme devours the ground.

"Andrew Duncan may be an awkward bugger, but he deserves a chance to have a say in his own future and that of his family. I don't like what sheep have done to this land, you know I don't, but I can't stand by and watch the only means of a livelihood for these people in this glen stripped away without a word in protest.

"You know, Mac, that meeting in Corran Bridge was great! It was damned good! It was real people expressing real feelings, although I could have wished it went in another direction. We got a bloody nose that night because Alec MacFee knew something we didn't, but for all that it was good. Do you know what it tells me?"

"Go on." Mac was listening intently.

"It tells me that these people really care about their land. Their land! It *is* their land, for God's sake, not van Fensing's or Denby's or mine, or yours for that matter! It's theirs. They're the poor sods who have to eeck a miserable living off it against the the the pissing rain and the wind and the acid soils and the damned deer chewing the hell out of everything that grows. Why would they do that if they didn't care for it? They love it, Mac. They love it because it's in their bones and their veins and the pits of their bellies. It's what's kept them alive all these centuries of being buggered about by politics and power in the hands of people who don't know what it means to turn the sod and mix your own dung with that of your cow and dig it into the soil in order to grow a bloody potato!

"I'm in it up to here." He whisked a finger across his brow. "I love that girl and she loves this place. That's rubbed off on me and just as I would go to the wall for her, so I will for this place. If we lose, we lose. But at least I will have had a go."

"You're right, Robbie, man, you're dead right! I never thought the day would come that I'd fight to keep sheep on these hills, but we can't just turf the folk out in the name of progress and enlightenment. Ever since the meeting I've been thinking about it. It's wrong because the man's so damned good at it. He's the best for miles around. We have to find a way of keeping folk like Andrew in the glens. I'm with you, you can tell that to your bonny red-headed lassie."

—24—

"—Slow down, Robbie! It's into the river we'll be in a minute!"

"We must catch them at their tea. If he's eating he won't just get up and storm out when we arrive." The car lurched round the corner of the single track road, down into the dips and up again to the tarmac horizon with no clue of anything coming the other way.

He had arrived at their cottage so flushed and angry she was alarmed. "We have to do this! Just get your coat and come." In the car he explained about van Fensing and the forestry threat. "But we're not even knowing if it's really going to happen," she argued, "are we not jumping to conclusions?"

"Yes, we are, but if we don't get to your father first, he will be led into a confrontation with van Fensing by some of those other bastards in Corran Bridge— Bob MacHurdle and his crowd, who will go to the papers and there'll be a right good row. Nothing will turn van Fensing against your folks quicker than that. We must persuade your father to put a well-argued case for keeping the sheep to van Fensing now, up front, in such a way that he can't ignore it. We can help him with that, and we can pull in Denby and Mac to back him up. It's a chance, Shiona, a slim one perhaps, but a chance we can't afford to miss if we're to be able to hold our heads up in this glen in the years to come."

The old van was there, and Andy's pick-up. They scuffed to a halt on the loose stone track. There was frenzied barking from within the dog shed. Shiona shivered as a chill wave passing over her: she wanted to see her parents again, and her brother, but she dreaded it. The cold looks, the silences. It was all so familiar, and the years of rows with her father had left their mark.

Rob thumped heavily on the door, and entered without waiting, passing straight through the tiny hall and into the kitchen. Three astonished faces stared at them. They were sitting together round the little table, Andy with his fork poised and cabbage falling from it like autumn leaves. Andrew's hands were pinned to the table with knife and fork protruding emptily, Mairi raised a hankie to her mouth and held it there. No-one spoke.

Shiona's eyes flew over their faces, the table, the white and blue ringed china, the kettle murmuring on the Rayburn, the yellowing wall-paper of tiny, imaginary flowers, the old dresser painted white once, now a dull cream; the clutter of bills stuffed into jam-jars with pens and coins and paper clips. Nothing had changed. It was all so familiar, so predictable. There was the teapot with the glued lid she had repaired herself aged twelve, the curled and stained photograph of a school girl in navy blue skirt and pullover, knobbly knees and white socks, still stuck into the corner of a picture frame. Was that really her? Was the same girl standing here now?

"I'm sorry for bursting in on you like this," Rob began, "but we've got something important to say to you all....".

Andy leapt to his feet, cutting him off with the harsh scrape of the chair. "I'll not listen to your rubbish!" he growled with his mouth full. He made towards the door, pushing past Rob. He found himself face to face with his sister. "Get out of my way, Shiona! I'll not stay in this house with the two of you."

Shiona was unprepared for this from her brother— her father, yes, but Andy had never been hostile to her. He had always lived his own life neither asking nor requiring approval from her or his family. She had never passed judgement on him and she didn't expect it in return. Her rage was instantaneous. The blood vanished from her face and she took a step back to block the door. Rob saw the defiance burning in her eyes, the set of her lips austere as they were that day in Lairg. As Andy came on, lifting his hand for the latch, Shiona pushed him angrily on the chest, and he reeled back towards his chair, his mouth open and eyes round with shock and disbelief.

"You'll not speak to me like that, Andy Duncan!" she cried

fiercely, still advancing, "not in this house nor anywhere else. Sit down! I belong to this family every bit as much as you do and I'll not be shut out nor yet ignored until I've had my say."

Rob opened his mouth and shut it again. This was his girl. This was the Shiona who had torn him to shreds that day in Lairg. She was invincible then and he knew it would be a mistake to interrupt her now. A smile came into his eyes. It was far, far better coming from her.

"Now you listen to me, all of you! You should know that van Fensing has already spoken to Bog Forestation and we think he has plans to put the sheep off, and you with it, and plant up the whole of Dalbattigh. We don't want that, Lord Denby doesn't want that, nor yet does Mac. It's on your side we are, and we want to be allowed to support you in a bid to stay on here." She paused. No-one moved a muscle.

"As I'm seeing it you have two choices: either you'll let us help you, or you go it alone—and I'm not thinking you have a hope in hell on your own. Mac and Lord Denby are most likely the only ones van Fensing will listen to, if it's not already too late. Now, will you let us help or won't you? Make your choice! We'll go away, or we'll stay and fight this with you like a family should. Which is it to be, Father? It's your job that's in it, and your home."

There was silence. It had taken her father days to recover from the broadside he received when she left home three years before and he knew better than to challenge her now. He had no words. He looked across at his son to see if Andy was about to make a counter attack. There was nothing. Andy too, knew when he was beaten. He was shocked. His sister had never raised her voice to him since they were teenagers wrangling over who should have the fun of standing in the wool sack doing the treading and who should have the much harder task of passing the fleeces up. None of his women had ever spoken to him like that, far less pushed him. Father and son shared clear, unspoken views about women. Their place was in the home, they should adopt a subordinate role to their menfolk and never, under any circumstances, contradict them. Mairi was their model. Andy had always sought out characterless girls who were easy victims to his rough hands and demanding masculinity. From that first hot summer night when, aged seventeen, he had discovered how to dominate a girl by trapping her in his powerful arms, smothering her with purposeful roving hands and rough wind-chapped lips, he had never failed. He had an ever-growing reputation in a small community so that no girl who returned his predatory eye was in any doubt about what to expect. 'Andy the Bull' he was, and that was fine by him.

He had no defence for, nor even experience of a defiant

woman. His mother had been unable to control or discipline him from the age of ten, and he had learned to keep clear of his father and do what he liked. He could think of nothing say. He japped his fork into a boiled potato and thrust the whole thing into his mouth as if to provide himself with an excuse for his silence.

"...I think we should all have a cup of tea," said Mairi, but still glued to her seat and quite unable to make a move. "I think that's a very good idea," Shiona said, raising the Rayburn lid and sliding the kettle across onto the hot-plate. "I'll do it, Mother. Stay you where you are." And then she turned to Rob. "Tell them what's happened."

"Did you see that helicopter two days ago?"

"Aye." grunted Andrew. Andy nodded imperceptibly.

"Good!" said Rob. "So you know how closely it looked at the ground here." He didn't wait for a reply. "Well, Mac and I watched it through binoculars and we think van Fensing was on board. Now, why would they have spent that time and money with van Fensing looking at this ground if they weren't trying very hard to sign him up to a major scheme? Not three hours ago he was in Yorkshire at Denby Hall. He was there to find out whether or not the sheep here are profitable. Mac spoke to Denby only an hour ago, who said he was very worried indeed that van Fensing had already made up his mind to put the sheep off and go into forestry. Not just a block here and a block there, but the whole place, Andrew," he paused, sweeping his arm upwards, "from the roadside here right up the hill to fifteen hundred feet and ring-fenced the entire length of the strath. Maybe as much as five miles of continuous plantation of sitka spruce and lodgepole pine from down below the falls pool right up through all your best grazings to the top of the Dalbattigh settlement. If you're very lucky you'd be left with the two river parks and a ten foot strip on the verge between the fence and the road. Enough ground for fifty ewes —only if you're lucky!"

There was silence.

"How are you so bothered?" demanded Andrew, his voice still acid with hostility. "You've already put the sheep off the south side. I've no' got a single ewe left on Carn Mor because of you and your damned conservation. You're no better than Bog Forestation yourself! If you had your way there'd be trees sprouting all over the grazings. Why should I listen to you?" The bitterness and confusion showed on his face and in his voice. His words came in staccato bursts as they had at the public meeting. Rob knew he had a long way to go.

"Andrew, it was never part of Mac's conservation plan to split this estate in half nor yet to put the sheep off altogether. All he wanted was to reduce the grazing pressure on the south side of the glen and to get some wild trees growing there for the exhausted soils. He wanted to concentrate the sheep on the north side with the best sunlight and the better soils because of your re-seeding. You must believe what I say. He had no hand in the estate being sold up. That was just bad luck. Denby got himself too thinly spread— he ran short of money and had to do something—I don't know the details any better than you do. The sale came as a terrible shock to us. A bitter blow—especially after that damned meeting. How do you think we felt about it?" He looked from face to face, letting his words sink in before pressing on. "I can tell you this, Mac and Janet were all for throwing it in and leaving the glen. —Anyway, all that's behind us now, that's past. We can't put the clock back. The estate is sold. Van Fensing has bought it, and I'm here to tell you that Shiona and myself and Mac together, and Lord Denby along with us, do not want you to be put off the hill and out of this house after all the years of work you've put into it, all of you! We do not want to see the Dalbattigh sheep stock—one of the best in the whole of the north—broken up and sold. And we don't want to see the best hill-farming ground in this strath ploughed up and down in parallel lines and planted stiff with trees forevermore."

He looked down. "And quite apart from all of that, I love your daughter and we plan to get married sometime soon." His voice dropped almost to a whisper, "I just couldn't live with myself if I stood by and watched her family evicted from this strath when there is a chance that we can do something to prevent it."

Andy and his father eyed each other blankly for several seconds. Andy spoke first. "And what would that be?" he growled, still chewing.

"We have to get to van Fensing as a united force, with the full backing of the community and Lord Denby, and to make it clear to him that he's not going to get away with it."

"That's the tea, now," Shiona poured the kettle into the old brown pot exactly as she had done a thousand times before. Her mother rose to her feet. "I'm awful glad you came, Shiona lassie, awful glad," she said with a voice hovering on the edge of tears. As she and her daughter hugged each other Andrew leaned forward to cut himself a large slice of fruit cake. Rob knew they had done the right thing.

"You've a real problem with the community," said Andy astutely, adopting a more conciliatory tone, at least with Rob. "That meeting did you a power of harm," he added. "No-one down the glen believes you didn't know about the sale. MacDonald's hated here now. He's seen to be the one that's caused all this, along with yourself, Rob. And most of the glen folk'll think that plantation trees is better than wild trees. At least there's work in plantations. There's no living in birch-woods."

"I know all that," said Rob. "I know it's going to be an uphill struggle, but it's important to tackle these things one at a time. Conservation has its problems, there's no doubt about that, especially with people and jobs. But the problem we're fighting is the one of the sheep and the forestry."

"And what makes you think van Fensing'll go for a big scheme?" asked Andrew.

"I don't really know," Rob said. "It's a gut feeling I have about the helicopter and about the guy himself. You see, he's not interested in sheep or sport or any traditional land use here. He's just a speculator. Highland sporting estates have done very well these past few years. Their value's gone up and up and up. I just have a feeling that he's in it for what he can get. He's been told he won't get much out of the sheep.

"You know better than anyone else, Andrew, what bad prices hill stock have fetched these past few years. That's the last thing he wants. Whereas the schemes Bog Forestation are offering carry big sums of taxpayer's money. They're investment schemes—nothing to do with producing good timber or looking after the land, or its people, or the wildlife or anything else. They're hard-nosed investment schemes for profit. That's what they are. They're for making money for Bog Forestation and for the investor who buys the land. That's what van Fensing's inter-ested in."

"Aye, well, you could be right there," said Andrew.

Shiona added, "Ach, it's a right muddle to understand," she said. "People were cleared out of the glens in the first place to make way for the sheep, now it's the sheep that still have a few jobs in them, but everybody knows that's been dwindling for years and there's not likely to be the money in it to keep anoth-er generation of folk up the glens. And seemingly the choice is either conservation schemes with jobs twenty or thirty years away, or forestry schemes which might produce a bit of work now but are likely to go damaging the land so that our grand-children can't grow anything here. Isn't that it Rob?"

"Yep! That's about the sum of it."

Shiona went on, "If I wasn't engaged to Robbie and had the chance to learn a bit about it all, I wouldn't have clue what was going on."

"So you don't believe in all this conservation stuff," Andy challenged, his courage beginning to return.

"I believe in it because I believe in Robbie," she replied qui-etly and openly. "But I do believe that conservation can live with good sheep farming, and deer stalking and grouse shooting, and all the wildlife and tourism and the other things that have gone on around us all our lives, whereas I can't see blanket forestry living with any of those."

"Yes, that's right." Rob agreed. "Close plantation forestry is very exclusive. It really doesn't allow anything much else to go on. It consumes a lot of deer wintering ground and grouse moor as well as the best sheep ground, and it harbours foxes and hoodies which then just destroy the grouse numbers and harrass the lambs. You shouldn't be in any doubt which is the friendlier of the two options. You've only to look around the Highlands to see how many glens are now dominated by forestry. And while they may have produced a few jobs during the planting, they haven't produced jobs to keep families like this one living in glens, that's for sure."

"Aye, aye. You're right enough there," Andrew nodded.

But it was already too late. Van Fensing had made the phone call. His lawyers had confirmed to Bog Forestation that very afternoon that he would sign up to the big scheme they had proposed to him in the helicopter. In their thick-pile-carpeted and knotty-pine-panelled Board Room a twelve year old bottle of single malt whisky had its golden seal cracked and the glasses chinked in celebration. Van Fensing returned to his similarly plush ofice in Amsterdam well pleased with his Highland acquisition.

Rob and Shiona left the Dalbattigh cottage in high spirits. It was a huge relief that it had gone so well. They too had shared a dram with the whole family and laid plans for a campaign which would raise the profile of the whole issue. Now they hurried to tell Mac and Janet about it.

"Hullo there! Hullo!" Rob called as he burst through the front door. There was no reply. Shiona followed him in without hesitation as they had done on dozens of occasions. Rob crossed the hall and stuck his head round the kitchen door. The lights were on and the lid of a stock-pot rattled a steamy tattoo from the stove. There was no-one there. "Try the sitting room," Rob said. At that moment the sitting room door opened and Mac's face appeared.

"Who's making all this noise in my house?" his half-smile seemed to lack his usual enthusiasm at their arrival. "Come on in," he said, and turned back to the room. "It's Rob and Shiona," he said to Janet. "Will you take a dram?" he asked with a wave to the bottle and glasses on the sideboard.

"Yes, please," said Rob, "we've got something to celebrate."

"Great!" said Mac, but Shiona intuitively knew that he didn't mean it. She saw with a glance that Janet was kneeling beside the fire, her eyes red with crying and her hair dishevelled. She quickly touched Rob's elbow with a worried look towards the fireplace. Rob hesitated.

"So what have you got to celebrate?" Mac asked holding out two glasses. "You both take water don't you?" He dribbled some water into their golden liquid.

"We've just been to see my folks, and we've made the peace."

"Good. Good," said Mac. "But that's great news. Come, sit down and tell us all about it."

Rob was uneasy. He knew they'd walked in on something. He was too fond of them both to act out a charade. "Mac, I can see this is a bad moment. I'm sorry we've burst in on you like this. I hope there's nothing wrong?"

"Ach, no." said Mac shaking his head. Janet smiled a wan, hollow smile; she remained kneeling and silent by the fire. Rob knew not to press them further.

"That's really great about your folks," said Mac. "I'm that pleased, Shiona." His voice was sincere; yet they knew he was distracted. He looked tired and stretched by something which had removed all his natural sparkle and brought Janet to tears.

"Are the children alright?" Shiona asked, now worried herself.

"Oh, aye, they're fine. Look, don't worry about us. We're okay. You're right, Robbie, it is a bad moment, but I'm very pleased with your news. We both are."

Rob knocked back his whisky and put the glass down on the sideboard. Shiona left hers unfinished. Somehow the taste for whisky had evaporated. Rob turned towards the door. "We'll see you soon, Mac."

They climbed into the car without a word and set off down the track. "What on earth was going on there?"

"I don't know," said Rob, " and I don't like it. I've never seen either of them like that before, especially Janet. She never spoke a word."

"No, I know. D'you think it was a row?"

"I don't think so. I've never heard them row. They're both such resilient characters I think if they fought it'd be hurling saucepans and slamming doors. I don't think it would be like that."

"No," said Shiona, "I agree."

It took them seventeen minutes to reach Corran Bridge. As they drove up to the crossroads they saw old Lachie Gunn leave the bar and hobble out into the road. To their surprise he flagged them down with his stick. As Shiona wound down the window he thrust his jaw forward, unshaven for several days and almost toothless. "It's Mac on the phone for you, Rob, in the hotel."

Rob pulled over and left the car without a word. He ran into the foyer and snatched up the dangling phone. "Mac? It's Rob. What is it, Mac?"

"I'm so sorry to do that to you, Rob. You know the both of you are always welcome in our house but I just couldn't bring myself to speak to you in front of Janet just then."

There was a pause and he heard his friend take a deep breath. "The thing is Rob, she's been called back to hospital. They've found something."

"What d'you mean, *something*, Mac?" Rob's voice reduced to a chill monotone.

"Something's shown up on a smear, Rob. It's cancer of the cervix, and I think she's got to have the lot out."

"Oh, my God!" said Rob. "Oh, Mac, I am so sorry."

"I think it's no worse that that, but we only found out this afternoon and it's shaken us both. I'm afraid we weren't very hospitable...."

—25—

The Highland spring arrived late and lasted only a week. The whole of April and most of May were more properly a part of winter than of spring. The delicate birch buds spread into first leaf in stinging squalls of sleet, and the new-born lambs at Dalbattigh stood and shivered in a bitter north-east wind. In the last week of May the wind withdrew to the Arctic and warm air flooded up from the Azores giving sunshine and heat to the long hours of daylight and the bright blue skies.

The wren was nesting deep in the wood pile Rob had built behind the cottage. Encouraged by strong sun the tiny bird perched on a rusty fence wire and spilled from that miniscule gullet a bubbling stream of song, louder and more jubilant than birds ten times its size. Cock chaffinches glowing pink in the strong light sat in the birches and trilled lustily. A hare thought she had hidden her three leverets unseen in the tussocky grass at the end of the little garden. Rob and Shiona watched them every morning from their bedroom window.

April had been a bad month. The daffodils which had

emerged as an unplanned surprise all round the cottage, had been broken by the wind and flattened beneath sudden drifts of overnight snow and Shiona rescued them in armfulls and filled the little cottage with extemporary vessels of bulging yellow; milk bottles, jam jars, a child's plastic bucket, a saucepan without a handle, a white enamel bread bin and even a polythene carrier-bag hung on a nail on the back of the kitchen door, which, like the roof, slowly dripped water onto the floor—all crammed with strident yellow trumpets as if to compensate for the lack of sunlight outside. The cottage abandoned its cosy winter smell of peat and woodsmoke and assumed the heady green fragrance of a flower shop.

It was as though the season was bewildered; uncertain whether to go back to winter or to push on into spring. High in the hills fresh snow filled the corries and thawed again every few days so that the Corran river persistently roared.

Lambing had been difficult. Just at the moment when Andrew had hoped to be able to boast high results, the percentage was right down. He withdrew into himself more than usual. The little kitchen at Dalbattigh echoed with the bleating of weakling lambs which surrounded the Rayburn in cardboard boxes in an often vain attempt to keep them in life, after only a few hours in the withering wind and the icy rain. On his way to his work at Ardvarnish, Rob dropped Shiona to help her mother with the circuitous chore of bottle feeding. Every morning there were little corpses to bury and more limp waifs brought in from the hill.

No-one knew whether the campaign to influence Ko van Fensing had had any effect or not. With slightly subdued support from Mac, Rob and Shiona had gone with Andrew and Andy to see Willie Ritchie and Bob MacHurdle. They had suggested another public meeting, but the response had been less than luke-warm. Bob MacHurdle lost no time in telling Mac and Rob that their credibility in the glen had evaporated forever. "You'll not get the folk in this glen to join in with your mad conservation schemes," he exclaimed with force.

"But that's not what we want the meeting for," Rob insisted, "it's to help Andrew. Same as before, the concern is about the loss of the sheep. You should be just as worried yourself, " he urged.

"Well then, Andrew can call the meeting like before, but you'll not get folk to turn out to listen to you two. I'll tell you that right now." Bob seemed to wrap each of his words in malice and contempt. The grazings he rented from Ardvarnish were north of the Corran and had been sold with Dalbattigh. He was determined to blame them. "The whole business is your fault. If you'd not come up with your crazy scheme Lord Denby would never have split the estate."

"That is rubbish!" said Mac angrily. As he did so they knew that any chance of getting the community united was lost. Willie Ritchie helpfully suggested that the best they could do now was to lobby those councillors who would listen and to talk to the local press.

"Aye, we'll do that anyway," said Andrew, "but Lord Denby's away to see van Fensing himself first and we don't want to antagonise the man until we know which way he's going to jump.

Gerry had fared no better. He had telephoned van Fensing in his office in Amsterdam and invited him to lunch in the Guard's Club next time he was in London. Van Fensing politely declined. Having already experienced the inhibiting pomp which surrounded the Lord Denby, and suspicious that Gerry wanted to bend his ear, he countered with an offer to meet in a rather mediocre but central hotel in Kensington. Gerry went. Two hours later he left empty handed but for an indifferent lunch of over-roast pork and stewed cabbage and an over-polite assurance from the now rather cool Ko van Fensing that what he had had to say would be carefully considered. Gerry knew that he'd blown it. It depressed him and he took it out on the cab driver by refusing to give him a tip as he stomped into his club to phone Mac.

"He listened, but that's all," he said. "It looks bad to me. I don't think he had any intention of taking any notice of anything any of us has to say. You'd better tell Duncan that the prospects of a reprieve are bleak."

"Did he give you any indication of what he was going to do, Lord Denby?" Mac enquired earnestly.

"No, not a thing, old man. I don't even know who's acting for him."

Andrew did. Roddie the Post thrust the bundle of letters into his hand as they met on the single track road. "It's a grand day that's in it now" said Roddie. "You'll be pleased for the lambs," he added, as he pulled away, leaving Andrew fingering the white envelope with the Edinburgh post-mark. It was from a firm of factor-lawyers specialising—so the enclosed information card said—in the management of sporting estates, woodlands and farms throughout Scotland. The letter was brief and to the point. A Mr Anthony Galbraith had been appointed, and the owners of Dalbattigh—now mysteriously plural—had decided to embark upon a series of commercial forest plantings with the locally based firm, Bog Forestation. Work would commence immediately and Mr Galbraith himself would soon be visiting

Glen Corran to discuss the future of the sheep unit in detail. Andrew knew in his bones what that meant.

After the initial shock, Mac and Janet had accepted the roll of the dice with dignity and calm. Janet travelled back and forwards to Inverness for tests, sometimes away for two or three nights at a time. Shiona met the school bus and escorted little Michael and Karen home to the Keeper's Cottage to give them their supper and get them off to bed in their mother's absence. Rob never heard a word of complaint from Mac or Janet, although anxiety increased for all of them when the date of the operation was brought forward a month sooner than they expected. Rob and Shiona agreed to move to the Keeper's Cottage when the time came for Janet to go in. Mac would stay down in Inverness until the operation was over. There was nothing anyone could do or say except Jessie MacChattin at the shop who had lost no time in fabricating sinister embellishments, titbits of spiteful and macabre speculation with which to feed her circle of parasitic gossips.

Buying a bag of caster sugar for her mother in the store one day Shiona overheard Jessie say to Megan MacHurdle, "Of course, they say that sort of cancer can be self-inflicted. I'm told it's to do with the number of partners."

"Aye, I've heard that too," said Megan, shaking her head.

"They say it's spread all over now. There's nothing can be done about it."

"Is that right? What a shame, with wee ones at school as well. It'll just be a matter of time then?" Megan questioned in a voice which begged for more details. Shiona, in her disgust, tossed the bag onto the counter in front of Jessie so that it burst, sugar showering in all directions, turned and stormed from the shop leaving the bell clanging angrily. The two women watched her get into the car and drive away.

"That girl's got a wicked temper. I've heard she's violent with it, too," said Jessie.

"Aye, so they say, so they say," nodded Megan, not wishing to admit that she had never heard anything of the sort.

Rob was sitting on a high heathery knoll looking down over the eastern sheep walk below Meall an Chollie, a mile from Dalbattigh. He had come here every morning for five days to wait for the hen harrier to leave the nest to feed herself and preen. It was good sitting in the sun. He was doing what he enjoyed most of all, on his own, out on the hill, working in direct contact with the wildlife he cherished. There was only one pair of harriers nesting in the whole strath and he was determined to monitor their progress from the laying of the first egg to the chicks fledging and exposing themselves to the ruthless persecution still practiced on so many estates. He had erected a brown canvas hide on a light aluminium frame about a hundred yards away from the nest and was moving it in closer to the site every day. The hide now stood only fifteen yards from the nest and so far both birds had ignored its presence. After more than an hour of waiting the hen bird stood up, looked about her and lifted off into the breeze to waft away over the ridge on nonchalant wings. Rob jumped to his feet and ran down to the nest. There were five dirty white eggs in a twiggy scrape well-hidden in deep heather. He quickly moved the hide in another few yards and climbed inside it to see whether the nest was yet visible. It wasn't. He would have to move it at least once more to get it right up close. He pushed the four corner pegs down into the peat with his foot, tightened the guys and withdrew to his heathery knoll as speedily as he could.

The harrier was only away for a few minutes. Rob spoke softly into his pocket dictaphone, enunciating his words slowly and meticulously. He started with his position; he noted the purpose of his visit; how many yards he had moved the hide and at what time of day; how long the hen bird was off the nest; and the fact that he had seen no sign of the male at all that morning. He fixed his binoculars on the hen bird as she stood preening beside her eggs. The heather around was too tall for detail and he could only just see her. A few seconds later she settled down onto the eggs and she disappeared from view. He glanced at his watch and spoke the time into his recorder. Once again she had taken no notice of the hide in its new position. "All going according to plan; turned for home at 10.47 am." He clicked the machine off and slid it back into the breast pocket of his camouflage jacket. He rose slowly and carefully and crawled down the back of the knoll into dead ground and away from the site.

Andrew knew he was out there somewhere. He stood on the roadside above the falls pool his eyes raking the hill in the hope of seeing him. Rob saw him first. He hurried on down the hill. "Aye, aye, Andrew!" he called, striding across the sheep-cropped sward towards the road. "What's up?"

"I think you should have a read of this, Rob." He held out the letter.

"Damn and blast!" Rob cursed as he read it. "Right! Andrew. We have no alternative now but to use the papers and stir up a right good row."

"I don't like the look of it, Robbie, lad. I think my days are numbered, papers or no papers."

"Oh, come on, Andrew, don't give up now. You can get decisions reversed if you work at it. You of all people mustn't falter now."

"Aye, that's all very well for a young fella like you, but I've not much fight left. I've seen this sort of thing happen over and over again down the years. It's always the people that come off worst. This'll be no different, you'll see. The likes of me and you can't touch van Fensing or Denby or any of the rich folk. It's no good, I'm telling you."

"Well, I'm not giving up, and Shiona won't either. One thing I'll make damned sure of is that the world knows that blanket forestry is the worst thing possible for this glen and its people."

Rob meant what he said. The story broke in the *Northern Gazette* with a front page headline 'It's a scandal!' A day later it was picked up by the other five Highland papers extending as far out as the Western Isles, Orkney and Shetland and Aberdeen. At the week-end a national Sunday contained a two-page feature on how people were still being cleared from Highland glens by large scale schemes funded from the public purse. Lord Denby appeared on the Scottish news and van Fensing declined to be interviewed. In the space of a week Ardvarnish and Dalbattigh became familiar names which tripped off the tongues of local radio commentators and dominated converstion in hotel bars across Scotland. A steady trickle of inquisitive visitors appeared in the glen. Many made the mistake of gleaning misinformation from Jessie at the stores which rapidly led to a rash of newspaper articles and reports which confused the issue so badly that even those who thought they knew what were the rights and wrongs, began to argue and disagree.

An embarrassed Mr Galbraith, in sports jacket, check shirt and corduroy trousers, gave an uncomfortable interview on Grampian television in which he stated that the sheep were unprofitable and regretfully had to go. Van Fensing had not budged. "Who is causing all this trouble?" he barked down the telephone to Galbraith.

"It seems to be that Bird Protection man who is living with Duncan's daughter. He's got the whole place stirred up."

"Have you been to see Mr Duncan?"

"Yes, twice, although it's a bit of a waste of time. He's the most uncommunicative devil I've ever met. I might as well talk to his sheep."

"Have you served notice on him that we'll be selling the sheep this summer? When is it the big sales are?"

"Yes, I have. The Lairg sales are in August."

"Oh yes. How did he take it?"

"Hard to say really. He shrugged his shoulders as if he was expecting it anyway. He didn't actually say anything."

"That's good. Maybe he is a wiser man than we thought."

"Hmm, we'll see. We've got the house to tackle yet."

"Yes, well..." said van Fensing. "We can leave that for a while."

The next morning Rob moved the hide forward to its final position. It was now only ten feet from the nest. He wanted to see at close range exactly what the bird's reaction to the hide was. He decided to stay inside. The sun was strong. The brown canvas tent, unventilated but for the small aperture for a camera lens through which he had to watch and breathe, acted like an oven. He could see the nest and a slice of moorland stretching away to the skyline, but little more. He had no idea from which direction the bird might return. Half an hour ticked slowly by. He was being slowly cooked. At least in the strong sunlight there were no midges.

Suddenly the bird was there. She arrived unseen from one side and tipped in to the nest almost as though she was pouncing on prey. She stood for a few moments fidgeting her long brown wings and eyeing her precious clutch before settling back on top of them. The round glossy eye stared fixedly at the hide. She looked composed and comfortable. There was not the slightest flicker of concern about the new position of the hide. Rob eased the thumb switch on his recorder forward and it clicked into the on position. The harrier heard it. Her neck extended a full three inches, head turning this way and that. Rob froze. He could see the wheels of the little tape cassette turning but he dared not stop it. Two minutes passed and slowly the bird relaxed again. "Eight-fifteen a.m," he whispered into the recorder held close to his lips. "Hide move successful. Remained inside to watch hen return. Now sitting on eggs at eight forty-three. Have to be very quiet."

Rob had no idea how long he would have to wait before she left the nest again. He didn't want to put her off her eggs, but neither did he want to spend the whole day in the hide. It was as uncomfortably hot for the harrier as for himself. Her bill was now gaping wide and her spiky tongue visible. She fidgeted the long wings across her back regularly to circulate some air among the mottled brown feathers. A leathery eyelid rose from beneath the eye to cover half the shiny orb; if not actually asleep, she was dozing. So was Rob. He fought to keep his own eyes open in the oppressive heat.

They awoke together. Rob wondered what it was he and the harrier had heard. Her shining eye was full circle again on extended neck. There it was again. A strange high pitched squealing noise. At first Rob thought it was a bird's cry distorted on the breeze. Perhaps it was the male harrier calling to his mate? But then it came again and he knew it was the cry of no bird he had ever heard. It was squealing of an inanimate, mechanical quality he couldn't place. The sound came to him in irregular snatches on what little wind fluttered over the moor. It was muted and muffled by the canvas and possessed a worrying quality which made him deeply uneasy. He knew these moors. He had walked them back and forwards in every season over many years. Every bird and animal that traversed the hills was familiar to him, and every call and sound that emerged from these great empty places beneath the sky. This was not the liquid call of the curlew, or the thin cry of the golden plover. It was not the drumming of the snipe, nor the rasp of the ravens among the high crags. It was neither meadow pipit nor lark nor the mew of the sharp-winged merlin they feared. Nor was it the squeaking of a rusty deer fence nor the sighing of the wind in the corries. He heard it again, this time accompanied by a rumble—a low, throbbing rattle. It was a long way off. Suddenly he knew only too well what it was.

A few minutes later the harrier stood up, looked around her, raised her wings and was gone. Rob snatched his chance. He unzipped the hide and stepped out into the glaring sunshine. He was just in time to see the hen meet up with her gull-like mate and the two of them float effortlessly together over the horizon. He looked around to see if the bird had been disturbed. There was no sign of any activity on the moor which might have put her off and he recorded the fact straightaway. "Hen off again at nine twenty-two. Left hide."

He ran quickly away from the site and didn't stop until he was well down the hill. He sat down to recover his breath and looked around for the source of the noise. It only took him a few seconds to locate it; and his heart sank. On one of the green swards beside the river his binoculars revealed a large articulated low-loader. Beside it on the fresh grass stood a bright yellow crawler tractor. A second tractor with a huge single furrow plough protruding like a scorpion's sting from its rear end, was grinding and squealing its way across the moor a mile to the west. There were two land rovers parked beside the low-loader and three men stood talking together beside the road. "Sod it!" Rob cursed. He knew that the day of reckoning had arrived. Bog Forestation had moved onto Dalbattigh to begin preparing the ground for their plantation.

He burst into the little Dalbattigh kitchen where Shiona sat drinking coffee with her mother. "Where's Andrew?" he demanded, unable to conceal the tension in his voice.

"You've seen the forestry boys, then?" said Shiona. "Father's away up to see Mac already. We're just discussing it....This is it, isn't it, Rob?"

"Not if I can help it!"

"What're you going to do?"

"I don't know, there's probably not much we can do, but I aim to try every last trick. I'd better get and find Andrew and Mac."

Andrew stood talking to Mac and Jockie Jack at the Ardvarnish sheds when Rob's car skidded to a halt beside them and he leapt out. They all looked glum. "What the hell can we do about it?" he began.

"I don't think we can do anything about it," said Mac shaking his head. "It's their ground, they've got the planting licences, the scheme's been approved—that's it." He shrugged his shoulders.

"It's a damned shame! That's what I say," said Jock.

"Aye, it's a shame, right enough," agreed Andrew dolefully.

"There must be something we can do. Even if we could get them to reduce the size of the scheme to try and keep the sheep in place," Rob tried.

"Why should they?" Mac asked. "They don't want the damned sheep. I shouldn't wonder if the best grazings are the first ground they plough."

"This is a hell of a bad day for Glen Corran," said Andrew shaking his head and poking his long crummack into the dirt with savage little jabs.

"There's one thing we could try," said Rob.

"And what's that?" Mac asked.

"We could go and talk to the plough drivers themselves and ask them not to start work because their actions are doing Andrew and his family out of their livelihood."

Mac thought for a moment. "Aye, aye, we could try that. Although, it's a job for them same as it is for Andrew. They'll not want to put their own jobs at risk. What you're suggesting would really amount to strike action."

"Aye, but we could try," said Andrew, looking from face to face.

"It'd be good idea to take Shiona with us," Rob added, "she is often more persuasive."

"Aye," agreed Jockie. "I think that's a good idea. I think you should try that."

"Right!" said Rob decisively. "I'll go and get her—come with me, Andrew? —what about you, Mac, you coming?"

"No, Rob, I can't. I'm sorry this has happened today, but you'll remember Janet goes into hospital this afternoon and I'm driving her down."

"Oh, God yes, of course. I'd forgotten that—I'm so sorry.

How is she?"

"Ach, well, she's not looking forward to it, of course, but she's as well as maybe."

"Of course she's not! Of course not! God, I hope it all goes well for you. Don't you worry about anything while you're away, Shiona'll guard the kids with her life." Rob stretched out a hand to Mac's sleeve and their eyes met. He was looking tired and stressed. Rob knew he hadn't been sleeping for weeks and that he was deeply worried. Rob looked away. He couldn't bear to see his friend so tortured. "Come on then, Andrew!"

The crawler plough was screeching and rumbling its way across the heather. Andrew, Rob and Shiona were climbing the shepherd's path behind the cottage at Dalbattigh in single file. There were now seven or eight men scattered across the south side of the glen. Marker pegs and flags were being hammered into position to guide the ploughmen and to mark the positions for the main drains. Men stood about in huddles of two and three holding plans and maps which fluttered in the breeze; others spoke to each other through crackling shortwave radios. The plough was grinding on up the hill. Rob forced his aching legs to take him up the path as fast as he could without actually breaking into a run. They aimed to get above the tractor on the path and then cut across to apprehend him as he turned round to make his first furrow down the hill.

"Hullo there!" Rob shouted. The tractor was facing downhill and the plough sunk like an anchor into the peat behind it. The driver had turned off his engine, opened his cab door and sat drinking his tea from a flask and munching a sandwich. He eyed them quizzically as they approached. Shiona knew him immediately. It was Finlay McGruer from Brora. He was a young fellow in his thirties she'd often seen with Geordie Hoggett at dances in the old days.

"Is it Finlay?" she asked, shielding her eyes with her hand.

"Aye, aye. It is, young Shiona. There's no mistaking you with that bonny red hair!" He smiled through his sandwich.

"This is my father," she said, " and Robbie, my fiancee."

"How d'you do?" said Finlay. "It's a grand day."

"It's not a grand day for us," said Andrew sternly. "You'll have heard about the dispute, Finlay, it's been in all the papers."

"Aye, aye. I've heard right enough."

"We've come to ask you not to drive the plough," Shiona said in her most appealing voice. "At least no' until the dispute's settled."

"Oh, now!" exclaimed Finlay. "That's a lot you're asking. This is my job too, you ken. The boss'll no' be pleased if I do something like that. You're asking me to walk away from my contract and the boss's reponse to that just might be, 'Keep walking, boy!' What do I do then, eh? That's two of us out of work!"

"Would you come down with us to see your gaffer just long enough to tell him you're not happy to begin ploughing while there's a dispute running?" Rob tried.

"Aye, I could do that," said Finlay. "I'm not happy about the job at all, but I don't see that I've got a choice." All four set off down the hill in the direction of one of the groups of map-holding surveyors.

Anderson Sinclair had been warned that there might be a demonstration of some kind at this job. He had been sent onto the site because he was tough and blunt and as hard as the grey schist boulder he stood on. "You can just get back to your bloody work, Finlay McGruer! This dispute's no business of ours. It's between the estate and their own employee, Mr Duncan here. It's got nothing whatever to do with us. And you three can bugger off and stop interfering with my work and my men!"

"Sorry, Shiona, Mr Duncan," said Finlay, looking embarrassed and crestfallen. He walked away from them, toiling slowly and dejectedly up the heather.

"And get a bloody move on!" shouted Sinclair after him.

"But, Mr Sinclair, you can't just expect Andrew here to allow you boys to plough up his best grazings while he still has thirteen hundred sheep on the place. Can't you see this has been very badly handled by the new owner and the factor," Rob argued.

"There's plenty grazing here, Mr Pearce, and there will be all summer. Our ploughing'll not do much harm to the grazings and we'll not be planting until the sheep are off it at the back end. There's no possible reason for not starting. Now, I've got a lot to do if you'll just get out of my way."

They turned angrily away and headed down towards the cottage. "Bastard!" said Rob.

"Aye," said Shiona, "he is that."

The glen was different now. The lines of parallel white scrapes on the smooth tarmac surface betrayed that the tractor had been there. Rob stopped and looked at where it had swivelled and left the road, cutting deeply into the grass verge, tearing at the pale blue speedwell flowers, crushing the yellow flags in the ditch, spewing the chocolate coloured mud over the sward, and clawing its way up onto the heather. A trail of broken woody stems and torn sphagnum moss marked its route, rising and falling out into the sultry moor. He felt as though his love affair with this place had been sullied. It was as though rough hands had forced themselves on his lover against her will. The image of Shiona treated in this way passed across his mind. He shivered, a tremor of revulsion passing the length of his spine.

Just then a bird flew out of the alders and crossed the river ahead of them, uttering a raucous rattling laugh. The sound was alien; that of an intruder who didn't belong there, its black and white plumage vulgar and mocking. They all stopped in surprise.

"Look at that!" said Shiona. "I've not seen a magpie in the glen before."

"Aye," agreed Andrew, "that's a rare sight in these parts, right enough." They both glanced at Rob.

"Yeah, you're right." he said in a far away voice. "They don't appear much in the Highlands. It'll just be passing through." They watched it fly away out of sight down the river. "One for sorrow," he said, almost to himself.

"What d'you mean?" Shiona asked, sliding her arm into his. Rob shook his head.

"Nothing," he said.

When they reached the road they saw the Ardvarnish Landrover heading towards them. It slowed as it approached and Janet wound down the passenger window. She looked pale and weary. Mac gripped the steering wheel with both hands and forced a smile.

"You'll be back in no time," said Rob, as they leant in to kiss her fondly.

"Thanks," she said quietly, unable to say more. Rob knew the tears were not far away. Shiona reached out to her and held her hand as Mac pulled away.

—26—

Anderson Sinclair was rattled. Never before had his workers been lobbied by people on the ground and he was suspicious that Finlay McGruer's resolve to do the job properly had been damaged. If one plough driver walked off the job he knew he would lose both and possibly some of the other local men as well. At lunchtime he climbed into his four-wheel-drive estate and drove aggressively down the single track road and out of the glen. At the first high spot where his car-phone would work he stopped and punched in the number of his head office in Perth.

"I want Finlay McGruer moved to another job straightaway and replaced with Alec MacFee who's on a plough up in Glencalvie just now. And I want Bob Grant, my other driver, taken off the job too. They're good friends, the pair of them, and I think it would be better to replace them both. Can you find me another driver?"

"I'll ask Alec MacFee and see who he recommends. It's a good idea to have them knowing each other, they work better that way."

"Aye. You're right."

"You know Alec MacFee's a local man to Glen Corran, don't you?" said his colleague, questioning his choice.

"Ach, aye, I know that well enough," laughed Sinclair. "But I've no worries about Alec. He's a good lad and has no truck with Andrew Duncan or with these green loonies. Alec's the right man for this job, I'm sure enough of that."

At eight o'clock the next morning Alec MacFee arrived in Glen Corran. Some of the men were already there and Sinclair was instructing them for the day.

"Morning, Alec. Good to see you again, mon," he called. "There's your plough," he pointed up towards the skyline. "It's already up in place. Here's your chart. Horse on into it and let's get some action here!"

"Very good, Anderson!" Alec swung his lunch-bag over his shoulder and set off into the heather.

"Oh, Alec! Come back here a minute." Sinclair signalled wildly with his right arm. "Did the office ask you to name another driver?"

"Aye, Anderson, they did and I've given the name of a very good man. He'll be here like a shot."

"Who's that?"

"You'll not know him. He's an old friend of mine—knows this ground like the back of his hand. He stays over in Aberdeenshire just now and drives on contract. I happen to know he's not working just now. He'll be here in the morning."

"Good lad! On you go!"

Jimmy Forbes arrived sooner than expected. He had been smiling to himself all the way across the Grampians. He was delighted to be coming back to the glen. He had followed the controversy in the local papers and had laughed to see the mess Mac, Rob and Denby had landed in since his departure. At Corran Bridge he stopped at the stores to buy cigarettes. He neither needed the cigarettes just then nor had he any desire to see Jessie MacChattin again, but he knew of old it was better than taking an advertisement in the local paper.

Jessie's eyes bulged when she saw his burly figure standing at the counter. "For any's sake!" she exclaimed, "it's Jimmy Forbes. Doolie! Doolie!" she shouted to her husband who was enjoying his afternoon nap in the sun. "You'll not guess who's just walked in the door."

"I've nae time for blethering," said Jimmy bluntly. "Gi' me twenty Embassy will ye, Jessie?"

"Here you are, Jimmy. It's good to see you back. How's Bella?"

"Just grand," he said coldly, pocketing his cigarettes and pushing a ten pound note across the counter.

"We've missed you both in the glen these few years, we have that," lied Jessie. The only thing she had missed was the regular source of gossip Bella used to feed her from up at the far end of the glen. "Will you be in the glen long?"

"Just as long as I'm needed," he growled, enigmatically.

"Ooh, you're back working in the glen, Jimmy? Is that it?" Jessie could scarcely believe her ears. "What's it you're doing?"

"I work for the forestry now and I'll be up at Dalbattigh for the next few weeks, so I dare say I'll see plenty of you, Jessie," and with that he strode out of the shop, not bothering to close the door behind him.

He drove very slowly down the strath. It was strange to be back here. He remembered every twist and turn in the road, every hump and hollow, every glimpse of the river where he paused to see if there was a fishing tenant plying the pools. In every broad mountain view between the trees he relived some of the hundreds of stalks he had performed during his long rule over this land. Little had changed. He spied deer fencing on the hill that was new, across the wide slope below Carn Mor, and wondered what it was for. He spotted a pair of goosander swimming side by side in Lady Margaret's pool, the glossy white drake dipping its green head below the surface to spy for the young trout and salmon it would grasp in its hooked and serrated bill. He though how easy they would be to shoot from the road side. They would never have survived a day in his time. He smiled to himself again. Whoever was keepering this beat of the river did not know his business. But there was little else he could find that was different until he swung round the corner at the falls and saw the Bog Forestation encampment on the river green. A large diesel tank stood on stilts for refuelling vehicles. A portable cabin was parked beside the road with 'Office' written on its side, and the assemblage of plant and equipment and vehicles indicated a large-scale forestry operation.

A group of men were unloading fencing materials from an articulated lorry. They were stacking strainers, posts and rolls of wire beside an old caravan which had been parked there to house the migrant forest workers during the week, who would be living on site and guarding the equipment. He entered the office without knocking and found Anderson Sinclair bending over a detailed map of the glen.

"Mr Sinclair?" he asked.

"It is. And who might you be?"

"Forbes is my name, Jimmy Forbes."

"Well, hullo there, Jimmy Forbes," said Anderson thrusting out his hand shaking Jimmy's enthusiastically. "I wasn't expecting you 'till tomorrow. Good of you to come across so soon."

"A job's a job, Mr Sinclair, and a man canna be choosy. I'm ready to start this afternnon if that's what you want."

"Aye, well, it is. The sooner the better. You'll get standard rates and your accommodation allowance. Do you have somewhere to stay?"

"Aye, I do that. I'll be staying at Braeside with the MacFees."

"You know Alec, do you?"

Jimmy laughed. "Ach aye, I know Alec right enough. I've known him since he was pissing his pants, and his father before him."

"Grand, that's fine. And you know the ground too, I believe?"

"I know it better than anyone else alive," he boasted defiantly.

"That's excellent. That's just what I wanted to hear. You'll know where the wet ground is and where to run the drains?"

"Aye, nae bother at all."

"Now, this is where Alec is ploughing at the moment." He jabbed a finger at the map. "He started up there this morning. You make your way over there and say hello to him and then come across the top to the east side here, and start on this section. Here's your ground plan and it'll tell you how deep to plough and what your spacing is and it marks the main drains."

"Aye, aye," said Jimmy pulling out his glasses and peering at the multi-coloured chart. "That's gey good ground up there. That's called the Cruachan, and there was shielings up there in days past. It's a good bit o' ground for the hinds in the winter and Andrew Duncan always had his ewes up there this time o' year for an early bite."

"Aye, well, you'll find the sheep are still there just now, but they're coming off this autumn and as long as you don't run any down they'll not be a problem to you."

"Andrew'll not think much o' that then?"

"That's as maybe," said Anderson sharply. "If you take my advice you'll keep well clear of that lot. You'll have seen in the papers what a stuchie they're making."

"Aye, I have," nodded Jimmy, leering, unable to contain his delight at the discomfort the forestry was causing in the glen. Sinclair reached to a hook on the wall and threw Jimmy a key.

"Your machine's outside the door fully fuelled and ready to go." He glanced at his watch. "It's twenty past two and I'll clock you in for two o'clock. Away you go, man, and get to it."

Jimmy left with only a nod. Moments later the tractor roared into life and clanked and screeched on massive steel tracks, across the road and into the heather, up the moor, pumping a plume of black exhaust into the clear blue sky.

Jessie was hard at work. She'd been unable to resist phoning Mairi in an ill-concealed attempt to alarm the Duncan family. "Ooh Mairi, dearie, I thought you'd better know that Jimmy Forbes is back in the glen. Now isn't that a surprise?"

"Aye, Jessie, it is. What's he doing back here?"

"He was in here buying cigarettes. He's working for the forestry, that's what he does now, so he says."

"Ooh, no," said Mairi.

"Aye, that's right. He's done very well by all accounts. He's some kind of manager."

"Oh, I see," said Mairi in bewilderment, not seeing at all. Jessie pressed on. "Aye, I heard he's going to be put in charge of the Dalbattigh forestry when it's all planted up. They'll be looking for a house as likely as not."

"Oooh my!" Mairi was unable to disguise her rising panic.

"I will not give up," said Rob to Andrew who sat despondently beside him in the car. "We must talk to Galbraith. We must try to get them to suspend operations until we've got your future sorted out."

"It's good of you to try, Robbie boy, but I think we're wasting our time."

"Never say die, eh Shiona?" he said glancing into a rear-view mirror filled with her smiling face and her radiant hair. He knew it was as much for her as for Andrew and the land that he was doing this. But it was more than that. He was doing it for generations of Highlanders past and future. It had become a personal crusade. He now passionately believed that the only future for the people living in these glens was for the world to treat the land and its people with greater respect and to promote sustainable systems which would support both. Not just for the forseeable future, but for the whole of the next century and beyond. In spirit he was already married to this girl. He was fighting for the survival of his own flesh and blood, for his unborn sons and daughters and their sons and daughters in turn, who would know the same sense of belonging to this wild and beautiful place.

Tony Galbraith met them in the Glen Corran Hotel. He shook them all by the hand and smiled in an open, friendly way Rob found disarming. He thought the man would be hard, a hired front-man to do van Fensing's dirty work. Instead he was a quiet, mild-mannered individual, gentle of voice and smile, who congratulated them on their engagement in a way which, for all his suspicion, Rob could not decry. For the first time he saw what an invidious task a factor had, sandwiched between the aspirations of an owner and the recipients of the systems which were his only tools with which to manipulate both. He was, after all, only doing his job and if the owner said, "Get them out!" it would be a strong man to risk his own neck by attempting to divert that policy when he was paid to implement it.

"I know how difficult this is for you," began Galbraith. "I'm afraid the whole business was very badly handled and I regret that I wasn't taken on earlier so that we could have consulted properly with all of you. But the decisions have been taken and the contracts have been signed and it's now beyond my power to interfere with that process."

"Can't you even get the ploughing delayed until the summer grazing is over and Andrew can take his stock off with a little dignity?"

"No, I can't. They need to have the ploughing done in the good weather to prevent making too much mess on the land and also to have it ready for autumn planting. I'm afraid Mr Sinclair is correct. The ploughing won't seriously interfere with the grazing for the rest of this summer. There's seven or eight feet between the furrows and there'll be plenty of grass left for the reduced numbers of sheep until they go to the sales in August."

"And what about Andrew's future?" demanded Rob. "Why has there been no negotiation about his house, his employment—just what are the estate's intentions? Is he going to be put out of that house as the rumours would have it?"

"Ah! Well, now. That is something I can do." said Tony Galbraith nodding. "I am making very strong recommendations to the owners that Mr Duncan is kept on and that he has security of tenure in an estate house. I can't guarantee it will be that one, but I shall certainly do my best to see that he and his family are properly housed for as long as he works for the estate. I'm confident that I can negotiate favourable terms and a fair contract for you, Mr Duncan, for the next few years."

"And after that?" demanded Andrew.

"I'm afraid I can't say just now, because I'm so new in this job myself. But I shall do everything I can to support the continuation of your family in the glen."

"Well, I suppose that's something to be grateful for," muttered Rob, who rather liked this man in his check shirt and tweed tie and his kind voice. He decided to have one last try. "Mr Galbraith, I know that down the hill ploughing is common practice. I've seen hundreds of thousands of acres go under the plough these past few years and I believe that it's bad for the land. I believe it runs the rainfall off the hill too quickly. It strips the nutrients and minerals out of the land and it leaves a scarred landscape for generations to come. Is it not possible to persuade Bog Forestation to plant some of this land with Scots pine which belongs here, instead of sitka spruce, and to do it by hand instead of having to rip the land to shreds like this?"

"Aye, Rob's right," said Andrew. "Once it's ploughed, that's it. It's no good for anything after that. It'll take hundreds of years for the plough furrows to fill and on the steep ground they never will. It's the end of hill farming in this strath, that's for sure."

Tony Galbraith looked at the table and drummed his pencil idly for a few seconds. He looked up at Rob. There was sadness in his eyes and his voice when he spoke. "I have a feeling you may be right, Mr Pearce. I confess that I don't like it myself, even though I've been involved in a good few thousand acres being ploughed around the Highlands. There's very little doubt that it grows better trees and it stifles the competition from the heather and the weeds for the first few years and gives them a really good start, but the other aspects of it—I agree with you— are probably not good in the long run. But I don't think I can do anything about that. It is the industry and the government which lead forestry in Britain, and to get such a radical change to established land preparation practise is a bigger task than I can undertake. I'm afraid you'll have to address your criticisms to a much more influential audience than me if we're to change that. There's nothing I can do to help you with Dalbattigh."

"It's rape! that's what it is," barked Andrew, his face reddening and his fists clenched. "Just bloody rape of the land!"

"Yes," said Rob, calmly. "It is. That's exactly what it is. Will you promise me one thing, Mr Galbraith?"

"And what's that, Mr Pearce?"

"That you keep the ploughs well away from the hen harrier's nest until the chicks have flown?"

"Yes, of course we will, of course. You can leave that to me. I know the law about wilful disturbance and I shall make it my business to inform Mr Sinclair personally."

"Thank you." Rob stood up and held out his hand. "And thank you for your time."

A dejected family group sat around the table in the little Dalbattigh kitchen with a dram, waiting for the MacDonald children to return from school. Mac and Janet's plight weighed heavily on their minds, and Rob had come to accept that there was nothing now that could halt the destruction of the moors. Assurances over protection of the harriers was small consolation. The whisky they shared did nothing more than dull the pain a little.

Rob and Shiona left the cottage hand in hand to walk down to the bridge to meet Hughie Clips and the school bus. They wore forced smiles for little Michael and Karen and walked them home to supper in their own home.

When the phone rang Shiona picked it up in the kitchen. "Rob, it's the hospital, it's for you." She called. She passed it over. He put down his whisky and pressed the plastic to his ear. "Rob here." A girl's voice said, "Mr Pearce, I have Mr MacDonald for you."

"Mac? Mac, it's Rob. What's the news?" There was silence. "Mac? Are you there?"

"Aye, I'm here Robbie."

"What is it Mac... Mac?" The voice was cracked and dry. "Mac...?" asked Rob again slowly and quietly. There was a deep trembling sigh at the other end of the phone. "What is it, Mac....?"

Rob's eyes roved about the room, across Shiona's anxious face, across the sparkling pictures of herons and tawny owls, and otters at the edge of the Falls Pool. He thought of that first night in this house when he'd met Shiona again, at the ceilidh, when Jockie's stained old fingers had danced on the strings of the fiddle and Lachie Gunn, smiling toothlessly, had danced like a twelve year old in front of the fire, clapping his hands and whooping with unbridled joy. He thought of the fireside suppers around the kitchen table with Mac and Janet and how they'd shared his love for Shiona and their plans to return to the glen. And he thought of the two little children upstairs in their beds beneath the grey slate roof.

27

Janet did not come home. The operation revealed advanced generalised cancer about which the surgeons could do nothing. By the time she recovered from the hysterectomy she was suffering extreme headaches from a secondary tumour at the base of her brain. She received massive doses of radiation and chemotherapy in an attempt to check the stampeding malignancy. After two weeks she was moved to the hospice in Inverness, a frail, hairless shadow of the strong, handsome young wife and mother the Glen Corran community had come to like and respect. She slid into a coma and died only a month after being admitted to hospital, only a few days away from her thirty-second birthday.

A pall of sorrow hung like a heavy cloud over Ardvarnish that summer. Jessie MacChattin was disturbed to discover how accurate her fabricated prognosis had been. Even her wildest exaggeration had not imagined that it could be so devastatingly sudden.

"Do hurry up, Dinah!" called Gerry petulently pacing the tartan carpet in the hall at the Lodge. "I do not want to be late." Dinah was arranging her hat in the large gilt-framed mirror in the cloak room.

"I really don't know why you made me come, Gerry," she said in a long-suffering voice. "I don't see why both of us had to be here and it's most unfair that you grumble at me for being late when you've forced me come to a house with no servants at all," she called through he open door.

"Dinah, the poor girl was your housekeeper, for God's sake! She ran your household here for you. Of course you had to come! What would the glen have thought if you hadn't?"

"Well, I'm here, aren't I," she said, appearing in the doorway looking, for all Gerry's inclination to be ungenerous, remarkably elegant in a black silk suit and dark red hat with a wispy black veil. He glanced down at her matching red shoes and wondered how much it had all cost. He decided it was better not to know. It was certainly unwise to ask; that lesson had been learned many years before. There was a price one had to pay for a tolerable existence and he continued to pay it without demur—but he was damned if he was going to acknowledge the success of the outfit. "At last!" he said, heading for the front door and the Range Rover waiting outside.

This was only the third Ardvarnish funeral he had attended in all the years of his ownership. The other two had been elderly estate workers: the old shepherd from West Dalbattigh whom he had scarcely known, and old Sandy MacDonnell, 'The Blower'—as he was universally known across the north for his long-winded opinions—who had been under-keeper and ghillie on the river for sixty years. Both funerals had, in their way, been celebrations at the end of long full lives ended as naturally and predictably as the first flurry of snow arrives on the summit of Carn Mor each October. They had both died in the place of their being, in the embrace of the community they knew, and both now lay in the shade of the rowan trees which surrounded the little walled graveyard at Craskie, returning at last to the land from which they had come.

This was very different. Janet was not of this community nor this place. She had been born a Fifer from Anstruther in the more genteel coastal setting of well-to-do farms and picturesque fishing villages. She was an incomer to Glen Corran and had been granted so very little time in which to make her mark. Mac, although a Highlander by name and lineage, belonged to the oak-wooded peninsulas of the west coast. Nevertheless, Gerry found the decision to bury Janet at Craskie encouraging. "I s'pose it means Mac might stay on," he said mostly to himself as they drove through the rhododendrons down towards the river. "The poor chap's taken a hell of a bashing."

"Yes, he has," she agreed. For a moment Gerry thought he detected a flicker of compassion in the tone of his wife's voice. But it was short lived. "I don't suppose you'll know for months what the situation really is. It's all most unsatisfactory. I'll have to find a new housekeeper before August."

Gerry wanted to tell her that she was hard and selfish and inconsiderate, but he knew there was no point; saying it today when he particularly wanted to avoid a row, was an idea he quickly abandoned. He sighed instead. He couldn't give a damn about the Lodge or August. He was deeply distressed, not on a personal basis, because his knowledge of Janet had only been in passing, en route to Mac, although he had always liked her, enjoying her smiling good humour and infectious enthusiasm for whatever she was doing. No, it was for her husband he griev-ed. He had come to rely on Mac. He had come to like him and trust him more as a friend than as an employee. Mac had taught him so much. He had helped him feel good again about owning his land. Stalking had taken on a new meaning for him with a stalker who explained to him the ecology of the land and its natural history in a way which made him care only a little about killing the stag and a great deal about enjoying the living hill.

All that was shattered. Fate had savagely wrenched asunder the lives of Mac and his little children and hurled a rock into the tranquil pool of mutual understanding between them and the estate.

"I wonder if the Duncan girl would be interested in taking on the Lodge?" Dinah broke into his thoughts.

"She might do it on a temporary basis," said Gerry, "but for God's sake don't ask her today."

"Why ever not?"

"Good God! Dinah. If Mac heard that you were filling his wife's job at her funeral he would be grievously hurt—and with every justification. I forbid you to even mention the subject."

"Oh, Gerry, you are so stuffy! Of course I wouldn't say anything in front of MacDonald. But there's no harm in mentioning it to the girl if she's there."

"Don't be so fatuous, it would be in the worst possible taste." said Gerry angrily. "It would get back to him within a matter of hours and you would do yourself and me and the estate a great dis-service. I forbid it." Dinah said nothing and they drove on in silence.

When they arrived at the little kirk Gerry was surprised to see a long queue of cars. The parking space for a small congregation was full and cars had pulled off the road onto the verge stretching away back towards Corran Bridge, out of sight down the winding road. "Good Lord!" said Gerry, "I knew Highlanders were keen on a funeral, but this is really quite a turnout."

"I hope there's no-one in our pew," Dinah said loftily.

The church was packed, but the appointed ushers, Jockie the mechanic, dressed immaculately in black jacket and kilt, and Andrew Duncan in his, had carefully kept two seats for Lord and Lady Denby when it had become known they were travelling up from Yorkshire. Rob and Shiona and her mother sat with Andy, also in the Duncan kilt and a green lovat jacket, in the pew immediately behind the two empty rows reserved for the MacDonald family. Rob glanced across at Gerry and they nodded sombrely to each other, acknowledging their shared sorrow with an expressionless eye. The coffin lay on trestles in front of the simple altar. The organ played tunelessly as the congregation silently awaited the arrival of the family.

Grief-weary and grey with sleeplessness the little party filed in. Mac was accompanied by Janet's parents and her brother, his own aged parents and his sister from Crinan. The hymns passed across Gerry like clouds, unnoticed and uncounted. The minister's anodyne words barely penetrated his consciousness; like the sun on a misty day, they appeared in momentary shafts and were lost again. "...loss to the whole community....hard to understand....a test of faith.... whole glen moved by the tragedy for Mac and his children." He found himself unable to look across to his bearded friend who had taught him so much. He was afraid of the anguish he would see written there and of his own reaction to it. The laird was supposed to be above a display of emotion, to be remote from the lives of ordinary people, as though moments like this were their doing not his, and his presence was perfunctory, to do with the responsibilities of a landowner and an employer, not as a fellow human being who wanted to cry out and share his friend's pain, and rage with him against the injustice of the world.

The undertaker from Lairg came forward and turned the coffin from facing the altar to feet pointing to the door. It was a signal for four men to come and bear Janet away, out of the little church into the summer sun and the birdsong and the whispering breeze in the rowans for the last time. Gerry wanted to carry her too. He felt a sharp little pain beneath his eyelids as he watched the stout figure of Willie Ritchie lead three other men from the glen forward to lift the wooden bearers and walk the coffin ponderously forward. The family followed. Gerry and Dinah stepped out to follow a discreet distance behind and the whole congregation stirred as strained faces turned to watch.

At the door Gerry was astonished to find the little graveyard also full of people standing in groups and huddles among the lichen patterned gravestones. The gravel path was lined and a crowd had assembled at the wall beyond the open grave, its mound of sandy soil covered by a green cloth. Somewhere behind him an air-filled bag jerked and groaned twice then to emerge on the breeze in the mournful strains of a lament. As they processed slowly forward the coffin was passed between pairs of kilted men lining the path, each taking the bearers and carrying it a few paces before passing it to another pair, moving back from feet to shoulders, men stepping forward to claim Janet for the community and saluting her in the only way they could by carrying her to her grave.

"This is a great honour," whispered Gerry to Dinah. "I've never seen this done to an incomer before."

The pipes floated past them on the warm air and the crowd closed around the minister and the family as the coffin came to rest on its bearers across the mouth of the open grave. A blanket of bright flowers made up by thirty or more wreaths and bouquets separated the throng from the grave. The piper stopped playing and the undertaker read out the names of the seven chosen men to take the cords to lower her into the ground. Janet's brother was the first, "Mr David Anderson..." The young man came forward and took the purple silk cord tied to a brass handle at his sister's shoulder. "..Mr Rob Pearce..." Dark-suited and grave-faced Rob took a middle cord. "...Mr Andrew Duncan..." Andrew stood solemnly at Rob's side. "..The Lord Denby..." Gerry stepped out and stood with military stiffness at

Janet's feet. "..Mr Lachlan Gunn.." Handing his stick to a friend Lachie, shaven for the first time in a week and in a green kilt of ancient colours, hobbled to his place. "...Mr Andy Duncan..." the burly wire-haired youth moved in beside Lachie. "..Mr John Jack..." the old mechanic stepped up. The last cord, held out in silence at the head of the coffin, was taken by Mac himself.

For a moment Janet was floating, borne up by her husband and the community she had adopted. The undertaker quickly removed the wooden bearers and the coffin was lowered slowly into the ground. The silent crowd was motionless. Rob looked glassily across the grave at Shiona. Her piercing red hair fluttered in the breeze, and he saw that tears ran freely down her pale cheeks. The scent of almonds from the yellow broom flowers wafted over them.

"Are you going up to the hotel, Gerry?" asked Rob as he and Shiona began to move away.

"Yes, yes I shall, but I must run Dinah back to the Lodge first. There'll be quite a crowd there, no doubt."

"I'm sure there will. This turn out was much bigger than I expected."

"What you prob'ly don't realise, young Rob," said Gerry paternally, "is that something very remarkable has happened here today." Gerry had a distant edge to his voice, almost of envy, as though he was acknowledging the existence of something available to others, not to himself.

"What's that?" Rob asked.

"The glen has turned out to support Mac in a way which speaks volumes. He is a Highlander and this community has accepted him, despite our recent problems, as one of their own. Am I not right, Shiona?"

Later that evening, with the grave filled and the flowers covering it like a patchwork quilt, a group of four figures stood quietly overlooking it. It was Mac holding the hand of his little son Michael, and Karen's tiny hand clutching Shiona's.

"Dad?" asked Michael, a troubled expression on his little face, "when Jesus has finished with Mummy will he send her back?"

28

Shiona lay in the crook of Rob's arm, her hair spilling over his shoulder. It was another bright morning. The sun had been up for hours and a yellow stripe cut across the counterpane from the open window, dust dancing in its beam. The clatter of young jackdaws on the corrugated-iron roof had woken them early. Shiona had come to love the cottage for all its shabby nonchalance and its constant attractiveness to anything wild which needed a roof. It was home, her home, where she and her Robbie could give of themselves and unto themselves. It was where she wanted for nothing. Above all it was away and out of the glen, an escape from the oppressive presence of the forestry gang and their snarling tractors and the hard-faced men who barked orders into crackling short-wave radios. It was a break too, from her discontented family and the gnawing sadness of Mac's plight. Yet for a few days there was respite. Janet's parents and Mac's sister had stayed on at the Keeper's Cottage after the funeral to help with the children and support him in the long, difficult task of rebuilding his life.

Dinah lost no time in approaching Shiona about the housekeeper's job for the months of August for the grouse, September, and into October for the stalking. "Would you care to come and do for us," she brayed loftily, "like you did before? I seem to remember Lord Denby thought you were rather good." Rob and Shiona had mimicked her, laughing at her affectation.

"I would do anything for him. He's been so kind, but she's really a bitch and I'm not sure I want to go back to what I was doing five years ago." she said drowsily. Rob yawned.

"I must get up."

"Not yet," Shiona said, coming alive and winding a leg round his and gripping his waist so that she pulled herself firmly to him. He turned towards her and kissed her tenderly on an eyelid. "My Highland lover," he murmured. They both grieved deeply at the loss of Janet. It drew them closer still; their love more urgent, hungrier and more passionate, as though, by holding each other closer and for longer, they could assuage their dread, burn out their fear of capricious fate.

"If you take the job you must do it on your terms, not on hers." Rob said seriously.

"What d'you mean?"

"You must lay down the hours you do and, more important, don't do. I'm not losing you to the Denbys for the rest of the summer just to please her and for a bit of extra cash."

"And you have Mac to think about—we both have. He is really going to need us."

"Aye, ...that I know."

She knew that she was the obvious person to help him with little Michael and Karen once the family had gone away. If she travelled in to Ardvarnish with Rob in the mornings she could be there to get them off to school, and then go on to the Lodge, returning in the afternoon to meet them of the bus, prepare their supper and get them off to bed. Rob had undertaken to spend as much time as possible with Mac once he was back in a working routine, and that fitted well with them both coming home to the Keeper's Cottage to Shiona and the children in the evenings. "I'm not sure how I can organise dinners at the Lodge as well."

"You can't. You must tell Lady Denby straight. You'll run her household for her but you're not sleeping there and you're not doing evenings or dinners, and that's that. She can take it or leave it. She's got to employ a cook anyway, and dailies, so she'll just have to organise her own damned dinners."

"She'll not like it, Robbie. You don't understand how important to her those dinners are. It's the big social event of her day."

"Tough! You're not to be bullied by that old dragon. Like I said, your terms, not hers!"

Gerry sat on the hill above Loch Stac. He had often returned to this spot, where he had fallen asleep that June afternoon and awoken, not only to find himself surrounded by deer, but also to the fuller implications of their presence. He studied the ground around him carefully. There was a difference, a marked one. He saw the little mouse-eared leaves of a willow protruding apple-skin green from among the brown woody stems of heather beside him. "That would never have survived," he said to himself out loud. He stood up and began to walk slowly back down the hill towards the loch.

It was very satisfying; even though so many other things had gone wrong. Beside the track the verge was bright with bird's foot trefoil and marsh orchids stood erect, varying pale pink and white to a subtle purple blue. Tiny flowers of milkwort and tormentil were everywhere, dotting the wet grassy patches between the heather with confetti of piercing blue and yellow. At the edge of Loch Stac fragrant bog myrtle thronged the bank, its powerful perfume rising from his footsteps. When he reached the highest of the new enclosures, now nearly three years old, he leaned against the wire mesh and marvelled at the thicket inside. The young birches were now three feet high and a rowan, perhaps from a seed carried by a redwing or a fieldfare migrating across these moors, had outstripped them all, standing nearly six feet high. He wondered if he would live long enough to see these trees form a free-standing wood in its own right, with the fence removed, and the deer returning to it for shelter from the early snows.

Further down the hill he came to the enclosure around the clump of old trees with the gnarled pine he so loved standing proudly amongst its offspring. He opened the gate and pushed his way through the thicket, waist high. Birches and pines were growing so tight together that he had to raise his arms to get through. He could see pine and birch and willow and rowan in abundance, and in a wet place, alder coming and several strong stems of bird cherry. There were broom bushes in bright yellow flower and to his delight he found the young green leaves of an oak. This, he thought to himself, was worthwhile. These were real results to show off to other people just what could be done with an overgrazed moor with a little time and thought and love. He closed the gate behind him carefully. Back on the track he looked across the glen again. His smugness drained away and he felt suddenly empty. True, he had achieved much on this side, but at a price—the full price perhaps yet unknown.

It was July and Bog Forestation had been working on Dalbattigh for a month. As he looked across the parallel stripes of the plough lines stood out, now covering the greater part of the green grazings and the high moor. He lifted his binoculars and saw the yellow tractor reversing up the slope beneath Meall an Chollie, lowering its great claw into the peat and a plume of black diesel exhaust shoot upwards as the tractor ground forward. He wondered if it was Jimmy Forbes. To him Jimmy epitomised all that was wrong with the estate in the old days, and all that had been wrong with his own management of it. He had become both the villain and a convenient scapegoat for his own ignorance and neglect. He certainly didn't want to see him.

Things had gone so very badly. The break up of the estate was galling enough, but van Fensing putting it to forestry was a bitter blow he couldn't come to terms with. And then there was poor Andrew Duncan and his family who looked like being the accidental victims of his own actions; and now, suddenly, almost as though some negative force was working against him and the estate—Janet MacDonald. He looked again at the tractor. It was now ponderously grinding its way down the hill, a long black furrow peeling out behind it.

At that moment the sun disappeared behind the clouds and Gerry looked up. A front was moving in from the west which drew a line across the sky, separating the piercing blue from the impending billowy grey; it might hold rain. He looked back at the plough, still powering down the slope. A new thought emerged, indistinctly at first, and then gathering momentum as he pieced together the snippets of information he had picked up from Mac and the NCC boys. He glanced up at the cloud again. It was blacker now and more menacing. That was definitely rain. He stepped out with a brisk pace.

What would happen, he wondered, to that rain if there was a sudden cloudburst, which, he had a nasty feeling, there might just be? On this side of the strath it would saturate the moor and sit about in pools in the peat and the heather, to be soaked up by the countless cushions of sponge-like sphagnum, and then slowly evaporate in the wind or be transpired back into the atmosphere by the vegetation. Eventually it would trickle down the burns feeding into the river to give a quick summer spate, perhaps just enough to help the salmon up the falls to their spawning grounds.

He stopped dead in his tracks. His old binoculars raised again to his eyes now scouring the opposite hill. "Dear God!" he said aloud. "Now I see what Mac was so worried about." The first fat spots of rain fell on his tweed coat and a little wind scurried through the heather. What would happen on the other side of the glen would be entirely different. Those plough lines would rush the water off the moor in long fast drains, carrying with it peat and silt. The low ground beside the river would be saturated and where the flood water forced its way into the tributary burns they would rise quickly, carrying debris into the river. That might be very bad for the salmon spawning beds. Then he thought of the winter, the seven months when he never came to Ardvarnish because the weather was so foul; long days of driving rain and sleet, often for weeks at a time without respite. He thought of the snows building up in the high corries and the meltwater streams traversing the hill in long lines of white when the warm winds came. What would happen to all that water now that the hill was ploughed? Surely it would tear the heart out of the ground and deposit it in the river? He was worried. He had to check this out. He turned up his collar and marched disconsolately down to the Lodge.

As he neared the Keeper's Cottage he thought it would be a good excuse to get Mac out and about again. The poor man had been beside himself these past three weeks and they had rightly left him alone, providing both time and space in which to face up to his loss. He knocked hesitantly on the door. Shiona answered.

"Oh, good afternoon, my dear," Gerry started amiably. "Is Mac about? I thought I'd see if he'd like to go for a walk to look at the river."

"Aye, Lord Denby, he is. He's through in his sitting room,

but I don't know if he'll come. For hours he sits, staring at the fireplace. He's been like this since....well, you know. He's not speaking or eating unless we force it on him. I'm thinking a walk'd be the very thing for him. It might just do the trick, especially since it's yourself. Come away through." Gerry followed Shiona into the little hall.

"Mac...it's Lord Denby to see you," she called, opening the door carefully. Gerry entered the room where he had so often shared their vibrant company and their generous drams, and where Mac sat now beside the unlit fire doing nothing. He looked older and greyer and his eyes seemed sunken, his cheeks hollow. He stood up.

"Hullo," he said, "come and sit down."

"No, I won't, thanks," said Gerry, smiling uncomfortably, not really knowing whether this was a good idea or not. "I'm just going down to the river and I wondered if you'd like to come with me, what? I'm a bit worried about the effect all this ploughing might have on the salmon. Do you fancy a stroll?"

"That's a grand idea," said Mac slowly, looking to Shiona as if for permission. She smiled, her eyes searching the haunted face for a flicker of the old self, the zest for life, the charm and wicked twinkle she had so loved before.

"Aye, I will come. I'm worried myself about the ploughing. We need to keep an eye on it for sure," he said deliberately. Gerry glanced at Shiona and saw tears welling at the rims of her blue eyes.

"I'll wait outside." Gerry turned quickly to the door and left.

"Oh Mac," Shiona whispered, "Go on out..." He came to her and they stood facing each other, deep brown eyes reflecting in hers.

"You and Rob have been so good to me..." He fell to her and she held him, hugging his broad shoulders and his beard buried in her hair and her neck. The cloud burst.

She felt she was drowning in his grief as his powerful body heaved and shuddered with venting emotion. She hugged him to her, holding him as a mother would hold her injured child. "That's good," she murmured, "let it all out, you can't be strong forever."

Mac and Gerry walked in silence until they reached the bridge. Gerry peered over into the black, motionless pools. "Precious little water at the moment!" he observed. "The fish won't get much beyond the falls until we get some good rain."

"That's not far away," commented Mac looking up. "That's heavy cloud coming in."

They walked down the road towards the Bog Forestation

camp. A man was hand-digging a hole for a strainer for the deer fence which would run along the roadside verge. "Aye,aye," he nodded to them. Mac returned the same acknowledgement of presence but with no particular desire to talk. They came to a drain which ran under the road.

"This is where the trouble's going to be," Mac began. "You see this is one of Andrew's old drains which runs away up the hill onto his re-seeds, following the natural fold of the land. Now the plough lines will cut across these drains, feeding into them all the fast water running down the furrows from hundreds of yards up the hill. The water will rush into this culvert, under the road and out to the river in a great splurge. That's bound to silt up the river in no time at all. I bet there are fifty of these old drains along the length of the new plantation."

"Aren't the plough lines supposed to stop every fifty yards or so and then start again so that they don't scour?" Gerry asked.

"Yes, they are, but it's hard to get the tractor drivers to attend to that, especially if the ground is steep and they're away up the hill with no-one looking. They don't like taking the plough out of the ground, either because they're lazy, or because there might be a hazard to it. Tractors have been known to roll."

"Should we be checking what they're doing and making a fuss if they are breaking the rules?"

"Aye, we should, definitely. It's us who will suffer, and the other owners downstream. Van Fensing has no fishing and won't give a damn what happens to the river. The tractor drivers certainly couldn't. They'll be away down the road with their money just as soon as the job is done and to hell with us!"

They walked on, Mac kicking the clods of turf and mud left by the tractors off the road in a way which revealed his inner frustration. "Change is always difficult to accept," he said quietly, "especially when it destroys something you love." Gerry thought for a moment he was going to say something else, to elbow the curtain of embarrassment aside and speak to him so that he could share the burden. But the moment passed.

"D'you know what saddens me most about all this, eh, what?" Gerry began.

"Tell me," said Mac kicking another sod into the ditch.

"This is not what forestry should be like. Growing trees and creating forests is one of the most noble professions in the world. It's a task a man can be really proud of and can watch develop all his life, so that in old age he can reflect on the value of his achievements." He kicked a large clump of grass to the side of the road. "But this is not forestry." He waved an arm across Meall an Chollie. "This is the exploitation of poor ground at the expense of the land, and its people and the wildlife, for hard profit. I have nothing against forestry. The old woods at Denby are my pride and joy, but I do not like this. This is not the place to grow good trees and these practices show a rough comtempt for the land and the profession."

Mac stopped and looked at his employer with a smile on his face. "That was good, Lord Denby. Well said, sir!" He walked on. "There was a time when I never believed I'd hear anything like that from a landowner." He laughed. "But you've certainly changed my views. I believe in years to come folk will speak of Ardvarnish in reverent tones as the place where Lord Denby began to put the clock back and return something to the land instead of taking all the time. It's a privilege to be part of it."

This was better, Gerry thought. This was the old Mac coming through. He was so pleased. He, too, had felt inadequate ever since the funeral, badly wanting to do something, but unable to, tied down by convention. They walked on in silence. The trouble with being the laird was that one couldn't step out of the laird's shoes. He wanted this man as his friend, not as his employee or his adviser, like Harry Poncenby or that useless man Holdingham had been. He was sick of the old order. Although there were plenty of his employees he didn't want as his friends and he was quite sure they didn't want him as theirs either. But Mac was different. Somehow he was right and he wanted to tell him that. But the words just wouldn't ring true. He sighed. He wondered if it would help Mac to be nudged back into doing some work.

"I say, old man, d'you think it'd be a good idea to do our own survey of the ploughing and submit a report to Bog Forestation if we find there are faults which will affect our interests?"

"Yes, I do," replied Mac with clear enthusiasm in his voice.

"Who d'you think we should get to do it?"

"Myself, of course. It's my job. I'll start on it right away, it'll only take a week or so."

"Oh—erm—are you quite sure you want to take that on just now?"

"Yes, quite sure. Leave it to me."

"Oh, well," Gerry gave in quickly. "I think that'd be an excellent plan."

Anderson Sinclair was pleased. The job was going well. Forbes had turned out to be a good driver and had put in extra hours to get the high ground finished to schedule. They were nearly half way through the job. About six thousand acres had been ploughed and a network of drains had been completed in the lowground. The fencing boys were well on and he reckoned he should be able to start planting in September. He had heard about MacDonald losing his wife. That was bad luck, but it suited him fine. It had taken the fight out of the conservation lunatics and no-one had been near him for weeks. He was due a week's break. Things were going so well he just might take it before the weather broke. He thought he'd leave Forbes in charge of the ploughing. He was the oldest man on the job and knew the ground best. He would be easier to brief than any of the others.

"Crack on with it, Jimmy, " he said. "I'd like to see all that high ground done before I come back. If it looks like the weather's going to break and you want to put in the extra hours, it'd make sense to get all the slippy steep ground done first. There's a bonus in it if you can get it done ahead of time."

"Very good," said Jimmy. "Wi' the light evenings it's nae bother to me to work late if the money's right."

"I'll see the money's right. You leave that to me."

Mac and Gerry saw a green estate car pull out of the camp and drive away down the road.

Jimmy and Alec called into the Glen Corran Hotel on their way home to Braeside. It was like old times. Lachie Gunn was there and Doolie serving behind the bar.

"A dram and chaser is it, Jimmy?" Doolie asked as he had done hundreds of times before.

"Aye, it is. And the same for young Alec here."

Bob MacHurdle came in smelling of sheep. "Aye, aye, there, Jimmy," said Bob. "I heard you were working up the glen. How's it going up there?"

"Will ye take a dram?" Jimmy asked.

"Aye, I will, right enough."

"The job's just fine. We're near half through now, it'll only be another few weeks and the planting'll start. I was that sorry to hear you'd lost your grazings. Hae ye been at the clipping the day?"

"Aye, we have, right enough. That's all the hogs done and we'll get the ewes tomorrow. I'm putting the half of them off this autumn now that I've not got the ground." There was silence for a moment and then he added, "Ach well, that's the way of it. I'd rather it was planted up with decent timber than those bastards up the glen got their way and turned it into scrub fit for nothing." Jimmy didn't know he had such a ready ally in Bob. He had still never met Mac, nor had he seen Rob since the trial, although his looks were branded on his memory.

"I heard thon man lost his wife. To the cancer was it?" Jimmy asked.

"Aye, she was riddled wi' it, through and through, so they say."

"That'll be why they've not been any trouble I shouldn't wonder. They tried hard enough to stop the forestry at first."

"Aye, although that bugger Pearce has worked his way round Andrew Duncan and his boy. He's no good, that one." Bob insisted.

"He's living wi' young Shiona out at Rogart, is he no'?"

"Aye, that's it, and coming into the glen every day doing some kind of fancy research work up at Ardvarnish. No good'll come of that I shouldn't wonder. They'll have some new daft scheme out of it for birds or birch trees or some such. Can you not creep up on him and push him into the river, Jimmy? We'd be well rid of him, that's for sure."

"That's what I should hae done when I first caught him in the bothy that day. I'd hae saved mysel' a deal o' trouble if I had." Jimmy spat out his words with venom.

"Aye, well, it's never too late, Jimmy. If it hadn't been for him I'd still have my grazings."

"Aye, and I'd still hae my job and my house." Jimmy took a long pull on his dram, tipping the glass back and banging it down on the bar again. Doolie came across from talking to Lachie Gunn.

"Another one, Jimmy?" said Bob.

"Aye,"

"And here for Alec."

"Is he going to marry that Shiona?" Jimmy asked, his malice for Rob burning inside him.

"Aye, they'd be married now if it weren't for that lassie dying of cancer, so Jessie told me." Doolie added. "It'll be before the winter, I shouldn't wonder."

Jimmy had often eyed Shiona as a teenager and thought of her slim waist and firm breasts. Bella had let herself go so badly that he'd almost forgotten what firm flesh felt like. He wondered if Doolie knew that he'd had Jessie years before when they were young and Jessie had worked a spell up at the Lodge. Lord Denby had sent her up onto the hill to look for him and she'd found him alright. He remembered it so vividly it might have been yesterday. She had found him fishing from the boat on Loch Meiklie and had taunted him from the bank, teasing him that if he didn't give her a fine trout for her supper she'd tell Lord Denby he was poaching. It was more than a trout she got when he reached the bank that spring morning. A leer spread across his face. She was good, he remembered that. He tossed the whisky back into his throat. Now Jessie was fat and old and so was Bella, but it still irked him that Shiona, whom he'd watched grow up in her tight jeans and her clinging tee-shirts, was now so bonny. "Damn that English bugger!" he said louder than he'd meant to.

"I'll drink to that," said Bob, "and any other English bugger! How long's he going to be here, anyway? That's no' a full-time job he's got, is it?"

"That's no' a job," said Alec. "It'll be taxpayer's money he's living off like all those other scientists who come sniffing round. What do they do that's any bloody use? You tell me that!"

"He's just watching bloody birds as far as I can see, that's all he does," said Bob.

"Aye, and vermin too," added Jimmy with relish. "He's got a hide up at a bloody hawk's nest on the moor, ye ken, and we've been told not to go near it, would you believe? If I had my way I'd blast the bloody hawks off the hill. They do nothing but snatch the grouse anyway."

"Are you telling me the forestry's being held up on account of some bloody bird?" "I am that! As sure as I'm sitting here," said Jimmy. "We're not to go near it till the boss says so. God knows when that'll be!"

"Can you no' arrange for an accident, Jimmy?" Bob threw him a glance, eyebrows raised. "I'm sure you've had plenty of practice." Jimmy laughed, emptying his glass again. He was enjoying this.

"Well now, there's a thought," he replied, as a thought really did pass across his blurred vision.

—29—

The weather broke. The clear skies of early summer passed into cloudier, sultry days of sharp showers and swarms of hungry midges. July saw the arrival of salmon fishers in their smart estate cars with long rods clipped to the roofs, pulled off the road onto the river greens, with rear doors gaping. Men and women stood about in small groups in a uniform of green waders and tweed hats with brightly coloured flies hooked into the peaks. It was a seasonal invasion from another world, apparel and loud voices strangely at odds with the scruffy old anoraks, the faded overalls and the acquiescent vowels of the locals.

Mac had rallied to the task of greeting them and welcoming back those he had known from previous years. He knew straightaway who had been into the Corran Bridge stores on their way up the strath because they had been primed by Jessie—probably the only good turn she had ever done him, and that unintentionally—about Janet's death. They came forward in embarrassed silence, avoiding his eyes for a fleeting handshake before quickly asking about the river or the weather. Some, visibly shocked by the news, whispered their condolences, "We were so sorry to hear..." or, "My dear chap, what a ghastly thing....we simply couldn't believe our ears."

He dreaded these exchanges, but was grateful for the consideration they showed, moving them quickly on to talk about the fishing and how a seventeen-pounder had been taken below the falls in the first week. At least he was busy, organising the ghillies and the beats, returning in the evenings to see what sport had been done. Several long-standing fishermen who had flicked their flies over the Corran for years expressed their horror at the forestry and the ploughing, standing open-mouthed at the changes it wrought. "This is the end of Glen Corran as I knew it," said an Edinburgh judge. Others were aware of the problems which might accrue to the river and remonstrated loudly, almost accusing Mac, saying "Couldn't you stop it?" and "Surely to God the salmon are more important to the local economy than a few damned trees."

At Dalbattigh Andrew was clipping. Alec MacMurchie the Ruddle had come in from Rogart and, with Andy, Rob and Shiona and Mac joining in when he could spare the time, the sheep had been brought in to the river park beside the fank where they were taken forward twenty at a time to be sheared of their scruffy hill fleeces. For two days the glen had been filled with whistling and yelling at dogs as the flock was gathered from the hill and driven down the road. The forestry men stood back and watched in silence as Andrew controlled the bleating sea of wool with Jess and Bran, his boots biting determinedly into the tarmac and his crummack swinging out as he strode past, not even acknowledging their presence, knowing that for the moment at least he had right of way, even if only for a little while longer.

At the fank the midges swarmed. "Why the hell couldn't you do this in June?" Rob shouted at Shiona, swatting wildly at his neck and arms. He straddled another ewe and half lifted, half dragged it forward to the pen. The air was rank with dung and urine and the lanolin made his hands feel unfamiliarly soft.

At tea time Mairi came out in her floral apron with thermos flasks and mugs and a tray laden with drop scones dripping with butter. They stopped for a few minutes only, under the rowan, where they ate and drank in silence, resting mind and body before pressing on. Alec and Andy rolled their thin cigarettes and blew smoke at the midges. Andrew leant back against the dry-stone dyke and closed his eyes, Bran curling in under his raised knees. Shiona looked across at Rob. He lay flat on his back with his arms behind his head and his eyes tight shut. Every few seconds he blew a fly off his face with a snort and a little shake of the head. She wondered what he was thinking—whether he realised that this was once her life, a ritual in which she had partaken every year from when she could first walk until she left the glen. To her people this was one of the milestones of the turning year, like Christmas or a summer holiday to southern folk, around which they planned their lives and which held memories of crystal clarity by which one could recall this year or that. She wondered if he realised what it meant to her for him to be there, with her family on the last year they were likely to be clipping, smelling the smells, hearing the sounds, knowing the lanolin softness, of her own beginnngs.

There were four hen harrier chicks. One was larger than the other three and still sat in the nest, looking as though it had evicted its lesser siblings. They had moved out into the long heather, a few feet away, probably more for security in the event of a fox coming across them than out of deference to their overfed brother. They were well-fledged, the straggly white down protruding from beneath brown feathers like wisps of hair about the head making them look like absent-minded professors.

Rob had watched them for two hours. It was uncomfortable and smelly. Blow flies buzzed angrily about the nest searching out the putrid remains of uneaten prey and crawling over the rim of acrid droppings around the nest, accumulated over the two months since the eggs were laid. He had seen the hen come in twice, once with a grouse chick and once with a slow-worm, the silvery tail of which had protruded twitching from the side of the bill of the large chick for several minutes before it was finally swallowed.

He had ringed the chicks quite early on. They wore their aluminium anklets almost with pride, and he planned to put a numbered wing-tag on them just before they flew. He was anxious to know whether any of this brood would return to Glen Corran in the years ahead now that they were not being killed here. He reckoned he had at least another week. He snapped on the dictaphone.

"Bully-boy looking good, about a week to go. He'll certainly lift off first. Gutsy won't be far behind, but Dainty and Wimp might be two weeks yet. Wimp might not make it. He got very wet in the cloudburst this morning and looks weaker than I've seen him before. Leaving hide 2.23 pm."

He was pleased to get out. It was wretchedly hot and sticky in there and the midges always found their way in. He stretched. He wiped the sweat from his glasses. He glanced at his watch again. He must hurry. He had promised to help Andrew stitch up the wool sacks before the lorry came to collect them.

He walked out to the west, down towards Dalbattigh cottage, cutting straight across the ploughed ground. He was alarmed to see that the furrows were now only about a hundred and twenty yards away from the nest and he did a quick calculation to work out how many more runs the tractor would need to do. It would only take a couple of hours. He climbed a little knoll and looked around for the yellow machine. He could see no sign of it. 'Perhaps it's gone down to refuel?' he thought, 'or maybe they've stopped there because of the strict instructions not to disturb the nest. Anyway, Jimmy wouldn't be stupid enough to tangle with the law again.'

As he crossed the furrows in a long diagonal down to the cottage he was alarmed to see the gravelly substrate showing up in the bottom of each trough. The rain had flushed them out cutting through the peat and carrying sand and gravels down the hill with the water. He followed one or two furrows down on the steeper ground and saw a fan of sand and silt spreading out from where it ended. There was no doubt the water was running off fast, just as Mac had said. In one furrow he found the bedraggled corpses of three tiger-striped grouse chicks which had been caught in the rain and swept down to be drowned in the pool at the bottom. He shivered. He knew he was witnessing the death of the moor.

Jimmy Forbes reversed his tractor back up the slope. He grimaced and rubbed his neck as the machine crawled backwards. He seemed to have been looking over his left shoulder for weeks now and he had a crick in his neck at the end of another long day. He rubbed the rear window of the cab clear with his hand to try and see the orange marker flag. The tractor lurched drunkenly as one track ground over a grey boulder. At last he saw the flag and straightened his line on to it. At the flag he throttled down and declutched; the powerful engine shuddering to a halt. He lowered the great plough share into the heather behind him and eased forward again a few feet to sink the plough to its full depth. He pulled the decompression stop and the engine died. Pulling his old pocket watch out of his jacket he saw that it was five to five. "That'll do just now," he said to the tractor and climbed out of the cab onto the heavy steel track, pulling his greasy haversack behind him. The door clunked shut and he jumped to the ground. He stretched and farted sonorously. He raised his hand to his eyes and stared down at the moor below him. The dim shape of Rob's hide was just discernable. He looked round the moor for several minutes to satisfy himself that there was no-one else about and then set off walking briskly through the long heather.

The female harrier sprang into the air and winged away in alarm, down the hill only a few feet above the ground, quickly disappearing into dead ground. Jimmy smiled to himself; if he'd had his gun that would have been a dead bird. He approached the hide slowly and carefully from behind. He was pretty sure it was empty because he'd kept an eye on it all afternoon and seen no sign of Rob since just after lunch when he'd been lying in the heather overlooking the whole slope from five hundred feet above. He had not been a stalker for all those years for nothing. No-one knew better how to be invisible on the hill when he wanted to. He stood silently at the hide for several minutes until he was entirely satisfied there was no-one in it. He bent down and briskly zipped it open. Inside was a folding camp stool with a striped canvas seat and a plastic lunch box with a sealed lid. He lifted a corner of the lid and saw a packet of digestive biscuits inside. He took one and stuffed it into his mouth, closing the lid and putting the box back where it was. He sat on the little stool and peered out through the round aperture. The plump chick sat with drooping wings in the centre of the nest, with its head on one side, eyeing the hide suspiciously. There was nothing new to Jimmy about a harrier's nest. He knew very well there would be other chicks hiding in the heather within a few yards. He peered sideways to left and right and saw two others lurking among the long brown stems, one bird pulling at the entrails of a well-grown grouse chick. He hated them. He'd been brought up to hate them and had it drummed into him as a boy that this bird was the most dangerous predator on the moor. He'd known of keepers who had been sacked on the spot if a harrier's nest had been found on their beat; it was a threat not just to the grouse stocks but to the keeper's very livelihood. "I'll get you, y' wee buggers!" he muttered and turned to leave the hide, zipping it carefully closed behind him.

Once he was well away from the hide he cut across the moor to where Alec MacFee was still ploughing. He stood on a knoll and lit a cigarette while he waited for Alec to grind back up the slope to him. He flicked the match away and watched it intently for a minute to make sure it had gone out—a habit learned the hard way many years before when he had accidentally destroyed three hundred acres of heather in the middle of the grouse nesting season. Alec parked his machine and they walked off the hill together to their cars beside the river. The air was very close. Just as they reached the road a clap of thunder rolled round the mountain and echoed from the corries of Carn Mor. To the west the sky lit up with a flash of sheet lightning and fat raindrops began to thud into the ground, drumming onto the car roof. "Just in time," called Jimmy. "I'll see ye at the bar."

It was deserted except for Lachie Gunn perched on a stool and Doolie polishing glasses with a brightly coloured tea towel. "Aye, aye," said Alec gruffly, but drew only an expressionless nod and an "Aye," from them both. Lachie studied his dram intently. He didn't want to make eye contact with either of them. Since Janet's funeral the glen had closed ranks around its own. She was one of them now, buried in their ground, and her husband and his children had earned a place in their hearts at the hand of misfortune. Jimmy Forbes's open antagonism to the MacDonalds and the estate had rankled and left its mark. There was discomfort in the glen about Jimmy's return; he was mistrusted, as were all the MacFees. "A bad lot," was the general opinion, and then there were disturbing rumours that Jimmy might be moving back permanently and managing the plantations. Without Bella in the glen to keep the world informed about her husband's doings and plans, there was widespread suspicion.

Doolie drew their drams without waiting to be asked and slid the two glasses across to them. "Cheers!" said Jimmy, throwing the golden liquid back into his throat. Doolie pulled the two half pints of beer and put them up without a word. Alec pushed a crumpled five pound note onto the bar and Doolie moved to the till, picking out his change coin by coin.

"Aye, well, that's me," said Alec, draining his beer.

"Ye'll take another?" offered Jimmy.

"No, no thanks, I'm away. I've to meet Jenny and take her to the pictures in Invergordon the night so I must get along. I'll see you t'morrow."

"Aye, you will." Jimmy sat a moment before easing himself off the stool and heading for the gents. He left by the back door and stood under the eaves staring out at the rain, waiting for a lull to duck across to his car. Once inside he sat drumming his fingers on the steering wheel watching the rain torrent streaming down the windscreen. His watch said ten past six. He knew most folks would be at their tea. When he started the engine the wipers swiped the rain aside revealing the empty car park. Slowly he nosed the car out into the road and turned right, back down the glen road. A late fisherman was dejectedly packing his equipment into a Volvo beside the river. The clouds were so black and heavy it was almost dark. He thought about putting his lights on but changed his mind. He knew every twist of the road and he had no desire to be seen.

When he came to the track leading off to the Ardvarnish sheds he turned in and coasted down to the yard. It was deserted, just as he expected. He looked across at his old workshop and wondered what went on in there now. Then he eased the car round behind the garages where Jockie Jack worked and parked under an old trailing birch at the edge of the rhododendrons. He remembered a buzzard he had once shot out of its upper branches and found himself looking up, almost expecting its ghost to be watching him there. He buttoned his coat up to the neck and pulled up the collar. A tug on the peak of his greasy old cap lodged it firmly on his head and he heaved his heavy frame out into the rain. A burst of thunder like canon fire echoed round the glen. "Perfect," he muttered, "only a bloody fool would be out in this." The rain re-doubled its intensity, hammering into the ground and crashing through the birch leaves in a hissing thunder of its own. In two paces he was into the rhododendron jungle and gone.

Shiona heard the distant rumble of thunder and guessed they were in for a storm. "Hurry up," she said to Michael, as he toiled over his fish fingers. "Karen's finished hers." She smiled an inner smile. She was excited and glanced up at the clock with ducks on its face. It was nearly six o'clock. Robbie would be back soon and she wanted to get the children off to bed quickly so that they could leave early. It was a special night, one she wanted to be perfect. She would wait until they were home at their cottage and the fire was lit. She had bought a bottle of red wine in Lairg. Perhaps she would light a special fire in their bedroom, although it was certainly not cold.

She'd suspected it, of course, for some time. She'd noticed her breasts were tender and tighter than usual and she'd found herself day-dreaming. She'd wanted to be sure. She bought one of those kits and did her own tests, but she still wanted to hear it from a doctor. Now she knew. The extra miles to Lairg on the pretext of shopping for Mac had been well worth it. It was true.

"If you're not going to eat them I'll give them to the cat, Michael."

Rob stayed later with Andrew and Mairi than he meant to. They had finished the wool sacks in the rain and gone in for tea. Mairi's scones were always a temptation and he was hungry. The rain made him reluctant to move. "We're in for a right good storm the night!" said Andrew as he flicked on the television for the six o'clock news. "God, is that the time?" Rob said. "I must get up the road or I'll be in trouble."

As he arrived at the Keeper's Cottage the sky flashed pink and white overhead and the thunder crashed again, much nearer now. Inside the cottage there was no radio playing, no bustle in the kitchen. It was empty and the sitting room too. He heard a child screaming upstairs and ran up. He met Mac on the landing, pulling a long face. "Wee Karen's frightened by the storm," he said bleakly. "Shiona's in with her now." The little girl cried out again and he added, "There's nothing I can do."

"I'm not surprised she's frightened. That's a hell of a storm and it's right over us now." Another crash of thunder and lightning together seemed to rock the little house. "Have you seen the rain? The track's running like a river and the road's awash at the junction."

"Aye, it's grim," Mac nodded. "The river'll be a torrent tomorrow."

Rob peeped in at Shiona through the half open door. She sat cradling Karen in her arms murmuring softly to her. "I may have to stay here tonight," she whispered, disappointment in her blue eyes. "I'll do some supper when I've got her settled."

"Okay," Rob nodded and smiled. He tiptoed away.

"Come and have a dram," Mac said, heading down the stairs.

"I will in a while," Rob replied, "but first I'm going out again."

"Whatever for?"

"I know you think I'm daft, but I have always wanted to see how birds cope with weather like this. I'm just going to nip back to the hide for a bit. I'm not sure anyone's ever written up harrier behaviour in a deluge."

" You *are* daft! but then I always thought birdwatchers were." Mac smiled at him. "Here, take my oilskin jacket, you'll need it."

"Thanks," said Rob pulling it on over his old pullover. "Keep that dram for me, will you?"

"Sure," said Mac. "See you later."

Rob drove down to the forestry camp and left his car beside the deserted site office. He had been to the hide almost every day so he knew his way even in the half dark. The hill ran with water and he slipped and floundered up the grass slope until he reached the long heather. When the lightning came it lit up the whole valley. Meall an Chollie stood out like a great black hulk, leaving its image imprinted on his retinas long after the light had gone. The rain was like a monsoon, drenching his soft cotton hat so that water ran down his face and neck in rivulets. His trousers were soaked to above the knees and he felt the rain running down his chest so that his shirt clung to him under the jacket.

At last he reached the hide. There was no fear of disturbing the birds. It was so dark between the lightning flashes that he had trouble finding it; the noise of the rain so loud that he didn't have to worry about stealth. He began to think it was all a waste of time. Perhaps he wouldn't be able to see anything anyway? He climbed inside and sat down.

Both adult harriers were there. The brown female stood in the nest crouched over her large chick with her wings spread in a broad canopy. The male, more easily discernable because of his silver grey plumage stood huddled at the edge of the nest apparently not doing anything. He couldn't see any of the other chicks. Rob settled down with his head resting in his hands and his elbows on his knees. They had neither seen nor heard him and there was nothing much to watch except for the occasional shake of the head and wings as the birds became gradually more and more bedraggled.

The rain was heavier now, drumming on the canvas so hard that he could move about without any fear of disturbing the birds. He reached for a biscuit. He looked at his watch. It was twenty past seven. The biscuit made him hungrier and he wanted to go home to Shiona and some supper by the fire. He reached for his dictaphone and tested it to make sure the water hadn't got in. It seemed fine. "Seven- twenty pm," he said, "in the middle of a storm. Both birds present, the hen sheltering one chick. Visibility very poor. Going home." He hoped the drumming on the tent wouldn't drown out the recording. It was very loud. He took a last look out at the harriers. To his surprise both birds were standing upright looking alarmed, the male twisting its head anxiously from side to side. Suddenly it flew. Seconds later the female leapt into the air as well, both birds instantly swallowed up by the darkness and the rain. Rob snapped on the recorder again. "Birds disturbed by something out there. Can't tell what it is, the rain is drumming so hard."

—30—

"What can he be doing, Mac? It's nearly nine o'clock." Shiona stood in the sitting room doorway drying her hands on a dish towel. "Do you want to start on and have yours? I can keep his warm in the oven...?"

"Aye, yes, I will, if that's okay. I'm sure he won't mind. How about you?"

"I'm not bothered, I'll wait for him." said Shiona, smiling and still trying to hide her disappointment. "He'll surely not be that much longer. I can't believe the birds are doing a great deal in this weather."

"I should think they've drowned, poor things. The water must be pouring off the hill out there." Their thoughts collided simultaneously. They looked at each other for a few seconds, reading the anxiety reflected in their faces.

"You're not thinking the river's broken its banks, are you," she said, "and he can't get back across?"

"I never thought of that," said Mac, getting to his feet. "I know the river has flooded in the past, and once the old bridge was swept away, but this one is much higher upstream, and anyway, it's stood for yonks." He dismissed the notion and then added, "...but I think I should go down and have a look, just the same."

"Oh, ...would you?"

"Yes, of course," he said, "I'll go now."

Outside it was still raining hard. Shiona watched the Landrover lights bumping down the track into the rhododendron tunnel. She stood at the porch for a moment longer listening to the insistent rain. She shivered. Maybe she should never have encouraged Rob to come back to the glen to work. She was uneasy. Their lives had changed so much since they came here—the sale of Dalbattigh, the forestry, her family being the losers and so much uncertainty there yet. What would Mac do without Janet? Would he stay on? And her father and mother? Would there be jobs, or a house? Would Lord Denby have to sell more land? Perhaps Ardvarnish would eventually go to forestry too? Nothing was reliable any more. She wasn't even very sure she wanted to stay here herself. Perhaps it was not a good place to think of settling and bringing up children—their children! She blushed. Her heart thumped beneath her hand. It was a curious sensation, an uneasy mixture of excitement and fear. She wished he would come back to her from that dark, wet night.

At the bridge Mac slewed the vehicle across the road so that the headlights shone through the parapet onto the angry water beneath. He left the seat and leant over the stonework. The river surged beneath him with awesome power. In just a few hours it had gone from being the gentle stream of mid-summer to a hurtling torrent which filled its whole bed. It had risen up the banks so that the overhanging alder branches were wrenched downstream and even the largest boulders had disappeared beneath its menacing waves. But there was no fear of it damaging the bridge and it still had several feet to rise before there was any fear of it bursting its banks.

Mac drove on. The ditch below the forestry had filled right along the roadside so that his wheels seemed to be cutting through surface water all the way. He could see nothing which might have delayed Rob. The rain seemed a little easier now and the lightning flashes were less frequent. Then he saw headlights up ahead, coming towards him a good way off. He pulled into a passing place and flashed his lights before dipping them. "Thank God!" he muttered.

'You're going to be in trouble when you get back, lad,' he thought with a grin. 'That girl of yours is flaming wild about her evening being spoiled. You'd better think up a damned good excuse! You know what the Duncan temper is like!' His smile collapsed inwardly and he uttered a little chill laugh. How often Janet had pretended to be cross with him, and he had feigned contrition and sat silently, on his best behaviour, until she couldn't sustain her crossness and burst out laughing. His eyes stung with the tears which wanted to come again. He snapped himself out of it and jumped out of the vehicle into the rain, and walked towards the oncoming car. It was Andrew Duncan.

"Have you seen Rob?"

"No, not since he left us early this evening. Is he not with Shiona?"

"Aye, he looked in at six but she was settling my wee Karen who was frightened by the storm, so he went out again to check his birds. He hasn't come back." Andrew glanced at his watch.

"That's three and a half hours. He can't be seeing much in weather like this."

"No, he can't," agreed Mac. "He's not had his tea either."

"Are you worried about him?"

"No, well, not really. I came out to see what the river was like in case it had burst its bank and Rob couldn't get back across to us. It's up okay, but it's not going to flood tonight."

"Aye, well, that's what I'm doing myself. I just went down the road and back to make sure my ewes were well away from the bank. I don't want to be losing lambs unnecessarily."

"Ach well, I'll go on back to Shiona," said Mac. "Rob'll show up shortly, I've no doubt. They'd better stay with me tonight, they'll not want to go back to Rogart now."

"Is that you, Robbie Pearce?" Shiona called from the kitchen. Mac went in.

"It's only me, I'm afraid."

"Have you got him?" she asked nervously.

"No, no sign, but the river's okay. It's up, right up, but there's no real flooding." Mac tried to sound reassuring. "Nothing to stop him coming back." It didn't work.

"...Then where is he?"

"I don't know. It is odd, I do admit." He was worried too and he couldn't conceal it. He wanted to hold her as he would have held his arms out to Janet when she was upset. He didn't know what to do or say. It was so unlike Rob. He wished the phone would ring and he'd be there, laughing and apologising, saying he'd dropped in to see Jockie and Cathy Jack and had got delayed by a dram in the time-honoured Highland way. There was more than worry in her face, there was anguish, and the pain of uncertainty clouding her lovely blue eyes. He took her hand in his. "You're such a friend to me, both of you are, and you've been so kind. I can't bear to see you worried. I'm sure he's okay. He's very sensible and experienced. He's not one to panic. If he's in a jam or got lost in the storm out there, he'll sit tight and wait until it's passed. Or he could still be in his hide, using it as a shelter. You know what he's like with birds."

"Aye, I do," she said slowly. "Maybe I'm being silly, but we've not been apart for months now, not for a single evening and it just seems so unlike him to do this without any warning."

"Well, we do know where he was going. Perhaps I should go up the hill to the hide. Would you like me to do that? The worst I could do is frighten his harriers away!"

"What time is it now?" Shiona asked.

"It's just gone ten o'clock. It's been four hours. " Mac pulled at his beard thoughtfully. "It's pitch black out there now, but the storm's passing over."

"Is it still raining?"

"Yes, a bit, but not like it was."

"Shall we give it another half hour and if he's not back by ten thirty you go up to the hide? How's that? Do you mind? I'm not being very silly, am I?"

"God no! Of course I don't mind! After all you've done for me? Of course I'll go."

"Have a cup of coffee, while we wait."

At ten-thirty there was still no Rob.

"Right," said Mac, "I'm off." He drove slowly down the glen, stopping periodically to point his powerful torch, out into the moor, swinging the arc back and foreward hoping to intersect a bedraggled Rob squelching back through the heather. When he reached the forestry camp he was surprised to see Rob's car parked at the site office. He got out and examined the car. It was unlocked. There was nothing unusual about that. The keys were in the ignition and Mac slid in to try the engine in case it had got wet and Rob had had to abandon it. It fired first time.

Leaving the Landrover there Mac set off up the grassy slope. It was arduous, slippery going until he reached a plough furrow and then he was able to walk up it. 'Well, at least it's good for something,' he thought to himself. The gravelly bed was firm under foot and he made rapid progress up the hill. When he emerged at the top of the furrow he came out onto the heather and shone the torch around. Everything was ploughed. He couldn't tell where he was. He walked on, climbing to a small rise and casting about again. The ploughing had completely changed the shape of the moor and he had lost his bearing. He was in a sea of furrows running in parallel stripes across the land and the old familiar heather with its wet flushes of grass and its undulating character was gone, submerged beneath a grid of linear uniformity. It was hopeless. He stumbled about for half and hour, trying this way and that to locate the area he knew was unploughed because of the harriers. He could find nothing. "Damn!" he cursed loudly into the storm. He turned back.

He banged on the Dalbattigh door and burst in.

"Andrew, I'm needing you," he said breathlessly.

"What's up, Mac?" Andrew jumped to his feet looking alarmed.

"Still no Rob, and I can't find the hide. It's bloody impossible in the dark with all that ploughing, everything looks the same. You know it so much better than me. Could you come out and see if we can find it together?" Andrew strode to the door without a word, lifting his heavy jacket from the hook and punching his arm into its sleeve. He snatched up his shepherd's lantern and his long stick, and pushed Mac out of the door.

"I'll get you there, no bother, but where the hell's that lad? You can't tell me he's still birdwatching." There was a dry edge to Andrew's voice. It was an edge of alarm.

They drove back to the forestry camp and Andrew took a firm line into the hill. After twenty minutes of crossing the plough lines, climbing all the time, Andrew stopped and threw his torch beam round about.

"...This is not supposed to be ploughed!" he said. He bent down and picked up a handful of ground from the top of the upturned furrow. It crumbled beneath his thumb and fingers. "That's fresh. It's not wet right through, this can only have been ploughed today. I thought they were to keep off this until the birds flew."

"Aye, they were." Mac answered soberly.

"The hide's only another couple of hundred yards off, we should come into the unbroken ground any moment now." They pushed on, climbing and dipping over the furrows, tripping in the cloying darkness and splashing into pools where the water had collected in low spots. They stopped again. Andrew stood silently raking the surrounding hill with his torch, Mac doing the same.

"It's difficult isn't it?" Mac said. "It's so featureless."

"Aye, it is that. We should be there by now." They moved on.

It began to rain again, but with a wind driving the raindrops into their faces making it harder still to see where they were. "All this has been ploughed since this afternoon," Andrew said. "Robbie came down to me to help with the wool sacks straight after leaving his hide. He was full of it, saying the big chick'd be away in a week and the others doing fine. I'm sure he'd have said if the ploughing had come this close. It must have been done after he left the hide. It's that bugger Forbes, I'll bet, just because Sinclair's off the site for a week."

"Oh Christ!" said Mac angrily. "I hope he hasn't ploughed up the nest site! There'll be all hell to pay if he has."

"What's worrying me is that if he has, and Rob's found out about it, that's where he is now, confronting Forbes. That would no' be good news, at all."

"Surely he wouldn't have done that on his own. He's a trained investigations officer. He'd have gone straight for the law. Nor do I think he'd have shot off anywhere without telling us." Mac shook his head. "Besides, his car's still down there. He couldn't have gone over to Braeside or even up to the hotel on foot, could he?"

"No, no, that's right enough. Where the hell is he then?" Andrew paused. "I'm not liking the feel of this at all."

"Nor me. Let's get on and find the hide and find out what's happened here."

"Aye, right, it has to be here abouts. You try below the contour and I'll take above." Andrew strode off up the hill.

For another quarter of an hour they cast about the moor, quartering it up and down and back and forth. They could see each other's torches flickering across the empty, scarred landscape, now coming closer together, now moving apart. Andrew came back down the hill.

"This is no good, Mac boy, we're wasting our time here. It's impossible to tell where the hell you are. Have you seen anything you recognise?"

"Nope, not a stone," said Mac emptily. "Are you sure we're in the right place?"

"I was when we started, but I'm not so sure now. What I don't understand is why we can't find the end of the ploughed ground. There should be a big stretch here that's untouched and we've not found ten bloody yards of open ground in any direction."

"If we walk straight down the hill from here we should hit the road half a mile east of the forestry camp just where there's that passing-place road sign with a bullet hole in it. D'you know the one?"

"Aye, I do, I know it well, it's been like that for as many years as I can remember," Andrew replied. "*That'll* have been Jimmy

Forbes, as like as not. He always was a trigger-happy bastard."

"Well, if we pitch up there we'll know we were in the right place here. Are you agreed?"

"Aye," said Andrew, "I am. That's about all we can do as far as I can see." They set off as fast as they could, each in parallel furrows running straight down the hill.

"There's the road now," said Mac, throwing his torch beam ahead. They jumped over the water-filled ditch and onto the tarmac and shone their lights left and right. "Do you know where we are?"

Andrew studied the riverside trees and the grass verge for a moment and then said "Aye, your signpost is a bit this way." He headed downstream, almost running now. "There it is!" Andrew's torch lit up the white diamond shaped sign with a round black hole in the middle.

"Right..." said Mac. "So we were in the right place."

"Aye, we were." They looked at each other bleakly.

"That can only mean that the site has been ploughed, and this afternoon. This is serious, Andrew. Where the hell is Rob?"

"What time is it now?" Andrew asked.

Mac shone his torch onto his wrist. "Good God! It's after half-past twelve. We've been at it for two hours. Shiona'll be worried out of her mind."

"Let's get back there quick and see if he's shown up."

Shiona was weeping. "Something's happened...I know it has," she sobbed on her father's shoulder.

"There, there, lassie, Mac's on the phone now, we'll soon get the authorities out and a proper search under way." He could hear Mac talking to Archie Bane the police sergeant in Lairg.

"...aye, Archie, we want the whole works, mountain rescue, the helicopter and an ambulance........No, it's not high in the hills, it's less than a mile off the road, but we've already scoured the moor and you can't see where the hell you are.....we need the helicopter for the searchlight so that we can see what the hell we're doing, and a proper gang of men.....I don't give a bugger for the rules, call them out now! If you don't I will.....and pick up that bastard Forbes while you're at it, he stays with the MacFees at Braeside. He's the only one who knows what's happened.....no, I can't prove that, but that's not a good reason for not hauling him in and questioning him to help us find Rob." He slammed down the phone and came back into the sitting room. "Jesus! I sometimes wonder whose side they're on!" he said in exasperation. "I wonder he didn't want me to fill in a bloody form!"

"Now, then, what's the plan, Mac?" asked Andrew.

"I've said we'll meet them at the forestry camp as close to

one-thirty as they can make it. It's gone one now. The helicopter will find us on the hill. Let's get going."

"I'm coming with you," said Shiona.

"No, Shiona love. I think you should stay." Mac said gently. But he saw the blood drain from her face and he knew he'd made a mistake. He raised a hand. "Alright, alright, of course you can come, and you'll be a big help. But you'll need some warm clothes." He turned to Andrew. "Would you be able to nip down and ask Mairi if she'll come up and spend the rest of the night here to keep an eye on the children?"

The three of them stood beside the Landrover next to Anderson Sinclair's office. The night was cool after the storm, but the rain had stopped again. A car came racing along the road from Corran Bridge and pulled sharply in beside them. Jockie Jack leapt out with his son Davy and came across to join them.

"I've got some of the boys from the village to come down," said Jockie breathlessly, pulling on a heavy black donkey jacket. "They'll be here any second." Even as he spoke another set of headlights could be seen filtering through the riverside trees. Four young men piled out of a rusty old van. Then came the flashing blue lights; first Archie Bane himself and then another patrol car from Lairg with two young constables.

"Did you pick up Forbes?" snapped Mac.

"No, he's not been back to Braeside tonight, I spoke to Willie MacFee myself."

"Curse it!" said Mac.

Mac and Andrew lined them all up on the road, each man with a torch, five yards apart, Mac on the left flank with Shiona beside him, and Andrew on the far right. Archie Bane left the blue light flashing on his car for the helicopter and they set off up the hill.

"Easy, now, lads, he could be anywhere! Take your time."

The helicopter came in down the river. They heard it long before they saw its halogen arc-light sweeping up the glen, a swathe of white light cutting through the alders along the bank and gleaming back from the swollen water. It hovered briefly above the police car and Shiona could hear Archie Bane's radio crackling in conversation with the pilot. The aircraft swung towards them and thundered up the hill about a hundred feet above the moor. It was over them in seconds. The downdraught hit them suddenly, picking up the surface water from the heather and hurling it about as if it was raining again. It passed overhead and a second wide-angle beam burst from its yellow belly, bathing the moor in brilliant light. They moved on, picking their way forward, heads down, eyes sweeping from side to side.

At the top of the moor Andrew stood still on the right flank and the men trailed past him to line up again facing down the hill now the length of the line to the east. Mac called out and they moved off, the helicopter still thundering a few yards in front of them. They passed down the slope, right to the road.

At the bottom Archie Bane called a halt and there was a protracted radio conversation with the pilot, the helicopter hovering a few hundred yards away. Andrew was called over and asked where they could land. He climbed into the police car and it sped off down the road to the first wide river park where there were no trees. The aircraft followed them. Archie and Andrew checked out the ground and the huge machine settled gently to earth.

One of the rescue team jumped down. They wanted someone on board who knew the land in the hope that he could direct the ground search team more accurately to where the hide was. Andrew was fitted with a helmet and a microphone and hauled on board. The rotors were still slashing through the night. As the engines screamed and the pitch of the blades twisted, the air hammered angrily, flattening the long grass as it lifted off again.

The men stood in huddles on the road, their anxious faces occasionally lit up by a match or the red glow of a cigarette. Shiona stood silently with Mac. She felt a little faint, but with no intention of admitting it. That something serious had happened out there she knew, but her brain was numb. She watched the events revolving around her in a daze. A robin broke into song from a birch tree beside the road, its crisp, tinkling song strangely at odds with the urgency of the moment. She glanced at her watch. It was ten to four. A thin line of light was spreading along the horizon behind Meall an Chollie. Another robin sang a little further away. Why wasn't she at home in bed, curled up to Robbie's back? What had she done to him by bringing him back to this place? Why had events turned against them so savagely? There was a lead weight forming in the pit of her stomach, dragging at her feet. She felt her hands trembling, a pulse thumping in her temples. The dawn spread rapidly across the mountainside spilling the grey morning light down to them and the river. More birds broke into the chorus she had known all her life.

The helicopter had roared overhead and passed up onto the moor with her father on board. Surely he would find her Robbie. He knew every hummock and dip, every grassy flush and sphagnum hollow, every boulder and crag, every gully and myrtle-scented marsh. She could see it hovering here and there, its fierce lights probing the ground. The radios crackled again and the men were being told to line up, Mac issuing orders crisply. He ran back to her.

"Come on, lassie," he said gently, taking her arm, "we're trying again. There's much more light now." He squeezed her
hand as they set off up the hill once more.

—31—

After a flight round the hill the helicopter returned to them and
led the line up the moor. Andrew now knew where he was and
he had placed them on exactly the right line. He now knew for
certain that the nest site had been ploughed, and all the surrounding ground with it. He was puzzled. Even though they
had quartered the ground carefully, there was no sign of the
hide. The helicopter now faced them, nose angled down and
moving slowly backwards as they advanced. The harsh white
lights, less bright now as the sky opened to the day above them,
still bore down on the scarred ground.

To Shiona the land seemed exactly the same as they had
already trudged over twice. She was confused. Why hadn't her
father been able to fly straight to the place? Were they still
searching for the hide and the nest site? Or were they now just
quartering the whole hillside for Robbie? She rubbed her hand
over her eyes. It was daylight now and she could see clearly the
ground up ahead. There was nothing there. They must have it
wrong. This couldn't be the place. She felt a flickering flame of
hope again, that after all Robbie wasn't lost on the hill, that
there was some other explanation. He wasn't here at all, he'd
found something illegal and had to go urgently and secretly like
that time in Lairg. Perhaps that's where he'd be, and he could-
n't contact her. If they'd only find the hide and discover he
wasn't there.

A shout came from down the line. Young Davy Jack had
found something, Jockie was shouting and waving wildly. Archie
Bane and Mac were running across. 'Thank God,' she thought,
'at last, they've found the hide.' It would be alright now, they
could leave the moor and go down to the road and someone
would bring her a message that Rob had phoned from a neighbouring estate, on the other side of the mountain. That was it.
That's why his car was still down there. He'd had to foot it over
the mountain to the next estate and he'd spent the night in the

stalker's cottage there. He'd often done things like that in the past. The storm would have put the phones out, for sure. She felt better now. She began to walk over to the little group of men. They must have found the hide, men were kneeling and the helicopter had roared in close, blowing her long red hair wildly about her face. She tried to hold it back with her hands but it kept escaping. It was hard to see. Mac was walking back to her. He was so kind, so thoughtful. He would tell her. It would be all right.

There were tears streaming down his face. She thought they were rain. "Is it the hide?" she asked, her eyes wide and looking up into his. He nodded, unable to speak. He held his arms open to her.

"Oh my God!," he said, drawing breath sharply through his running nose. He held her, trying to turn her away. She resisted, fighting him.

"What is it?! Mac!" There was panic in her voice now. "Tell me!!" She broke free and stumbled across the furrows to the huddle of men.

"Shiona! No!" called Mac, running after her, "no!" But it was too late. She was there, looking down at the crumpled figure in the heather. They were uncovering him from beneath the furrow, pulling the huge peaty turves back to reveal his broken body and twisted limbs. The heavy steel tracks had passed right over his head, smashing his glasses into his face as the life was crushed out of him. Beside him lay the tangled wreckage of the canvas hide, its torn edge fluttering in the down-draught. And at his side, squashed like a ripe fruit, lay the carcase of a hen harrier chick.

A cry broke above the roar of the helicopter. It was a cry which contained the anguish and torment of this sad and lonely land, as poignant as the strains of the pibroch, echoing the voice of people long gone from this place. It was a cry which was to ring in the hearts and minds of all those who heard it, for the rest of their days.

Mac turned her gently and slowly away. The helicopter landed on a knoll and her father leapt clear, running to her. "Shiona, my lassie, my own lassie," he threw his arms round her as the tears welled into his own blurred vision.

Over the shoulder of Meall an Chollie a brown bird wafted on languid, gull-like wings. It seemed to hang there for a moment, reluctant to go despite all the activity. Its own long, thin cry was lost on the wind.

Jimmy Forbes sat up and stretched. He was sore and stiff. He opened the car door and peered out into the damp morning. It was seven thirty-five. He didn't like sleeping in the back of his car, but the accommodation allowance was good money, and anyway, he thought Willie MacFee was charging too much.

Something hard was sticking into his back and he felt down for it. His hand brought up a half-bottle of whisky—empty. He tossed it over into the boot. No wonder he'd slept so soundly. Then he began to remember. He lay back again and closed his eyes, reliving the moment. It had fallen into place very well—far better than he had thought it would. He hadn't been quite sure how he would explain it all, but it was so obvious. Events had provided him with the perfect set of excuses. He had been urged to get the ploughing done if it looked like the weather was breaking. Anderson Sinclair had told him so himself. It was hardly his fault that the storm had come at that moment, at exactly the right moment for him. There he was, doing as he was bidden and it came from nowhere; the skies just opened and before he knew it the visibility was so poor that he'd lost his way. They could hardly blame him for carrying on for a while in the hope the storm would pass, and anyway, when you're ploughing you're concentrating so hard on getting it right, watching the depth behind you and the spacing and the lie of the land, that ploughing the nest site by mistake was perfectly understandable. That sounded good. He liked that. And then it got dark, exceptionally dark for a July evening, and even though he'd got out and had a look round and thought he knew where he was, the conditions were atrocious. He hadn't got a hope in that torrential rain, so he just kept going, doing his best for the company. Just as he'd been told to do. He didn't think he'd have any trouble with Anderson Sinclair; he hated those conservationists as much as he did.

He sat up again. He struggled out of the car and pulled on his boots. He urinated into the rhododendrons and spat loudly-collected spittle at the same time. He lit a cigarette and stood in the wet grass with his bootlaces trailing as he blew the pale smoke upwards. It seemed to hang in the fronds of the birch tree, unwilling to disperse. The tea in his flask was tepid. He swilled it round his mouth and spat it out in a long stream. "Hmmm," he said to himself, "it could still be a bit dodgey." The great thing was to turn up for work as normal as if nothing was wrong. He was good at playing innocent. He'd often fooled Archie Bane in the past. He'd got away with those dogs dying of strychnine poisoning by playing the 'daft laddie'—and if it hadn't been for that nosy bastard Pearce he'd have got away with the eagles too. He thought through it again, the fat chicks passing under the steel tracks, their bellies splitting and the entrails spewing out onto the moor.

There'd be a stink, he knew that, but they'd never be able to pin anything on him. There weren't any witnesses, no-one in their right mind would have been up on the moor in that weather. They would just have to accept his story whether they liked it or not, however much fuss the SSBC made. He'd probably lose his job, but it was only a contract with a week to run, and there were plenty more where this one came from. And as for the glen, he didn't care a damn about the place. It didn't bother him if he never set foot here again. He'd got his own back, that was what really mattered, on the whole bloody lot of them. He spat again and threw the cigarette end into a puddle.

He turned his car slowly out of the workshop drive and down the road. He was surprised to see a police car at the forestry office, and Anderson Sinclair's green estate too—he wasn't due back for another three days. And wasn't that the factor's car? 'That was bloody quick', he thought. They'd found out much sooner than he'd reckoned. "Aye, well," he mutterd, "here goes." He swung into the camp exactly as he had done every day for weeks, parking his car in exactly the same place as usual. He got out slowly and stretched again, as he always did. He looked at his watch. He was dead on time. The office door opened and Anderson emerged. "Jimmy!" he snapped, jerking his head towards Archie Bane behind him. "In here!"

Harry Poncenby knew this was not a job for the telephone. He left the estate office and drove slowly up the west drive to Denby Hall. 'Dear God, things have gone wrong up there!' he thought. He tried to predict Gerry's reaction. It would be sad if he decided to pull out of Scotland altogether because of this. He enjoyed his annual stalking expedition and the chance to flick a fly over the river. The car crunched onto the yellow gravel beside the front door. He thought he could catch him at breakfast.

The French windows were open wide and the scent of wisteria from the orangery filled the morning room. Gerry was lost behind the pages of the *Financial Times*. Harry coughed. A corner of the pink paper folded down and Gerry peered over the top of his bifocals. Harry at the house at this hour meant one of only two possibilities—very good news or very bad news.

"What is it, Harry?" There was no smile on Harry's face. He knew it was going to be bad. He'd guessed that was it, anyway. There wasn't any good news these days.

"Good morning Gerry", he began politely, "I'm afraid it's bad—very bad." He pulled out a chair and sat down. "Do you mind if I have some coffee?"

"Go ahead, help yourself." Gerry calmly folded his newspaper. It couldn't be that bad or it'd have been on the morning news. "The government hasn't fallen, has it, Harry, and the bloody socialists are in again?" He joked lamely.

"No, sir, I'm afraid it's much more serious than that." The coffee trickled into the cup from a tall silver pot. Now Gerry knew it was bad, Harry never called him 'sir' unless he'd got his coldly professional hat on. He'd heard it often enough. He could be so pompous. "I regret that it's my duty to inform you that...." He dreaded that voice. It couldn't be the bank, they were still dazed by the success of the Dalbattigh sale and he'd managed to defer some of the payments to Lloyds. Then he guessed. "Oh, no," he said, "has poor old Mrs Spink died at last?

"No, sir, she's still hanging on, but it is a death."

"Not—not one of the boys?"

"Dear, God, no! Thank heaven, nothing like that, although he's the same age. No, I'm afraid it's that nice young chap Pearce. I think you quite liked him—up at Ardvarnish."

"Rob Pearce? What on earth's happened?"

"There seems to have been an accident, Gerry. Mac MacDonald phoned about half an hour ago. It seems that Pearce was run over by a forestry plough on Dalbattigh yesterday evening."

"Good God! Killed?!" Gerry pulled off his glasses and looked at Harry with hooded eyebrows.

"'fraid so, killed outright. The tracks went right over him. He was in a canvas hide at the time, watching hen harriers at the nest."

"Why the hell didn't he get out of the way? He must have heard the tractor coming! And what was the bloody driver doing, for God's sake? You don't just run down hides! I've never heard anything so bizarre!"

"I know, the whole thing sounds very strange, although there was a hell of a storm going on at the time, thunder and lightning and torrential rain."

"What, you mean the tractor driver couldn't see where he was going?"

"I think so. That seems to be the story." He paused, as if plucking up courage. "I'm afraid it was that man Forbes."

There was a long silence. The two men looked at each other bleakly. Gerry spoke first.

"Forbes, eh? Hmm. I didn't like the sound of it when I heard he was back in the glen. What does Mac say?"

"Not much, Gerry. He's shattered, of course. They were very close and after everything he's been through recently I think he's been knocked sideways by this."

"I'm not surprised," said Gerry quietly, feeling sideways himself.

"He was very calm, but he had trouble talking to me. He was badly cracked up; I didn't like to press 'im for too much detail."

"No, I can see that, old chap." He paused. "Jimmy Forbes, eh?" He drummed his fingers on the polished table. "Well, well. Well, well, well."

Dinah swept in wearing a long silk robe. A cigarette protruded from a black holder. She ignored Harry.

"Gerry, Elsie Mountgarron's coming over for lunch today. I take it you're going to be out?"

Gerry sat staring at the table. He was studying the reflection of the tall silver candelabrum. He reached out a finger to touch it almost as though he expected to be able to feel something on the shiny surface. If he heard Dinah he took no notice.

"Poor beggar!" he said.

"Gerry? Gerry? Did you hear what I said?" Dinah yapped irritably.

"Yes, dear, as you wish." Gerry replied abstractedly.

"Good." And then, "are you two conducting business of some kind...?" She might as well have added "...because if you are this isn't the place to do it." But it was not necessary. Gerry knew perfectly well he was not wanted around the house today. He looked up at her for a second or two, withdrawing his hand from the reflection.

"I shall be going to Scotland later today and I may be away for a little while. Young Rob Pearce has been killed in—er—well, an accident, and I shall probably stay up for the funeral."

"Pearce? killed?" She drew on her long cigarette. "How very careless. Not on Ardvarnish, I hope?"

"No, thank God!" Harry said too quickly, "Not on our ground." He knew the emphasis was wrong, but it was out before he could stop it. He hadn't meant it to be so heartless, but he was very relieved not to have to handle the police and the agricultural-safety people and all the endless red tape such incidents spawned.

Gerry looked up sharply. "I do not see what difference it makes whose ground it happened on, he is still dead. And he was working for us—at least partly for us." There was admonition in his voice. He had always thought Harry was a cold fish.

Harry Poncenby adjusted his tone and described the news to Dinah, adopting his professional role again. This time he made it sound as though he really cared, ending "...he seemed such a nice young fellow too." Dinah slowly focused on what Gerry had said.

"You can't possibly go to Scotland," she complained with indignation. "We've got the Lord Mayor's Dinner in York the day after tomorrow, and we've got Fiona Biddlestone's wedding on Saturday. I've never been to Thorpe Priory and I've been looking forward to it for months!"

"Then you must go to it on your own, Dinah," said Gerry firmly, getting up from the table. "And I'm sure you can persuade Harry to take you to the dinner in York. I shall be in Scotland." He was sick of both of them. He wanted some fresh air. He wanted to go to Mac. He was sure that there was more to this than they knew and he had to go. And what about Shiona? 'Poor girl,' he thought, pursing his lips and a deep frown spreading across his brow. He remembered his conversation with her that night in the study at Ardvarnish, and her frustration with her father and the tears that came that day at the back door of the Lodge. She had done nothing to deserve this. They were such a handsome couple together. They had looked so happy and so right for each other. Even at the funeral he had been struck by how well-suited they were. Now this. He moved towards the French windows. Sparrows were chirruping jauntily in the wisteria out in the orangery. He walked out in a daze, failing to notice the sparrows or Dinah calling after him "You needn't think I'm coming to another funeral....."

Jessie McChattin was beside herself with frustration. She had had a bad night. She knew something was going on. Long after midnight she had heard cars driving at speed to the crossroads and roaring off down the glen. Four times she had jumped out of bed and run to the window to see if she could see who it was. Each time she was too late. Then the flashing blue lights of a police car and an ambulance and a little while later the unmistakable hammer of a heavy helicopter. She could contain herself no longer.

"Doolie, Doolie, wake up, there's something going on." But it was no use. Doolie had taken special precautions against interruption of any kind. The precautions had started quite early in the evening, in a modest way, with old Lachie Gunn who had drawn his pension that afternoon and had money to burn. Doolie was never one to say no to a dram—they had, after all, known each other for fifty-seven, or was it fifty-eight years—he could never quite remember how old he was—so a modest celebration when there was apparently nothing else to do was quite in order. But it had got a little out of hand. By closing time at the bar, and once he'd shut up and bade goodnight to old Lachie, the feeling had come on him and he had taken a half-bottle on tick and departed with it to the shiny new bus shelter the Council had generously provided at the crossroads. He sat there watching the storm, happy in the knowledge that Jessie would not come looking for him in that weather. When he reached the house an hour later he was past caring about the storm inside or out. He had made it up the narrow stairs with only two stops and tumbled into bed in his vest and socks. He knew nothing and cared less about Jessie's frustration until late the following morning. By then everyone knew.

The men had trickled home, grim-faced with tiredness and shock. What they had seen out there on the hill had been no ordinary accident. There were those who thought it could not have been an accident, but even those who did, had been rent inside by what they had witnessed. Every one of them had heard the cry ring out across the moor and watched Shiona, devastated and stricken, being led away by Mac and her father into the grey morning. The police had thanked them and sent them home, declining any further offer of help until the CID arrived from Inverness. A little after six o'clock Dr Ferguson arrived from Lairg and struggled puffing and blowing up the hill with a young constable to declare Rob dead. He turned away from the mangled corpse, pushing his stethoscope back into his bag saying, "In all my years of attending accidents in these glens I've never seen one so sickening as this. The poor man's skull is crushed."

Jessie McChattin saw Jimmy Forbes being taken away in a police car at ten to eight. "That's him arrested now," she said to Megan on the phone before the car was out of sight. "I always said he had violence in him," she said. (She remembered the violence clearly enough, but it was a violence she had not minded at the time.)

Anderson Sinclair was a very unhappy man. This was the last thing he needed. "When can I get my men back to work?" he demanded of Sergeant Bane.

"Not today, sir. I can't allow any machinery to be moved until the homicide team have given me clearance. That may not be until tomorrow. I think it would be better if you closed the operation down for the rest of this week. We'll need to take statements from a number of your men."

"I'll do nothing of the kind!" he retorted angrily. "It's not our fault Pearce has got himself killed and you've got the driver who can give you the whole story. I have a job to do here and I want my men back on the hill tomorrow."

"My advice to you, sir, is to forget it for this week." Archie repeated himself. "If you'll forgive me for saying so it might be considered insensitive if you put the men back too soon."

"Insensitive my arse!" cursed Sinclair. "It was bloody insensitive when these people tried to stop our work last month, and

Pearce was at the heart of it. I had to replace my drivers because of their damned insensitivity. My men go back to work tomorrow morning at eight o'clock, and that's that!"

"Is that you, Ishbel?" Jessie asked in her politest telephone voice. She was far from content from the snippets of information she had gleaned from her usual ring of contacts. She wanted hard information and she was prepared to use all her guile to get it. She knew too well that Ishbel MacFee was close to Jimmy and, of course, her son Alec, so she trod warily. "I was just ringin' because I heard Alec was the driver of the tractor which killed Rob Pearce, and I just wanted to say how sorry I was. What a terrible accident to happen." Ishbel rose to the bait immediately.

"Oh, no, Jessie, it wasn't my Alec, he was nothing to do with it. It was Jimmy seemingly, although I've not seen him myself. He never came back to the house last night."

"Is that so, Ishbel, I'm so glad it wasn't your young Alec. What a terrible stramash, eh? You'll be very upset."

"Oh, I am Jessie, I am that. Alec's not long back in. They're no' working today out of respect and he's come home again. He's very upset himself."

"I hope it'll no' affect his job, Ishbel. I know he was very friendly with Jimmy." She cast another fly.

"Now why should it, Jessie? Alec had nothing to do with this at all. It'll not affect him." She insisted defensively. "It was just an accident and Jimmy'll only be going in to make a statement. He'll be back soon I shouldn't wonder. I doubt they'll even bother to speak to my Alec about it. In fact they've been told to be back on the job at eight o'clock tomorrow morning. It's very sad right enough, but it'll not affect my Alec."

Cheered by her success at Braeside Jessie dialled the Dalbattigh number praying it wouldn't be Andrew who picked up the phone. "Ooh Mairi, dearie, it's Jessie here. I just wanted to ask how poor Shiona was, poor lass. That was such a terrible thing to happen."

"Aye," said Mairi wearily. "It was right enough. It's been a dreadful shock for Shiona. The doctor's here just now and she's been given something for her nerves. We'll not know how she is for a day to two yet. It was good of you to ring."

"I heard they'd taken Jimmy in for questioning. It was just a terrible accident they say?"

"Aye, it was." Mairi was confused by what the men had been saying. She thought it best to agree. She didn't want to go on with this conversation.

"Ishbel MacFee was saying they'll be back at the ploughing tomorrow morning first thing.... but I'll not keep you, Mairi dearie, you'll be wanting to get back to poor Shiona." She rang off. She knew Jimmy Forbes better than most and she was sure there was more to it. She dialled a friend in Lairg near the police station, she might know....

"What did that bloody old bag want?" asked Andy who was pacing the little kitchen like a sentry.

"Now Andy, you shouldn't speak like that. She was only phoning to ask after Shiona. It was very kind of her."

"Hmmph!" said Andy. "I doubt that! What did she want to know?"

"Nothing at all. All she said was that the forestry boys were starting again tomorrow morning first thing."

Andy stopped pacing and looked at his father slumped exhausted and dejected in the old chair beside the Rayburn. Andrew looked up, dazed for a moment. Their eyes met and anger burned through the tiredness and the calamity which had overtaken them all. Father and son read each other's thoughts.

"Are they, hell!" said Andy. "I'll see about that." He went out and pulled the door sharply behind him. They heard his pick-up tyres spurt on the loose dirt road and speed away down the glen.

Gerry did not go straight to Ardvarnish. He caught the inter-city express to Edinburgh for a meeting with his old Oxford chum Sir Peregrine Monteith who happened to be Minister of State for Agriculture, Fisheries and Forestry. They had shared rooms in Hertford in the old days of endless expeditions to the Highlands to shoot and fish without a thought for the future, or the impact the war had had, or capital taxation, or nationalisation or any of the cataclysmic changes which had subsequently derailed the life he had so confidently expected for himself in those laughter-filled days.

"Perry? I say, old man, can you see me for lunch today? I know you're frightfully busy. I want to bend your ear I'm afraid."

"It'll cost you a good lunch then, Gerry." Gerry did not feel like lunch, but he was determined to make the effort.

Gerry had not been into Muffins Club for many years. Nothing had changed except that Peregrine had got larger—quite a bit larger. They headed for a corner table.

"Look, Perry, I may be speaking out of turn, what? but feelings are running very high about the mass afforestation of Highland glens and across the peatlands in the far north—I don't have to tell you that, it's in the newspapers every week. Well, you won't have heard yet—it won't break 'till tomorrow—but yesterday evening a young chap was killed up near my place by getting in the way of a forestry plough—the forestry's not on my ground, I hasten to add, I sold it to a Dutchman earlier this year. Now I wish I hadn't. This young fella was a bird man. He worked for SSBC and he was in a hide at the time, watching hen harriers. The tractor ran him down—a very nasty business. I'm on my way up there now. He was engaged to the daughter of one of my old employees." Gerry forced a little smoked salmon into his mouth.

"What a remarkable tale," said Sir Peregrine "Go on."

"It is, indeed. I don't know the full facts yet, but what I do know is that there is going to be an almighty stink about this. SSBC can muster one hell of a membership and they have a lot of clout with the press. You can be damned sure they'll run this story long and hard. Added to that, there is a great deal of local feeling against the forestry. It's going in the wrong places, Perry, and we're pushing people off the land, not just for a while, but forever. I don't think you should underestimate the depth of feeling about this. Those people want to stay in the glens. There is a place for forests, of course there is, but not whole glens like the scheme where this boy's been killed. There's no room left for a sheep or a cow or anything that will keep a family in place there. I'm damned sure we can arrange it better than that if we put our minds to it."

"Hmmm. I see. You think we're in for a storm, do you, eh?"

"I'm damned sure of it. I've come here today to tip you the wink, Perry. You've got a real chance to be ahead of the game here. I think it'd be a smart idea if you could announce a review of forestry grants or something."

"Let me get you right, Gerry, old man. Are you saying the grant system is wrong or the forestry is wrong, or is it both?" Sir Peregrine helped himself to another glass of Vouvray.

"It's both. The grants are open to exploitation against the interests of the nation, in my opinion, and they result in bad forestry practices which put trees in the wrong places, damage the land and displace people from the countryside. —Look, I know you can't wave a wand, and changing the system will inevitably take a good while, but it would do you no harm to be seen to be on top of this issue, and it would be a very good start to changing things if you could announce a review. I'm very keen to take the heat out of this particular case. The whole thing's been a tragedy for that glen and I'm wound up in it because I sold the ground. I want to do everything I can to help those people." He hoped he hadn't said too much. Ministers were funny. Sometimes you could bend their ears and sometimes it was counter-productive. He thought he'd better leave it at that.

"I'm having the Dover sole." Sir Peregrine spoke to the black-coated waiter. Gerry didn't want anything more to eat. He wanted to be in Glen Corran. He needed to support Mac and

Shiona, Andrew Duncan and his family. He owed it to them. He'd got them into this mess and he was going to do everything he could to get them out of it again, or at least to ease the pressure on them so that they could reassemble their lives without worrying whether they had a roof over their heads. He picked at his scallops in a slippery white wine sauce.

"I do enjoy potatoes at this time of the year, don't you, Gerry....?"

After lunch Gerry took a taxi to a fine Georgian crescent overlooking Arthur's Seat. The headquarters of SSBC was engraved on his memory from the lengthy correspondence which followed the Forbes affair—the first Forbes affair, he thought to himself as he pressed the brass bell. He asked at reception if he might see Mr Michael Stone.

A tall young man came tripping down the stairs in an open necked shirt and with his sleeves rolled up. "Lord Denby?" he asked.

"Yes, we've not met, I don't think." He held out his hand. "Can you spare me a moment?"

"Yes, of course." Mike showed him into a meeting room.

"I have come to say that I am simply aghast at what has happened. I am on my way there now, so I don't know the full story, but I am deeply suspicious of this incident and I want to assure you that I shall do everything in my power to see that all the facts emerge."

"What do you mean, you're deeply suspicious?" Mike asked, looking slightly alarmed.

"I don't know, but there was, of course, a great deal of animosity between Rob and Forbes. I can say no more than that, other than—well—it seems to me to be a very unlikely accident."

"Are you suggesting Forbes knew Rob was in the hide?" Mike asked.

"No, no, I'm not. I have no grounds for that whatsoever, but I cannot bring myelf to accept that he didn't know he was ploughing up the nest site. It seems to me very likely that he ran down the hide on purpose. I intend to make sure that point is very thoroughly investigated. I feel very responsible, not only as a part employer, but also because I encouraged him to set that hide up to find out exactly what the harriers were eating. Does anyone know what he was doing in the hide at that time of night?"

"Yes," Mike said. "I've spoken to Mac MacDonald this morning. Apparently he went to the hide sometime after six o'clock because he'd always wanted to see how the adult birds sheltered their chicks in really heavy rain like that. It was an amazing downpour."

"I see," said Gerry quietly. Perhaps he was being unfair to Jimmy Forbes? Perhaps it really was exceptional weather and visibility? "Well, we'll just have to wait and see about that, won't we? In the meantime I sincerely hope the SSBC will use this tragedy to maximise publicity about persecution of raptors, and, even more important, the inappropriate location of forestry."

Mike looked at this strange man. Outwardly he was the epitome of an establishment figure. The tweed jacket, the glasses, the little moustache, the faded silk tie, the silk handkerchief stuffed carelessly into the breast pocket, the gold signet ring, baggy khaki drill trousers and brown brogues, almost a uniform which could be seen the length of the country at race meetings, game fairs, and to be found liberally scattered across the pages of country magazines. The name, the voice, the fastidious manners, the filigree veins on his cheeks which gave away an excess of good living, the handshake and the formality, the implied wealth and land and connection to a stately home, all suggested that this man was traditional English country and that his views would be rigid and, as likely as not, stuck in the pre-war era. Yet that was not what Rob had said to him. Rob had called him a revolutionary landlord and a friend. He'd nick-named him 'Lord Renaissance' and told him about his sudden awareness of the deer problem and the disappearance of the old birch and pine woods on Ardvarnish; about his sudden passionate interest in ecology and in the life of the glen. He was a paradox and Mike felt, despite all his instincts, that he could trust this man.

"Why did you really come here?" he asked, mobilising the directness and perception which had won him his senior position. Gerry was a little taken aback.

"I'm sorry?" he said.

"What was the real reason you came here today?" Mike repeated. "There is another reason apart from courtesy, isn't there?"

Gerry opened his mouth to refute any such suggestion, and then closed it again. He smiled. He liked this direct young man. "You're right," he began. "I am deeply concerned not just about this incident, but about the future of the glens. They are such wonderful places. I think Rob felt like that. There is a very special role for the Highlands in our lives, for people, for wildlife, for the rural economy, and sadly, for a very long time now we've been doing it wrong. That is why I liked Rob so much; he wanted to put back—to rebuild the natural habitats man has destroyed with one extractive scheme after another. We need to rethink upland agriculture, forestry and sport and to do so in the context of the people whose land it is—I mean the Highland people, like poor Rob's Shiona and her father

273

Andrew Duncan who live and work there and give their lives to the place..." he paused, realising too late what he had said, "...like Rob has."

"What do you want us to do?"

"I want you to use Rob's death to blow the whole thing wide open, to really make people sit up and think about those land issues. Use it to achieve something for Rob and Shiona and her people, —please."

—33—

Anderson Sinclair had told all the men to be there at ten to eight and to be on the job by eight. He was determined to be there first. To his surprise he saw a farm tractor and trailer parked in the passing place, apparently deserted. He drove on. He rounded another bend and breaked sharply. A second tractor and trailer was blocking the road ahead. "What the hell's going on here?" he asked himself. There was a gang of men standing about on the roadside and he could see a number of vehicles and cars jammed into a passing place further on. He thought there must have been another accident. He wound down his window.

"What's happened?" It had still not occurred to Anderson that he might be the target of the blockade.

"The road is blocked, Mr Sinclair. We're not allowing any forestry cars through at all. It's been decided. There'll be no more forestry until after the funeral."

Sinclair threw the car door open and lurched out. Several men came forward, headed by Andy Duncan. Sinclair strode forward to meet them. He did not wait to hear what they had to say.

"Get these bloody vehicles out of the road right now, or I'll get the police to do it for me." At that moment a tractor and trailer appeared round the corner behind Sinclair's car. "You'll find the road is blocked behind," said Andy calmly. Another man stepped forward from the group. It was Donald Swanson, the crofter from Alltbuie.

"Mr Sinclair. We mean you no harm, but you've to understand we won't allow any forestry to resume until Rob Pearce is buried properly and in his family's time. Now, we'll let you leave the glen as soon as we have your word that there'll be no attempt to return until after the funeral."

Another car drew up coming from Corran Bridge. A man got out and began to walk down towards them. "Hello, Donnie! What's going on here?" asked Gerry.

"Morning, m'Lord—we weren't expecting you. It's a blockade, sir, we're not allowing the forestry to resume until after the funeral."

"Why are you doing this, Donnie?" asked Gerry.

"The community have met, m'Lord, and all agreed that its not fitting for the work to go ahead until Rob's buried. There's thirty men and women prepared to support the blockade."

Gerry looked at Sinclair. "It seems there is a lot of local feeling about this. Perhaps it would be wise for you to agree to withdraw until after it's all over."

"Are you supporting this lawlessness, Lord Denby?" asked an incredulous Sinclair.

Gerry's eyes passed across Donnie's lined face, past him to Andy's with his shock of wiry hair, and then back to Sinclair's set jaw and bulging veins. "Yes," he said clearly, " as a matter of fact I am."

Gerry went first to the Duncans. He didn't know how he would be received, but he had to go.

As Andrew Duncan opened the door Gerry felt the pall of sorrow well out into the sunshine. He looked thinner and taller and older. His eyes were cloudy and uncertain and for a moment Gerry thought he had not recognised him.

"Oh, it's yourself, Lord Denby. Come in." The little kitchen was hot and stuffy.

"I have come to find out how poor Shiona is."

Mairi's eyes were red-rimmed with tiredness and weeping. She looked old and frail. "She's taken it hard, there's no denying that. Aye, she has that," said Andrew. "Will you take a dram, Lord Denby?" A bottle stood on the table. It was the last thing he wanted or needed but he knew very well that its presence and its offering at that moment was of special symbolism in this Highland household. It was the ultimate gesture of welcome and he was glad to accept.

"She's upstairs on her bed. The doctor's given her pills to calm her. She was that distressed we thought she might lose the baby," said Mairi.

"A baby...oh, I didn't know. I'm so sorry."

".No, well, nor did we," said Andrew, "and worse than that, nor did he, she was to have told him that night."

"Will you let me see her, please? We got on very well together, you know."

"Aye, of course," said Andrew. "This way."

The ceiling was too low for both of them on the tiny landing. Gerry had to stand stooped at the bedroom door. It was hot under the slate roof. She was not asleep. Her red hair was spread across the pillow like the wilted petals of a huge poppy. She looked at him out of hollow eyes which seemed to register nothing, no recognition, no acknowledgement of another human being, no life.

"Shiona?" he whispered. The eyes moved to his face. He sat down on the edge of the bed and took her hand in his. There was no flinch, no flicker of life in the limp, clammy fingers or the thin, unmuscled wrist. He held it gently between both his hands. "Shiona?" he tried again. It was a relief to see even the throat muscles moving. "I am so very sorry."

He sat with her for fifteen minutes. Andrew followed him to the door when he left, and out to the little gate. The midges were bad. They were always bad at Dalbattigh.

"Thank you for coming, m'Lord," said Andrew.

Gerry seized his chance. "Andrew—erm—I wanted to say to you that whatever happens, with the estate, I mean, when the sheep go off, there is a job for you on Ardvarnish and a house, I promise you that."

For the second time that summer the little church at Craskie was crowded with silent mourners. For the second time the whole community turned out, now to support Shiona and her family and to salute the young incomer who had died in their midst. For the second time that summer, on a warm August morning, bright with sunshine and birdsong, a piper stood at the gate to the little graveyard and a lament sounded among the rustling rowans.

Only after a long and difficult discussion with Mac and Gerry had Roy and Brenda Pearce agreed to allow their son to be buried at Craskie. Their inclination had been to return him to his own kind on the outskirts of Tunbridge Wells. It was hard for them to understand how much in love he had been with the glen; that he had wanted to make this his home and had chosen a Highlander for his wife and the mother of his child.

Jimmy Forbes was released without charge. Archie Bane could not bring himself to phone. He drove the twenty-three miles from Lairg, down the long glen road to the Keeper's Cottage to break the news to Mac himself.

"I've not seen such a thorough investigation in years," he said, accepting a dram from Mac, abandoning, as he did so, a rule he had struggled to observe for eleven years. "We just have to accept that it was simply a terrible accident."

"Can't you even prove he was intentionally destroying the nest site?"

"No, we can't, and Rob's employers can't. There isn't a shred of evidence we can hold against him. I'm sorry, but we shall never know."

The newspapers ran the story for days. The SSBC came as close to suggesting that the ploughing of the site might have been intentional as their lawyers would allow, and they lost no time in revealing Forbes's previous conviction and its remarkably coincidental connection with Rob. The case again aired the issue of the ploughing of peatland for commercial forestry and the loss of hill grazings. A new word crept into the debate. The 'sustainability' of down-hill ploughing and the monoculture of huge blocks of sitka spruce and lodgepole pine was questioned by many feature writers; the Forbes-Pearce case became a watchword for environmentalists who had long been opposed to commercial forestry practices. The plant and machinery stood idle beside the river and somebody had hurled a rock through the site office window.

Ko van Fensing fumed in his Amsterdam office refusing to speak or comment. The press hounded him day and night. A tabloid paper researched that he had neither sent flowers to the funeral nor condolences to the family. The headline appeared two days later: *'van Fensing the Heartless—The millionaire who couldn't afford a wreath.'*

In a rage of humiliation he snatched up the telephone to his London solicitors. "You can cancel the contracts with Bog Forestation and put that estate on the market immediately. I do not want to have anything to do with the place again!" The Highland newspapers loved it. *'Dutchman pulls out after death and forestry row.' 'Birdman tragedy evicts forestry and Dutch laird.'*

For the second time that summer the community closed in around a coffin and carried it out into the sunshine. They passed it from hand to hand to the poignant strains of the pipes. Crofters, shepherds, lorry drivers, roadmen and teenage boys in borrowed kilts too long for them, and hobbling pensioners like old Lachie Gunn, men and boys together, lined the path each to carry Rob a few yards on his last journey, their tribute to Shiona and her incomer who had fought for their land.

At the graveside a mass of flowers shrouded the grass in a wide arc around the open grave beside Janet MacDonald. There were wreaths and messages from all over Britain. SSBC staff had travelled north in large numbers to be there and friends and colleagues from school and university days had read of the accident in the national papers and felt moved to make a response. Shiona's friends had gathered from many glens and townships for miles around. Jeannie and Geordie Hoggett were there, Sandy and Betty Macronie, and Doolie and fat Jessie The Stores. There stood Dunc MacRail the fencing contractor from Altnahara, Morag and Davy Phimister down from Lochinver, Iain and Debbie McLardy beside Danny Stott, his hands rougher than ever. Old Hughie Clips and Alec MacMurchie the Ruddle stood proudly in their old muted kilts and white stockings, black jackets gleaming with silver buttons.

For the second time that summer Jock Gordon, the part-time undertaker from Invershin, solemnly called the seven names to take the green silk cords. "Lord Denby...." Once again Gerry stepped forward to take the first cord at Rob's shoulder. "...Mr Andrew Duncan...." Andrew's gaunt figure took a middle cord. "...Mr Andy Duncan..." Andy took his place beside his father, the two Duncan kilts in ancient and modern colours side by side. "Michael Stone..." Mike wore a dark grey suit and came to the grave blowing his nose on a bright white handkerchief. The undertaker paused momentarily before continuing. "...Mr William Ritchie...." The stout, genial figure of Willie Ritchie edged through the crowd in a red kilt with a broad leather belt and fine Harris tweed jacket with antler buttons. "...and Mr Roy Pearce." Rob's ageing father was a stranger to the Highland ways and Jock Gordon held the cord out to him as he slowly made his way to his place at Rob's feet.

For the second time that summer Mac stepped forward to the head of the grave. His eyes drifted the five feet to the mound of fading wreaths which still covered Janet's grave. They seemed held there for a second before returning to this new coffin suspended over the darkness beneath. The minister opened his prayer book. The thin pages fluttered in a little wind which ruffled his flowing white surplice and seemed to whisper his words for him in the rowans all around. "...we therefore commit his body to the ground..." The minister stooped to scoop up a handful of gravelly soil. "... earth to earth, ashes to ashes, dust to dust..." Jock Gordon withdrew the bearers and slowly, as slowly as a passing cloud, the coffin disappeared from view. One by one the cord-bearers dropped their silk cords into the grave and stepped back. The handful of stony ground rattled on the lid of the coffin. Only Mac was left. He seemed reluctant to let go, staring emptily down at his friend. At last, with a flick of the hand the cord was gone. The tears running silently and helplessly into his beard.

Four hundred men and women stood motionless for what seemed to be an age. Somewhere a long way off a sheep dog barked excitedly. A man's electronic watch bleeped three o'clock and he blushed that it seemed so loud, placing his hand over it just too late. A muffled cough came from somewhere at the back of the throng. Very slowly Shiona left her sobbing mother's side and walked forward, proud and erect in a plain grey coat. A black velvet band restrained her long red hair. She looked taller and thinner; her face had remained pale and expressionless throughout the service and the committal. There was no sign of emotion. Her composure seemed to lift her above and transcend her from the crowd. Robbie Pearce had been taken from her people by the cruel events of their turbulent history. In her hand she held two bunches of bright purple bell heather plucked that morning from the hill where he died. She had finished her weeping there, out on the empty moor among the black plough furrows where the cushions of early heather flowers seemed to defy the destruction all around. She had gone there with Mac, onto whose strong shoulder she had, for one last time, unleashed her grief.

The heather bunches were tied with soft red bands. Only she and Mac knew they were the delicately and lovingly-braided strands of her own hair. She handed one to Mac. He raised it to his nose to breathe the honey fragrance of the hill he and Rob so loved. He gazed at the purple radiance of the blooms for a few seconds before tossing them into the grave. Shiona's followed, her white hand hanging poised in the air after it had gone. Then Mac led her away.

The drive to Ardvarnish Lodge was lined with cars which stretched back through the rhododendrons to the stone bridge and the junction. Men and women stood about on the lawns and the gravel drive. The French windows into the dining room were thrown wide. The long table was spread with a white damask cloth and and a line of gleaming silver candlesticks. Silver platters crowded with smoked salmon, vol-au-vents, king prawns, colourful tomato, pepper and cucumber salads, dainty sandwiches and bowls of fresh rasberries, strawberries and cream, covered the entire table. White uniformed caterers from Inverness busied among the crowd, passing round the food and delivering copious wine and whisky to the assembly. Gerry had been determined to do it properly. At last there was something he could do for Shiona and the people in this glen. He experienced a powerful desire to throw the whole place open. He wandered among them, smiling here and chatting there, "...Oh, hello Mrs Mackinnon, how nice to see you again...A sad day, indeed!.....How is poor Angus these days? A little better I hope?...." and "...Well, Doolie, have you caught a fish yet this summer?" knowing full well that he'd caught several down below the falls in the early hours of the summer mornings, as he had every salmon run for the past forty years.

"Oh, no, m'Lord. I've had to give up the fishing since a few years on account of the arthritis in my elbow," Doolie smiled amiably through the gaps in his teeth, nursing his arm in which he held a large glass of whisky: his elbow didn't seem to be giving him much trouble this afternoon.

Tony Galbraith stood quietly to one side. He did not belong there and he had come to the funeral reluctantly, feeling he had to attempt to redress the negative press coverage the estate had received. Only as he was leaving his office that morning that had he been informed that it was back on the market. For a few minutes he had stood with his hand on the car door wondering if he could duck it, and then his professionalism claimed him.

"Hullo Galbraith, I'm so glad you could come." There was genuine warmth in Gerry's voice.

"Hullo, Lord Denby. A sorry business, the whole thing."

"Yes," said Gerry meaningfully, "the whole wretched thing."

Tony Galbraith was not sorry the estate was to be sold again. He had not liked van Fensing and felt badly let down by him. He saw a chance to express his own feelings diplomatically.

"You may not have heard, Lord Denby, but van Fensing is selling up. I only heard myself this morning."

Gerry stared at him for a moment and then said emphatically, "Good! I'm glad. I hope that means that crazy forestry scheme will be abandoned."

"I don't know about that, sir, but I'm not sorry to see the land change hands," said Tony cautiously, "I'd prefer it to be someone British next time."

"Yes," said Gerry, but he was no longer listening. He was looking round for Andrew Duncan. There was hope and he wanted to be the one to deliver it in person.

The sun had gone now, lost behind the dark hulk of Carn Mor and only a burgundy afterglow remained along the mountain skyline. They stood at the head of two flower-covered graves. Someone had removed the faded wreaths from Janet's and replaced them with those left over after Rob's had been covered. They were two patches of brilliance in a field of green grass and grey, lichen covered stones. A card wired to a large wreath stirred in the breeze. Shiona bent down to read it. *'To my friend Rob,'* it said, and then underneath *'Thank you.'* It was signed *'Gerry.'* She stood up and her hand reached out for Mac.

There is a special healing in the hill. Mac and Andrew sat down in the heather beneath the summit of Carn Mor. It was hot. Mac shed his jacket and threw it down, collapsing into a quilt of purple flowers. "At least we're above the midges," he sighed with relief. Andrew sat on a rock and poked at the sphagnum with his crummack.

There were only three days to go before the twelfth. Mac had offered Andrew a few day's employment helping with the organisation of the shooting which, to Dinah's outrage, Gerry had instructed Harry Poncenby to lease to an agency for the whole season. Gerry had no stomach for a grand shooting party of his own. Mac and Andrew were walking the ground to see where the grouse were and whether the young birds were flying strongly. The weather was not conducive to walking the steep ground. It wasn't so bad up here because there was a breeze and the sultry moor was left behind, but they were glad of a rest.

They lay in the strong sun for several minutes without speaking. Mac's eyes were closed, his hands behind his head. He could easily have gone to sleep. Andrew had spent his whole life on the hill. He never tired himself, always walking with a measured pace of elegant economy. The tiredness within him was not that of lack of sleep. It was of the uncertainty which had landed on them yet again— about the future; about his daughter and her growing baby, about the new owners of Dalbattigh estate, whatever new scheme they might pursue. He looked across the glen to the north side, to the wide sheep walks where he had tended his flocks for as long as he could remember. It was scarred now, striped up and down with the ploughing like great claw marks across the face of an old friend. He realised he was looking straight at the moor where Rob had died. He studied it intently for a few minutes, trying to make out exactly where the hide had stood. It was very hard to see. The distance was too great.

He sat up and looked harder, straining his eyes and shielding them from the bright light with his hands. "Mac! Mac!" he said sharply. "Give me your binoculars."

Mac opened his eyes and sat up. He passed his binoculars over, wondering what Andrew had seen. Andrew studied the moor carefully for several minutes.

"What is it?" Mac asked.

"You have a look," Andrew handed the glasses back. "See if you can work out where the hide was."

Mac gripped the binoculars to his eyes in silence. "Aye, I've got it, what about it?"

"Do you see the ploughing above it? The furrow which runs down through the site?"

"Aye."

"Can you see anything that's odd about it?"

There was along pause before Mac spoke. "Do you mean the spacing?"

"Aye, I do. That line's not parallel with the rest. It seems to take a direction of its own from higher up."

"That's right," Mac said, still looking hard, "there's a kink in it. What about it?"

"Do you not think that's a bit funny? If it was pouring with rain that heavy surely he'd have wanted to keep parallel for guidance?"

"Aye, he would, unless there's a big boulder there or something else to make him kink like that." Mac looked at Andrew.

He was standing now, leaning on his crummack staring across the valley. "The more I look at it the more I think he's taken a direct line, aiming at a fixed point below him," he said.

"That means the visibility couldn't have been all that bad," commented Mac.

"Unless there's another possibility." Andrew's voice possessed an ominous edge.

"What's that?"

"That one line was ploughed first, straight through the hide, on purpose, and all the other ploughing was filled in later— after Rob was dead."

The two men looked at each other in horror. "So you think he knew he'd killed Rob and ploughed the whole of the rest of the area to make it look like an accident?" Mac said slowly.

"Unless there's a good reason for that line taking a different course. I want to get over there and see for myself."

On their way past the Lodge they met Gerry looking at the new trees he had planted along the west drive. "Good God!" he exclaimed when they told him. He jumped into the Landrover with them and Mac flung the vehicle carelessly down the track.

When they arrived at the site the bamboo canes erected by the police still stuck out of the ground, linked together with blue string. Blow-flies buzzed among the heather although Mac had buried the harrier chicks as soon as the police had allowed him to. The three men stood on a knoll overlooking the whole scene.

"You can't see a damned thing from here," Gerry said. "We're far too close to it to see whether the lines are parallel or not."

Andrew strode off up the hill, following the main furrow

upwards over a hump and out of sight fifty yards away. There was an urgency in his pace. A few seconds later he shouted to them. They hurried across. "The line only starts here," he said. "That other one's come down later and run into the end of it. It's not a kink at all, the plough line which killed Rob only started here." He jabbed his crummack angrily into the furrow. "Look! You can see where the plough share has been dropped and sunk into the peat. Also, the line which killed him is a good eight inches deeper than the others, it looks as if he wanted an extra heavy furrow turned to do the maximum damage."

Andrew pulled his crummack out of the peat and laid it flat on the heather between the furrows, turning it end on end like a yardstick to measure the distance between them. He was excited now. He ran from line to line. "There you are! Different spacing too! There's no bloody doubt about it. That furrow was done entirely separately!" He jabbed at the scar which killed Rob.

Mac stood on the hump where the plough was first sunk. "Go and stand where the hide was, Gerry!" he shouted. Gerry stumbled down the slope and stepped over the blue string. He turned and faced Mac. Mac dropped to his knees and squinted down the furrow. "Absolutely dead straight!" he shouted. "Pace it out, Andrew."

Andrew counted out loud as his long sure pace strode down the furrow: "....seventy-five...seventy-six....seventy-seven..." until he stood beside Gerry.

Mac followed down behind him. "So the visibility was at least seventy-five yards. It may have been raining hard, but the visibility was nothing like as bad as he made out to the police."

"The bastard!" said Andrew.

"This is damned serious," said Gerry. " I think we need the CID boys back here sharpish."

Andrew crossed the string again and stood back from the site to look at it from another angle. He came forward again shaking his head. "Ach, this was no bloody accident," he said. The sunlight flashed on something in the deep heather at his feet. He thought it was a cigarette packet and he walked on.

"We mustn't get carried away, boys," said Gerry, taking his glasses off and wiping the sweat from his eyes with a red and green silk handkerchief. "I think we've all made up our minds that Forbes ran down the hide on purpose, but we mustn't forget he had no way of knowing Rob was in the hide. He must have got the shock of his life when he discovered what he'd done."

Andrew stopped and turned back. Maybe that wasn't a cigarette packet. Perhaps it had shone too brightly for that. He retraced his steps, looking from side to side. He couldn't find it.

"What are you looking for?" asked Mac.

"I'm thinking I saw something shiny in here somewheres about." He was parting the long heather stems. Mac and Gerry walked over to join him.

"What d'you think it was," Gerry asked.

"I don't know. I just thought it was something metallic."

"Is this it?" asked Gerry, holding up a hand dictaphone.

"Christ!" cried Mac. "That's Rob's field recorder! God, I am a bloody fool! I never missed it when they handed in his effects. He recorded every move on that." Gerry handed it to him.

Mac eased the play button on. Nothing happened. "Damn! It's buggered. The rain's got into it."

"The tape might still be all right," Gerry said.

"Is it still on record?" asked Andrew.

"Aye, it is," nodded Mac. "Of course! The batteries will be flat, but I can play it on mine when we get back...."

"No," said Gerry gravely. "Police first."

Detective Sergeant MacMillan was at Lairg tying up the ends of the accident. He said he would be with them within the hour. He would bring Archie Bane as a witness and another tape recorder in case the tape was damaged and might only play once.

"What are we expecting to find?" asked Gerry while they waited.

"A lot of field notes about the harriers," replied Mac. "There could well be information on the weather and the ploughing."

"You'd think he'd have heard the tractor coming," said Andrew.

"Aye...you would that," Mac agreed.

The patrol car drew up.

"Have you touched it?" asked Archie.

"Not the tape," Mac said. "We haven't even opened the machine. I tried the play button once, but nothing happened."

"Can you vouch for that, sir?" the CID officer asked Gerry.

"Yes. Yes, I can."

"Good. Right, now," he said. "We'll see." He carefully lifted the mini-casette out of the recorder, examined it, wiped a bead of moisture off it with a clean white handkerchief and placed it in Mac's machine.

"Are you ready Archie?"

"Aye, I am," he replied, "running now." He pressed the record button on the police recorder.

The play button revealed nothing but an empty silence. They stood around the machine gripped by the tension of the moment. "Right," said Mac, "nothing there. Now I'm rewinding to the beginning of the tape. Here we go...." The tape crackled and a roaring sound emerged. "Testing...testing..." said Rob's voice.

"That'll be the rain on the canvas hide," said Mac anxiously.

"Ssh!" said Archie.

Rob's voice came again "Seven-twenty pm...in the middle of a storm....both birds present....the hen sheltering one chick.. ..visibility very poor....going home." The tape went blank again.

"Damn!" cursed Andrew. Gerry reached out to restrain him. Then the same roaring sound came again, louder now, followed by Rob's voice. "...birds disturbed by something out there...can't tell what it is...the rain is drumming so hard." He was almost shouting into the recorder now. "...both adults have left the site...this rain is amazing...my God! It's not rain, it's a bloody tractor!...."

Gerry gripped Andrew's arm, digging his fingers into him so that it hurt. More of the roaring sound. "...I'm leaving the hide now. It must be Jimmy Forbes and he's close!..." They heard the zip rip down and crackling sounds as Rob clambered out of the hide. Then his voice came again, shouting. "...he's coming straight for the nest...I must stop him....Jimmy! Stop! Stop, you bastard!...Oh,God, I don't think he's going to stop!....I can see him looking straight at me... he's shouting something back at me....I'm not going to move...he'll have to stop...Jimmy! Stop!......" The thunder of the huge diesel engine was now a roar. There was a crackling sound through the roar, and a thud as the recorder landed, and then the roar seemed to get quieter, running on and on until it slowly faded to nothing and the tape went quiet.

Gerry released Andrew's arm. They both looked at Mac in stunned silence for several seconds. The detective-sergeant turned off the machine with a loud click. He spoke very quietly and deliberately. "That, gentlemen, is murder."

"How do I tell Shiona?" said Andrew with his head in his hands.

"Let me, please?" said Mac.

"Yes," said Gerry calmly. "Let Mac do it. They share so much now."

He set out on foot, down the stony track to the bridge over the river, now quiet again after two weeks of dry, sunny days. Oystercatchers piped frantically to their chicks amongst the stones on the river shingle and a common sandpiper flicked and bobbed on the grassy bank, emitting a long thin call. At the junction he turned left and walked on, along the riverside towards the little cottage.

The gate creaked and he saw her standing in the open door.

"Hullo," she said, smiling. "I saw you coming. How did

Father get on today?"

"Very well. He did really well. It's great to work with him on the hill." For the first time he noticed a slight rounding of her figure, the slightest hint of her growing baby. He smiled one of his old smiles. "Shiona?" he asked, "Will you come for a gentle walk into the hill?"

The End